NECESSARY PURSUIT

A TRINITY MASTERS NOVEL

MARI CARR

LILA DUBOIS

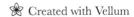

PROLOGUE

"Lover, come back to bed."

Oscar Hayden looked up from his computer toward the woman sprawled out on the mattress and grinned. He could see the peaks of her nipples through the sheet.

He usually didn't like pet names because they brought up some past shit for him, but it didn't bother him with her. Probably because the sex they'd just had was so fucking incredible.

He glanced back at the laptop, tablet, external hard drive, and tool roll he had open on the hotel desk. "Give me a second." The tablet was in pieces—he'd had to use the hotel room hair dryer plus his heat roll from the tool kit to melt the special glue that held the tablet's glass front to the body of the device. With that off, he'd been able to dissect the innards, connecting directly to the external hard drive and his computer in order to run the tests and analysis he hadn't had the time for until now.

Selene Tanaka wrapped the sheet around herself as she

slid gracefully off the bed. Her bare feet were silent as she walked over to where he sat. He'd pulled on a pair of boxers when he left the bed, but hadn't bothered with a shirt.

It had been a wild couple of weeks due to an insane series of events started by his dipshit brother and an inadvertent tablet switch. Well, one of his dipshit brothers. He had two, the three of them identical triplets—his mother had occasionally remarked that if the fourth divided zygote had kept growing, giving her identical quadruplets, she'd have changed her name and left the country.

Langston, the current dipshit in question, had agreed to join a weird secret cult. The cult had dangerous enemies, and Oscar had come to Boston to help Langston track down a bomber. Langston hadn't exactly asked for his help, but Oscar needed to protect his brother.

To give credit where it was due, the cult mobilized an effective strike team. They'd come close to capturing the bomber, a man named Luca Campisi, two days earlier, but he'd managed to escape by setting off a series of trash can smoke bombs around the Boston waterfront.

Langston would bitch if he heard Oscar calling the Trinity Masters—a secret society that had been around since the United States rebelled against England—a cult. The colonists traded King George for George Washington, and in addition to proclaiming that freedom, the founding fathers had opted to create a secret society that would bolster and protect the fledgling nation, modeled on a similar society—the Masters' Admiralty—in Europe.

His sister Sylvia had joined the Masters' Admiralty and moved to Europe. Now Langston was in the Trinity

Masters. Oscar had been invited to join both cults as well, but the price of admission was too steep.

While being a member of the Trinity Masters had clear benefits—access to influential people, with the accompanying benefits of also accessing the money and power those people had—there was, in addition to loyalty and secrecy, a marriage requirement; specifically, an arranged marriage between three people.

Oscar had spent the last couple of years trying to recover from having his heart dropkicked by Faith, the woman he'd truly believed to be the love of his life.

Dating was an unholy nightmare, so he couldn't deny there was a bit of appeal to the idea of having someone choose a spouse—wait, spouses—based on intellectual affinity and potential to innovate, and not anything as sticky as emotions.

However, Oscar had seen for himself that just because it was an arranged marriage with purpose didn't mean the unions were wholly cerebral. Langston and Sylvia both fell in love with their trinities. If there was something the Haydens had in common, it was that they all tended to lead with their hearts. And if there was one thing Oscar didn't have to give anymore, his heart was it.

He wasn't going to join, but he had to admit the cults had good taste in members. After all, they wanted *him* to join, and his siblings, which clearly showed they knew quality.

And Selene? She was a member. And she was fucking amazing.

"What are you doing?" she asked, looking at the items he had spread out on the desk.

A brilliant theoretical atomic physicist at Cornell, she

was rational, perceptive, and intelligent to a level that, if he was being honest, was a little intimidating. He and his brothers were all smart and successful, all *hoping* to change the world in their own ways. Selene *would* change the world. She was one of two dozen people who were in a position to design and propose things like new nuclear energy paradigms that would be both safe and far more sustainable than fossil fuel.

The bomb Langston had been trying to track down? A portable nuclear device large enough to level a city. That pants-shitting, terrifying idea had barely seemed to rattle Selene, who'd been brought in to interpret the bomb plan.

He'd met her at a tense gathering in a dramatic underground conference room beneath the Boston Public Library —because of course the cult had underground meeting rooms. The moment Oscar looked at Selene, there had been a spark. Something he hadn't felt in a very, *very* long time.

He relaxed as she leaned against him, her lovely breasts brushing the back of his head. Relaxed wasn't his default state. She leaned down, which meant even more boob contact, and peered at what he was doing.

While she wasn't a computer engineer like he was, he was pretty sure there wasn't anything she couldn't understand if it was explained correctly.

Well, that, and she liked it when he pulled her hair.

Oscar had been studying the local storage of the bomber's tablet. This whole shit show started when Langston had inadvertently switched tablets with an Italian man named Luca. Langston had been unknowingly carrying around the plans for the city-killer bomb with a potential twenty-kiloton output. Luca had followed

Langston to the U.S. and was apparently willing to do anything to get the tablet back. Considering what was on it, that made sense.

Oscar tapped the external hard drive he had sitting in a cradle. "When I copied Luca's data, I put it on here. I've opened up a similar tablet to attempt to recreate, not just mirror, his." He pointed to the disassembled tablet he had propped up on a book, which looked almost lewd with its glass gone and thin wires running out of it. "And my laptop is running the data."

He scooted his chair back and patted his lap. He liked touching Selene, being close to her. It had been a long time since he'd been with a woman, and Selene knew how to push all his hot buttons. The two of them shared a chemistry that was off the charts. She slid onto his knee, the sheet parting so her bare ass was against his thigh. His cock thickened.

"And what do you hope to find?" she asked.

"I don't know. Maybe nothing, but the tablet had even the pre-programmed apps stripped out. I want to see when and how that happened. Or if they were never there, it might mean the tablet wasn't bought retail, but as part of a bulk custom order, shipped out pre-consumer interface."

"And that could potentially be traced?"

"Exactly."

Selene cupped the back of his neck and smiled at him. "A clue."

"Yes. And my program can run in the background." Oscar nipped the soft skin at the crook of her elbow.

"Oh? Well then." Selene let go of the sheet.

Was there anything hotter than a naked woman on your lap?

5

Oscar licked her nipple before sucking it into his mouth. When she started to whimper, he stood, hoisting her up with his hands under her ass. She wrapped her arms and legs around him, head falling back as he nibbled on her neck.

He carried her to the bed, dropping her on the mattress. He was just about to strip his boxers off when something caught his eye.

Glancing back toward the desk, his heart practically stopped. "Fuck."

Selene tensed. "What?"

He leapt across the room and slapped the tablet face-down on the desk, then quickly shut his laptop. Selene jerked up, his tension clearly spreading to her, but her voice was calm as she asked again, "What's wrong?"

"The camera turned on."

"Perhaps you accidentally hit a button when you stood up?"

Oscar shook his head. "Not my computer. I have tape over it." Most hackers, whether white or black hat, blacked out their cameras—aka, put a piece of electrician's tape over it—or custom built computers without a camera. This was his travel laptop, and though he'd customized it, he hadn't bothered to mess with the screen, except to black out the camera.

He'd done the same with the tablet he'd brought in order to test his theory, but the tape had been on the glass.

The glass he'd removed.

"Fuck," he snarled. "It shouldn't even be possible to…I mean, the functionality beyond the internal storage is all disabled."

Selene rose, not bothering with the sheet this time. "The tablet—you're saying it was the tablet's camera?"

"Yes."

"Maybe your test triggered something that turned on the camera. Perhaps your test activated a program or application that needed the camera."

Damn, she was smart. And sexy. And sexy because she was smart.

"Possibly," Oscar said slowly.

"But unlikely?"

"A malfunction or unanticipated hardware activation is the simplest explanation."

"But we are not in a simple situation. The law of parsimony may not apply."

He'd google that later. "The worst-case option is that Luca had some sort of backdoor alert in his system that I haven't found yet."

"Which would...allow him to turn on the camera remotely?"

"Possibly. I basically recreated his tablet, so..." Oscar closed his eyes, hoping it would make his brain work faster. He needed to be thinking worst-case scenario. Not that he didn't always think that way. "Yes. He could have."

Now Selene looked worried, and he felt like an almighty asshole. Goddammit, he always ended up feeling like an asshole with women, and the fact that a psycho bomb maker may have just seen the start of their sexy times was a very good reason for her to hate him.

"How do we know?" Her question was still calm, even if her expression was pinched with worry.

Oscar scrubbed his face. "I'm going to open the laptop.

There's a physical barrier on the camera. Hopefully the program captured the hardware toggle."

Selene stepped to the side, out of range of the camera, and picked up her phone.

Oscar sat, then slowly opened his laptop. The window of the analysis program was still up, the program running. He scanned through the lines of code captured from the tablet via the hardwire connection.

There it was. A remote code access. Somehow Luca had found the replica of his own hard drive, used a back-door access, and then, since the tablet was connected to the hard drive, he'd been able to turn on the camera. Without the glass, the image was probably out of focus, but he would have seen something.

He kept scanning, his heart in his throat. Oscar was good, but to manage this, Luca must have had concealed backdoors and traces on his tablet unlike anything Oscar had ever seen before.

"Fuck this fucking fuck," Oscar snarled, enraged at his own incompetence.

Selene lifted her phone to her ear.

"Who are you calling?" Oscar snapped. He winced internally. He shouldn't yell at her. She wasn't the fucking dipshit in his room. He was.

Selene, however, was unfazed by his anger. "I know you don't want to hear this, but we need help, Oscar." She paused, clearly listening to whomever had answered. "Hello, Mr. Stewart, I need to speak to the Grand Master."

CHAPTER ONE

"We don't need to involve them," Oscar snapped at Selene for the third or fourth time.

Selene merely arched a brow, not even bothering to look up from her phone. Ten minutes ago, she'd called the Trinity Masters. They'd rushed to dress and were now simply waiting. Well, she was waiting, perched in the desk chair, legs elegantly crossed. He was pacing while berating himself for being a moron, with the occasional terse comment to Selene, which made him berate himself more because he knew he shouldn't be snapping at her.

She was unconcerned by his anger and, apparently, by the implications of what had just happened. If Luca had seen them, it was Selene who was at risk. Luca had met Langston, which meant Oscar's face wasn't exactly a major surprise, but now he might be able to identify Selene.

Never mind the violation of privacy she must be feeling.

He stopped pacing, took a deep breath, and turned to her. "I'm sorry."

Now she looked up. "For?"

"I fucked up."

Her cool, almost remote expression softened and she rose. "Mistakes were made, but it was hardly enough of a miscalculation to be a fuck-up."

His lips quirked. "You have a quantifiable definition of fucked up?"

"A gradient scale from oops to the advent of agriculture."

Oscar snorted in amused surprise. "The far end of that spectrum is the advent of agriculture?"

"Arguably one of homo sapiens' greatest mistakes."

Oscar hooked a hand around her waist and tugged her body against his, his anger melting away. "Says the nuclear physicist."

He lowered his face to hers, and just before their lips met, there was a knock at the door.

Selene smiled and slid out of his arms even as he snarled silently.

She opened the door, and Sebastian, Franco, and the Grand Master walked in.

The hotel room, which had seemed palatial, now felt crowded. The Grand Master wasn't particularly tall or imposing, but she carried an authority that made her presence fill the room. She wore a cape-like jacket with a hood pulled up. Langston had told him that members of the cult weren't supposed to know who the Grand Master was. He and his brothers had seen her without the hood, thanks to the extraordinary circumstances during which they'd met when her husband, Franco, had been shot.

Selene inclined her head. "Grand Master."

"Dr. Tanaka." Though her face was somewhat shadowed by the hood, the light from the lamp on the desk allowed them to see her features, making the hood more of a pro-forma gesture. As she looked at Selene, the Grand Master's lips quirked. "You were here with Mr. Hayden?"

"Yes." Selene paused. "Having sex." She looked at Oscar out of the corner of her eye, and he resisted the urge to make a face at her. Something about Selene made him want to kid around with her, laugh even. What the fuck was that about?

Oscar rubbed the spot between his eyebrows as Franco snickered. Luckily his complexion meant a blush wouldn't show.

"What happened?" the Grand Master asked, turning to him.

He quickly went over what he'd been doing. Sebastian came over to the desk, examining the components and wires. The tablet was still facedown, though cocked at a drunk angle, thanks to laying on the wires and cords still hard-linked to its exposed components. He'd disconnected the other ends from both the laptop and external drive.

"You kept a complete copy of the bomber's tablet for yourself?" the Grand Master asked coldly.

He'd known this was coming. "Yes."

"And why would you do that?"

"Because the guy designed a backpack nuke. I thought maybe it would be a good idea to learn everything I could." Oscar didn't usually bother with sarcasm, but in this case it felt appropriate.

"*You* could." The Grand Master arched a brow. "And what would *you*, a lone man with limited contacts, do with whatever information you discovered?"

Oscar's back teeth ground together. He hated feeling stupid and useless, and right now he felt both.

She's not wrong. Who, besides the Trinity Masters, could you go to with the information? You're the dipshit now.

"How sure are you?" Sebastian asked, breaking the tight, silent tension.

"That the camera turned on? One hundred percent."

"And that Luca Campisi was the one who did it?"

"Zero percent. I'd have to try to trace it back, and given that this fucker had a completely hidden backdoor, I wouldn't attempt anything outside my lab." Oscar took a breath, shoved his ego to the side, and added, "Or have someone more specialized than me look at it."

Sebastian looked surprised at that statement.

Oscar raised his hands. "I know computer security, but only because cracking it is sometimes necessary in data mining. That's my real specialty."

Everyone fell silent, waiting.

The Grand Master's face was turned away, so he couldn't read her expression, but when she cleared her throat, they all stood a little straighter.

"We assume the worst-case scenario," she said. "Luca knows you copied his tablet and has a way to actively seek out that copy. He was successful, and in doing so, was able to turn on the camera of this tablet. He has seen both of you and the hotel room. He could potentially identify each of you, and maybe even the hotel, via the decor."

Oscar looked around the room and then at Selene. She might be in danger because of him.

"Dr. Tanaka, we will protect you until this situation is resolved," the Grand Master finished.

Selene inclined her head, but then frowned. "What about Oscar?"

"While we appreciate Mr. Hayden's help over the last week, we did not seek his assistance, and he is not a member."

Oscar stared at her. Was she about to…?

"I would advise you not to return to your home," the Grand Master went on. "We know Luca is aware of the location, given the fact he ransacked Langston's lab while searching for his tablet. He was able to bypass your security."

He ground his teeth again. Damn it, she *was*.

"Grand Master, surely we can protect Oscar, given—" Selene stopped talking when Sebastian reached out and put a hand on her shoulder. Oscar repressed the urge to tell him to get his fucking hands off her.

"I would suggest leaving the East Coast for some time. While we think Luca returned to Europe, we have no confirmation of that. I'd also suggest not contacting your family. You, and those you love, will be safest that way."

"Just get to it," Oscar snarled, furious with the thought of being forced to walk away from his own life by some asshole bomber. He'd do it, if he had to, but it would hurt the people he loved. They were safe. She hadn't said it, but they both knew it. Sylvia and Langston were both already cult members, and Walt was half a world away.

The Grand Master smiled. It was cool and touched with a hint of satisfaction. "Or you could finally accept my invitation."

Fucking fuck. If he'd just left well enough alone, hadn't insisted on messing with this stupid shit, he wouldn't be in this position. He glanced at Selene, whose eyes were wide with surprise. He didn't know if she was shocked at the fact that he had a standing invitation to join or that the Grand Master would strong-arm him. Brilliant as she was, clearly Selene wasn't manipulative enough to have seen this coming. The Grand Master cleared her throat, pulling his attention back to her. Their gazes locked, and he knew his life was about to change.

"Become a member and we will protect you."

JULIETTE TOSSED the jacket on the floor the moment she and Franco were inside. One of her now-extensive collection of black, hooded pieces, it was warm enough to serve as a snow coat in Boston, which also made it uncomfortably warm to wear inside, and by the time they left the hotel room, she'd been sweating, only to walk out into the chilly air of the Boston night.

The jacket landed half on top of a pair of polished dress shoes and a black briefcase that hadn't been there when they'd left earlier.

"Devon?" Franco called out, even as he put his hand on her shoulder protectively.

"I'm here," their husband called out, his voice floating down the stairs.

The Beacon Hill mansion they'd bought last year was light and airy during the day, thanks to being a corner lot. It had been their sanctuary, and until last week, she'd managed to keep the business of the Trinity Masters separate from their home, their trinity. The whole Langston debacle had resulted in her meeting with Sophia Starabba in her home. Sophia, a smart, fashionable Italian woman, appeared to be the acting leader of the Masters' Admiralty, since Eric Ericsson, the fleet admiral, was missing.

Based on information from her sources—though calling Sylvia Hayden a "source" when the woman was woefully bad at subterfuge was laughable—Juliette was fairly certain there hadn't been some sort of coup within the Masters' Admiralty. Still, the longer she went without talking to Eric, the more suspicious she felt, even though she respected Sophia.

In fact, she and Sophia had innovated a new, collaborative endeavor, the MPF—Masters Protection Force—and based on tonight's crisis, they'd gotten it off the ground just in time.

One night, she, Devon, and Franco had sat down in their pajamas on the living room floor with a bottle of wine to talk through the plan for the MPF, which Franco had started referring to as "The Plan" with capital letters. She'd tried to rope in Sebastian, but he'd made an aggravated noise and hung up on her when she'd called him at midnight to see if he wanted to be part of the discussion.

Sebastian had given up his job—well, jobs—after she'd assigned him to his trinity with Elle and Grant. Since he was permanently in the country now, he was able to serve as one of her counselors, a position that seemed to take up even more of his time than being an international aid worker and CIA asset had.

And speaking of the CIA…

Devon came down the stairs wearing nothing but a towel.

All thoughts of the Masters' Admiralty, Sebastian, and the latest crisis fled when Franco walked over, kissed Devon, and yanked the towel away.

. . .

AN HOUR LATER, lying naked on the foyer floor, their clothes and that one towel strewn around them, Juliette sighed in contentment. No matter what else happened in the world, she had this, had them. Their little family.

That thought sobered her enough that she sat up, only to have Devon hook an arm around her and pull her back down, this time with her head pillowed on his chest. "I'm not ready to let you go yet."

"What time is it in London?" she asked.

"Six a.m.," Devon answered without hesitation.

"Frankfurt?"

"Seven."

"Then I have time." Juliette settled in, the floor hard under her, so she draped her legs across Franco to get comfortable.

"Wait." Devon cupped her cheek, turning her face toward his as he held his head off the floor. "London, Frankfurt…you're talking about activating the MPF. What's going on?"

"This floor is hard," Juliette said.

Franco rose, helping her and Devon up as well.

As they headed upstairs to their bedroom with its Alaskan King bed, Franco and Juliette took turns explaining what Oscar had done, and the aftermath.

Once he had agreed to join, she'd pulled in two of the Warrior Scholars as bodyguards for Selene and Oscar, and they'd also served as a security escort to get everyone safely to the Boston Public Library.

Juliette may not have called on the Warrior Scholars, thanks to the guilt she felt over poor Levi, if Sebastian

16

hadn't insisted. Levi Hart was one of the Warrior Scholars, an elite group of soldiers-turned-grad-students and Trinity Masters' members who functioned as her Boston-based on-call security team. Levi had ended up in the hospital after their last run-in with Luca Campisi.

The ceremony to initiate members wasn't long, and this particular one had been even shorter, thanks to Oscar's terse replies. Sebastian had handled the post-initiation discussion with Oscar since Franco had screwed up his brother Langston's onboarding. While that was going on, Juliette had spoken privately with Selene, offering to send her, along with a bodyguard, to a safe house on the West Coast.

Selene had opted to remain with Oscar. The Hayden boys were good-looking, but Oscar must have been really good in bed for Selene to decide staying with him was worth the risk.

Following his initiation, Oscar—who now wore a triquetra pendant on a long gold chain—had seemed surprised Selene was still there. A personal protection detail from Price Bennett's security company would arrive first thing in the morning to take them to a safe house in rural Pennsylvania, far enough from Boston to provide some geographic security, especially since the safe house was, according to Price, in the middle of the countryside and easy to defend against a lone assailant.

Until the Bennett Security team arrived, Oscar, Selene, and their Warrior Scholar guards were safely stashed in headquarters. It wasn't the nice accommodations of the Boston Park Plaza, but they'd survive.

Juliette let Franco finish the explanations while she went to select pajamas. She didn't plan to get on a video chat with Sophia, and given the late hour, putting clothes back on seemed counterintuitive. They'd just had some incredible sex, so a satin teddy was thematically appropriate, but she pulled on sweatpants, a long-sleeved T-shirt, and put her hair up in a bun that made her look like a pineapple.

"And then we came back here and had floor sex," Franco said as she walked out of their massive dressing room closet.

Devon crossed his arms. "If we want to catch Luca, instead of putting them in the—"

"I'm not going to use them as bait," Juliette declared.

"We need Luca Campisi. He is a direct threat to national security."

"He's a threat to worldwide security, and we will catch him. Oscar's computer, the hard drive, and the tablet he was using are on their way to San Francisco with a trusted courier. Norah Douglas is going to run an analysis and see if she can trace where the search originated from."

Norah, a member, was a forensic computer investigator, brilliant hacker, dark web expert, and one of the secret leaders of an anonymous "hacktivist" collective. Silicon Valley companies hired her to attack their systems as a way to test the security. It wasn't a matter of if she could get in, but how long it took. Both the FBI and CIA used her as an outside consultant for particularly difficult digital investigations. If anyone could back trace Luca based on Oscar's tablet, it was she.

"We could keep them safe while making it appear that they were vulnerable." Devon was stern and serious. "The simplest course of action would be—"

"You're the one who said you thought he'd returned to

Europe, so we have time to focus on a digital trace, because travel time alone—"

"His travel time back to the U.S. would mean we have time to construct a secure plan for using—"

Juliette ignored the doubt gnawing at her and held her ground. "I'm not risking the lives of our members in order to—"

Franco slid his arm around her, tugging her to lean back against his chest. "'Logic clearly dictates that the needs of the many outweigh the needs of the few, or the one.' But that only applies when it's self-sacrifice. Or if you're Spock."

The tension that had been building vanished, as if Franco had taken a pin to a balloon. As always, he managed to keep her and Devon grounded, keep them from their natural inclination for drama and self-flagellation.

Devon hung his head and snorted out a laugh. "I can't deal with you when you throw geek quotes at me."

"Geek is the new cool."

"Sure it is."

"Before you two have this argument—again—let's make this phone call." Juliette slid out of Franco's arms and then out of the bedroom. She and Franco had a first-floor office for Trinity Masters business, which they hadn't used until this last week. Tonight, they'd need it since the hardline phone in there, totally separate from their personal phone and internet, was secure and encrypted.

Sophia picked up on the third ring. "Grand Master."

"Ms. Starabba."

"To what do I owe the pleasure?"

"The timing of our last meeting, and the plan we developed, was fortuitous."

There was a brief pause. "The bomber?"

"Yes."

"He's in the U.S.?"

"Not as far as we know, but he knows we have a copy of his data and is searching for it. Digitally. We have people working on tracking him, but once they do…"

"We must be ready." Sophia's voice was hard and merciless, her accent making it sound elegant. Like a beautifully crafted dagger.

Juliette glanced at each of her husbands, then said, "We need to activate the Masters Protection Force."

OWEN FRASER OPENED the drawer of his desk. There were four cell phones inside. It was the one way in the back, the newest but least used, that was ringing. Calm settled over him as he picked up the phone and answered it.

"Fraser."

"Mr. Fraser, I didn't anticipate needing you so soon." The woman on the other end of the line spoke with a crisp New England accent. He hadn't been at the now-infamous all-society meeting where the new Grand Master had been introduced—and where it had been clear from her voice that for the first time in the secret society's history, they had a female leader—but he now recognized her voice from the series of conversations they'd had over the course of the last few days.

"I'm here to serve, Grand Master."

"There's been a development in the situation with the

Italian bomber. There's a potential lead, and we need the Masters Protection Force ready to mobilize."

"In Europe or in the U.S.?"

"Current intelligence says he's in Europe, but it's possible he will return to America in an attempt to locate Oscar Hayden and Selene Tanaka." The Grand Master quickly summarized the situation while Owen jotted notes in his personal code language.

Outside the window, the city of Frankfurt was bustling with morning traffic. Through the glass wall of his office, he could see the activities of the small team of agents and employees who made up the Frankfurt sub office of the FBI's International Operations Division.

"Has Percival been notified?" he asked when she'd finished.

"The Masters' Admiralty's acting leader was going to call him right away. They're most likely on the phone now."

"I will wait ten minutes after we finish and then call him."

"You know how to get ahold of my counselors if you need anything…or if you have any information I should be made aware of."

"Yes, Grand Master."

"Excellent. Thank you, Agent Fraser."

The call ended and Owen sat back in his chair, whistling. As an FBI agent working abroad, his job was fairly complicated. Taking on the role of leader of the U.S. half of the Masters Protection Force would only add to the complexity. Regardless, he'd accepted the position without hesitation.

Owen unlocked the lower drawer on the long, low filing cabinet he had in his office. Amid all the other files was a slim one he'd labeled "MPF" in Devanagari script. Carrying it back to his desk, he flipped it open, using the action of re-examining the file's contents as mental preparation time before he made the call.

The Masters Protection Force was an international, interagency law enforcement task force. At least that's what it would have been called if it had been organized by governments or Interpol. The Trinity Masters and Masters' Admiralty were not adversaries, but they also weren't allies. Rumors of the existence of a European arranged-ménage-marriage secret society had been swirling through the Trinity Masters membership for months, even reaching him here in Germany. When he'd first heard, he'd tried to poke around and see if he could confirm the existence of the European society, but there'd been nothing.

Then the Grand Master called, he was read in, and, more interestingly, she'd asked him to head their side of this new task force, which had been the brainchild of herself and Sophia Starabba—the acting head of the Masters' Admiralty. Sophia herself was a law-enforcement agent with the Italian Carabinieri and Interpol. Or she had been; according to her record, she'd given up her position and moved to London and was currently unemployed. Acting head of a secret society wasn't the kind of job that people declared on their LinkedIn pages.

The shiny new Masters Protection Force was an elite task force of fourteen people, each of them a member of their respective secret society. Right now, he and the rest of the Trinity Masters MPF agents were severely outnumbered —there were only five of them, including himself, while the Masters' Admiralty representation was nine people strong.

He and the Grand Master had deliberately tapped individuals from each of the major U.S. federal agencies— NSA, Homeland Security, CIA, with himself representing the FBI. The fifth member was one of the Grand Master's advisors, a historian named Franco, who was quick-witted, friendly, and smart in the way one would expect a historian to be.

The man would be a nightmare out in the field.

On the other side of the MPF were the nine people from the Masters' Admiralty, one from each "territory." He had their names, and most of them had civilian jobs, the majority of them working for various well-established and exclusive security firms like *Cohortes Praetorianae*, where Milo Moretti, the MPF member representing Rome, worked.

Figuring out what the significance of the territories were and their borders was Owen's new pet project, but in the few conversations he'd had with Percival Knight—his equivalent, and the representative from England—Owen hadn't been able to get any information about it out of the Englishman.

The MPF had the broad and daunting mission of investigating and neutralizing any and all outside threats to both societies.

The city-killer bomb and the hunt for its maker fit that criteria, with the side benefit of potentially saving the world.

Owen picked up the phone and dialed Percival Knight's number.

"Mr. Fraser," he answered. "I was about to call you."

"You've spoken with your chief?"

"My admiral, yes."

Owen jotted down the word "admiral" in his notes. "Our first official investigation."

"This only works if we truly collaborate," Percival warned.

"I'm not the one holding back information," Owen pointed out. "This bomber started out targeting your society. I'd like to know more about why. And who exactly the Bellator Dei are."

There was stiff silence for a moment, then he heard Percival sigh. "Perhaps this information would be best shared in person."

Owen smiled, knowing the other man couldn't see the expression. "Let's meet in the middle. Brussels."

"Tonight in Brussels."

CHAPTER TWO

S elene smiled at Oscar as he placed her suitcase and his bag down by the front door of the safe house. The five-hour car ride from Boston to the small, rural town of Lenoxville, Pennsylvania, had been relatively uneventful. She and Oscar had discussed movies and books with Bill and Wayne, the two bodyguards from Bennett Security who had been assigned to protect them. Bill had done a quick yet thorough walk-through of the house before allowing her and Oscar to enter. Now Wayne was circling the grounds as Bill stood sentry at the front door.

While Selene knew she should feel safe with guards and Oscar, it was difficult to relax knowing that her life may be in danger. That Luca Campisi, a man capable of designing a deadly bomb, and tracking down electronics in a way Oscar—who was brilliant—hadn't anticipated, was looking for them.

"Thank you, Oscar," she said softly, slipping off her winter coat, as she looked around the large farmhouse the Grand Master had provided for the two of them. The

Grand Master had offered to split them up, but when faced with the possibility of being separated from Oscar, Selene had insisted on remaining with him. She wasn't sure what it was about the handsome, grumpy man from Charleston, but Selene was intrigued and...dammit...smitten.

The front door opened into a large room that was a combination living room and dining room, with well-worn hardwood floors covered with a smattering of rag rugs. There were no overhead lights, so the interior was lit by lamps. Between that and the too small, too few windows, the house was quite dim, considering it was early afternoon and sunny outside. Not that they expected the sunshine to last. The weather forecast included a freak snowstorm, the word blizzard even mentioned as a possibility.

It was certainly cold enough to snow. The safe house was quite chilly, and she glanced around wondering where the thermostat was. Or if there was a fireplace they could use.

"I wonder how long we'll be here." Selene hadn't expected to be away from home longer than a few days, so she hadn't packed enough clothing. If this adventure lasted more than another week, she was going to have to do laundry. Luckily she wasn't teaching this semester, but focusing on a research project. All she had to do was reschedule some meetings with grad students and she'd be okay on the work front.

"Who the fuck knows," Oscar grumped. But then he put his arm around her, pulling her against his side and rubbing his hand over her upper arm. On the surface, he was off-putting because of the anger, but she'd gotten to peek under the surface, to see the core of the man, and he was caring and brilliant.

And very, very good in bed.

Selene sighed. "I might have to do laundry if it drags on too long."

Oscar gestured to his small overnight bag. "Yeah. All I've got in there are a couple clean T-shirts, two pairs of socks, another pair of boxers, and some lounge pants. Didn't realize this trip was going to go into overtime. Or that it was going to be cold as a witch's tit."

Selene grinned at the Southerner's lightweight jacket. As an upstate New Yorker, she was no stranger to frigid weather. The same couldn't be said of Oscar.

Selene lifted her laptop case. "At least I can do some work while we're here. Though given my current research, I can't really be away from my lab for more than a month. What do you think the chances are there's good Wi-Fi out here in the middle of nowhere?"

Oscar shrugged. "I'm not holding my breath. At least you've got a computer."

Sebastian had confiscated Oscar's laptop, the hard drive and his tablet, something Oscar was not handling well at all. "Not that it matters. The good equipment is in my home office. Couldn't have accomplished much from here anyway."

Selene followed him down the hallway, the two of them exploring the downstairs. Besides the living space at the front of the old farmhouse, there was a small room set up as an office, a half bath, and a doorway that appeared to lead to a basement.

Selene's eyes widened as they stepped into the last room on the first floor—the kitchen. "I didn't expect this," she said, as they entered the large, bright, modern kitchen. "This room has obviously been remodeled recently." Black dome pendant lights hung over the breakfast island, which had four tall woven stools. The room was far more inviting than the rest of the house, feeling like the type of place guests would gather at a party, standing around the counter, eating, drinking, talking.

It instantly became Selene's favorite room. As a single woman who lived alone, Selene didn't cook very often, though she enjoyed it. Cooking for one always felt like more effort than it was worth, and in truth, she was typically too busy with work to make the attempt. As such, she lived on microwave meals, takeout and the occasional bowl of cereal for dinner.

"The whole house beats the hell out of my place," Oscar mused.

"Really?"

He nodded. "Not a lot in my Batcave except the bare necessities. A bed, a couch, my workroom."

Selene turned to study him, curious about what his home might look like. Their association had been very short —the two of them only meeting just over a week ago. And while they'd had sex several times a day since they met, there was very little she knew of the man beyond the physical realm.

Last night, they'd been given separate sleeping quarters within the Trinity Masters headquarters, something she suspected they were both somewhat grateful for, considering the strange turn of events that had occurred during the day. Selene had lain on the air mattress, playing over everything that had happened over the course of the past two weeks, and she suspected Oscar, who'd been unhappy about his initiation into the Trinity Masters, had needed the time alone to assimilate to his new future.

Selene's work typically kept her too busy for socializing. Instead, she preferred to share a night or two with men she found physically attractive, rather than someone with whom she might form an emotional bond. After all, as a member of the Trinity Masters, she wasn't searching for a Mr. or Ms. Right. She was simply biding the time until she was called to the altar, by indulging her sexual needs and expanding on her experience.

She was both curious and adventurous by nature, a combination that had given her parents gray hair, but which were assets in a scientist. The truth was that science was rapidly approaching, or perhaps had already passed, the point where the question was no longer "could" they do something, but "should" they. The bomb Luca had created was a prime example. A small, portable nuclear detonation device, as opposed to a street-corner reactor that could power a few square city blocks, was scientifically thrilling and morally horrifying.

When Oscar turned her, pulling her against his chest so they were flush from shoulder to knee, her thoughts turned to sex. The same curiosity and lust for adventure that drove her scientific inquiry guided her sex life.

The feeling was undoubtedly aided by the fact that lust was a far more enjoyable sensation than vague unease and fear, which were what she'd been feeling since the body-guards had picked them up.

She wasn't sure if saying she wanted to stay with Oscar so she could continue to have sex with him was better or worse than saying she was smitten.

While Selene didn't regret sleeping with him, she was struggling to walk away, something she'd never had a problem with before.

Now that they'd gone into—as Oscar said—overtime, she was interested in getting to know him on a more personal level. What she'd learned of him so far had left her equal parts fascinated and curious.

"So, you're from Charleston…" she started.

"Yep. Born and raised. I built a small cottage on a large piece of property my family owns just outside the city. My brothers also have houses there…well, places to live. Langston converted the barn into his apartment-slash-lab and built a Tesla coil in the stable area."

"I've been to Charleston a couple of times. It's a lovely city."

"You'll have to come visit me sometime. I'll show you all the best locals' haunts, the places that never make it into the travel guides."

"I'd like that very much. Sounds like you and your brothers are close." She had met Langston, but had yet to meet the third triplet, who was apparently a doctor and out of the country.

"We're very tight, got that triplet link thing going. You have any siblings?"

She nodded. "A younger sister, Theia."

"Yeah. I have one of those, too. Sylvia."

"Oh yes. I remember the Grand Master mentioning that you had a sister the first time we met. What does she do for a living?"

"She's a successful poet."

Selene's brows rose. "Sylvia Hayden is your sister?"

It was Oscar's turn to be surprised, though she also detected some pride in his expression. "You've read her work?"

Selene nodded. "My best friend is a literature professor

at Cornell. She claims I have the potential to become a supervillain and is on a mission to make sure I maintain my moral empathy by exposure to fine arts—music, literature, poetry. She gave me a copy of one of your sister's books for Christmas last year. I enjoyed it so much, I went out and bought the rest of her work."

"Supervillain?" Oscar snorted. "Well, teaching STEM without also teaching humanities is how we get Spider-Man villains."

Sylvia laughed, thrilled he hadn't been shocked or horrified by the joking reference to her line of work's potential for evil.

"I'll tell Sylvia her art is keeping you from joining the dark side. She'll be touched."

"As I recall, the Grand Master advised Langston not to contact her when we were analyzing the bomb schematics at headquarters. Why?"

Oscar sighed. "She lives in England now. Moved over there and joined the Masters' Admiralty."

Selene had been shocked to learn that there was another secret society, much like the Trinity Masters, that functioned in Europe. "I'm curious how Sylvia became involved with a secret society in a different country. Why wouldn't she have joined the Trinity Masters?"

Oscar casually shrugged one shoulder. "The answer to that is simple and complicated. She fell in love." There was something in his voice that Selene wasn't sure she was hearing correctly, something that sounded perilously close to distaste.

"Explain, please."

"Two members of the European cult, Lancelot and Hugo, were in Charleston looking for a woman they

31

believed was working with an enemy of the Masters' Admiralty. The woman, Alicia, was my sister's former teacher and friend. They came to Sylvia for help locating her. Somewhere along the way, she fell in love with them, and they with her. Eric, the fleet admiral—head dipshit of the Europeans—invited Sylvia to join the cult, then married her to Lancelot and Hugo. Actually, he offered all of us membership to his cult."

Selene had heard Oscar refer to the Trinity Masters as a cult a few times, and it amused her. "Perhaps you should reconsider the cult descriptor, given the fact you are now a member."

Oscar rubbed his jaw uncomfortably. "Don't remind me."

"It's not so bad." She patted his chest. "We have cookies…and access to DOD research contracts."

There was no mistaking he hadn't been happy about joining the Trinity Masters. She had been surprised to discover he'd had a standing invitation, as she didn't realize that was a possibility. Selene, a legacy, hoped that with the passage of time, he would change his mind about the secret society and all it had to offer.

"So the arranged marriages in the Masters' Admiralty aren't made based on innovation capacity or protection of intellectual assets and arts, but rather love?" she asked.

Oscar shook his head. "I don't know a lot about the Masters' Admiralty, but from the things Sylvia has said, I get the impression her trinity was an exception rather than the rule."

"She was very lucky then."

Oscar studied her face, his brows furrowed. "If you

think so, then why did you join the Trinity Masters, knowing love might not be part of your future marriage?"

"I'm a legacy, Oscar. I grew up in what I knew was a nontraditional household, and when I was old enough to be trusted with the secret, my parents, all three of them, told me why. I know that love can grow between strangers in an arranged marriage, and that, quite frankly, parenting with three people seems preferable to two. It's normal to me because that's how it was in my family. My parents didn't know each other—besides by reputation—before they were called to the altar, however, the three of them found a deep and abiding love. Is that why you were resistant to join? Because you'd prefer to marry someone you love? If so, I hope you'll believe me when I say I've seen many, many trinities formed between strangers who have fallen in love."

Oscar hmphed. "You're a romantic."

She laughed. "I believe that's the first time I've ever been called that. I prefer to think of myself as a realistic optimist because I know myself well enough to know I don't wish to live my life in a cold, emotionless marriage. One of those might *really* turn me into a supervillain."

His lips twitched. "For the good of humanity, you need to be in love?"

"I want affection, companionship, and good sex."

His hands slid to her hips. "Just good?"

She winked. "Fine. Amazing sex. Now that you're a member, are you saying you wouldn't prefer the same?"

Rather than answer, Oscar released her and walked over to the refrigerator, pulling it open. "Fully stocked," he murmured.

Selene got a sense he was uncomfortable with the turn

the conversation had taken and was attempting to stall. Or change the subject completely.

Unfortunately for him, she'd been described as tenacious on countless occasions in the past. If there was something she wanted to know, she asked the questions until she discovered the answer. "Oscar," she prodded.

"I'm not worried about finding love. In or out of a cult."

His response was vague...and compelling. And it drove home exactly how little she knew about him.

"Why not?"

Oscar ignored her question. Instead, he pulled an IPA from the refrigerator and held it up to her. "Want one?"

She nodded, watching as he grabbed a second bottle, uncapping them both before handing her one. She glanced at the label and saw that the beer came from a local brewery.

He walked around to where she sat, setting his bottle on the counter after taking a long drink. He leaned closer, placing a soft kiss—his lips cold after the beer—against her neck. "Should we check out the second floor? Find the bedrooms?" he murmured, his mouth still exploring her neck and the sensitive spot just below her ear.

The man was an accomplished lover, and she was tempted to extend their tour to the bedrooms—just one bedroom, actually—as he suggested. But she recognized his actions as a diversion.

"Yes, I would, but I reject you using sex to avoid answering my question."

Oscar lifted his head from her neck. Then upped the ante, his hands grasping her waist as he stepped closer, forcing her legs apart so that he could stand between them.

It was an invitation she didn't want to decline, but there was a tightness around his eyes and mouth that spoke of a pain she wanted to understand.

"Selene," he whispered, kissing her cheek before nipping her earlobe. "The only thing that matters now is I'm a cult member. Stuck."

She pulled away. "Is that truly how you feel?"

Oscar huffed, stepping back, then moving to the other side of the island. Leaning across, he reached for his beer, taking another long drink. Two sips in and he'd nearly polished off the whole bottle. "Yeah," he said, with a surprising amount of heat. "That's how I feel."

She sighed. "I'm sorry to hear that. May I ask why you feel stuck?"

Oscar shook his head, the gesture not one of rejection, but rather reluctant capitulation. She was wearing him down.

His attention was focused on the large bay windows that created a small breakfast nook off the side of the kitchen. "I've been in love before. It didn't work out."

"Heartbreak isn't an uncommon occurrence, Oscar."

"It was more than that."

"More?"

"Forget it," he said dismissively.

"Did this relationship end recently?"

He shook his head, still not looking at her. "Two years ago."

Selene wasn't sure what to make of that response. "Two years," she repeated. That was a long time. "Why did the relationship end?"

His gaze swung in her direction, and he was scowling deeply. "She said the only emotion I was capable of was anger. She was right." His tone and dark expression certainly seemed to mirror that accusation.

She held his gaze. "I see."

Oscar finished his beer with one last sip, and once again, she recognized his reluctance in continuing this discussion. The silence dragged on, lasting a few moments too long, passing from companionable to awkward.

She and Oscar didn't have a long acquaintance, so any reassurance she might offer would no doubt ring false to him, though she'd certainly witnessed many emotions from him. Not the least of which was lust, her personal favorite.

So she wouldn't dismiss her own instincts, which told her whoever this woman was, she had indeed been mistaken.

She expected Oscar to change the subject, so she was surprised when, once again, he stared out the window as he spoke. It was as if by avoiding her eyes, he could pretend she wasn't there, wasn't listening.

"We were high school sweethearts. She was my first love, and I was hers. I'm not going to say it was all sunshine and roses. We were off as much as we were on. Langston used to tease us, called us Ross and Rachel, but I did love her. And I tried to be the man she wanted, needed."

Selene wanted to point out that love wasn't truly love if it required change. Growing together and adapting, yes, but not one-sided change. She remained quiet, afraid he'd stop talking if she interrupted.

"We fell apart and came back together five times over the course of twelve years."

Her eyebrows raised. "That is a long time."

He nodded. "When you've been together that long, I

guess it's easier to return to something comfortable, familiar."

"Is that why you continued dating her?"

Oscar shook his head. "No. That's why I think she kept dating me. I loved her. Loved her so much, I tattooed her damn name on my back."

She'd assumed the large tattoo, Faith, that was written across his back had been a declaration of spirituality.

"She broke things off for good the night I'd planned to propose."

"Oh, Oscar. I'm sorry." Selene was curious about a woman who would date a man twelve years if she was truly that unhappy with him. It seemed the height of cruelty to expect a man to change rather than to love him for who he was, and Selene found herself angry with a woman she'd never met.

Oscar studied her face and sighed. "You have more questions. I can see it."

"I don't wish to make you unhappy."

Oscar snorted. "If you ask my family, they'd say that was my normal state."

Selene considered that. Oscar was unlike any of the other men she had taken to her bed. She preferred adventurous, passionate lovers who saw sex as an outlet and an expression of self. In short, she preferred people with relatively few sexual hang-ups who were GGG—"good, giving, and game"—and didn't take it too seriously. Oscar was gruff, and yes, she had noticed he was quick to anger, though not in a way that frightened her.

"I wouldn't say that."

Oscar frowned and she could tell she'd surprised him

with her observation. However, he recovered quickly. "Stick around a few more minutes and you'll change your mind."

She gave him a smile. "I don't believe I will."

His brows relaxed, giving his eyes a softer, less intense look. "So ask what you want to know."

"Her name was Faith?"

He gave her a curious look, which she answered. "I've seen your tattoos, including the one on your back. I'd assumed you'd meant faith as a noun, but I can see now it is a name."

Oscar shrugged. "At least it's on my back and my stupidity isn't thrown in my face day after day." He sighed, and Selene sensed he was working hard to center himself to calm down. "Have to admit I'm sort of partial to the name Selene. Goddess of the moon, right?"

She smiled. "The original Titan goddess. Not one of the lame Greek hangers on. Though when I was in college—physics major with a minor in applied chemistry—I jokingly told people I was named after Selenium, the element. That I had to go into chemistry because of my name."

"And what is Selenium?"

"A metalloid. Dangerous, but beautiful—it can be used as a pigment."

"Dangerous and beautiful? Suits you."

"Flattery will get you everywhere," she said, perfectly aware that she was flirting with him, while he was still attempting to change the subject.

Oscar was a thorough, considerate lover, and while part of her longed for another night in his bed, there was a more realistic, practical side that issued a warning. In the past, she'd never been in a position to confuse physical attraction with affection, but there was something about Oscar that tugged at her heartstrings.

"Everywhere, you say?" he asked suggestively.

He had a slight Southern twang that Selene found extremely appealing, sexy. But she wasn't going to let him distract her with that honey voice and sexy body.

"Why would Faith accuse you of being angry all the time?"

Oscar seemed somewhat surprised by that question. "Surely you've noticed I have a temper."

Selene blinked as she thought back over the past few days. His reactions had seemed perfectly reasonable in the face of what had been going on around them. "Not a particularly scary one."

If her question had surprised him, her response had shocked him outright.

"Two years is a long time to harbor a broken heart, Oscar. Why haven't you moved on?"

He toyed with the label on the beer bottle and glanced over his shoulder. She suspected he was debating whether or not to have another.

"Because I don't blame her for leaving. Her reasons weren't wrong. And they won't be wrong with the next woman. It's just...I'm not..." Oscar rubbed his hands over his beard. Selene had observed him doing the same thing several times, typically whenever he was thinking, tired or, like now, frustrated. "I'm not like my brothers and Sylvie. I don't wear my heart on my damn sleeve, and I suck at saying sweet shit."

Selene fought not to grin, aware that Oscar might take her humor badly. She attempted but failed to force a more serious expression. "And Faith wanted you to compose her poems, write songs about her?"

Oscar realized she was joking and barked out a loud laugh. "Not exactly. I think she would have been okay if I'd just...fuck...I don't know...talked to her. She said I was emotionally distant. That the only emotion I was capable of expressing was anger."

"Anger is far from a dispassionate emotion."

Oscar nodded slowly. "Yeah. Well, I lost my shit the night she told me it was over for good. I told her she should know how I felt about her. I mean, Jesus, she was fucking everything to me."

"I'm guessing the," she repeated his words, "'lost my shit' response didn't help your case."

"All it did was prove her right." He blew out a long, harsh breath. "We got into the biggest fight we'd ever had. Ended with her storming out. She left me alone with a hole in my heart and a useless diamond in my pocket."

Selene reached across the island, placing her hand on top of his. He turned his over, grasping hers to hold, giving it a squeeze before he released it.

"And there's been no one since?"

He shook his head and she could see him shutting down, pulling away from the conversation. And her.

"And Faith is the reason you didn't want to join the Trinity Masters?"

"I rejected joining the cult because I don't like taking orders, and I'm not planning on getting married. I'm no good at relationships and not looking for love."

"I don't believe that."

Oscar didn't appear to hear her rejection of his reasoning. Instead, he said, "I prefer my life the way it is. Falling in love means giving someone control over you, and I'm not doing that again."

"Is it about control, or love?"

"They're the same thing," he shot back.

Selene raised an eyebrow, but he wasn't looking at her.

He was quiet for a moment, then said, "The way Langston and Sylvia and even you talk about these arranged marriages, I can tell that even if falling in love isn't necessarily an expectation, it's a hope most members seem to have."

"I suppose it is."

"And now that I've been shanghaied into this cult, I have to hope," he stressed the word, "that whoever is placed in an arranged marriage with me doesn't expect me to fall in love with them." He straightened, still not looking at her. "Because I had the love of my life, and losing her hurt too fucking much."

CHAPTER THREE

"Sir, ma'am, we need you to move to a more secure room."

Oscar sat bolt upright, jerked from sleep by the calm but brisk tone of the guard. He glanced over at Selene, who was rolling over, her hair a mess around her face. Oscar yanked the sheet up to make sure she stayed covered.

The two of them had ventured to the larger of the two bedrooms after their conversation in the kitchen, moving their luggage into the master bedroom by tacit agreement. He'd left home just over a week ago, expecting to spend a few nights in Boston bailing Langston's ass out of trouble. He'd stayed afterward to spend time with Selene, and when it had been just them in the hotel, the fact that he hadn't packed much hadn't mattered.

Then the camera had turned on. And his and Selene's vague comments about both needing to get home were forgotten.

Their current situation meant more time in each other's

company, and Oscar wasn't about to look a gift horse in the mouth. His attraction to the beautiful physicist continued to grow the more he got to know her. What had started out as merely sexual chemistry was quickly turning into something akin to friends...with benefits.

"I need you up," said the guard, who he could now see was Wayne. "Right now."

"We need clothes." Selene was propped up on an elbow, holding the sheet over her chest with the other hand.

"No, ma'am. You need to move to a more secure room."

Oscar swung his legs off the bed, not giving a fuck about his own nudity. His shirt and boxers were on the floor, and he grabbed them, though he didn't have time to pull them on. Selene rolled across the bed to get out on his side, reaching for her glasses on the nightstand. She tried to bring the sheet with her, but when it wouldn't come untucked, she dropped it. Modesty was far less important than safety.

Both naked, they followed the guard through the dark house. As they tiptoed down the stairs, Oscar caught sight of the second guard, Bill, standing beside a window in the front room, carefully positioned in shadow. Outside, the sky was a deep gray; it had to be close to dawn, but there was a blanket of heavy-looking clouds that meant it was still fairly dark.

A laptop was open on the floor near Bill's feet, the screen tilted so that he could see it.

"What's going on?" Oscar whispered.

Wayne didn't reply right away, instead leading them down the hallway. He opened the basement door, the well-oiled hinges silent.

"There's a vehicle with a lone occupant on approach. It passed by several times before finally turning onto the driveway."

"Who is it?" Selene asked. "Can you see?"

"Not yet." Wayne nudged Oscar down the steps into the basement. When Wayne reached for Selene, Oscar grabbed her, pulling her in with him before the other man could touch her.

"When the vehicle is in range of the main camera net, we may be able to. The distance cameras are infrared, so all we know is it's a single occupant."

"What are you going to do?" Oscar demanded.

"Our job...protect you." Wayne closed the basement door.

With the door closed, the basement was pitch black.

"Fuck," Oscar snarled as he started feeling around on the walls for a light switch. When he hit it, the cavernous room was lit by a bare bulb hanging from the ceiling of the space below where they stood, at the top of the stairs.

"Do you think it's safe to have a light on?" Selene asked. Her lovely body was haloed by the dim glow.

Oscar passed her his shirt. "It's an interior, underground room. Also, if he didn't want the light on, he should have given us a fucking flashlight."

Selene slipped on the shirt, then started down the stairs. The basement was unfinished, more cellar than useable room.

Oscar followed her down, slipping on his boxers when he reached the bottom. No more than three minutes had passed since Wayne had woken them up, but the peaceful night's sleep he'd been having with Selene by his side seemed hours ago.

After revealing more than he'd intended about his relationship with Faith, the two of them had moved upstairs to the bedroom. He wasn't sure who had made the first move. Maybe they'd both shifted closer at the same time. All he knew was, one second, they were unpacking the few clothes they had in their possession, and the next, they were naked on the bed, kissing and touching as if their lives depended on it.

Oscar was no stranger to one-night, even two-night stands, and while he knew they were in serious danger and this was far from a vacation, he was unnaturally happy to have this time with Selene. He wasn't anxious for it to come to an end. Which was ridiculous, considering the very deadly threat to their lives.

"Do you think it's Luca?" she asked.

"I think we should assume so and be pleasantly surprised when it's not," he snapped.

Selene merely raised an eyebrow, the corner of her mouth twitching. "Is something wrong, Oscar? You're normally so easygoing and sunny..."

"Ha. Ha." Actually, her teasing did help him relax. He'd warned her about his temper, yet his gruff tone didn't seem to bother—or even faze—Selene.

They were silent for a moment, both straining to hear anything. In the silence, he started to work through the possibilities and iterations of what could be happening.

And the more he thought about it, the more he second-guessed the current plan of hiding in the basement.

"If it is Luca..." He glanced at Selene.

Her brow was furrowed. "He said their job was to protect us. But shouldn't the priority be to take Luca into custody?"

"Exactly what I was fucking thinking." Oscar scrubbed his hands over his face. "If he gets out of the car with a gun—"

"More likely a bomb."

"—will they kill him to keep us safe?"

"And if they do, our chance at answers about that bomb dies with him."

They glanced at each other and then both bolted for the stairs.

The guard by the window, Bill, glanced over when they emerged from the basement, his gaze hard. He gestured emphatically for them to go back down the stairs.

Oscar ignored him and ran at a crouch through the living room, scooping up the laptop from the floor before Bill could stop him. Cradling it with one arm, he ran back to Selene. Together, they looked at the camera feeds displayed on the computer.

A nondescript car sat about fifty yards from the house. The farmhouse, owned by Bennett Security, was regularly used as a safe house, so it had cameras set up around the perimeter. One of those cameras was capturing this feed. Because the car was still a fair distance from the camera, the picture was grainy.

Despite that, they could see the driver, who had both hands on the wheel, and as they watched, he bowed his head.

"Tired? Praying?" Selene whispered.

Wayne, who Bill must have signaled to come back downstairs to deal with them, clamped a hand on Oscar's shoulder. "Sir, you need to get back in the basement, where you're—"

"What are you going to do with him?" Selene demanded. "We need information from him."

"Information?" Wayne frowned.

"Fuck, they're not members of the cult, so they weren't told shit."

"What cult?" Wayne demanded.

"The fucking cult I just joined like a moron."

Selene put her hand against his back, rubbing it in a circle, while addressing Wayne. "The man you're protecting us from may have answers we need."

"About a cult?" Wayne asked.

"Ignore the cult comment. He wakes up grumpy."

Oscar snickered at her comment. It was rare for someone to not only find his gruffness inoffensive, but funny. Selene not only didn't care when he snapped, she found a way to make him laugh.

"We need you to capture him," Selene told Wayne. "But be careful because he may be wearing a bomb."

In the silvery blue light that filtered in through the windows, Oscar thought he saw Wayne's face go pale.

"You want us to capture a suicide bomber?"

"What?" Bill hissed, turning away from the window. "There was no mention of a suicide bomber."

"*This*...this is what secrecy gets us." Oscar kept his attention on the laptop. The man-who-might-be-Luca still sat in the driver's seat, bent over the wheel.

Selene hastily explained. "We don't know that he's a suicide bomber. All we know is he kidnapped a woman and put a bomb vest on her."

"If you think the assailant is in possession of an explosive, we need to fall back and—"

"Your only orders are to protect us?" Selene demanded.

"Yes, ma'am, which is why—"

Selene dashed down the hall. Unlike Oscar, she didn't bother to crouch when running across the parlor. Bill lunged for her but missed.

"Fuck," Oscar and Wayne snarled almost in unison as they leapt up to follow her.

Selene was already at the front door. Hand on the knob, she glanced back. "Please make sure I don't die."

Then she opened the door and stepped out onto the porch.

Selene stood in the doorway, silhouetted by moonlight, her feet bare and her lovely, long, naked legs making her seem fragile. Vulnerable. His heart thumped its way to his throat, making it difficult for him to breathe, to swallow. Fear kicked in as he played out all the ways this could go very, very wrong. He envisioned the way her body would jerk with the force of the shot and then drop, crumpling into a heap, her blood pooling under her, long black hair forming a halo around her beautiful, angelic face.

Jesus, now was not the time to have a morbid poetry moment. That kind of stuff was Sylvia's territory. He was the one who kept everyone safe and in check.

Selene was neither at the moment, yet he was out of his element here.

He preferred digital battles. The closest he'd ever come to combat was when he'd seen Franco get shot. The image of watching the man go down, the blood, Juliette's cries, it had all come back to him too many times since. Bullets struck fast, and if they hit their target, there was fuck-all anyone could do to stop the destruction.

Oscar was hampered by the fact that he still held the computer with one arm, so it was Wayne who grabbed the back of the T-shirt Oscar had loaned her and yanked Selene back inside.

"Wait, he was getting out of the car!"

"Call it in," Wayne snapped at Bill while hauling Selene toward the basement door. "The situation is FUBAR."

Oscar could run to Selene's defense, demand Wayne release her, stop him from forcibly keeping her safe…

Or he could finish what she'd started.

Snapping the lid of the laptop closed, he tossed it onto a chair, and walked out the door.

It was Luca Campisi—now that he was half out of the car, Oscar could confirm his identity based on the photos they'd been shown in the aftermath of Langston's drama. When Oscar walked out, he hesitated for only a moment, then finished exiting and closed the door.

"Langston," Luca said in an elegant Italian accent. "I'm here to teach you how to defuse the bomb and to beg you to destroy your copy of the plans."

Langston.

Oh fuck.

More than once, he and his brothers had played identical triplets' tricks, switching places in an attempt to fool teachers or friends. He'd portrayed Langston more than a few times in his life, but never when the stakes were so high.

"I'm listening." Oscar held his hands up to show that he meant no harm, on the off chance Luca did have a weapon and got nervous. He lowered them quickly, not wanting Luca to mistake his trembling as fear. In truth, it was fucking freezing outside, and Oscar was only in his boxers.

Luca hesitated, remaining by the car a full minute before taking a couple tentative steps toward Oscar. He stopped for just a moment when Selene stepped back on the porch, then continued to the house.

Oscar did his best to look nonthreatening while placing himself slightly in front of Selene and ignoring the sounds coming from inside the house. Bill and Wayne had better keep quiet or Luca would hear them.

Luca looked like he'd seen better days. His medium-brown hair was shaggy and in bad need of a trim, and his clothing looked as if he'd slept in them more than a few nights. He was still too far away for Oscar to make out the shape or color of his eyes, but he could see the black-framed glasses he wore. If Oscar had passed this man on the street, he never would have noticed him. At first glance, he was the very definition of nondescript. No wonder he'd managed to evade capture. There wasn't anything in the man's face that screamed "mad bomber." Instead, Luca just looked like any other Joe Schmoe.

"Did you—or you, Dr. Tanaka—give the plans to anyone?" Luca asked, sounding both resigned and worried.

"No," Selene said slowly.

"No. How do you defuse it?" Oscar countered. The question was a test because what Luca couldn't know was that they already knew how to defuse the bomb.

Luca sagged…in relief. He muttered something in Italian, then glanced at Selene and smiled. "Dr. Tanaka, it's a pleasure to meet you. I've read many of your papers."

"Crap, I'm a supervillain by association," she muttered.

Oscar snorted out a laugh. Their reactions were completely at odds with the seriousness of the situation, but it was either make a joke or freak the fuck out.

"You want to make sure you're the one who gets to start the nuclear war?" Oscar asked.

Luca shook his head frantically. "No, no. The plans are…" He stopped and looked away.

Oscar narrowed his eyes. Something wasn't right here.

Selene adjusted her glasses and cleared her throat. "The particle accelerator in your schematics wasn't detailed enough to explain how you were going to get an accelerator that size to get a neuron up to the speed necessary to break neptunium. You could—"

"Don't give the bad guy suggestions!" Oscar yelped in alarm.

Selene pursed her lips.

Luca was frowning as he looked back and forth between them, pointedly looking at their attire—a pair of boxers and a T-shirt all they had between the two of them—as both eyebrows crept up. "I had thought you were with Ms. Edwards."

"The woman you kidnaped, strapped a bomb to, and terrorized?" Oscar snarled. Luca was talking about Mina, his new sister-in-law. He might not have been a fan when they first met, mostly because, as Langston's arranged-marriage wife, she was walking/talking proof he wouldn't be getting his brother out of the cult, but now she was family, and Luca needed to pay for what he'd done to her.

Luca looked away. The guy was a good actor because he looked genuinely ashamed, almost sickened.

"Why neptunium?" Selene asked.

"Never mind why." Oscar frowned. "Why are you here?"

"We probably should have started there," Selene muttered.

"I came to tell you how to defuse the bomb. It is an unholy thing."

"So it works…you've tested it?" Selene's voice trembled a little.

"I've tested individual components, never a full-scale test, and run computer models."

"Again. Why are you telling us this?"

"Because those who would make the bomb must be stopped."

"'Those who would make the bomb.' That's *you*. You're the one who wants to make it," Oscar snapped.

"No, no…I…" Luca stopped then seemed to sag again. "I designed it, yes, but I do not wish to see it used."

"He designed it," Oscar murmured.

"Remember the thermal exhaust port," Selene breathed so low, he could barely hear.

"I do," he replied in the same nearly inaudible whisper. "Fuck. Why is this cult shit always so complicated?" To Luca, he called out, "You designed the bomb?"

Luca nodded slowly. "Yes. What I have done is unforgivable, but that does not mean I want to see it used."

He was the designer, not the builder. Well, shit, that changed things.

"'In some crude sense the physicists have known sin.'" Selene looked grim.

"And become destroyers of worlds," Luca said in apparent agreement.

"Oppenheimer?" Oscar asked, fairly sure that's what the destroyers of worlds' comment was in relation to.

"Yes." Selene tipped her head to the side as she studied Luca. "You're the city-killer bomb's designer?"

"City killer. Yes, that is a good name for it." Luca walked toward them until he stood at the foot of the steps. "And I would build it, if I had to."

"If you regret designing it, then why would you build it?" Selene demanded.

Luca held out his hands. "*Nessun sente da che parte preme la scarpa, se non chi se la calza.*"

"Do you speak Italian?" Selene asked Oscar.

"Nope. You?"

"Translated, it is 'no one feels which way the shoe is pressing, if not who is wearing it.' But the meaning is…" Luca lowered his hands. "I think the meaning is close to 'needs must, when the devil drives.'"

Selene touched his arm, and Oscar looked at her. He had a feeling they were both thinking the same thing. The combined brain power of himself, his brother, and Selene had been enough not only to figure out that the schematics were for a nuclear bomb…

…but to find the built-in redundancy.

An exploitable flaw, like the thermal exhaust port on the Death Star. A flaw whose existence only made sense if the designer had been working under duress.

Selene started walking down the stairs. Oscar grabbed the collar of his shirt, stopping her, though she was now only two steps above Luca. He loosened his grip when he remembered she had nothing on under it, so if he pulled it up too much, this would become a peep show on top of everything else.

"Who made you design the bomb?" she asked Luca softly.

His eyes widened. "How did you—"

Bill and Wayne chose that moment to storm out onto the porch, guns in hand.

Luca cursed and backpedaled toward his car. Bill leapt down the steps and grabbed him in a choke hold. Wayne wrapped an arm around Selene's waist, hauling her up the steps and shoving Oscar, forcing him back into the house. The instant they were inside, Oscar yanked the other man's arm off of Selene and pushed her behind him.

"What the fuck are you—"

Bill hauled Luca inside and forced him to his knees. Wayne grabbed his arms, holding them—though Luca wasn't struggling—and Bill placed zip cuffs around his wrists, binding them behind his back.

"I'm glad you listened and aren't shooting him," Selene said.

"He has friends incoming." Bill jerked his head to the laptop, which was open on a beat-up oak console table near the front door.

Oscar and Selene looked at the camera feeds. Oscar now knew the emotional reality of the phrase "pants-shit-tingly terrified."

The thermal image cameras—the ones farthest from the house—showed half a dozen red and yellow shapes, people walking at a crouch, moving toward them. The camera feed switched, and another half dozen figures were approaching from another angle.

"What the fuck?" Oscar snapped, anger so much easier than fear.

"This house is good for protection and defense against a lone assailant," Wayne said grimly. "If we'd known we would be defending against a military-style assault…"

"Who are they?" Bill demanded as he hauled Luca to his feet.

"I don't know," Luca blinked at them.

"You'd better hope you do because you're now our

hostage," Bill said coolly. "Your life depends on them standing down."

"They won't," Luca said quietly. "Because I do not know them."

"I think he's telling the truth," Selene said.

"Ma'am, he's a clear and direct—"

"Listen," Oscar snapped. "You don't have all the information. We do. He designed the bomb under duress. We knew from the plans that the designer wanted to have a way to stop the bomb."

Bill blinked. "Like the guy who designed the Death Star?"

"Exactly."

"Then who are they?" Wayne asked, gesturing to the computer.

As one, they turned to look at Luca. "I truly do not know."

"Think hard," Bill snapped.

"Who cares who they are?" Selene asked. "How do we stop them?"

"We've called it in and Bennett is making a formal request for a police SWAT unit to support us."

"Can't we just call nine-one-one? Would that be faster?" Oscar demanded.

Bill pointed at the computer. "They're moving like a military unit. Nine-one-one would send a single squad car. and the cops would be dead before they got to us."

"Who do you work for?" Wayne shook Luca by the shoulder.

"Hey," Oscar snapped. "Let's focus on the other bad guys."

"Our orders—"

"The situation is fluid. Keep up," Selene interjected.

Oscar grinned. Damn, she was amazing.

"Langston, Dr. Tanaka, you…you found the defect I made?" Luca sounded relieved and maybe a little hopeful.

"Yes." Selene glanced at Oscar. "I'm putting on clothes."

"Bring me pants."

She dashed up the stairs and Oscar went to face down Luca. He looked at the other man, hoping he could see… he wasn't sure what. He wasn't the one who was good at reading people. That was Sylvia. He thought he saw… sadness, resignation. The other man looked almost weary.

"What the fuck's going on, man?"

"I thought I could change the world."

"With a bomb?"

"With a powerful, renewable energy source."

"Harness the power of the sun?" Oscar asked, recalling what Selene had said at that now-infamous meeting, which felt like it had happened a lifetime ago instead of only last week.

"Yes. But my personal situation is…" Luca looked away. "Langston, you must understand—"

"Actually, I'm Oscar."

Luca sputtered. "What?"

"I'm Oscar. Not Langston."

"Your name is not Langston?"

"I'm Langston's brother. We're triplets."

"Ah, that explains why you seemed so different." He glanced toward the stairs. "And I'm glad Langston was not cheating on Ms. Edwards."

This conversation was surreal. Oscar had had enough. "Listen, dipshit—"

"Dipshit…" Luca sounded it out.

"What the fuck is going on? Who made you design the bomb? That's who is probably coming toward us."

Selene—who'd thrown on jeans, a hoodie, and tennis shoes—raced down the stairs and threw pants, shoes, and a shirt at him. She nearly got knocked down by Wayne, who raced by securing the house. Heavy metal internal shutters now blocked all the windows, leaving them standing in murky darkness.

"I cannot tell you that."

"Try again," Oscar snapped, pulling on his pants. "You're going to tell us."

"I. Can. Not." Luca enunciated slowly, some of the resignation retreating as his shoulders stiffened with anger.

"You don't know," Selene said.

Luca shook his head. "There is no other way to say—"

"You made some sort of unbreakable vow or promise," Selene cut him off. She was studying the Italian man intently. Oscar realized what she was doing and stayed quiet.

"If I could—" Luca began apologetically.

"They have something on you."

Luca went completely still, but then shook his head a little too quickly. "No, no, it's not—"

Selene refused to relent. "They have some*one*. They have someone you love as a hostage."

Luca looked at her, his eyes unblinking, his body unnaturally still. Oscar wasn't sure the man was even breathing at the moment. He was obviously terrified to show any sign of emotion, that by doing so, he would reveal the truth. What he didn't realize was his utter motionlessness was the most revealing tell of all.

"Fuck," Oscar said quietly as he slipped on his shoes and shirt.

"We can help you," Selene assured Luca.

Bill raced to them, shoving all three of them toward the basement. The man's face was stark. If Oscar hadn't thrown out a hand, he would have tumbled headlong down the stairs, Bill was pushing them so hard.

"What the fuck, man? We—"

"They have a breaching device. SWAT isn't here. You three hide. We'll hold them off."

The last word was lost when the sound of something heavy hit the front door, reverberating through the whole house.

Oscar grabbed Luca, whose arms were still behind his back, and hurried him down the stairs, Selene steadying him from behind. Bill watched them as they made it to the bottom, then he closed the door, sealing them into darkness.

The house shuddered again, and a moment later, the sound of gunshots rang out.

CHAPTER FOUR

The sounds coming from the house above them quieted and then stopped altogether.

"Is the SWAT team here?" Selene whispered.

"Hopefully, they don't shoot us." Oscar, who had been pacing, stopped and looked at them. "Well, me."

While she appreciated Oscar's attempt at grim humor, her stomach, already knotted with anxiety, heaved. How had the situation gone so bad, so fast?

They hadn't had time to deal with the revelation that Luca, the man whom they'd all painted as the villain, appeared to be another victim. Selene glanced up, taking in the silence above them, then went to Luca, who was leaning one shoulder against the wall.

"I'm sorry. There's nothing in here I can use to take the cuffs off." She'd checked, but the basement lacked the sort of things basements should have, like tools or random pieces of metal or other building supplies sharp enough to cut the zip ties biting into the skin around Luca's wrists.

Luca looked up, and the intelligence in his eyes was startling. Appealing.

"You would do that, Dr. Tanaka?"

"Selene," she said. "We knew whoever designed the bomb purposely made it easy to defuse. We therefore extrapolated that the bomb designer either had doubts about their decision to create it in the first place or was trying to create a fail-safe in case things took a bad turn."

"We?" Luca looked between her and Oscar. "You mean yourself and…"

Selene stiffened, realizing she might have made an error.

Did Luca know about the Trinity Masters? If he didn't, she wouldn't tell him. Secrecy was one of their most important rules.

"Langston and Oscar."

"And Mr. Blake and Ms. Edwards?" Luca's lips curved into a wry smile. "I am aware they are both in a relationship with Langston."

"Because you were following them around and spying on them," Oscar snapped.

Luca straightened as if he were going to snap back at Oscar, but took a breath and remained silent.

"Say it," Oscar demanded, arms crossed. He could certainly be intimidating when he wanted to be.

The sound of footsteps overhead made them all fall silent. Oscar nudged her against the wall beside Luca and stepped in front of them both. Selene slid around to the front, hip-checked Oscar back into the wall, and hissed, "I'm the one they're least likely to shoot."

Oscar's eyes scanned her face. "I'm not—"

"—going to be a dumbass. Excellent choice."

In tense silence, they listened to people moving around above them. There were more than two sets of footsteps.

It might be Bill, Wayne, and the SWAT officers.

Wishful thinking on her part. She'd seen the infrared, counted the number of people approaching the house. It didn't take a genius to know the odds were definitely against them.

The door to the basement opened, and a second later, a man's voice said something terse in a language Selene didn't immediately recognize.

"Hide," Luca breathed. "Let them take me and maybe they won't—"

"Who are they?" Oscar's low words rumbled with rage. After what he'd told her about his temper, Selene wondered if perhaps it was the men above them who should be frightened.

"I don't know," Luca said. "But they're speaking Serbian or Croatian."

Boots pounded down the stairs, and Oscar's arm slid around her waist, pulling her beside him. In a line, their backs against the wall, Selene, Oscar, and Luca watched as eight men in anonymizing black riot gear spread out across the basement. Each held a gun, and three of the eight had their weapons trained on them.

One gun for each of them. How equitable.

Selene had never had a gun pointed at her before, and the feeling of helplessness was nearly overwhelming.

One of the men near the center stepped forward. Before he could speak, the man beside him snapped his gun up, twisting his hand palm down in a position that seemed at odds with his tactical gear. "You do what we want and we won't hurt you."

The speaker spoke American English with a Chicago accent, which, like the sideways gun, seemed at odds with the terrifying commando-unit appearance of the group.

The man in the middle, the one who'd first moved, shot the speaker a look. Their faces were hard to see through the tinted visors of their helmets, but whatever the expression, it made Chicago Henchman lower his gun.

The leader focused on Luca. "The plans."

Before Luca could reply, Oscar jumped in.

"The plans to what?" Oscar demanded. "Also, who the fuck are you?"

"You don't talk, motherfucker," another of the men snapped. "You want me to shoot your bitch ass? Because I will. I'll fucking shoot you in the dick." This one also sounded American—with a flat midwestern accent—and young, his voice cracking at one point. It was almost embarrassing, listening to him attempt to intimidate Oscar. Even with the gun, this henchman had far less personal gravitas than Oscar or even Luca.

The leader, who she decided to think of as Boss Henchman, snapped something at Teenager Henchman. Then, ignoring Oscar, he refocused on Luca. "Give us the plans."

Did Boss Henchman have an accent? She couldn't tell. His terse sentences weren't enough for her to make a determination. But there was a slight oddness to the way he'd said "the"—the th sound more of a z.

If he, like Chicago and Teenager henchmen, was an American, who spoke Serbian or Croatian, that would mean...something? She realized she was cataloguing this information as if it were vital. And maybe it would be, if they made it out of this situation alive and she could provide valuable information to…to who? The Trinity Masters? The Masters' Admiralty? The FBI?

"No," Luca said simply. He looked at Selene out of the corner of his eye as he said, "I'm the only one who has them, and I will not give them to you."

I'm the only one who has them.

Luca was warning them not to say they'd seen and copied the plans.

Boss Henchman jerked his head at the man next to him —not Chicago, the guy on the other side—who started toward them. Oscar slid in front of her, the muscles of his back tense as he pressed against her front.

The man reached not for her, but Luca. Henchman Two grabbed him by the shoulder and jerked him away from the wall. Luca stumbled, off-balance without the use of his hands. He glanced back at them as he was hauled away, and Selene's heart clenched at the resignation in his gaze.

She dug her nails into Oscar's back, wanting him to get out of the way so she could try to…to what?

They were in the middle of a deadly situation, which meant this connection she felt to Luca was nothing more than crisis bonding. At least, that was the logical reasoning to explain her sudden desire to protect Luca, a stranger, at all costs.

They forced Luca to his knees.

And then they beat him.

It was a night of horrible firsts. The first time she'd had a gun pointed at her. The first time she'd witnessed such cold and deliberate violence. The first few blows, delivered by Boss and the man who'd grabbed Luca, were cold and calculated—a punch that rocked his head back, then a knee to the chest that made him double over.

Then the others, including Chicago and Teenager, took over. They weren't silent and methodical, the way the two clearly more senior men had been. They taunted Luca. They swore and cursed and made a show of it, clearly enjoying the violence for violence's sake.

The sounds surprised her; below the cruel, stupid comments and jeers were other noises. The slap of Luca's body hitting the concrete when a backhand to the face knocked him off his knees and sent his glasses skittering across the basement floor. Luca's wet coughs after he was kicked in the stomach.

Oscar squatted down to pick up the glasses. Selene took them from him, shoving them in her front hoodie pocket.

Every few blows, Boss would order the others to stop, and he would question Luca, switching to what she was fairly sure was Italian. Luca's answers, when he gave them, were terse, just one word.

"No" was the same in most languages.

"Fuck," Oscar snarled. "Just give them the damned plans." His words weren't loud enough for Luca to hear; it was more as if he were willing Luca to do it.

"We could give them the plans," Selene whispered against Oscar's back.

Oscar turned his back to the room, hugging her, as if comforting her when, in reality, he brought his lips to her ear, continuing their conversation. "Right before they grabbed him, he was trying to warn us not to say we have them."

Selene nodded, then winced at the sound of another vicious blow landing. "They're going to kill him."

"Actually, I don't think they are. I've been watching him, and Luca is shifting right before the blows land."

"What are you talking about?"

"He's leaning out of the way, or twisting so they aren't hitting his kidneys."

"They're still hurting him."

"Yeah, but they're not killing him…and they don't seem to realize what he's doing. Not even the smart one."

"I think the two senior guys might have accents, but the dumb ones sound American."

"The leader and the guy standing beside him are the dangerous ones."

"Boss and his number one henchman. I agree. But they all have guns."

"And we're trapped in a fucking basement with them."

"We have to do something, get all of us out of here. I can't just stand here listening to," a thud sounded, followed by a low moan from Luca, "that."

"What the fuck can we do?" Oscar snapped.

"I don't know," she said, irritated, which was a far better feeling than sick and scared. "This feels like some sort of low-budget gangster movie."

"Yeah, well, you're the one who's halfway to supervillain. Out bad-guy the bad guys," Oscar grumped.

Selene repressed the insane and inappropriate urge to howl with laughter. "Okay, you're my loyal sidekick."

"I was joking."

"I wasn't," she said with a smirk.

Oscar grunted, but turned away so he was standing beside rather than in front of her.

Selene started walking. She walked right past Luca, who was curled on the floor, his face bloody, and through the line of henchmen, Oscar next to her every step of the way. They made it as far as the stairs before Boss barked, "Stop."

She turned to face them, trying to ignore the four guns that were now trained on her.

"You will not leave," Boss growled. She could see now he wasn't a particularly strong man. In fact, his bulk was more fat than muscle.

"I have no interest in remaining. My time is valuable." Selene adjusted her glasses and looked at each of them. "This man approached me through improper channels. We were addressing the break in decorum when you arrived. Clearly you have a preexisting arrangement. Therefore, my men and I are leaving."

From the way Boss Henchman shifted uneasily, she was fairly sure her use of unnecessarily large words had worked. She was banking on his English not being good enough— and the others not being smart enough—to realize she'd just said a whole lot of nothing.

"We should shoot them," Chicago said with relish.

He was clearly not the brains, but stupid was dangerous.

"We were just supposed to get the Italian guy, right?" Teenager asked, looking around. Several of the henchmen had a quick conversation before Boss waved his hand at them and snapped in Serbian (or Croatian) something that didn't really need to be translated. Telling someone to "shut the fuck up" was all about the tone.

The others fell silent as Boss turned back to Selene. "Why did he come?" He gestured to her, the meaning clear enough.

There were more of them, and they had guns, both of which made them dangerous, but despite their military-style equipment—which implied both experience and discipline

—they lacked the level of confidence she would have expected.

Certain that Boss was, in truth, just a henchman like the others, Selene settled into her role as a badder bad guy. She'd been to many a faculty meeting, which meant she could turn what should have been one well-worded email into a forty-minute conversation.

Stall for time.

All she had to do was stall for time until SWAT got there. And, if possible, get them out of the basement. As it stood right now, they were hemmed in with too many weapons and too many loose cannons.

"Because I'm the one people come to when they have that type of need," she replied vaguely.

Another low-voiced conversation between the henchmen. Between their legs, she could see Luca, who lifted his head. One cheek was magenta, but he didn't look as bad as she'd thought he would. Oscar was right, he'd been exaggerating his reactions.

Or they'd concentrated on body blows and he was bleeding internally.

Luca widened his eyes and shook his head at her.

Selene ignored him and folded her arms, as if impatient. It helped hide that her fingers were shaking.

"Who are you?" Boss asked.

"Who are *you*?" she countered.

"No." Boss raised his gun, pointing it at her head, his Eastern European accent stronger now with his irritation. "You answer."

"Shoot me and you'll never *know* the answer."

"Answer!"

"Selene," Oscar hissed. "This isn't—"

67

"I have access to resources," she said, maintaining her calm facade, while inside she was barely holding it together. "Resources no one else has, and which he wanted."

Another statement that was open to a variety of interpretations.

Boss looked at the man next to him, the one who'd first dragged Luca away, as if seeking input. If all of them had been like those two, attempting a bluff would have been suicidal.

Chicago scratched his elbow with his gun, while the second man said something in Serbian. Boss listened, then refocused on her.

To her everlasting shock, Boss lowered his weapon, a definite glimmer of what looked like respect in his eyes. "Ah, we are in the same business."

Crap. She totally was a supervillain.

"You buy or sell?" Boss gestured to Luca, without looking back at him.

Lying on the floor, Luca mouthed, "Sell."

"Sell," Selene said, then she narrowed her eyes. "What does he have that I would want to buy?"

Boss shrugged uncomfortably, aware he may have revealed something he shouldn't have.

"If she sells the chemicals and stuff, let's take her t—" Teenager started, only to be cut off by Boss, who reached out and shoved him.

Selene looked back at Oscar. "Perhaps we were too hasty, leaving—" crap, she'd almost said Luca, and knowing his name might not be what her supervillain persona would know. "—the Italian to them, if he has something to offer."

"He is ours." Boss raised the gun once more.

Selene paused, pretending to consider it. "Then as a

matter of professional courtesy, I leave him to you. However, my presence here is not necessary."

"You and I are not finished talking," Boss said. "Maybe we buy what you sell."

"You didn't follow proper channels, either." She turned away from him and approached the foot of the stairs. She expected to feel a bullet rip through her body any minute. Mercifully, it didn't.

"This is taking too long," Chicago muttered, clearly unhappy with the way Boss was running the show.

Boss ignored that complaint, then turned to the other men and gestured to Luca. "Take him upstairs. We finish there."

Selene remained at the base of the steps and tried to take a deep breath, grateful they would be going upstairs. Upstairs where she and Oscar wouldn't be trapped and would at least have somewhere to run and hide if the opportunity presented itself. And if they were more spread out, maybe there'd be a way for them to grab Luca...

But upstairs would also mean the henchmen might see SWAT coming and take her and Oscar hostage again.

Then again, if they were in the basement, they'd be even easier to grab and use as human shields when SWAT arrived.

Oscar stepped next to Selene when Chicago waved his gun at them. "You two next. And don't try any funny business."

Yep. Bad movie.

"Go," Oscar breathed, putting his hand on her back and urging her to move.

As she started up the stairs, she saw Henchman Two and Teenager reach beneath Luca's arms, half-carrying, half-dragging him up the stairs. Selene couldn't tell if Luca was too weak to walk up the stairs on his own or if he was simply pretending he was more seriously injured in order to make their job harder.

Or maybe Oscar was wrong and Luca was in far worse shape than they realized.

If they'd hoped to have a few moments to themselves upstairs, they were disappointed because the henchmen were right on Oscar's heels.

There was definitely a power struggle/language barrier situation going on between Boss and Chicago. Perhaps Selene could exacerbate that situation, turn the henchmen on themselves. She tried to recall if Bill or Wayne had mentioned how long it would take for SWAT to arrive.

The thought of their two bodyguards had her looking around. "Where are my men?" she asked with forced bravado.

Granted, this situation had been out of her control since practically the beginning, but that didn't change the fact that two men had risked their lives to keep her safe. She needed to know they were okay.

Teenager leered at her. "Taking a little nap."

She gave him a once-over and sneered.

When he stormed toward her, Oscar stepped in front of her, his arms folded.

Boss barked something from the kitchen, where he'd led the henchmen. Teenager hesitated, but it wasn't until Chicago said, "Leave the bitch," that he turned away.

Definitely a power struggle.

For a moment, they were alone in the hall.

Oscar turned to her. "We'll get him back. They aren't going to kill him. They want the plans."

"They're torturing him."

"Hold it together, Tanaka. We've gotta find Wayne and Bill. They're probably locked in a closet."

"Why are you whispering?" she asked.

"Because we saw twelve of them on the security cameras, and only eight were in the basement."

"Fuck," she hissed.

"That's my line." Oscar kissed her, quick and hard, and then stepped away. "We need to stay with them." Oscar jerked his head toward the kitchen. "If we run into the other mercenaries before the head guy gives them the message that you're dangerous and we should be allowed to leave…"

"And if we stay with them, we can keep an eye on Luca."

Oscar nodded in agreement, the corners of his eyes tight with what other people might say was anger, but which she was sure was worry.

They stepped into the kitchen, Selene in the lead.

They were just in time to see Henchman Two shove Luca to his knees once more. Chicago then kicked him in the stomach.

If Oscar was correct, and Luca was attempting to soften the blows by slight body adjustments, there was no denying he'd been unprepared for the kick. He lurched forward, grunting in obvious pain.

Selene tried to ignore Luca's groans and the muted thuds of the beating, which started again—and with renewed vigor—fighting to listen for some sound from outside that would mean help had arrived.

They could have left. Could have gone to find Wayne and Bill and then left.

But she felt as if she needed to be here for Luca. Not that she was doing a damn thing to help him.

How long could they stand here before Boss or Chicago realized how weird it was that they were hanging around? Selene tried to come up with their next move, but her nerves were slowly getting the better of her. They were lucky to have fooled the men this long, and she knew enough to know they were currently living on borrowed time.

Where the hell was the SWAT team?

Her fingers dug into Oscar's back after one particularly hard slap that sent Luca's head back.

"Enough!" Boss yelled as Luca lay on the floor, a trickle of blood dripping from his nose to the tile beneath him. The boss henchman knelt by Luca. "Give me the plans," he demanded.

Luca didn't reply to Boss's request, not even to repeat his standard "no." Instead, his eyes remained closed, and Selene wondered for a moment if they'd knocked him out.

Selene caught Oscar's quick intake of breath, her gaze leaving Luca's still frame lying on the ground.

"What?" she whispered to Oscar, whose attention wasn't on the activity in the kitchen, but rather on something outside the window. Either Bill and Wayne hadn't had a chance to close the metal shutters in here, or Boss's group had opened them.

She followed his gaze, but saw nothing. Then, she squinted and stared harder, certain she'd seen movement.

"Give them!" Boss shook Luca's shoulder roughly.

She saw Luca's eyes open slightly, slitted just enough for him to see. He was faking unconsciousness.

She was trying to decide what she should say, what else

she could do to stall any more of the beating, when Oscar stiffened, his hand dropping to his side, his fingers wrapping around her wrist.

Through the kitchen window, she could see movement on the back porch, and the sense of relief made her light-headed.

A figure, clad in black, in almost identical riot gear to what the henchmen wore, slid through the shadows.

"We have a problem," Oscar breathed, squeezing her wrist slightly.

"How to get him away from them?" she asked.

The henchmen had split into two groups—Boss and Number Two talking quickly in Serbian. Chicago, Teenager, and the other four huddled together, speaking quietly in English. They occasionally threw looks her way. Looks that said the unimaginative assholes were tired of abusing Luca and looking for their next target. Between her and Oscar, she was the far more obvious victim.

"Or are you worried about the way they're looking at me?" she asked when Oscar didn't reply.

"Black SUV."

"What?" Was Oscar losing it? Maybe the stress of the situation had gotten to him.

"I think I see a black SUV in the distance."

Selene's heart stopped.

Oscar turned toward her. "There are men approaching. Black clothing, no markings. Not SWAT. Not police. I don't think they're—"

Glass shattered, and she had a brief view of a small black canister sailing through the air before the world exploded with light and sound.

CHAPTER FIVE

O scar slitted his eyes open. Red spots danced in his vision. They went with the ringing in his ears.

He could see just enough to make out that around the room, everyone—including Selene—had hit their knees. Most had their eyes squeezed shut and hands over their ears. Only the two less stupid guys—the two he was pretty sure were foreigners with limited English—had managed to hold on to their guns.

Luca, bloody and lying on the floor, blinked, seeming to stare into middle space. He'd had his eyes closed when the light and sound bomb—a flashbang—had come through the window. Oscar had been turned toward Selene, which had saved his vision.

Plus, he'd had experience in the aftermath of a flashbang. Langston had gone through a period where he'd developed a couple of versions of the explosive with various levels of light exposure, decibels of sound, and also a few that gave off smoke.

Oscar had learned to work through the blindness and deafness so he could chase down his brother and beat the shit out of him.

There was no point in talking, Selene and Luca wouldn't be able to hear him, so he dashed forward and yanked Luca off the floor.

Luca started to fold, dropping back to his knees, so Oscar shook him. Luca blinked, focused, realized who had grabbed him, and miraculously was able to stand.

Oscar gave him a shove toward the interior kitchen door, and Luca stumbled into the hall. He hauled Selene up. She started to shove him away, her eyes open but completely unseeing. Damn it, she didn't know it was him. Oscar cupped the back of her head and kissed her.

That worked.

She stopped fighting and reached blindly for him. He grabbed her hand and dragged her out the door and into the hall. He glanced back in time to see the presumed leader of their first attackers look up, notice Luca was gone, and then raise his gun.

The fact that, with his ears ringing, he wouldn't hear the sound of the shot before he felt the bullet rip through him somehow made this worse.

Just before he slapped the door between the kitchen and hallway closed, he saw the back door explode inward and two men, moving at a crouch, their faces obscured by black face shields, entered the house. Their gear was uniformly black, no "police" or "sheriff" or "SWAT" patches anywhere in sight.

Fan-fucking-tastic.

How many people were after these fucking plans?

Oscar grabbed Luca again, hauling both him and

Selene toward the front door. As they passed, he looked around, hoping to see Bill and Wayne, but they were nowhere in sight.

A quick glance out the front windows showed two black SUVs flanking Luca's car and a team of four men standing on the porch.

He was not waiting around to find out who those jokers were.

With a snarl he couldn't hear, he changed course. Bill and Wayne had parked on the side of the house, so he led his people into the small makeshift office that was just off the main living area. The window shutter probably made a racket when he unlatched it, but hopefully everyone was still in partial hearing loss. The window itself was heavy duty, dual-paned, but after he unscrewed the sash lock, it slid open easily. Knowing his luck, the damn thing had probably screeched, so he waited, muscles tense, but no black-clad men appeared.

He slid out the window, dropped to his feet, and waited, ready to be shot at any moment.

Selene was shoving Luca, who threw a leg over the windowsill and slid out. Oscar caught him, wishing he had a way to cut the zip ties so Luca could use his hands.

Selene practically threw herself out the window, and together they raced for the car. Oscar jumped into the driver's seat while Selene and Luca dove in through the door behind him, clambering onto the back seat awkwardly. The keys were right where he'd seen Wayne leave them—in a compartment in the center console. He jabbed the button, turned the car on, and threw it into drive.

Men came running from the porch as he sped past. He

saw one raise a gun. In the rearview mirror, he saw Luca and Selene duck.

The crack of the shot was just barely audible over the ringing in his ears.

The car lurched, but the windows remained intact. He had no idea where they'd been hit—fuck, if they'd shot the gas tank, would the car explode or just lose gas and leave them stranded?

He put his foot down, speeding along the rural drive until he hit the main road, which wasn't much of a road. Outside the window, white flakes started to whip by. He thought it was damage to his vision until they started to fall faster.

Snow.

Because, of course, it was starting to fucking snow.

What they needed was a main road—a real main road, not a country road. A highway or interstate. Someplace with people, or that would get them to people. He kept driving, far faster than was safe, hoping he'd recognize something and know when to turn.

Far behind him, barely visible through the flurries, a black SUV appeared.

"Fuck," he snarled, surprised he could almost sort of hear his own voice.

He spotted a turnoff and took it, the vehicle rocking up onto two wheels. Selene scrambled from the back into the front passenger seat. She opened the glove compartment and took out a gun.

Hey, look, now they were armed.

"Do you know how to drive in snow?" she yelled.

He shook his head, grateful his hearing was returning.

She made a face. "Slow. Down."

He slowed even though it made him feel frantic.

Outside the window, the snow started to stick.

He turned right, then right again, hoping to find his way back to the main road they'd been on, behind the SUV, so he could once more try to nose his way back to a freeway.

Instead, the roads twisted and turned, the scenery outside becoming hilly and even more rural, a dangerous thin white layer of slippery snow covering the road, making it hard to see. If it wasn't for the vegetation that now sported layers of snow on the upper branches, he might not have known where the road was at all.

"We need to pull off. We can't keep going in this," Selene said, her voice slightly distorted. His ears were still ringing, but he could hear.

"If we do and they find us—"

"If we can't drive in it, they can't, either." The fact that Selene, who was an upstate New Yorker and knew her snow, was more worried about the road and weather than the bad guys was telling.

On their right, a gentle slope led down to the base of a small ravine. Trees, close enough together that they only caught glimpses of a stream at the apex of the valley, would provide some hiding if he could find a place to pull off.

Then, through the trees, he saw the top of a roof, visible only because the geometric rectangular white of the snow-lined roof caught his eye amid the natural landscape. A second later, he glimpsed a small break with a mailbox beside it. He turned onto the drive.

The slope down to the house seemed much less gentle when he was trying to keep the heavy car from sliding down it through the snow than when he'd just been looking at it.

The tail end of the car started to fishtail, but he managed to keep control—barely—and they reached the bottom without damage.

"No lights," Selene said. "Or other vehicles. Doesn't look like anyone is home."

Oscar nodded, glancing in the rearview mirror at the driveway they'd just slid down. He didn't have to be a snow expert to know this car wasn't going to make it back up to the road they'd just left. Not that he planned to try. The snow was falling so thick and hard, he was struggling to make out the hood of the car anymore.

This wasn't good.

"Come on," he said, twisting to look at Luca, who had managed to push himself upright in the backseat despite his bound arms.

Opening the doors let in a blast of ice-laden cold air. Oscar left getting Luca out of the car to Selene while he ran for the cabin. A quick look in the windows showed no signs of anyone. On one hand, that was good because it meant there was no chance of someone mistaking his asking for help as an attempt to break in. He'd just left the scene of one shootout, and he'd like the "not getting shot" track record to stand.

On the other hand, it meant he was going to have to actually break in.

He didn't see a video doorbell or security company sticker. That didn't mean those things weren't there. It just meant he didn't see them.

Selene and Luca joined him on the covered porch.

"We need to get him inside." Selene's tone was urgent.

Oscar looked at her, worried, but she was looking at Luca, who was hunched forward, his head hanging.

Oscar went to one of the windows, braced himself on the porch rail, and then kicked out the bottom pane of the window with his heel. He knocked the rest of the glass free, then started to climb in when Selene thrust Luca at him and edged her way in front of him.

"I'm a better fit."

She climbed in, careful but quick, and a second later the front door opened.

The cabin was small but comfortable, the decor featuring far more chicken-themed items than he'd realized even existed.

Selene raced for the kitchen and started opening drawers. A second later, she returned with a pair of kitchen shears.

Luca's wrists were bloody, and he made a small noise of pain as she slid the scissors under the wide zip ties and snipped them.

"Thank you," he said, then groaned as his wrists were finally free, his arms falling to hang at his sides.

Over Luca's bowed head, Selene looked at Oscar and they shared a grim expression.

They set Luca in a chair at the round kitchen table. "Find something to cover that window. I'll figure out the heat situation."

It was warmer inside than out, but it wouldn't stay that way with the cold air pouring in through the window. He did a quick search through the house, including the miniscule root-cellar-style basement.

It was there he found a small toolbox and a few oddly sized pieces of plywood.

Wood in hand and carrying the toolbox, he came back

up. Luca was at the kitchen sink letting cold water run over his wrists.

He found Selene on the front porch, loading a bucket with coal.

"Saw this on the way in. We're in coal country." She carried the scuttle inside and walked over to the coal-burning stove. Oscar was very impressed when she grabbed the heat gun that rested on top and held it against the coal. "It will take a while, but this should heat the house."

Oscar fitted the largest piece of plywood over the window—it only covered half of it, then awkwardly tried to hold it in position with one knee. Luca came and silently braced the wood while Oscar nailed it to the wooden window frame.

Together, he and Luca finished covering the window, working quickly and quietly. Once they were done, Luca retreated back to the kitchen table, while Oscar added a layer of black garbage bags and duct tape to the remaining open space, sealing up the frame.

Selene was rubbing her arms. "It'll take a minute to warm up but we have heat."

"What we need is a phone," Oscar said. Now that the adrenaline high from their escape had faded, Oscar was thinking about all the things they didn't have—their phones, wallets, or Selene's laptop.

He didn't have any electronics. For the first time in his adult life, he was totally tech-less.

Oscar bent, braced his hands on his knees, and tried not to panic.

"Oscar, what's wrong?" Selene asked.

"My phone. Your computer."

A chair squeaked across the floor loudly as Luca stood. "The copy of the plans? They have it?"

"No, but it's a computer. I *don't have access to a computer. Any computer.*"

"I...do not understand," Luca said slowly.

"Oscar's having a small breakdown." Selene patted him on the head. "There, there."

The anger-laced panic was interrupted by a surprised snort of laughter. Oscar straightened, then folded his arms. "Did you just pat me on the head?"

"Would you rather I pat your ass?" she asked with a smile.

Luca cleared his throat. Oscar's reply died on his lips. Now was not the time for sexy banter.

Though really, was there a bad time for sexy banter?

"Thank you," Luca said quietly. "For rescuing me. It was kind, and more than I could have imagined."

Selene opened her mouth, but Oscar put a hand on her shoulder. "We saved you because we need answers."

Luca nodded, as if that was what he'd expected.

"Who are—" Oscar started.

Selene held up a hand. "No. First, we contact the Grand Master."

Oscar snarled, and Luca looked confused. "Who?"

Selene winced, realizing what she'd said.

"We could do that," Oscar added. "If we had phones, but we don't."

Luca once again cleared his throat. "Isn't that a phone?" He pointed to a decorative chicken phone mounted on the side of a kitchen cabinet. "A, uh, chicken phone."

Selene picked up the chicken-leg-shaped receiver and started stabbing the egg-shaped number buttons.

"You know the number?"

"If you had access to the number for the Batphone, wouldn't you memorize it?" Selene asked.

"She's not Batman," Oscar muttered, aware he was perilously close to sounding sulky.

"Sebastian, it's Selene Tanaka. Yes, we're alive." Then she frowned. "Wait, what rescue?"

Oscar stomped over and made her twist the receiver so he could hear.

"We sent in a rescue team, but they said you fled with Mr. Campisi," Sebastian was saying.

"The second set of bad guys was actually..." Oscar ground his teeth.

"Hello, Mr. Hayden. And yes. You ran away from your rescue. We were briefly concerned that perhaps you had changed allegiances."

"What?" Selene demanded.

"You *took* Mr. Campisi and fled."

"Because we were expecting a SWAT team. That's who Bill and Wayne said they called."

"Well, shit." Sebastian's tone had relaxed. "That makes sense."

"You should have had them identify themselves," Selene snapped.

"Or wear the cult logo on their uniforms," Oscar added.

At the table, Luca started at the word *cult*. Oscar glanced at Selene, who raised a brow. What did Luca know?

"Bill and Wayne, we looked for them…" The anger was gone from Selene's voice, replaced by worry.

"They're alive. On their way to the ER to be checked out. Both in stable condition, but they were drugged so we need to be sure."

Oscar felt almost sick with relief. He'd been trying not to think about the fact that they might have left Bill and Wayne to be either captured or killed.

"You took Mr. Campisi as a hostage, then?" Sebastian asked. "Dangerous, but there are no doubt some benefits. We will reroute the strike team to pick you up—"

"We're in the middle of what looks like a blizzard. I doubt you'll be able to get to us," Selene said grimly.

"Fuck. How? It's not even that cold here in Boston."

"Well, Bum-fuck, Pennsylvania is now covered in a foot of snow." Oscar looked out the window. The world outside was blindingly white, the wind whipping the falling snow sideways so it even coated the trunks of the trees.

"Are you safe?" Sebastian asked.

"Yes. Did you catch all the Serbian henchmen?" Selene asked.

"We have twelve men in custody."

"That was all of them," Oscar confirmed.

"How did you know they were Serbian?" Sebastian asked.

"Luca guessed, based on the language they were speaking."

"Ah. I…hope to be able to speak to Mr. Campisi soon." Sebastian's words were carefully chosen.

"He's the bomb *designer*." Selene stressed the last word.

There was a long beat of silence. "I see. That changes things," Sebastian murmured.

"Exactly, because this whole thing wasn't already fucked," Oscar said.

They spent a few more minutes on the phone. Selene rummaged until she found some mail with the address of the cabin on it, and they gave that information to Sebastian, who stepped away for a few minutes to confirm that the rescue team, who apparently had been out looking for them, had been forced to stop because of the snow.

The three of them were stuck until the roads were passable. It was safe to say if they couldn't get out, whoever lived here couldn't get back.

Oscar poked around the kitchen enough to confirm that there was food and they weren't in danger of starving. Ten minutes later, they ended the call with Sebastian, and Oscar realized that there was nothing they could do but wait. If he hadn't pushed them to run, hadn't literally driven the getaway car—away from their rescue team—they could have been on their way back to Boston and back to their normal lives.

Except he'd joined the cult, so what the hell did normal even mean these days?

Oscar scrubbed his hands over his face. "What do we do now?"

Selene opened a cabinet and pulled out a dusty bottle of red wine. "Would anyone like a drink?"

CHAPTER SIX

L uca smiled as Selene handed him the glass of Merlot. The Bellator Dei didn't allow consumption of alcohol. He'd sip, but not drink it all, as the few glasses of wine he'd snuck over the years had made him feel pleasantly languid and libidinous. It wasn't the time, place, or company for those sorts of feelings.

"Oh." Selene reached into the front pocket of her hoodie. "I forgot I had these."

Luca could have kissed the beautiful scientist when she produced his glasses. While his vision wasn't terrible, it also wasn't great. He was nearsighted enough that he would have spent the next few days squinting at the blurry blobs around him. The frames were slightly bent from the backhand that had knocked them off, but mercifully, they weren't broken.

He bent the frame back into shape, then slipped them on, nodding his head gratefully. "Thank you. I feared they were lost."

Oscar, who had disappeared while Selene was pouring

drinks, returned and set a white pill bottle in front of him. Pain medication.

Luca looked up in surprise. Oscar was frowning, his expression almost angry, but his actions were caring.

He still couldn't believe that Oscar and Selene had rescued him. It was unexpected…and undeserved.

"Thank you." Luca read the label, carefully took out two, and then closed the bottle.

Oscar snatched it up, shook out two more, and smacked them down on the table. "You just got your ass beat. You can have four."

But he deserved the pain.

Luca found it increasingly difficult to face the man in the mirror every morning when he considered what he'd done. What he'd become.

Everyone was silent until he put the pills in his mouth, washing them down with a small sip of the wine. The smell of it reminded him of Italy.

He didn't think of Italy as home. No place was really home.

The instant he finished swallowing, Selene and Oscar both started to talk at once.

"How were you planning to resolve the distance discrepancy needed for the particle—"

"Who the fuck are you, and what the hell is going on?"

Selene looked at Oscar, cleared her throat, then said, "Fine, start with the less interesting information."

Oscar was staring at her. "You thought specifics about the bomb was where to start?"

"Well, we know he's not the bad guy."

"He designed, and said he was willing to make, a city-killer bomb. He's at least two-thirds of the way to bad guy."

"He designed it under duress," Selene countered.

Oscar pointed at her. "You're way too close to being a supervillain."

"You're a hacker. Between the three of us, we're basically a modern-day Manhattan Project." Selene gestured to all of them, and Luca felt ridiculously pleased about being included, even in such an offhanded way.

Oscar snorted. "More like the Masters of Evil."

"Who?" Selene propped her chin on her fist, seemingly at ease arguing with Oscar, whose frown was intimidating.

"Team of Marvel bad guys."

"Hydra," Luca said. Both turned to look at him. "If this were a comic book, I would be a Hydra scientist."

Oscar leaned forward. "Start talking."

Luca opened his mouth, closed it. He'd been about to tell them his story. How he'd ended up sitting at this table with them, and he was compelled to start with his childhood. A story he'd never shared with anyone.

But that was not what they cared about.

His head felt foggy, not because of the wine, but due to a lack of sleep, and exhaustion from the pain and fear of the last few hours. He'd been up nearly thirty-six hours straight now, and while it was only midafternoon, he wasn't going to be able to keep his eyes open much longer.

"You know much of the story already, if you know that I added a flaw to the bomb design."

"You created the bomb design for them because they're threatening someone you love." Selene's eyes were soft.

"Yes," Luca confessed. It seemed pointless to deny it, when he'd already admitted as much, thanks to his failure to hide his reaction.

"Who made you design the bomb?" Oscar asked.

Luca looked at them, these strangers who felt familiar, who felt like compatriots. It was an odd feeling after so many years of having to keep his own counsel. One he was about to destroy with just three words. "The Bellator Dei."

Neither of them reacted.

Luca had expected his words to have the conversational equivalent of detonating a bomb.

He thought the Bellator Dei was well known amongst members of the Masters' Admiralty. They were ancient enemies, the Bellator Dei having almost been destroyed by the amoral and powerful Masters' Admiralty until eight years ago, when a benefactor, a man who knew the Masters' Admiralty's secrets, had stepped in to raise the Bellator Dei to its former glory. The man had supported them in their ordained quest to rid the world of the corrupt and evil secret society that controlled the world governments and promoted unholy unions between one woman and two men.

He'd stopped believing the doctrine years ago, when he realized exactly what the Bellator Dei was, though he'd assumed at least some part of what he'd been taught about their "enemy" was true.

But none of the stories about the Masters' Admiralty mentioned that the secret society also operated in America.

Luca took another sip of the wine, wincing as the tart liquid stung a cut on his lower lip.

Selene noticed his discomfort. She rose and walked around the kitchen, opening several drawers until she found a towel. Then she went to the freezer, grabbed some ice, and wrapped it up.

His eyes widened with genuine surprise when she handed it to him.

"Here. This might help until the pills kick in." She leaned closer, inspecting the injuries on his face.

"You know how to take a beating," Oscar observed. "You were moving away from the worst of the blows."

Luca nodded. He'd learned at a very young age how to disassociate, how to accept the physical pain while blocking the emotional impact of the beating—the sense of helplessness, the fear. "I have suffered worse beatings than this."

"From the Bellator Dei?" Oscar asked.

Luca searched Oscar's expression for any hint of duplicity, still doubtful that these two, who were clearly members of the Masters' Admiralty, had never even heard of them. How humbling that, while for the members of the Bellator Dei, defeating the Masters' Admiralty was everything, to members of that secret society, they were nothing.

"Yes, and from earlier. From my childhood." Luca purposefully didn't look at them, not wanting to see the pity he knew would be there. "It made me easier for the Bellator Dei to indoctrinate."

"Indoctrinate?"

"I believe this is the word." Luca's English was good, but not perfect.

"I think I know where you're going with this, and yes, that's the word," Selene said.

"The Bellator Dei, the warriors of God, are a cult."

Oscar put his head on the table and thunked it there several times while muttering "another fucking cult."

Selene patted Oscar's back while looking at Luca. "Ignore him. Keep talking."

"I, uh…" Luca relaxed back into the chair. Their reactions were not what he'd expected, not the anger or derision he'd anticipated. The sense of camaraderie was probably an act, a subtle way of getting him to drop his guard and reveal his secrets. They needn't try so hard. Luca had no one else to turn to for help.

"They found," *us*, "me when I was young. Thirteen. In an orphanage in Tbilisi, Georgia. My name then was Nikoloz."

"You were adopted by a cult?" Oscar raised his head. "Fuck."

"I was, and I was grateful for what they did for..." He took a sip of wine. "I was desperate for the new start, anxious to leave the boy I'd been behind. I was happy to forget who I'd been, that poor Georgian orphan, to become an Italian. Become a man. The Bellator Dei filled my hungry stomach, gave me responsibilities and a good education. I worked very hard to become a man worthy of them. I embraced my new home, my new country. I was devoted to them and their mission."

"Which is?" Selene asked.

"To eradicate the Masters' Admiralty."

Oscar and Selene stared at him for a moment, then looked at one another.

"They blame the corrupting influence of the Masters' Admiralty for the current ungodly state of the European governments."

"Corrupting because...of the trinity marriage?" Selene asked.

"Yes, the union between two men and one woman is—"

"Don't forget two women with one dude," Oscar said.

"What?" Luca blinked at him.

"Or three men, three women. It's *any* combination of three."

Luca opened his mouth, then closed it.

"Bet the religious nuts wouldn't have objected if the trinity marriage was only one man with two women." Selene's mouth curled up in a sneer.

"Of course not," Oscar said. "The whole point of most religious cults is so gross old men can rape teenage girls."

Luca wanted to run to that chicken phone and call Joli. Wanted to see if this information—which he'd, suspected based on his own observations—would be enough to break their hold on her.

"I saw your brother with Ms. Edwards and Mr. Blake, and I thought they seemed…"

Happy. They'd seemed happy.

Luca looked out the window, at the near white-out conditions outside the now pleasantly warm cabin. Speaking of Mina Edwards reminded Luca of what he'd done. He could justify his actions, remind himself that he had no choice, but those reassurances paled in the face of the pain he'd caused.

"How is Ms. Edwards?" he asked softly. He would never forget the terror in her eyes when he'd strapped the bomb to her. His actions were unforgivable.

Oscar slammed his fist on the kitchen table. "You don't get to ask about her after you terrorized her. I don't care if you designed the bomb with a gun to your head. You strapped a bomb to my sister-in-law and sent her out in public. Then you fucking set off smoke bombs in *Boston*. You gave the city PTSD flashbacks, and—"

"Oscar," Selene murmured, but Luca cut her off.

"No. He's correct. What I did to Ms. Edwards was reprehensible." The sense of camaraderie was gone, burned away by Oscar's justified anger. It was good that

Luca was reminded that he was far past the point of redemption.

"I have done many evil things," Luca said softly. Perhaps the violence of his childhood and adolescence had broken something inside him. Some moral compass that would have stopped him from doing evil things for a good reason.

"I stopped believing in their mission years ago, but I could not leave the Bellator Dei. I became what they asked, did what they needed. I infiltrated your society by working for *Cohortes Praetorianae,* which allowed me to both monitor what you knew on behalf of the Bellator Dei, while also truly analyzing the bombs they brought to me. Sometimes I was analyzing the remnants of a bomb I might have designed."

"You're a double agent," Selene said.

"No, because I have no allegiance, but to my…"

"Spit it out," Oscar growled. "Who? Your parents, brother, sister, wife? Who do they have?"

What was the point of keeping the secret? Perhaps… perhaps they could do what he had not been able to. "My sister. Joli."

"You did all this to protect your sister." Selene raised an eyebrow at Oscar. "Something I'm sure you can understand."

"I wouldn't force someone to be a suicide bomber."

"Wouldn't you? To protect your sister?"

Oscar ran his hand over his jaw, drawing Luca's attention to the other man's dark beard. He could just make out the edge of the tattoos on Oscar's upper arms. Luca wondered what a man like Oscar would ink onto his skin.

"I'd do anything for Sylvia. I mean…Jesus—fuck."

Oscar didn't finish his thought, though Luca understood why. It couldn't be easy to admit the lengths—the horrible, unimaginable lengths—a person would go to for a loved one.

"My sister has no life outside of the Bellator Dei. She still lives with our parents and works for the Bellator Dei. Every day, she is there at their headquarters. She had no way to see what they are. I was never as…devout…as she is, and my calling…" He paused, snorting in grim amusement at the term he'd used. "My *orders* meant I was able to have a life outside of that place."

There was silence for several minutes. Selene refilled Oscar's empty glass, then her own. She extended the bottle toward his still mostly full glass.

"No, thank you," Luca said quietly. "The Bellator Dei insist on purity of body. No alcohol."

"Fuck that," Oscar snorted. "Booze is how God intended all of us to get through this fucking shit show that is life."

Luca considered that. "When I realized that the Bellator Dei were not warriors of God, but a cult, the first thing I did was get a bottle of cheap vodka and drink it."

Oscar's expression relaxed into a smile. "Cheap vodka is not where I would have started."

"It was…not pleasant," Luca admitted.

Selene laughed softly and took a sip. The pain medication had kicked in, and Luca's whole body weighed heavily with exhaustion, both from the dulled edge of the pain and the relief of finally talking about what he'd been doing.

It wouldn't change his fate, but maybe if the rest of the Masters' Admiralty thought the same way Selene and Oscar did, he could bargain with them to ensure Joli was safe. The Bellator Dei had to be stopped, and he'd been desperately searching for a way to keep his sister from ending up like…

He would not allow Joli to become collateral damage in a battle she should never have been forced to wage. She'd been young and hungry and desperately seeking approval, love, and their adopted parents and the cult preyed on those things.

Selene and Oscar gave him hope. Hope for Joli.

Hope that she would not end up like Greta.

He had no hope for himself. His life was forfeit, thanks to his actions. A fact that he'd accepted years ago.

Luca pushed himself up from the table, his ribs aching, his shoulder muscles hard as rock. He couldn't keep going. "If you'll excuse me."

"What about food?" Selene asked. "I can start dinner now. None of us has eaten anything."

He shook his head. "I'm not hungry. Right now, I simply need to rest."

Selene nodded, and Luca walked stiffly toward the couch.

"Take the bed," Selene said.

"No, there is only one bed, you should have it." Luca gestured between them.

"Right, he knows we're sleeping together because he spied on us with that webcam," Oscar said, but the anger in his words had no heat behind it.

I didn't look. I respected your privacy.

Those were the things he should have said.

Instead, what he said was, "I was rather disappointed when you stopped."

Oscar threw his head back and laughed, and Selene arched a brow at him while smiling.

"Go get in bed," Selene said. "I think the couch pulls out. We'll sleep there tonight."

He should offer to sleep on the floor. He should insist on taking the couch.

But he hurt.

His whole body ached, he was tired, and more than that, it felt good to let Selene and Oscar keep taking care of him, even if all they were doing was letting him have the bed.

CHAPTER SEVEN

Selene made Oscar memorize the phone number for the Grand Masters' advisors—"Call them before nine-one-one unless you're having a medical emergency"—before making him dial the newly memorized digits on the chicken phone.

"Yes?" Sebastian answered.

"It's, uh, Oscar Hayden." God, he hated talking on the phone. What was this, fucking nineteen-ninety, that he had to talk to someone on an actual landline phone?

"We're working on extracting you, but it's not going to happen for at least twenty-four hours. Maybe more, if there's no break in the weather."

Oscar glanced out the kitchen window. The snow was really piling up. If he had to guess, he'd say they'd already gotten a foot and it was showing no signs of stopping soon. As a Southerner, he wasn't accustomed to weather like this. He didn't like the feeling of being so completely trapped by nature.

"Yeah, I could have told you that."

Sebastian snorted. "Is there a reason for your call?"

"We have new information." Selene snatched the chicken leg away from him. Oscar wrapped his arm around her waist and pulled her against him so they could both hear. And because he liked the feel of her body against his.

"Tell me."

Selene briefly outlined what they'd learned from Luca about the Bellator Dei, who stood in righteous moral opposition to the Masters' Admiralty. About his sister who, unlike him, was still a devout member and therefore essentially a hostage.

"Ohh, plot twist." Franco's accented voice sounded distant, but the words were audible, and when Sebastian sighed, Oscar couldn't stop the snort-laugh.

"That answers some questions," Sebastian said. "But raises others." There was a long pause. "Be careful."

"You think he's lying?" Oscar asked, all amusement gone.

"Possibly. Right now, we have no proof other than his word that he's the bomb designer. It could be a ruse."

"But it was his tablet that Langston accidentally grabbed."

"It was a tablet in his possession. If he were the man ordered to actually build and test the bomb, wouldn't he need a copy of the diagram?"

Oscar and Selene frowned at one another. Sebastian had a point, but he hadn't been in that house. Hadn't seen the way Luca had taken the beating, heard Luca help them by cluing them in about what to say and not say.

"And there are still too many questions we don't have answers to," Sebastian continued. "Including how he found you at that safe house."

"We'll ask him," Oscar said.

"Wait, and we'll question him once we extract you."

Oscar glanced at Selene and shook his head. Selene frowned, but then nodded in agreement.

"There's one additional piece of information," Selene said. "He thinks we're members of the Masters' Admiralty. He admitted that until he met Langston, he hadn't known that the Masters' Admiralty also operated in America."

Another long silence, then Sebastian said, "Keep it that way. Don't offer any information, and whatever he *does* think about the Masters' Admiralty, confirm the information as if it's correct, even if it's not."

"Very well. Is there anything else we should do?" Selene asked.

"Don't get close to him. You can't trust him." Sebastian paused, then sighed. "And whatever you do, don't fuck him."

Oscar sat up slowly and tried to work the kinks out of his back. He knew sleeping on the pull-out couch was going to suck, but after the beating Luca had taken, he'd agreed with Selene on giving him the bed. Having Selene on the pull-out beside him made it suck a lot less than it would have otherwise.

Last night, after their phone call to Sebastian, they'd found a jar of spaghetti sauce and some noodles in the kitchen pantry and shared a peaceful dinner, pausing occasionally to check on Luca. It was only after he was asleep that they'd considered maybe he shouldn't have been allowed to sleep in case of a possible concussion.

Once dinner was over, they'd cleaned up the kitchen, then pulled out and made the bed with some sheets and a blanket they'd found in a trunk in the corner of the living room. Selene had curled into his arms, put her head on his chest, and fallen asleep within moments.

He hadn't been too far behind her, given the fact they'd only gotten a few hours' sleep the night before.

He glanced through the remaining front window—outside, the world was white and gray, a blanket of snow on the ground and trees and an overcast sky above.

He felt Selene's hand stroke his bare back, and he twisted around, smiling at her sleepy expression, admiring how beautiful her hair looked, tousled on the pillow.

"This bed is crap."

He chuckled and nodded. "Never slept on a pull-out couch that was comfortable. Tonight, if Luca feels better, we're flipping a coin for the bed."

"What time is it?"

Oscar glanced toward an honest-to-God cuckoo clock that hung on the wall. The damn thing had squawked every hour on the hour, waking him up with the stupid racket from three in the morning on. Prior to that, he'd been too dead to the world to hear it. "Not quite eight. At least the snow stopped."

Selene sighed. "For now. Looks like it could start again any minute. There's at least two feet of snow out there. I doubt, even if it doesn't start up again, they'll be able to get us out today."

"We could be here a while," Oscar grumped. "Thank God there's enough food." He and Selene had gone through the pantry and taken stock of their stores while investigating dinner possibilities. While there was no fresh food—no milk or eggs or produce—there was enough soup and canned fruit and vegetables and spices. And, mercifully, the freezer had been stocked with quite a bit of frozen meat. He'd found a pound of bacon amongst the chicken and pork chops and steaks and moved it to the refrigerator to fry up for their breakfast this morning.

Clearly, they'd broken into someone's weekend cabin. The owners had two distinct interests—farmyard animal decor and hunting. In addition to all the chicken shit, there were three deer heads—Jesus, he hated those things—mounted and hanging on the living room walls. He'd felt their glass eyes on him all fucking night.

Given this didn't appear to be someone's primary residence, at least the worry of anyone actually making their way through the blizzard in an attempt to return home was lifted.

Oscar scratched his chest as he rose slowly. He'd opted to sleep in just his boxers. None of them had a change of clothes, though he planned to see if there was anything in the bedroom they could pilfer.

Oscar was just bending over to retrieve his jeans when Luca came in.

"*Buongiorno,*" Luca said, before recalling himself. "Uh, good morning."

Selene sat up and smiled at the Italian. Oscar was still trying to decide how to feel about the man. The stories he'd heard from his brother of Mina's torment, the haunted look he'd seen in her eyes when she'd returned to the hotel after her captivity, were still fresh in his mind, but now that he'd learned the reason for Luca's actions…Oscar couldn't fault the man for trying to save his sister.

Of course, it didn't matter *how* Oscar felt about it. If Rich and Langston ever got their hands on Luca, there would be no minimizing the beatdown they'd give him.

"How about some breakfast?" she asked Luca. "We found some bacon last night. Or there is leftover spaghetti, though I hesitate to give it to someone who lives in Italy."

Selene obviously didn't share his reservations about Luca.

Luca gave her a grateful grin. "Food would be good. I am very hungry."

Selene stood up and crossed the room, gently touching Luca's slightly swollen, bruised cheek. Oscar felt an unexpected tightening in his chest as he watched the compassionate way her fingers caressed Luca's face. Faith had accused him of being a jealous bastard a time or three thousand during their relationship, and he figured she hadn't been too far off the mark. Of course, hindsight was twenty-twenty, and Faith, during their "off-again" times, had dated plenty of other men, which always provoked in him the other fault she constantly complained about. His temper.

None of those anxious, angry feelings were present as he watched Selene with Luca. And he tried to tell himself that was normal because Selene wasn't his. Not truly. But… fuck…over the course of the past week or so, he couldn't deny wishing she was. So why wasn't he jealous of that touch, or of the genuine—shit—desire he saw in Luca's eyes as he looked at her?

"Does anything still hurt? Would you like more medicine?" she asked.

"The pain is tolerable. Thank you for your concern."

Oscar pulled on his jeans, but didn't bother with his shirt. Selene, like him, had shed her jeans, sleeping in just a T-shirt. There wasn't a shy bone in the woman's body, her lack of inhibitions one of the things he admired most about her. She was confident and direct.

"I'm going to fry up some of that bacon we found last night," Oscar said. He was risking grease splatter on his chest, but he'd rather deal with that than having his one shirt get dirty.

Luca's eyes lit up at the mention of food, but he said, "American bacon?"

"Similar to fried pancetta," Selene said.

"I've seen it on American TV and movies…"

Oscar waited. If Luca tried to turn down the bacon the way he had the wine—talking about religious purity—the other man was going to find himself on the receiving end of a *proper* "Come to Jesus" lecture.

"…and I've always wanted to try it."

"Right answer," Oscar said.

The three of them made their way to the kitchen, and Oscar rummaged around in the fridge and pantry while Selene and Luca sat at the table.

They both offered to help, Luca hesitantly mimicking Selene's offer, but Oscar had waved them off, telling them they'd just get in his way. Pulling the bacon out of the fridge, he placed half a dozen slices in the pan, then opened a can of whole potatoes he planned to turn into hash browns. He'd kill for an onion, but beggars couldn't be choosers.

While he cooked, Selene and Luca had a supervillain

conversation while sitting at the kitchen table drinking coffee out of novelty chicken cups.

Oscar tried to remember if any comic book villains had the equivalent of Alfred. It was odd, because in his family, he was the morally ambiguous one. Walt saved lives, Langston blew shit up, but also built robots to help blow up things safely, and his sister was an artist who used her platform to address social justice issues.

He wrote programs that could find almost anyone and anything. Data mining wasn't what most lay people thought of when they heard hacking, but it was infinitely more valuable than being able to send someone a computer virus or steal credit card information from big box stores.

Maybe this was one of the reasons he objected so strongly to the idea of the Trinity Masters. It was exclusive and secret. The kind of secret that he would never have even known to look for.

SELENE WISHED they were having this conversation in her office at Cornell, or even better, one of the labs. Either place would have had the tools she wanted, even if that "tool" was as simple as a whiteboard or a full-sized piece of paper. Instead, she was sitting on one end of the couch, which she had converted back from a bed while Oscar dealt with the breakfast dishes.

The blank backside of a junk-mail envelope was the best she'd been able to come up with for her notes.

"I want to finish our talk about the bomb."

Luca looked uncomfortable. "I'll tell you what I can."

"You'll tell us everything," Oscar yelled from the kitchen.

"I'll tell you what I can from memory. I do not have every detail memorized."

"First," Selene said, pulling Luca's attention back. "Where did you learn about nuclear physics and bomb making?"

Luca shifted in his seat, taking a moment during which he frowned.

"When I was sixteen, I was switched from a regular secondary school to a…a training program. The Bellator Dei had just been blessed with a new facility, part of which they turned into a school."

"A training program that taught a sixteen-year-old how to make bombs?" Selene felt sick at the idea.

"Fuck." Oscar popped his head around from the kitchen. "So an extremist terrorist organization, not just a cult."

"Terrorist…" Luca looked away.

Selene cleared her throat. "Next question. Where's your data? The math to back it all up?" They'd talked through the top-level details while Oscar cooked breakfast, but now it was time to get into the fine-grained details.

Luca's lost, remote look faded as he focused on her, his eyes bright and intelligent. "Ah, I did it on a non-networked computer and paper and then threw both away. I knew what I was doing was dangerous, and I didn't want anyone to find it."

"But you had the schematic to build it on your tablet."

"I had the schematic for an easily disabled version on my tablet. There is no unaltered version any longer."

"Why actually create it?" Oscar asked as he walked out

of the kitchen. "Why not just put a bunch of random shit on a piece of paper and tell them you made a bomb."

"I wasn't the only person in that particular training program."

"Your work was checked by other members who would have known how to read the schematic," Selene said.

"Yes."

"But bomb making and nuclear physics are distinctly different. Did they teach you atomic physics? Nuclear weapons training?" she asked.

Luca shifted in his seat, looking uncomfortable. She and Oscar shared a glance.

"Actually, I taught myself," Luca said slowly.

"You taught yourself theoretical nuclear physics."

"Yes."

Selene was hard to surprise but that had done it. "How? I mean, where did you get that kind of information from a very small and regulated academic discipline?"

"Er…your TED talks," Luca muttered.

Beside her, Oscar started to laugh so hard, he began to wheeze. She hit him with a pillow. "Shut up, Oscar."

"Super…villain…" He dissolved into gales of laughter.

It didn't help that Selene was fairly sure she was blushing.

"Ignore him. He thinks I'm going to go nuts and become a supervillain."

Luca nodded solemnly, then paused, seeming to consider his words before saying. "You would make an excellent villain."

She threw the other pillow at Luca.

When the boys had settled down, she pointed at Luca. "I want to talk specifics. Why neptunium?"

One by one, she asked Luca the questions that she hadn't been able to answer for herself when all she'd had to look at was the bomb design. They discussed how and why he'd selected that particular heavy atom. The answer— because it wasn't as tightly regulated as uranium and plutonium—is what she'd guessed, but it was good to have confirmation.

The next question was how he'd planned to create a particle accelerator that was both portable and able to generate the needed speed. The answer—responsive nanotech pathways—theoretically sounded possible. However, she would need to investigate more thoroughly as she didn't know much about nanotech.

And her final, and most important question. "How did you exponentially increase the output from existing known levels given that amount of base material?"

Luca talked her through it. They passed the envelope back and forth until both sides were covered in squiggles. Luca was brilliant, and if he'd had a different life, he would be an incredible and innovative scientist, rather than the manager of a small, private forensic explosives lab.

But, the more they talked, the more she began to suspect that his calculations were, quite simply, wrong.

Selene frowned down at the envelope. "I don't think this is possible."

"I did the math." Luca took the paper, looking it over. "I should not have destroyed my original calculations."

"Does that mean the bomb doesn't work?" Oscar asked.

"I'm certain it will explode, but not, perhaps..." Selene closed her eyes, eliminating the visual stimulation so she could focus on running and re-running the calculations in her head. "I need to get back to my lab."

"Blizzard." Oscar was up and pacing.

Luca was staring down at their notes. "If I'm wrong, then it doesn't matter. We can release the plans." He swallowed hard. "But it also means…"

"Don't get ahead of yourself," Oscar warned.

"We need to know for sure what the bomb output would be. I need someone with access to Pleiades."

Oscar whirled around. "We know someone with access to Pleiades?"

"Yes."

"Wait, can *I* get access to Pleiades?"

"What's Pleiades?" Luca asked.

"NASA's fucking sexy super computer." Oscar was all but purring.

Selene was already on the phone. A quick call to Sebastian got her Preston Kim's number, and ten minutes later she was on the phone with him. He'd done some consulting work with JPL and had contacts at NASA. There were undoubtedly NASA scientists who were members, but Preston had been read in—he knew the situation. She quickly explained, and a second later his husband Lance was also on the phone. She made Luca give her the envelope so she could read the notes.

Lance was already running first-level simulations and had promised that they wouldn't even need to involve other people for access to Pleiades. He could access DARPA's supercomputers, which he declared had double the processing power of Pleiades.

Oscar, who had been shamelessly eavesdropping, looked like he was going to have a stroke at that particular piece of information, which was not common knowledge, the way Pleiades' existence was.

After telling Preston to contact Sebastian in order to get ahold of her, she hung up the phone and shook her head at Oscar.

"You can't hack DARPA to find out about the super-computer."

"Can't or shouldn't?" he asked.

"Okay, shouldn't."

"Yeah, I'm going to do it."

"Enjoy federal prison."

"Fuck that, the Grand Master better bail my ass out. The least I should get for having to join this stupid…"

Selene left Oscar muttering and pacing and went back to Luca in the living room. "Luca?"

He was still sitting, elbows on his knees, head in his hands. "I hope you are right. What I created was an abomination. I did it because I thought…I thought it might be enough to allow me to free myself and my sister from them. I thought if I could get out, and then give modified plans to the world…"

"You were thinking small nuclear power plants." Her colleagues at MIT were working on that too.

"Yes. I could give, or sell, plans for a stable nuclear energy source in exchange for protection, resources, a…a life."

"But first you had to follow orders, build them a bomb, so you built in a flaw."

"If I didn't create it, they would have asked one of the others."

"So you made sure you were the one to design the bomb. That way, you could make sure it had an exploitable flaw."

"Yes, but…but that doesn't mean people wouldn't die."

"True."

"I am not a good man." Luca looked so cold and grim that she wanted to hug him.

"Well, you'll have to do a bit better than a maybe-bomb if you're going to be a supervillain like me."

That got a small smile out of Luca.

Oscar, apparently done with his rant, came to sit on the couch. "I have a question."

"About the bomb?" Selene asked.

"No, I'm not stupid and I could follow that conversation. About your sister."

Luca stiffened.

"You said she's bought into the cult." Oscar leaned forward.

"Only because she has not—"

Oscar held up a hand. "Not judging. But I'm wondering why you think they'll hurt her to get to you. I mean why would they do that, if she's loyal?"

"I don't know why they do *any* of the things they do, but I know they will hurt her."

"Maybe they'll just think—" Selene started.

Luca shook his head. "They did it to someone else."

Selene knew that what he said next would be something heartbreaking. Something terrible.

"The school is not just for bombs. They also train programmers. They create applications, games for your phone, and they use that for income and to embed spyware. My sister was a student there."

"That's how you tracked the tablet and found us?"

"Yes. All my electronics are coded with a special…software?" Luca shook his head. "I am not sure of the terms."

Oscar scrubbed his hands over his face. "Okay, spyware

piggybacked on a game app. And also some sort of digital tracking coding."

"I think there is a physical element," Luca said. "I watched Piero work on my tablets and computers. He disassembled them."

"Ah-ha!" Oscar sat up. "I fucking knew it had to be something like that."

"Who is Piero?"

"My age; like me, he was one of the first to be put in the Bellator Dei's school, but for computers."

Selene knew she didn't want to hear the end of this story. That it wouldn't end well.

"Piero was making money for the Bellator Dei. A lot of money. But it all went to them. He lived at the facility. Had nothing for himself, despite all that he brought in. He stood up to them. Demanded that he be allowed to marry and leave, to be a supernumerary, like my parents. He wanted some of the money he was making for himself so he could have a life of his own."

"What did they do to him?"

"To him? They denied him, again and again. And when he stopped working, when there was no longer enough money…" Luca took off his glasses, hooked them on the collar of his shirt, and pressed the heels of his hands to his eye sockets. "Do you know what it means to be a…I'm not sure of the precise term in English. A martyr soul? A victim soul?"

She and Oscar shook their heads.

"The leaders, they went to Piero's parents and his sister. They said that they'd had a revelation, a vision of Saint Sebastian who said Greta had a victim soul. That she was put on this Earth to suffer as Christ did. Her suffering would save many, and make her a martyr, ensuring her place in the kingdom of Heaven."

"Oh my God," Selene breathed, seeing where this was going.

"Greta was a loyal numerary. A valuable member of the church." Luca lifted his head, put his glasses back on. "They tortured her to death and made sure Piero was there to watch."

Oscar's whispered "fuck" was full of horror. Selene felt helpless just listening to Luca's story. She couldn't imagine how he felt. He had to design a horrific nuclear bomb because doing it himself was the only way he could ensure that there was a way to dismantle it, all while making sure that he outwardly seemed loyal so that he wouldn't have to watch his sister be tortured to death.

"That is what I'm protecting my sister from."

For a long time, none of them said anything.

CHAPTER EIGHT

O scar sat silently, letting the implications of what was at stake for Luca, and what Selene might have discovered about the bomb, sink in. Now that he was over the whole secret military supercomputer situation, he could focus on the important part of what they'd just learned.

The bomb might not actually be the city-killer they'd feared, and Luca was undeniably being coerced. If the option was to kill some people or watch Sylvia be tortured to death, Oscar wouldn't have hesitated long, even if taking another life went against everything he believed.

"Is your sister safe right now?"

"Yes. I told them before I left, I had to go no-contact for several weeks due to an assignment with *Cohortes Praetorianae*. I've done so in the past, so they won't be looking for me."

"What about the monitoring hardware and software they had?" Oscar asked.

"My phone. I have an app they made me that let me track my tablet, but they must have…" Luca frowned.

"There's probably a way to backtrack, which is how the Croatians—"

"Serbian. They were speaking Serbian."

"—Serbians tracked you."

"But does that mean they're on to him?" Selene asked anxiously.

"If it was the Bellator Dei, they would not have come to me like that. Why would they bother? They know I would do anything to protect Joli."

"So the Serbians somehow followed you, maybe with your cult's tracking software, to get a bomb plan that no one outside your cult knows about," Oscar summed up.

Selene's brows rose. "Sounds like the cult has a leak."

"That's what I was thinking too," Oscar said.

Luca shook his head slowly. "I don't know enough about the numeraries to know who, or why?"

"The who?"

"Those who live at the headquarters, devote themselves to the organization."

There was a long silence before Selene said, in a brighter tone, "On the plus side, the bomb might not work."

Luca smiled. "In this case, I am glad to be wrong."

"Though I think with some of your ideas we could—"

"No." Oscar folded his arms. "No more supervillain shit, you two."

The quiet relief, mingled with amusement, that filled the cabin made it easy to sink into the silence while outside the snow began to fall again.

Luca was still on an ancient, overstuffed yellow-and-green plaid armchair. The entire cabin appeared to have been furnished by Yard Sales R Us.

"I wonder…" Luca began hesitantly.

He paused just long enough that Selene prompted him to continue with a quiet, "Yes?"

"I wonder if I might ask a few questions of my own."

Oscar had expected this. Luca had been patient so far, answering their questions honestly. Or at least Oscar believed the answers had been the truth.

It wasn't like him to trust someone quite so quickly, but his gut told him that Luca wasn't a liar. He was a man with his back against the wall and a reluctant cult member, but not a liar.

"Of course," Selene replied.

"I am curious about the Masters' Admiralty. The only knowledge I have of the organization is what the Bellator Dei has told me. And I think it's clear from last night's discussion, they've shared some untruths."

"Or radical thought. The insane religious cult doesn't care too much about facts or truth," Oscar said.

Luca nodded once. "I must admit I am curious about the ménage relationships within your society. These are assigned, correct?"

Oscar decided to let Selene take the lead on this, as his association with the cult—oh, fuck it—the secret society was relatively new. Selene had grown up in the Trinity Masters, so she was a better authority to speak on the subject, as well as knowing what they should tell a nonmember, and what they shouldn't.

Then he chuckled to himself, aware the brilliant woman was probably better suited to speak on most matters. Oscar had dedicated his life to three things: data mining, his family, and Faith. And look where that had gotten him.

Trapped in a blizzard with these two.

Suddenly, his outlook changed as he realized this was probably one of the best times he'd had in years...if he didn't take into account the city-killer bomb they were trying to keep from the not-too-bright, well-armed Serbian mobsters and the crazed religious zealots in Europe who were looking for it.

"The arranged trinity marriages are assigned by...our leader, yes."

"And is there a reason behind the assignments?" Luca asked.

"The..." Selene cleared her throat, speaking slowly and precisely. "The society was formed in order to form lasting, complex bonds that provide hidden security to societal structures."

"A cord of three strands," Luca said softly.

"Exactly. And this also means that scientists and scholars, artists and inventors, people who might otherwise give up on their passions, are protected by their spouses."

"Patronage."

"Yes. And sometimes specific trinities—that's what we call them, or triads—are created because our leader thinks that together, those three people might, given intimacy and time, create something, invent something...that will change the world in some way."

"What do you mean?" Luca sat forward, clearly interested.

Dude had a thing for cults. Oscar covered his mouth with his hand so neither of them would ask why he was smiling.

"The man I called earlier, Preston, is a chemist. His wife owns a video game company and his husband is a mathematician for the U.S. government."

"Chemistry, mathematics, and...computer programming? Business development?"

Oscar knew where this was going. He had a voice mail from Carly Kenan, founder and owner of Nexus Six, saying she wanted to talk to him. He'd geeked out about that until he figured out she was a member of the Trinity Masters and was probably just going to try to recruit him.

"Computer programming. They created TideForm."

"The environmental monitoring software?" Luca asked, clearly impressed.

Selene nodded. "TideForm is the tech infrastructure of Carly's gaming company, plus Preston's chemistry knowledge to create the analysis component inside the bots. Their husband's military contacts got the devices aboard U.S. military ships, who dropped them in the oceans. They came up with the idea one night while watching a documentary about oceanic climate change."

Oscar pictured it—sitting around in pajamas, Selene beside him, their husband or wife on the other side of her, as they heckled the TV. How fucking awesome would that be? A casual moment at home with his spouses that could turn into something that might change the world.

"I see. And these marriages..." Luca paused for a moment, and Oscar knew by the slight flush of his cheeks where this conversation was headed.

Sex.

It was one of the primary things Oscar had been interested in—and given his brother the most shit about—when Langston joined the Trinity Masters.

And while Sylvia had joined the Masters' Admiralty and been placed in a trinity marriage first, Oscar refused to think about his kid sister shacking up with two men.

He didn't give a shit if Hugo and Lancelot were pretty cool.

"The marriages are consummated by all three members?"

Selene smiled and nodded. "They are."

Luca leaned back as he processed that information. "Are the two of you in a trinity?"

Oscar shook his head. "Nope."

"Yet you are lovers."

"We are," Selene answered.

"Just the two of you?" The second the question flew from his lips, Luca raised his hands, waving them, as if he could erase the words. "I apologize. That is a personal question and none of my concern. I'm just…confused about how these relationships are formed. It's clear the two of you have a bond, yet you do not know if you will be placed in a marriage together, yes?"

Selene nodded, then leaned forward, resting her elbows on her knees. "That's correct. Many members of the society…practice."

Oscar snorted. "I'm supposed to start practicing ménages? Jesus." He hadn't meant to blurt that out, and he internally kicked himself when Luca's curious gaze shifted to him.

"I'm, uh, new to the cu—society," Oscar quickly added.

Selene grinned, her head turned so only Oscar could see the way she rolled her eyes in amusement. "I've participated in ménage sex…with one man and one woman, two men, two women, and on one particularly fun weekend there were four of us, two of each gender."

"Of course you have. And by the way, that's fucking

hot," Oscar teased Selene before looking at Luca. "Let me guess, your crazy cult demands chastity as well as sobriety."

Luca shook his head. "No, of course not. The Bellator Dei follows the Catholic doctrine. Marriage between a man and a...w-woman, procreation, these things are highly regarded, required even."

Oscar noticed the slight stutter in Luca's comment about marriage. A quick glance at Selene proved she'd heard it as well.

"So one man and one woman," she clarified. "That's all that's allowed?"

Luca nodded, his gaze shifting to look out the window. Oscar didn't think the Italian was suddenly taking an interest in the blizzard as much as trying to avoid making eye contact with them.

"So," Luca began again after several quiet moments, turning slowly to direct his next question to Oscar. "Your brother and Mr. Blake...they..."

He knew what Luca wanted to know but was too uncomfortable to ask, so he gave him the answer. "There is butt stuff."

Selene snorted, then stuck out her leg and kicked him gently.

Oscar sighed. "I don't hang out in the bedroom with them, Luca, but...I'm pretty sure they're lovers too, if that's what you're asking."

"Fascinating. The Bellator Dei believes that homosexuality, bisexuality—these things are abominations against God, terrible sins that must be severely punished, expunged from a person's soul through brutality."

"How fucking surprising," Oscar growled, his temper

flaring hot. "Your cult is filled with those beat-the-gay-away dickheads. God, I hate those motherfuckers."

Selene reached over and placed her hand on his knee, squeezing it. His shoulders started to relax.

Luca didn't respond to Oscar's violent outburst, but there was pain in his expression that told him he was right about the cult's unsavory control tactics.

It told him something else as well, as Oscar felt a few more pieces of the Luca puzzle click into place. And he started to understand why the man was no stranger to beatings.

"So it is true the Masters' Admiralty embrace, even encourage…" Luca ran his hand through his shaggy brown hair as he considered what they'd told him so far. Obviously, the guy hadn't had time to stop in for a haircut while running all around the East Coast, chasing a tablet.

"Are you gay, Luca?" Selene asked quietly.

Luca lifted his face, swallowing heavily, and Oscar knew the second the man began to speak that Luca was not only *not* a liar, he trusted them. And considering everything the man had suffered in his life, Oscar recognized that as the gift it was.

Luca squared his shoulders, tension radiating from him. "I'm bisexual."

Oscar's stomach clenched with pain on Luca's behalf. "They found out. The fucking bastards found out and tried to beat it out of you, didn't they?"

LUCA GAVE OSCAR A SINGLE NOD. He wasn't sure how to respond in the face of the other man's obvious rage in his defense. He had noticed over the course of the past day or so that Oscar wasn't the type of man who shielded his emotions. Everything he felt was written plainly in his expressions and in his tone, yet Luca felt as if he could see through the man's outbursts to the passionate person beneath.

Luca had spent his entire life repressing his feelings because he'd learned from a young age that sadness or fear were easily exploited, while anger and love were easily snuffed out through violence.

"Luca," Selene said softly. "I'm sorry they did that to you."

Luca didn't doubt for a moment that Selene's compassion was as genuine as Oscar's anger, and his throat began to tighten. He couldn't recall anyone—with the exception of his sister—ever stepping up to his defense. These people were strangers, yet in just a day, they'd shown him more compassion than the orphanage or those who had raised him in the Bellator Dei and had claimed to love him.

Unlike Joli, Luca, who was older, had vague memories of their real parents, who were killed when his sister was just a baby. She'd waited eight years for a family, her entire lifetime, when the couple from the Bellator Dei found them at the orphanage, claiming they were good children of God who would grow up to answer His call, just as Signore and Signora Campisi had.

They'd been indoctrinated—baptized—within two days of arriving in Italy, and he'd been enrolled in a private Catholic school, while Joli was homeschooled by their new mother. He, like Joli, had readily embraced the teachings, the faith, so grateful to finally have a place in the world.

When he was fourteen, the Campisis pulled him out of

his beloved secondary school and placed him in a new school, if it could be called that. "As I told you, the Bellator Dei opened their own school. It started as a few confused young men stuffed into a single room at the new headquarters of what we thought was simply a very strict church. We were taught to make explosives by a man with dead eyes. Now the Collegium Sanctorum, where they teach children to become terrorists—you used the word, and I think it is right—is far more than it had been."

They had shared so much, taken care of him...if there was anyone he would trust with this story, it was Selene and Oscar.

"His name was Roberto. He was two years older. He and his family were devout members of the Bellator Dei."

Luca was proud of the strength in his voice, considering his heart was now racing. He hadn't spoken—or even thought—of Roberto in years.

"Did you love him?" Selene asked softly.

Luca smiled sadly, Roberto's face in his mind's eye. "I was only sixteen. What did I know of love?"

"I was sixteen the first time I laid eyes on Faith. I might have been young, but I knew enough to know I was in love with her," Oscar said.

Luca looked at him curiously. "Faith?"

"First love," Oscar grumbled before giving him a sheepish grin.

Something always tightened in Luca's body whenever Oscar's stern expression gave way to a smile. The man was extremely attractive, with dark hair, skin, eyes, muscular build, and a well-trimmed beard. His handsomeness was a perfect counterpoint to Selene's incredible beauty...while Luca was perfectly aware there was nothing beautiful about him, either physically or spiritually. There was nothing about his looks that made him stand out, which had actually been a blessing more than a few times in his life. No one ever gave him a second glance, so it was easy for him to blend in, make himself invisible.

The only person who'd ever truly seen him was…

Roberto.

"I do believe I felt genuine love for Roberto, and he for me. We both said the words, and for my part, I meant them sincerely."

Selene smiled. "I'm beginning to believe it's not in you to lie easily, Luca."

"You're wrong. I have told many lies to many people."

Selene was not deterred. "People who didn't have your trust, who were unworthy of the truth. I suspect you are a loyal friend."

"What happened with Roberto, Luca?" Oscar prodded.

"We knew Bellator Dei frowned on our…kind of love. Knew that we would be punished if discovered. But we were young and, well, a young man's body wants what it wants. We were each other's firsts, and that can be a very powerful thing. Our hunger for each other made us less careful than we should have been."

"You were caught together?" Selene asked.

Luca nodded. "The technical institute was just one building and part of a small campus that also included the Bellator Dei headquarters, as well as a small chapel. There were dormitories on the lower floors of headquarters, the offices on the upper floors and off-limits to students. A numerary caught Roberto and me in my room together one afternoon. He'd had suspicions about our relationship, so he followed us back to the dormitory, waited long enough to," Luca swallowed heavily, "catch us in the act."

"What did he do?"

"He called for another numerary."

"Wait, what the fuck is a numerary again?" Oscar asked.

"A celibate member who lives to serve the Bellator Dei. They lived there too and served the Prelate—the leader."

"You don't have to tell us any more if you don't want to," Selene said softly. "If it's too painful."

But he did want to tell them. He'd remained silent about that time in his life for so long.

He was living on borrowed time. Of that he was certain, and it hurt him to think so much of his life would be lost forever, never shared, never known. He was tired of being invisible.

There was something about Oscar and Selene that told him his secrets would be safe with them. More than that, he felt as if they'd even understand.

"Roberto and I were not allowed to dress. Instead, we were dragged naked across the campus in full view of our classmates to the chapel, where we were told we would confess our sins and have our bodies purged of Satan's influence."

Luca had been focused on the floor as he spoke, but Selene's soft intake of breath, the horror behind it, had him lifting his eyes to hers.

"Luca," she whispered.

He gave her a sad smile he hoped would comfort her. "It was a very long time ago, *tesoro*."

"How bad was it?" Oscar asked.

Luca glanced in his direction. "It was bad. We were

placed in cells beneath the chapel across from each other. They said *mortificazione* would cleanse us." He had to think about it for a minute to translate a word, a term that for him held such horror and fear, it seemed impossible to translate. "The mortification of the flesh."

"A fucked-up term for beating a kid," Oscar growled.

"They ordered us to cleanse ourselves—beat ourselves." Luca nodded toward Oscar in acknowledgement of the term. "When we would not, I was forced to watch as they beat Roberto with a flail. He was forced to do the same when they used the whip on me. Through it all, we were made to repeat the rosary. All seasons. Over and over. Every few hours, a numerary would come down to our cells and ask if we were ready to make amends with God. The numerary assistants—women—would come and beg us, plead with us, because they feared for our souls. They cared for our wounds, which was not the mercy we thought at first. They took away the pain so that it was fresh again the next day.

"Roberto repented on the third day. He picked up the whip they offered and used it on himself. Before he passed out, from pain or blood loss, he forsook me, and swore before God that he would never look at another man with lust in his heart."

"Did you do the same?" Selene asked gently.

Luca's lips tipped up in a grin. "Lust is not my greatest sin. Pride is. I remained in that cell for another week, beaten each day, forced to repeat the rosary on my knees for hours. They came every day to offer me the flail. Demanding my repentance. I would not give it, and would not beat myself, so they did it for me."

Oscar's expression was half horror, half respect when he asked, "How did you get out?"

"In the end, it was my sister, Joli. She'd pleaded, begged, cried to our adopted parents, until at last they intervened—I would like to say they did so on my behalf, but the truth was my actions reflected poorly on them. Something they would not stand for. So, they assured the Prelate that our family would devote itself to prayer and mortification of the flesh."

"And did they?" Selene asked.

"They did. I was sent home from school, where Signore Campisi continued the beatings and they slowly starved me. That lasted another week. Until…it was Signora Campisi who figured out what my Achilles' heel was. She was the one who discovered how to break me."

Oscar stood up and walked to the front window, tension in every step. "Your sister. They threatened Joli, didn't they?"

Luca nodded. "She was twelve at the time. Joli was—is —truly brilliant. I believe your word is genius. The Bellator Dei had taken notice of this and hired tutors for her, claiming her calling was different from that of the other young girls in our congregation, who were expected to marry and have lots of children who would be raised in the faith."

"They planned to use her for something else?" Selene asked.

"A mind like hers, well…the Bellator Dei believed she was a gift from God, sent to help them in their battle against the Masters' Admiralty. She reminds me a great deal of you," he added, looking at Selene. "Signore and Signora Campisi threatened to end her schooling, to wed her to a 'good and faithful' man. Signore Esposito. He was nearly fifty at the time and everyone knew of his predilections, his preference for young girls."

Oscar slammed the side of his fist against the wall. "Jesus."

"I turned the whip on myself, confessed my sin, and repented. The beatings stopped after that. Eventually, I was sent back to the institute."

Luca bowed his head as shame washed through him. He'd put that time away, locked it tightly in a box he never opened.

Selene stood up and walked over to him, kneeling before Luca and taking his hands in hers. There was a strength in her grip that revived him.

"You did nothing wrong."

Luca knew that, deep down inside, he knew it, but…

"Knowledge is often cast in shadows, obscured by the blinding light of emotions." Luca had been told a million different ways—through words, scripture, fists—that for him to love a man was a sin. And if he had *only* been told in those ways, he would have remained strong, would have held on to his convictions that he was right and they were wrong.

"What happened to Roberto?"

Luca glanced up. Leave it to Oscar to see there was more.

"He had returned to the school as well. He never spoke to me again." Roberto hadn't needed to speak. The hatred, the disgust, the pure, unveiled disdain in his eyes as he'd looked at Luca had said it all.

And that was when Luca had suffered his first—and

only—broken heart, and the shame of his actions had been born.

Luca cleared his throat and said the rest. "Six months after…after us…Roberto married a girl from our order and became a supernumerary. He works as a builder, devotes himself to supporting the Bellator Dei and his family. They have three children now. He chose his path, just as I have chosen mine."

"You *chose* to be adopted by a bunch of religious freaks and forced to design bombs?" Oscar's voice boomed in the stillness of the room. The snow outside had muted every sound until all that was left were the subtle noises from inside—the occasional crack of the fire in the stove, the ticking of the cuckoo clock, and their voices.

"My feet may have been placed on this path—"

"Slammed on it is more like it."

Luca grinned once more at Oscar's passion. While he suspected some may have found his anger, his aggression off-putting, Luca was drawn to it like a moth to flame. Perhaps because he found it so difficult to express his own feelings. He was envious of the man's ability to show what was in his heart.

"What I am trying to say is I have made very conscious decisions in the past few years, decisions that were necessary. Even though I am aware they will lead to my death. Either at the hands of the Bellator Dei or the Masters' Admiralty."

"What?" Selene dropped Luca's hands and stood quickly. "What are you talking about?"

"I have betrayed the Bellator Dei. They will learn of my subterfuge eventually. I was granted mercy when I was a boy, but—"

"You call that *mercy*?" Selene cried.

Luca ignored her outburst even though it warmed him to see and hear her outright anger on his behalf. "The Bellator Dei is but one enemy. You saw those men the other night. They were willing to do anything to get the designs. And once they had, my life would have been forfeit."

Selene was shaking her head.

"And then there is your society. The Masters' Admiralty. Do you think they will forgive me for what I did to Ms. Edwards? To Boston? I am their—*your*—enemy."

Oscar crossed back to them, standing next to Selene. "We can explain it to the Masters' Admiralty. We can make them see you had no choice."

"You have kind hearts. Understanding. Compassionate. Not all will feel that I am deserving of the forgiveness you have granted, even if my bomb does not work. Your brother, for one."

Oscar waved that concern away with the flick of his wrist. "Langston's a dipshit. I'll make him understand."

"I do not understand dipshit."

Oscar barked out a laugh. "It means my brother is an idiot."

Luca's eyes widened. "Ah. A sibling term of endearment. I have the same for Joli. She is my *piccola pulce*."

"I recognize the word little, but not the other?" Selene said.

Luca grinned. "It means little flea. She is forever buzzing in my ear."

His smile faded slowly. It had been several months since he had seen his sister, and while logically he knew she was safe, the overprotective brother in him longed to fly to Italy and steal her away from the tiny apartment she lived in, to drag her away from the people who would do her harm.

Selene reached out and touched his forearm. "Your sister will be okay."

He nodded, grateful for her reassurance.

Selene released him and returned to the couch, gesturing for Oscar to sit down again as well. "I think we need a distraction, and to talk about something that's not so…"

"Fucking heartbreaking?" Oscar asked.

After the revelations of the past few minutes, Luca expected to feel heavy, overwhelmed. Instead, he was… happy. He felt a thousand pounds lighter, a hundred years younger, and more comfortable in his own skin than he'd felt in his entire life.

Oscar smiled as he rose. "Luca, do you know how to play poker?"

CHAPTER NINE

Oscar had found the pack of cards in the kitchen's junk drawer, which, as anyone with any sense knew, was where a pack of cards should be. Luca had sheepishly admitted to playing poker on phone apps, but he had never played with other people.

"Then you were playing the cards, not the table." Oscar shuffled and set the deck on the table in front of Selene.

She tapped it with two fingers and Oscar arched a brow.

"I see you, Dr. Tanaka."

"I try to replicate the power of the sun for a living." Selene adjusted her glasses in a sexy librarian way. "You think I'm scared of taking risks?"

"It's like watching sexy American TV," Luca said, glancing back and forth between them.

"You think we're sexy?" Selene asked. "I mean, me too. Obviously Oscar is sexy."

Luca blushed. "Yes. I mean, you're both... It's..." He

stared at the cards as Oscar dealt. "Remind me of the rules."

"Straight poker. Five-card stud. Nothing wild. Keeping it simple this first round. Selene, deal out the chips."

Selene gave them each ten sauce packets, also gathered from the junk drawer.

They glanced at their cards, discarded, took more, and placed their bets. To his surprise, Luca raised, then raised again.

"You must have a very good hand," Selene said.

Luca glanced at each of them. "I build and design bombs for a living. Maybe I am simply taking a risk."

Oscar whistled and slapped the table. "It's going to be a game of who has the biggest nerd balls." He pushed the rest of his hot sauce packets toward the center of the table. "Too bad for you two, that's me."

"Call," Selene snapped.

Selene had a flush—all hearts. Appropriate.

Luca had three of a kind.

Oscar lay his cards out. "Full house, tens, and queens."

Selene drummed her fingers on the table, anxious for a rematch. It appeared his nuclear scientist was competitive. "Deal."

She won the next round, but he'd bet conservatively, losing only two hot sauce packets. On the third round, Oscar folded, losing only one in the process.

By the fourth hand, he still had most of the packets in his bank and was humming "The Gambler."

"Deal," Selene snapped. "Wait, I'll deal. You're cheating."

"Don't get too worked up, Tanaka. It's just poker. Now, if we were playing spades..." Every game of spades between him and his siblings had ended in violence. Every. Single. One. Always followed up by one of them yelling, "I will never play cards with you again!"

Selene dealt, and Oscar's smile had grown in time with his pile of hot sauce packets. He was waiting until Selene realized something she'd missed.

"I raise…" Selene trailed off as she finally noticed she was out of "money."

"You have to fold?" Luca looked up from frowning at his cards.

"Socks," Selene said.

"Strip poker." Oscar sat up, staring across the table at her to try to read her mind. She glanced at Luca, then back to him, and shrugged slightly.

"What is strip poker?" Luca asked.

"You bet with your clothes. You lose and you have to take off something."

Luca cleared his throat and tugged at the front of his shirt.

The bi guy who grew up in a nutso religious cult was probably wishing he was a thousand miles from here.

"Let's not." Oscar picked up some sauce packets, prepared to pass them to Selene.

"If she keeps losing…will she, will you, take off all your clothes?" Luca asked.

"Those are the rules," Oscar said, grinning when he realized Luca wasn't as averse to the idea as he'd assumed. "But you'd have to take off clothes as well."

"If I lose."

"Oh, you're going to lose." Oscar let the hot sauce packets spill from his hand back onto his pile.

"In or out, boys?" Selene asked.

"I'm in. I'm happy to see both of you naked," Oscar declared.

"Big talk. Call." Selene laid out her cards.

Luca took the round with a full house and Selene took off her socks.

Once the clothes started coming off, Luca suddenly got a whole lot better. Over the next half hour, Selene lost her pants and shirt, Oscar lost his socks and shirt, and Luca had all the sauce packets and was fully clothed.

"Did you just hustle us?" Oscar demanded.

"What's 'hustle?'"

"Mmmhmm, nice try. How do you say shark in Italian, Selene?"

"*Squalo*," she replied.

"Nice try, *squalo*. You're a hustler."

"In the Old West, you would have been shot," Selene snapped.

"You're salty 'cause you're losing." Oscar was enjoying this far too much. "You can always back out."

"I don't quit."

"So what are you taking off next? Bra or panties?"

"Bra," Selene purred. "And I plan to play with myself. We'll see how good you two are while I do that."

Luca froze. "Uh…"

Something else occurred to Oscar, and he shot Selene a sharp glance to let her know that this was serious. She paused in the middle of unsnapping her bra, then lowered her hands without removing it.

"Luca, after what happened when you were a teenager…" Oscar had to stop and think about his next words. There was nothing worse than making someone feel shitty about themselves or their sexuality. "After what you went through when you were a teenager, it would make sense if you stayed away from any kind of sexual situation, avoided...uh, images..."

"What kind of porn do you watch?" Selene asked.

"I'm supposed to be the unsubtle one," Oscar groaned. "You can't just ask people what kind of porn they watch. Dude might not even watch porn."

"I watch porn," Luca said. "For a long time, I tried watching what I thought was very heterosexual porn. But I primarily watch, uh..." He glanced at Selene apologetically. "Gangbangs."

Oscar shook his head. "This conversation is fucking surreal."

"One woman, multiple men?" Selene clarified.

"Yes. And some bondage stuff."

"That can be pretty heterosexual," Selene said, elbow on the table, chin on her hand. "Just bondage? Are we talking light hentai tentacle porn stuff, or full BDSM?"

"No pain, no discipline," Luca said sharply. "Well, uh, some domestic discipline."

Oscar had a brief fantasy of turning Selene over his lap for a spanking while Luca watched and made suggestions. Under the table, his dick hardened in his pants.

After that, they could take turns fucking her.

"But power exchange..." Selene seemed to consider it. "I'm guessing you aren't fantasizing about being the powerless one."

"No. I have been powerless enough in my life."

Selene shuffled. "I think we should keep playing."

This round, no one bothered to bet with the sauce packets. Selene bet her bra, Oscar bet his pants, and Luca also bet his pants.

When Oscar raised a brow at him, Luca cleared his throat. "My chest doesn't look like yours."

They all took a minute to look at Oscar's pecs.

"They're very pretty," Selene said.

"Agreed," Luca breathed.

"Are you two objectifying me?" Oscar asked

"Oh, I'm sorry——" Luca's apology stopped when Selene put a hand on his arm.

"Yes, we are," Selene purred. Her fingers flexed on Luca's arm, and Oscar saw the other man go still.

"Deal," Luca demanded.

Ah-ha. Now they were starting to see the real man underneath all the hurt and shitty life crap.

Selene won.

Oscar stood up and shucked his jeans, then adjusted his boxer briefs so his hard-on wouldn't stick out through the hole. There was no way to hide how hard his dick was, so the least he could do was make sure little Oscar didn't play peekaboo.

Luca was in the same boat, and both Oscar and Selene unabashedly watched as he adjusted his black boxers. Luca tried to take his seat again, but Selene stopped him with a little tsk.

"Twirl," she said. "Both of you."

Oscar spun around on his heel, then struck a body-building pose, pointing toward the corner of the room to show off his arms.

"Show off," Selene said, but the tone of her voice was pure appreciation.

"That's…" Luca abruptly took his seat.

"I didn't get my twirl."

"You don't want to see me twirl."

Selene put her hand back on Luca's arm. "Actually, I do." She ran a single finger from the crook of his elbow down to his wrist. "I guess you can do it naked, after I win."

"Keep dreaming, woman." Oscar took his seat and shuffled the cards.

Oscar won the next hand. Luca lost his shirt and Selene took off her bra.

Though her breasts were lovely, Oscar watched Luca rather than Selene. Luca's gaze slid down what he could see of her naked body, from her face to her breasts, and when Selene ran her fingers down between them, then gently pinched a nipple, Luca stopped breathing.

Oscar reached out and clapped him on the shoulder. "Breathe."

Luca exhaled noisily. "Yes. Breathing. It's my first—" He clammed up and blushed.

Oscar's brows rose as he realized what Luca hadn't said. While he and Selene were playing around, enjoying the high-spirited, erotic game, what was happening here meant a hell of a lot more to Luca. Just the thought of that had Oscar's cock growing even harder. "Your first time seeing tits in person?"

Luca nodded once. "I have wondered at times if I was gay, but no, I am most assuredly bisexual."

"Where's our twirl?" Selene played with her other nipple and from the way her breathing had changed, Oscar knew she was seriously turned on.

The woman had an incredible sex drive. She knew what she liked and wanted. That was the opposite of Faith, who'd always been too self-conscious to ever truly get into sex. It didn't matter how many times or ways he told her she was beautiful, she spent too much of their between-the-sheets time fretting over how she looked naked. Which he was able to admit to himself now, really fucked with his own confidence. He'd worked his ass off to rock her world, but she never got out of her head long enough to enjoy it.

Selene held nothing back, neither her praise nor her enjoyment, and it was fucking amazing.

Luca hesitated, considering her request, then stood. His boxers weren't going to be able to hide that erection much longer, and from the look of it, Luca was packing serious inches.

Luca turned—and the sight of his back damn near killed the mood.

If the light hadn't struck the other man's pale skin just right, the crosshatch of scars that spanned his upper back wouldn't have been visible, as the white lines were old and healed.

"Your back." Selene rose from her chair so fast, she nearly toppled it.

Oscar stood too, his heart heavy.

Luca turned around. "Ah, I forgot." He glanced between them, his expression hardening. "Don't pity me."

"The whippings?" Oscar asked.

Luca sighed, seeming resigned. "Yes. The horizontal scars are from where they beat me. The vertical ones are from my self-mortification." He pantomimed flicking a whip back over his own shoulder.

"You whipped yourself hard enough to leave scars," Selene breathed.

"Of course he did. To protect his sister."

Luca looked at Oscar and nodded. Then he started to reach down for his shirt, puddled on the floor. Selene put her foot on top of it. Luca froze, half bent, and looked up.

"Do you need to stop? Do you need this to be over?" Selene asked quietly.

"If you want a few minutes to yourself..." Oscar wasn't used to feeling so protective, so watchful, when it came to a man who wasn't one of his brothers.

Though what he felt for Luca wasn't brotherly.

Odd, he'd never really questioned his own sexual orientation. He'd loved Faith, was going to be with her forever, and so there'd been no point. But something about Luca drew him in.

Then he considered Langston's newfound relationship with Rich. He'd never questioned his brother's orientation, either. The guy had been a man slut since puberty hit, chasing anything in a skirt. And while Oscar had teased Langston about doing butt stuff now with his new husband, the idea of it hadn't bothered him. Now that he considered it, he was intrigued.

"I thought you would want to stop," Luca said quietly.

"Not me." Selene toyed with the waistband of her panties, then ran her hands up her belly to cup her own breasts. Luca had an up-close view since he was still hunched over, his head level with her breasts, and his breathing grew heavy.

Oscar put a hand on Luca's shoulder, his body tingling as he touched the other man's bare skin. He yanked Luca back to his seat.

"Place your bets." Oscar shuffled, though badly. It wasn't about the cards anymore. Hadn't been for several hands now.

Rather than sit down, Selene pushed her chair away and bent over, elbows on the table, back arched so her sweet ass was sticking up, her pale-green panties molded to her cheeks.

"That's…I think that's cheating," Luca said.

"It is. But it's the perfect position for a spanking," Oscar spoke before he thought it through.

Fuck.

Mentioning any kind of corporal punishment might be a trigger for Luca.

Selene seemed to have the same thought because she glanced at him and then they both looked at Luca, who swallowed hard. "If you hurt her, I would stop you." Pause. "Try to stop you." Pause. "Unless…"

Selene smiled. "Unless I knew I was a bad, bad girl and deserved a spanking?"

Luca braced both hands on the table, his fingertips white. "We're going to have sex, correct? Because if not, I'm going to…"

"We're having all the sex," Oscar assured him.

Luca jumped to his feet, slid his arms around Selene, forcing her upright, and kissed her.

Oscar put away the cards and tidied the sauce packets. The man deserved some space for his first girl kiss.

Though for a first time, he was doing a fucking good job.

Luca had one arm around her waist, the other hand cupping her head. Despite how frantically aroused he clearly was, the kiss was long and deep. Hell, Oscar was just an observer, and he was more turned on than he'd ever been in his life.

Oscar finished putting everything away and then walked over to the couple. "My turn."

Selene and Luca broke apart; Selene arched a brow and

smiled a little. Oscar returned the conspiratorial look—and then kissed Luca.

It was clear from the momentary stiffness Luca had thought Oscar was going to kiss Selene. Luca had just had his first girl kiss, but now it was Oscar's turn to pop his own I-kissed-a-boy cherry.

Luca's lips were soft at first, but when Oscar licked his bottom lip, Luca got unexpectedly, and thrillingly, aggressive. Oscar had never been the proverbial little spoon, and he kinda liked it. Luca's tongue slid between his lips, running over the front of Oscar's teeth. Damn, he'd never known the inside of his top lip was an erogenous zone.

Luca wrapped his arms around Oscar, his touch tentative and at odds with his masterful kiss.

A hand on Oscar's ass—a third hand—startled him, until he felt Selene's breath whisper across his cheek. "This is hot. Do it again, but with your dicks touching."

Luca broke the kiss, and they were both panting. Selene was apparently done waiting because she grabbed the waistband of Oscar's boxers and yanked them down. His dick rebounded, and he snarled at her. "Careful, woman. You don't wanna snap that off."

"Oh? Was I a bad girl?"

"Very bad," Luca breathed. "He should spank you."

Oscar hid his avaricious grin, more than happy to take the lead on Selene's punishment. Pretending to focus on stepping out of his boxers, he was able to take Selene by surprise as he turned, grabbed her, and pulled her over his lap, plopping down into the chair she'd shoved away from the table.

"Oh!" she cried.

He landed a couple of swats on her ass and she wiggled, her hands gripping his calf.

"Pull down her panties for me," Oscar said to Luca.

Luca ran his hand along her back, almost reverently, then paused as his fingers hit fabric. "Selene, you are not frightened? You are willing?"

"You have my affirmative consent." She twisted to look at Luca. "But after this, I reserve the right to pretend I don't like it. Adds to the fantasy for me."

"For me as well." Luca yanked her panties down to her knees.

Oscar spanked her a few more times. He was more of a slap-an-ass-in-the-heat-of-the-moment guy, but he'd watched enough porn that he could figure out how to make this hurt in all the best ways. For Selene and...

He glanced up at Luca, whose eyes were glued to Selene's slowly pinkening ass. The other man clenched and unclenched his fists, clearly desiring a piece of the action.

After half a dozen or so swats, he ran his fingers along her slit. She was hot and wet, and Oscar gritted his teeth, trying to get an iota of control.

Jesus. There was no way he wanted this to end too soon, but fuck if he wasn't ready to blow now.

"My turn," Luca breathed. It wasn't a question.

It was a demand.

Oscar slapped her ass once more for good measure, then helped her stand.

Luca, however, never got to the point of spanking her because as Selene straightened and stepped out of her panties, he just stared at her.

"*Bellissima*," he murmured.

Oscar stood behind Selene, pulling her back against his

chest. "Arms up," he commanded. Selene raised her arms, sliding her hands behind Oscar's head. He kissed her shoulder, the side of her neck, then nipped her ear. "Spread your legs. Wide."

Selene did, as Luca looked her over, then shucked his boxers.

"Damn," Selene breathed. "That is a very nice cock."

Oscar had never been intimidated by another man's dick, but he'd also never been in a position to think about another man's dick in relation to possibly having it in his ass.

"We're both fucking *you*," he whispered to Selene.

"Chicken."

"Yup."

"May I…" Luca's gaze darted over Selene's naked body.

"Look?" she asked. "Touch?"

"And taste," Luca breathed.

Selene's fingers dug into Oscar's head. "God, yes, please."

Luca dropped to his knees. He ran his hands up her legs from ankles to thigh, hesitating there.

"Spread her pussy open with your thumbs," Oscar suggested. "Take a good look at how pretty she is."

Luca murmured something quietly in Italian. Oscar didn't speak the language, but from the tone, he was pretty damn sure it was a prayer of thanks.

Though Oscar couldn't see—a situation that he was going to rectify real fucking quick, he knew when Luca touched Selene because she arched in his arms.

"Ah, this is the clitoris?"

"YEP, THAT'S IT!" Selene jerked in his arms.

143

"I wondered if the sensitivity of it was exaggerat—"

Selene hooked a leg around Luca's neck and jerked his face against her pussy. A second later, she shivered and moaned.

"Hold me up so I can ride his face," she demanded, trying to pull Oscar's arms around her waist.

"Fuck that, I want to watch." Oscar tugged Selene away from Luca. "Also, the man has a fuckoff huge bruise on his cheek. Be careful."

Luca inhaled heavily and then licked his lips. "It didn't hurt."

"Now, you're getting it," Selene said with the sexiest smile Oscar had ever seen.

Fuck, that was hot.

"Bed. I want to watch." Oscar knew he sounded angry, but he wasn't. He was so fucking turned on, his cock was already wet.

Selene raced for the bedroom. Oscar hauled Luca up and shoved him after her. By the time they reached the bedroom, Selene was already on her back on the bed, legs spread, arms up by her head.

"Luca should get to decide how this goes," Oscar said. "It's his first time with a woman."

"He can, as soon as he finishes eating my pussy."

"Wonderful plan." Luca threw himself down onto the bed between her legs and spread her open with his thumbs. This time, Oscar got to watch as Luca started by carefully licking her clit with just the tip of his tongue, Selene's back arching with each flick.

"Suck my nipples," she pleaded, tugging on Oscar's wrist.

He wrapped one hand around his cock, squeezing the

base to keep himself under control, and then bent his head to her nipples. He sucked long and hard, then scraped the tip with his teeth. Lifting his mouth, he blew across her wet flesh, watched her areola tighten, then leaned over to repeat the action with the other breast.

"I'm close," Selene breathed. "But I want to come with one of you inside me."

Luca lifted his head. "I want that too."

"To be inside her?" Oscar asked. "Or to have me inside *you*." He wasn't sure what wonderful, insane impulse made him add the second part.

Luca's eyes lit up. "Both."

"Don't fucking move. Either of you." Oscar jumped to his feet and raced for the kitchen. He'd seen Crisco there. Because, of course, the lunatics who owned this chicken-themed, dead-deer-heads cabin cooked with Crisco.

When he came back, Luca was on his hands and knees above Selene. She had one arm hooked around his neck, raising her upper body to facilitate their kiss.

"Fuck her," Oscar barked. "Then I'm going to fuck you, and when I fuck you, it will make you fuck *her*."

They broke the kiss, Luca holding eye contact with Selene as he adjusted his knees and dropped to his elbows. Selene pulled her heels toward her ass, creating a cradle of her legs.

"Condom?" Luca asked.

Selene looked at him. "I'm protected and clean. Do we need one?"

Luca swallowed heavily as he shook his head. "I...no... we don't."

"Fuck yeah," Oscar muttered as he shifted so he could watch as Luca lowered his hips. It took him a few tries to get his cock lined up correctly. Selene reached between them to help guide him in.

"Right there. Can you feel it?" she asked softly.

"Yes. You're so hot…and…and soft."

Oscar popped the top off the Crisco tub, scooped some out, and greased his dick.

"Slide into me, my angel," Selene whispered.

Luca's ass flexed and his big dick disappeared into Selene's pussy. He started trembling. "That feels…that feels so fucking good."

"You have two minutes to fuck her, then I'm coming for your ass," Oscar warned.

They both looked over.

"Crisco?" Selene asked. "What kind of redneck bullshit—"

She stopped speaking and moaned as Luca pulled out all the way and thrust in again.

"She's tight all the way, along the whole length of my cock."

"Do it again, but shift your hips down, angle your cock up. That way you'll hit her G-spot."

Luca frowned in concentration and thrust again. The frown turned into a very satisfied grin as Selene arched under him, her nails digging into his back.

"If there were four of us, we could have someone playing with her nipples," Luca breathed.

"We're one short for a gang bang, but while I fuck your ass, you can play with her tits." Oscar climbed onto the bed.

"Have you fucked a man before?" Luca glanced back over his shoulder.

"No, but I've fucked an ass before. *Her* ass, actually,"

Oscar said, looking at Selene, whose eyes were unfocused with her arousal. She was seriously close to coming. "Relax."

Luca slid deep into Selene and then dropped down, his pelvis and chest flush with hers.

Oscar spanked Luca just because he could, enjoying the other man's groan of pleasure, then rubbed his Crisco-covered fingers between the cheeks of Luca's ass, feeling his tight entrance. He should go slow, work Luca up to this, but they were all too fucking close. Oscar held Luca's hips, angled his cock, and pressed.

For a moment there was resistance, and then Luca's tight hole relaxed, and the tip of Oscar's cock slid through the ring of muscle. He stopped, panting.

Under him, Luca was trembling, and Selene was writhing uncontrollably.

"Fuck him," Selene demanded. "Fuck him and make him fuck me and oh shit…"

Oscar widened his knees, forced both Luca and Selene's legs apart another few inches, held tight to Luca's hips, and thrust his cock in deep. That shoved Luca's hips forward, and Selene moaned in pleasure.

"Again," Luca demanded. "Again, please. Don't stop!"

He wasn't sure he *could* stop. This whole thing was so fucking good, so hot and dirty, that he knew there would be no way of stopping the orgasm that was already making his lower back and balls tight.

Oscar pulled almost all the way out, then thrust in again.

And again.

He fucked Luca, Luca fucked Selene, and he had a beautiful view of both of them.

"I'm coming," Selene breathed. "Harder, faster. Make me come."

Luca took control then, thrusting in and out of her pussy, and with each back thrust, he fucked himself on Oscar's cock.

Oscar shuddered as the first pulses of the orgasm claimed him, his dick twitching inside Luca. Selene cried out, nails on one hand digging into Luca's back, the other hand wrapping around Oscar's wrist as he held Luca.

"Yes, yes!" Luca groaned. For a wonderful moment, he jackhammered in and out of Selene, his ass working Oscar's cock through the orgasm.

Oscar closed his eyes, arched his back, and groaned in deep pleasure. It wasn't just the physical, but the emotional affinity. The way they were connected, the way Selene had, in her climax, grabbed both Luca and him.

Oscar's pleasure was so encompassing and complete that when the orgasm was over, he collapsed forward, lying across Luca for just a moment before he slid to the side, aware that he had been forever changed.

CHAPTER TEN

Luca stood in the middle of the kitchen, shirtless, wearing just his pants. He'd only gotten dressed an hour ago even though it was late afternoon.

Luca stared unseeingly out the window above the kitchen sink, his mind playing over everything that had happened last night and today. He'd slept with Oscar and Selene…both of them…at the same time. And it had been incredible. The most perfect night of his life.

They'd all fallen fast asleep last night after—*dannazione*—after, not stirring until nearly noon when first Oscar, then he, had made love to Selene.

Luca couldn't wrap his head around how amazing it was to come inside a woman's body. The slick heat that enveloped and caressed his cock was the greatest physical pleasure he'd ever known. And it had been made even more incredible when Oscar reached between his legs as Luca fucked her, cupping and squeezing his balls until his eyes rolled back in his head and he dove headfirst off the cliff, his climax so powerful, he could still feel the effects of it now.

A large part of him wondered if he'd actually died in that safe house and, by some miracle, made it into a Heaven he'd stopped believing in long ago. It was the only way he could believe the past twelve hours were real.

Selene was the one who'd insisted they needed to rise. For one thing, the coal stove had burned out, and while it was cozy and warm in the bed, the cabin had rapidly chilled, thanks to the broken-out window.

Begrudgingly, the three of them climbed out of bed. Selene was currently feeding the fire while Oscar had gone outside with a shovel he'd found in the cellar to try to dig them a path to the car, now that the snow had stopped. He wasn't sure what the point of that was since the drive was still coated in snow, but Oscar seemed to be enjoying himself.

Luca had been charged with scrounging up dinner. There weren't many choices, though he had found some minced beef and a bag of fried potatoes in the freezer, which, according to the instructions on the back, could be baked in the oven.

He was fairly certain he had the makings of a hamburger. Or at least the start. Hamburgers were in fashion in Italy right now. He'd eaten them before, but never made one.

Luca searched but didn't find anything that looked like buns, but he did find ketchup—which was sugary tomato pudding he personally found disgusting—but he also found mayonnaise. The meal felt very American to him, and he liked that.

He walked to the pantry to find a vegetable to add to

the plate. He sorted through the various cans, and had settled on a can of corn when he decided to investigate a large cardboard box tucked into a corner on the floor of the pantry. The cartoon elephant on it meant it wasn't likely to be vegetables, but he was curious. He bent down to open it.

Peering inside, his eyes widened and he whistled.

"What's in there?" Selene asked as she walked into the kitchen and over to the sink to wash the coal dust from her hands.

Rather than answer, Luca pulled the box out and lifted it to the counter.

Selene, drying her hands on a towel, glanced inside, her smile growing. "You just hit pay dirt, Luca."

He wasn't sure he agreed, but before he could suggest they simply put the box away, Oscar shuffled in, rubbing his hands together briskly. "Jesus. It's colder than a brass toilet seat on the shady side of an iceberg out there."

Selene and Luca shared a laugh. Luca was amused by Oscar's colorful way of speaking, but right now...his clever turn of phrase was overshadowed by his ridiculous outfit.

Oscar grinned and rolled his eyes before striking a Superman pose. He'd found a camouflage jacket in the bedroom closet that he'd paired with a quilted blaze-orange hunting hat, complete with fur-lined ear flaps, before venturing outside.

Selene pointed to the box. "I don't think you'll be cold for long."

Curious, Oscar tugged off his hat as he walked over and looked in the box. "Hot damn. I think I just forgave the owners of this cabin for all the stupid-ass chicken shit."

The three of them each took turns pulling different bottles of liquor from the box.

"Oooo. A full bottle of Hendrick's...and tonic," Selene exclaimed excitedly. "G and T's are like mother's milk to me."

Oscar chuckled, even as he shook his head. "No, thanks. I'll stick with a classic. Crown Royal. I think I saw some cans of Coke in the refrigerator."

Luca wrinkled his nose as he pulled out a bottle of vodka disdainfully. "Vodka."

"*Good* vodka," Selene stressed. "Grey Goose. Top shelf. Not cheap. You should give it another try."

Luca shrugged noncommittally.

"It's happening. We need mixers." Oscar had the refrigerator open and he was pulling out different cans of soda. Opening the freezer, he grabbed a tube of frozen orange juice concentrate and handed it to Selene, who immediately found a pitcher.

"Happy hour before we eat?" Selene asked.

"The meat is frozen," Luca pointed out.

"Happy hour," Oscar declared. Selene put the meat in a pan and took it to defrost on the coal burner.

Luca finished emptying the box before moving it off the counter. With the soda, juice, tonic water, and seven different bottles of liquor, they'd managed to create a small makeshift bar.

Oscar rubbed his hands together again, but this time, the gesture wasn't due to cold, but excitement. Obviously Oscar was seeing possibilities. Possibilities that both excited and potentially worried Luca.

"Okay, I think we should start light. You're a G and T girl, right, Tanaka?"

Selene was way ahead of Oscar, already popping ice cubes from trays into glasses. "I'd kill for a lime, but beggars can't be choosers."

She expertly poured out the gin and tonic water over ice, explaining to Luca that the best G and T, in her opinion, was a one-to-one ratio.

Oscar argued with her and added more tonic to one of the glasses. When Oscar argued, the anger in his voice was intimidating. Except, apparently, to Selene, who rolled her eyes then handed Luca the glass with additional tonic in it.

Luca had vowed never to touch liquor again after the unfortunate cheap-vodka night—he'd spent hours on the bathroom floor, promising abstinence forever—but that vow seemed silly now in the face of their enthusiasm. Besides, considering last night, Luca trusted them. He'd trusted them with the secrets of his past, with his remembered pain. Trusted them enough to finally live out a fantasy that had been so much more than his imagination could have ever created.

Luca took a tentative sip of the gin and tonic. Given his previous experience, he'd mentally prepared himself for the liquor to burn. So he was shocked by how smooth the drink was.

"That tastes like…" He took another sip, trying to nail down the unusual flavor, but he couldn't figure it out. It was very mild, but not sweet.

"Juniper? Cucumber?" Selene supplied.

"Juniper. That's it. How unusual."

"Like it?" she asked.

"Very much," Luca said, taking a larger sip.

Oscar downed his gin and tonic in one quick swig,

clearly not as impressed as Luca. "That's okay for a start, but this is a real man's drink."

Oscar tried to take Selene's glass, but she held on to it and hissed at him. Luca relinquished his glass and Oscar rinsed out their glasses, joking he didn't want the gin to taint the flavor of his masterpiece. Grabbing another glass for Selene, he then poured Crown Royal and Coca-Cola into the glasses. He lifted a jar of maraschino cherries to show them. "Found these in the pantry. My secret weapon." He added a couple cherries to each glass. "Since we don't have Cherry Coke. Give that a try, Luca."

Again, Luca was surprised by how easily Oscar's drink went down. "That is delicious."

Selene sipped her drink and gave Oscar a one-shoulder shrug, clearly not willing to admit how much she liked his cocktail. He liked the casual way she had a glass in each hand.

"Perhaps it's just vodka that I do not like," Luca said.

"Two iterations are not enough of a test," Selene declared.

"Nice try, Luca," Oscar said, uncapping the Grey Goose. "You're still doing a vodka tasting."

Selene considered their options, then consulted with Oscar. "You could go for the classic," she suggested. "A screwdriver."

Oscar shook his head. "Feels too safe, too boring."

"I thought that was what the orange juice was for?" Selene stuck a wooden spoon in the pitcher and gave it a quick stir.

Oscar grinned. "I just like to have options. I mean, there's amaretto here too, and there's nothing like OJ and amaretto."

"Amaretto?" Luca picked up the bottle, read the label, and brightened up. "Oh. I love almonds."

Selene ignored him, reaching for a different bottle. "There's a little thing of Bacardi. OJ isn't pineapple juice, but maybe with a cherry in it."

"Too tropical for the middle of a fucking blizzard."

"True," Selene agreed with Oscar.

"What I'd really love to make him is a Bloody Mary, but there's no tomato juice. Damn," Oscar said after a few minutes. "There's not much here. It'll have to be simple." He returned to the refrigerator and pulled out a tiny plastic lime.

"Seriously?" Selene asked. "There was lime juice in the fridge and you didn't bother to tell me?"

Oscar gave her a shit-eating grin. "Didn't feel right wasting it on a G and T." He cracked open a Sprite, pouring that and a splash of the lime juice over the vodka.

Selene scowled. "But you'll waste it on a vodka and Sprite?" Her question was laced with outright disgust. "Is there Seagram's? A seven and seven—well, seven and Sprite—is more blizzard appropriate."

"Says the woman who started with a G and T and suggested Bacardi and OJ."

"Crown and Coke? That was your life-altering suggestion?" Selene scoffed.

"I added cherries," Oscar said hotly.

Luca was starting to feel warm, thanks to the alcohol. Warm and...happy.

He was happy.

Unable to contain it, he started to laugh, enthralled by these two wonderful people. They were so open and honest with what they thought and felt. He'd spent his life hiding. From others. From his own emotions. They, in contrast, could bicker and argue, then smile and laugh together.

They stopped arguing when his laughter continued, Oscar tilting his head and leaning closer to him.

"Drunk?" he asked Selene, though it was Luca's face he was looking at. "I mean, he's only had two drinks. Talk about your lightweights."

"I'm not drunk," Luca said, still chortling.

"You might be a little bit drunk," Selene pointed out.

"Is that why I feel…happy?" Luca set his drink down. "In that case, I want to always be drunk."

Selene's expression softened. "You haven't been happy very often, have you?"

"No."

Oscar put a thumb on Luca's eyelid and pulled it up, staring at his eyeball. "Not drunk. Tipsy."

Selene knocked Oscar's hand away from his face. "Leave his eyeball alone. You're not a doctor and you can't diagnose levels of drunkenness like that anyway."

"Walt's a doctor. I absorbed some of that med school shit by sibling osmosis."

"Is that possible?" Luca asked.

Selene shook her head. "No, it's not. He's full of shit. But I agree with his conclusion. You're probably just a little tipsy. Here." She added more Sprite to his glass.

"But what about more vodka? I think I like it after all."

Oscar snorted. "We're going to pace you. After this one, you chug water."

"Aww, it's like he's a new pledge to our frat and we have to make sure he doesn't die of alcohol poisoning," Selene said cheerfully.

"Where the fuck did you go to school again?" Oscar asked.

"MIT."

"What the fuck was going on in your Greek system?"

"What about those other bottles?" Luca pointed. "I'm a scientist. We should experiment."

"Look at me, buddy." Oscar cupped Luca's face in his hands. "I'm going to make this simple. If you drink too much, your dick stops working."

"That's…that's not acceptable."

"It's one of life's great injustices," Oscar agreed solemnly.

"I, however, can keep drinking," Selene said. "And then I can be drunk while you two pleasure me."

Luca held very still as his mind crafted one sensual, sexual fantasy after another.

Oscar squeezed his face. "What are you thinking right now?"

He should prevaricate. But he didn't want to. He wanted there to be no secrets from these two.

"There are things…things besides drinks I'd like to try."

"Sex things?" Selene said hopefully.

Luca sighed, long and slow. "So many sex things."

"Damn blizzard, we're short at least one person for a gang bang," she grumped.

"I'll share you with *him*. I'm not sharing you, either of you, with a stranger." Oscar had crossed his arms and sounded grumpy once more.

Selene ignored him. "Luca, tell us what you want to try."

"I should make dinner. Hamburgers. We're in America, so I was going to make hamburgers."

"Luca, spit it out," Oscar demanded. "What do you fantasize about when you jerk off in the shower?"

If he hadn't had the drinks, he wouldn't have said it, or at least wouldn't have blurted the words out as if he were entering terms into the search bar of a porn website.

"Gang bang. Bondage. Forced Voyeurism. Fem Dom."

Selene and Oscar stared at him, and his buzz started to fade, replaced by embarrassment.

"Fuck dinner," Oscar breathed. "Take off your clothes."

SELENE PUT a hand on Oscar's chest to stop him as the big man reached for the hem of her shirt. He froze, muscles tense under her palm. The fact that she could stop him, a man so physically dominant that there was no way she could have stopped him if this were a purely physical contest, excited her.

That thought sparked another fantasy, but they already had a deliciously long to-do list.

"We have to decide on a logical order for this," she insisted.

"How about we just talk about it while we fuck?" Oscar demanded in exasperation.

"Don't you think Luca deserves the full experience?"

Luca stiffened. "If this is motivated by pity because of my..."

Whoops. She'd put her foot in it. "Luca, no, of course not."

"Selene just wants to do some Fem Dom so she can make us eat her pussy."

"When you say eat, you actually mean lick, correct?" Luca cleared his throat. "The available pornography doesn't make it clear exactly what is pleasing."

Selene licked her lips. If they kept talking rather than doing, she was going to jump one of them. Literally jump on them. Oscar was used to her and would catch her. If she could get them to the bedroom then maneuver Luca so his back was to the bed, then at least if she knocked him over, they'd have somewhere to land.

"What are you thinking?" The question came not from Oscar, but from Luca.

"Why do you ask?"

"You have your sexy face on," Oscar said.

"I have a sexy face?"

"You do," Luca said.

"He just met you and he knows it." Oscar stepped closer, effortlessly closing the space between them, her hand still pressed to his chest. "You are a fucking sexy woman."

Selene briefly considered doing exactly what Oscar had suggested—just going for it. Another session of sweet ménage sex.

Ménage sex, like what she'd have with her trinity.

She looked from Oscar to Luca and let her thoughts take her down a road they had never traveled. She was wishing for, hoping for, something that was impossible, something that wasn't hers for the taking.

What would she give to live in a committed trinity with Oscar…and Luca? Luca, who was not a member of the Masters' Admiralty or the Trinity Masters. Selene couldn't help thinking of Oscar's sister, Sylvia. After all, she was an American admitted to the European secret society. Perhaps Luca, an Italian, could…

Selene silently rebuked herself. Luca was part of a religious sect working against the Masters' Admiralty. He wasn't a part of the world she lived in. What she longed for was absurd, inaccessible, unachievable. She wasn't living in a fool's paradise and it was time to stop pretending she was.

Shoving those thoughts aside hurt, but also helped her control her arousal. Selene stood on her toes, placing a kiss on Oscar's cheek.

"Oscar?"

"Yes?"

"Tie Luca to the chair and make him watch while you fuck me."

Luca had just taken a sip of his drink—they should probably take it away from him before the poor guy got well and truly drunk—and choked on it. He swallowed and then coughed a few times. Oscar went over and patted his back. Once Luca had finished sputtering, Oscar took his drink, set it on the counter, and then wrapped his arm around Luca's shoulders.

"Is getting tied up going to give you PTSD flashbacks?" Oscar asked him.

"No, I don't—"

Oscar spun Luca around and forced him down into a kitchen chair.

"Selene, get me the duct tape from the drawer."

"Which drawer?"

"What do you mean 'which drawer?' *The* drawer."

Selene rolled her eyes, but started opening drawers until she found the one where he'd sourced the cards and hot sauce packets. There was a roll of duct tape at the back.

Selene brought it over, examining the very sexy tableau.

Luca was in the straight-backed chair. Oscar knelt behind it, his arms wrapped around Luca from behind, both holding Luca to the chair and keeping his elbows at his sides.

Selene found the end of the roll and pulled some off, with that distinctive, loud ripping sound unique to duct tape. Both men looked at her, and for a moment, she considered taping both of them to the chair, just as they were. Then she'd sit on the table, spread her legs, and make them watch as she played with herself.

Selene tore off a piece of duct tape and slapped it over Luca's mouth.

Damn it, she *was* a supervillain because doing that had felt way too good.

Luca mumbled behind the tape, his eyes wide. Selene unwrapped a long section—grateful this was a fairly new roll, and slapped it across Luca's chest, then passed the roll to Oscar.

A few passes around his chest and then Oscar tore the tape, patted the end in place, and stepped back.

"Why gag him?" Oscar asked.

"It seemed like a good idea at the time."

"You're terrifying."

"You like it."

"I do. I never claimed not to be cracked in the head."

"Are you saying only crazy people would want to fuck me?" Selene asked.

"Like attracts like."

"Then maybe you're a supervillain too."

Luca grumbled from behind the tape, an exasperated sound. They'd wrapped the tape around his upper arms and chest, which meant he had no problem bending his head to meet his raised hand and ripping the tape off his mouth. "Talk less, fuck more."

Selene let out a delighted laugh, which quickly turned into a yelp of surprise as Oscar spun her around and bent her facedown over the kitchen table. Selene shivered in delight as Oscar hooked a hand into the back of her pants and jerked them, and her panties, down around her thighs.

"You can give orders all you want," Oscar told Luca. "But you just have to watch while I fuck her."

Luca's breathing was heavy. "Get your hands off my wife!"

There was an awkward pause.

"Um, can I do that?" Luca asked quietly. "Pretend?"

"Role play it is," Oscar declared. "Why the fuck not?" He pinched Selene's bare ass.

She yelped, and Oscar pinched the other cheek.

"Please don't spank her," Luca said.

Selene lifted her head slightly. "I thought you liked bondage, not—"

Smack.

Oscar spanked her ass hard enough that she yelped.

"—S&M," she finished, panting.

"We're apparently going to do all the kinks." Oscar shoved her pants down to her knees. "Now be a good girl, don't make me get a wooden spoon."

"Oh yes—I mean no, no, don't get a wooden spoon," Luca panted.

Oscar put one hand between her shoulder blades and smacked her ass with the other. It felt good, small stings that turned to pleasant warmth, a warmth that made her pussy, already wet, pulse with need.

Selene lifted up on her elbows, twisting to look at Luca

while she spoke to Oscar. "Oh no, please don't fuck me in front of my husband!"

"I will." Oscar jerked her up. Her pants and panties fell to the floor. "But first I'm going to make him watch while I play with your tits.

Oscar grabbed the front of her shirt with both hands. He was going to rip it off her. That was so hot.

You don't have anything else to wear.

Selene elbowed him in the stomach, then as Oscar wheezed, removed her own shirt. "I'm not wearing one of those camo monstrosities in the closet if you ruin my clothes."

"You get a wooden spoon and punish him," Luca breathed.

"All in good time, sexy." Selene winked at him.

Oscar had recovered his breath. He yanked the straps of her bra down her shoulders, using them to trap her arms at her sides.

Then he slid his hands into her bra and twisted her nipples.

"I can't see," Luca moaned in distress.

"I know you can't. She has to tell you what I'm doing."

Selene licked her lips, arching into Oscar's hands as he first kneaded her breasts, then pinched her nipples.

"He's pinching my nipples," she breathed. "Now he's rolling them. Sort of twisting them with his fingers. Now he's pulling—oh God, do that again—pulling them as he twists."

Luca's whole body tensed, and the chair groaned as he flexed against the tape.

Oscar turned and once more bent her forward, but this

time toward Luca. Selene braced her hands on Luca's thighs, their noses nearly touching.

Luca wrapped his hands around her wrists, holding her in place. Behind her, she heard the zipper of Oscar's jeans. Then his hands were on her hips, his cock sliding into her. Selene shivered in pleasure, her eyes closing, at least until Luca sealed his lips over hers. Oscar's cock filled her from behind, Luca tongue-fucked her mouth, and she knew if they didn't stop now, they wouldn't get to all the other delicious perversions on Luca's list.

The sense that these were stolen moments, that time was running out for them, washed over her. It should have made her want to stop and savor, but instead she felt frantic with the need to connect with them, to have them here and now because there was no surety about what would come next.

No. She knew what was on the way. And she was desperate to hold those hounds at bay.

Selene wiggled her right arm, freeing it from Luca's hold so she could slide her palm over his erection. Luca tore his mouth from hers, head tipping back. She watched his throat work, watched the tendons flex.

"Can you undo your pants for me?" Selene breathed. "I need to keep one hand braced because of Oscar's fucking. So deep. So hard." She said the last not only as a description, but as a plea for more, and Oscar heard it, gave it to her.

Luca's fingers fumbled, but he managed to get the zipper undone. That was all she needed. Selene nipped Luca's chin as she reached into his pants and boxers. His cock was seriously huge, and as she pulled it out, she considered the logistics of giving him a blowjob. Maybe it would be better if—

"I've never had... No one has ever..."

"For fuck's sake, suck the man's dick." Oscar punctuated the order with a slap to her ass.

Selene jerked forward, the top of her head bumping Luca's chest.

She dropped down, bracing her forearms on Luca's thighs, and wrapped her lips around the head of his cock.

There was something so wonderful and powerful about knowing her touch could deeply affect another person. A swipe of her tongue over the tip of Luca's cock and he started swearing in Italian, the words sexy, even if she didn't know what they were.

Oscar's cock thrust in, hard and hot inside her. She swallowed Luca's cock, taking as much of it as she could into her mouth, which wasn't much, but she stroked the underside with her tongue as she withdrew.

"I cannot...I am going to..." Luca muttered.

"Come in her mouth," Oscar commanded. He spanked her again. "And you better swallow it."

The sexy, arrogant asshole. Selene would make him pay for that. She'd put him on his knees and make him lick her pussy while Luca fucked him and then—

The first ripple of pleasure tightened her sex around Oscar's cock. She shoved her mouth down on Luca's dick, and the fullness there, mirroring what was happening at her pussy, ignited her orgasm. Selene swallowed hard around Luca's dick while thrusting her hips back against Oscar.

Luca was back to shouting in Italian, and a moment later, his salty come hit the back of her tongue. She swallowed, and swallowed again. Behind her, Oscar was cursing, and she felt his cock twitch inside her.

They were joined together in pleasure—Selene was no stranger to that. And if that was all she was experiencing, if she wasn't also inundated by a million different overpowering needs, hopes, and desires, she wouldn't be so overwhelmed by this sudden desire to cry.

SELENE LAY on the kitchen floor, her bra still tangled around her middle. Oscar used a kitchen knife to cut through the tape, then peeled it off Luca's shirt. He slid off the chair to sit beside her on the floor. They were both still panting. Oscar, like Luca, was still dressed, but he'd tucked his cock inside his pants.

"Do I have to carry you two to bed?"

"Fem Dom doesn't need a bed," Selene declared from the floor. "That's what we're doing next."

Luca grinned, a big, goofy, heart-on-his-sleeve grin that Selene adored. "I never thought I would actually get to try the things I fantasized about."

Selene rubbed his back without moving anything but her arm. "If it's not what you thought it would be like, that's totally normal."

"It's not." Luca looked over at her. "It's better."

"We're clearly not doing Fem Dom right now," Oscar declared. "You two are practically dead on the floor in the chicken kitchen. We need a fucking nap."

"I'm just lulling you into a false sense of security," Selene assured him.

Luca snorted and started to laugh.

"But the floor is hard." Her butt was starting to hurt. "You may pick me up, servant."

Oscar hooked his hands under her armpits and yanked her to her feet. Selene looped an arm around his neck, ready to be carried like a princess to the bed.

Oscar briskly unlooped her arm, planted his shoulder against her hips, and slung her over his back. Selene yelped as he straightened, his hard shoulder digging into her stomach.

Luca rose to his feet. "The urge to, uh, spank her. You…"

Oscar smacked her ass. "Go for it. Her ass is very spankable."

Selene shrieked as a wicked slap landed on her ass.

"Too hard?" Luca sounded so worried.

"No," she breathed. "It hurt in a good way." Luca's unexpected dominance, followed by his seemingly endless compassion, just made everything that much hotter.

"My turn—"

Oscar's words were interrupted by the clucking ring of the chicken phone. They all turned to look at it, Selene bracing her hands against Oscar's ass.

"Fuck," Oscar breathed.

"I'll get it. Back up." When Oscar had brought her close enough, Selene snatched up the receiver, still slung across Oscar's back. "Hello?"

"Selene?" It was Preston Kim.

She poked Oscar, and he seemed to get what she wanted. He lowered her to her feet. "Hello, Preston."

"Lance and I ran the calculations."

She swallowed, her stomach knotted. "And?"

"The numbers don't work."

Selene closed her eyes in sudden, earth-shattering relief. "The bomb doesn't work."

Luca sank into a chair, his whole body slumped. Relief...or disappointment?

If these results had come a few days earlier, she would have suspected—worried—it was the latter. But there was no doubt in her mind now that Luca was grateful to know his designs couldn't be used to snuff out countless innocent lives.

"You're sure?"

"Yes. We've tried several iterations."

The city-killer bomb wasn't the horrific thing they'd all feared.

"Did you inform the Grand Master?"

"Yes. They wouldn't give me this number until I informed them of our results."

"Thank you, Preston. And please thank Lance for me."

"I will."

Selene hung up the phone and turned to look at Oscar and Luca.

Luca raised his head, and he was smiling. "I have never been so happy to be proven a fool."

"It's over," Selene said. "The bomb doesn't work, so it doesn't matter who has the plans and—"

"I wish that were true," Luca said quietly. "But it isn't over."

CHAPTER ELEVEN

O scar said, "Right. Uh-huh," for the third time since answering the phone, and Luca sucked in a deep breath, forcing a fake calmness when the other man turned to look at him.

They'd been awakened at the crack of dawn this morning to the phone ringing, er, clucking. They hadn't managed to answer it the first time, but when it began clucking again almost instantly, it was clear whoever was calling didn't intend to stop until one of them answered.

Oscar, dressed in only his boxers, had managed to grab the chicken leg receiver first, and the look on his face had made it clear who was calling.

The Masters' Admiralty.

Meanwhile, Selene was pacing back and forth across the kitchen floor.

She stopped when Oscar turned to hang up. He continued to face the wall for a moment, his back to them.

"Well," she said impatiently. "What did Sebastian say?"

Oscar turned to look first at her, then at Luca. "They're

getting us out of here. There's a helicopter en route as we speak. Should be here within the hour."

"Helicopter?" Selene said, not bothering to hide her alarm. "But there's at least a foot and a half of snow on the ground."

Oscar shrugged, though it was obvious he wasn't any happier about their so-called approaching rescue. "Sebastian says the pilot is experienced, knows how to safely land and take off in deep snow. We're supposed to make our way back up to the main road. There's a clearing half a mile to the north, where the helicopter plans to pick us up. Now that the weather has cleared, Ju—they don't want to leave us here in case anyone is still looking."

"Me," Luca said quietly. "If anyone is looking, they're looking for me." Luca had known this was coming. While the past few days had been the greatest of his life, he hadn't allowed himself to forget it wasn't going to last.

Regardless, he had hoped for at least another day or two.

"Doesn't matter who they're looking for...we're in this together." Oscar spoke with such authority, such confidence, that for a moment, Luca could almost imagine they *were* a team, a unit.

God knew there was nothing he wanted more.

And nothing he could have less.

"We all knew we were living on borrowed time here," he said, proud—and somewhat shocked—by the strength in his voice. "I will never be able to express to the two of you how much these past few days—"

"Stop." Selene put her hand up. "Stop right there. We're not saying our goodbyes right now. This isn't over yet, Luca. Not by a long shot."

"As I have said before, *tesoro*, I have made peace with my decisions. I'm not afraid to die."

"Whoa. Seriously, dude," Oscar said loudly. "Enough of that. Selene is right. You're going to speak to the Tr— Masters' Admiralty, and you're going to tell them your side of the story. We're going to get your sister away from the psycho religious fuckers, figure out what to do with the bomb plans, now that we know it doesn't work, and then you're getting on with your life."

Luca nodded, offering a weak facsimile of a smile, hoping it was enough to fool his lovers.

Dannazione...his lovers.

If only time could stop...right here...right now.

Selene narrowed her eyes. "He doesn't believe us," she said, speaking to Oscar, though her gaze was locked on Luca's face.

"If there is anything I have learned these past few days, it is to trust you. Both of you. I do believe you will remain with me; however, you cannot predict the actions your society will take, nor would I..." He sighed heavily. "Nor would I allow you to place yourselves in the crosshairs of the Bellator Dei. If I was a good man, I would have left before—"

"Not gonna happen so you can save your breath," Oscar interjected.

"Oscar—" Luca started.

"Doesn't matter. This debate—that Tanaka and I are going to win—is going to have to wait until we get back to Boston," Oscar said, glancing at the clock. "We don't have long before the chopper arrives and we're going to need every minute of it to slog through that fucking thigh-deep snow."

Luca looked around the kitchen with all the crazy chicken stuff and smiled. He would think back on this odd, magical place every day for the rest of his life. A life that was probably only a few days long.

"What about the car?" Selene asked.

"Sebastian said they'd send someone to retrieve it once the roads were passable again. Get the feeling he's also going to settle up our debts with the owner of this place—replace the window and pay him for the food we ate."

"Might want to tell him we put a dent in the liquor," Selene joked.

"I'm glad he will reimburse them," Luca said. "This place provided us sanctuary. I'm not sure we would have survived outside in the car during this blizzard for so long."

"I don't know," Oscar said. "Seems to me the three of us are pretty good at generating our own heat."

They all took a few moments to get dressed, Selene looking around as if she was missing something. Then she laughed. "I keep forgetting we broke in here with nothing but the clothes on our backs."

Oscar grimaced. "All I know is, I'm a few hours away from computers and cell phones and—"

Selene silenced him with a kiss. "I think it was good for you to unplug for a few days. You look less grumpy."

"The fuck-fest is what made me less grumpy."

Selene hummed. "Fair, and imagine how much more fun we could have had if we had an internet connection and access to weird inspirational porn."

She put out the coal fire while Oscar and Luca attempted to put the place somewhat back to rights. There was no way the owners wouldn't realize someone had been there, considering the broken window, the garbage in the kitchen, and the sheets they'd stripped from the bed, but there wasn't time to do more.

As Oscar said, they were in for an uncomfortable, cold hike to the helicopter landing site.

And forty-five minutes later, Luca had decided uncomfortable was an understatement.

They'd found a pair of relatively thick coveralls, something Oscar referred to as Car Hearts, that they'd put Selene in. Oscar had managed to scrounge up a second pair of gloves and another *cappello*—toboggan, according to Oscar—in addition to the gloves and silly hunter's cap he'd been shoveling snow in earlier. Both were thin, better suited to a chilly fall day than a frigid winter one, but Luca was still grateful for the extra layer of warmth they provided.

As it was, he was concerned they might all be flirting with hypothermia. Trudging through the deep snow was strenuous and exhausting, and his pants, socks, and shoes were soaked through. Luca clearly spent too much time sitting at his station in the lab and not enough time working out. Though he was certain they hadn't walked more than two kilometers, he felt as if he'd run two consecutive marathons.

It offered him a small amount of comfort that Oscar and Selene, who were both in good shape, didn't appear to be faring much better.

They reached the clearing, but all that meant was they were now standing still in the snow.

"Jesus. If that helicopter doesn't show up soon, my nads are going to break off," Oscar grumbled.

Selene nodded, her teeth chattering loudly enough that Luca could tell speaking was beyond her at the moment.

Mercifully, Luca heard the buzz of a helicopter approaching.

"Thank g-goodness," Selene stuttered. She was currently stomping her feet, bouncing in an attempt to keep warm.

Oscar held his hand over his eyes, shielding them. It was amazing to Luca how absolutely blinding all this white snow could be. "I hope the pilot thought to pack us some dry clothes and blankets."

They huddled closer, watching as the helicopter hovered overhead. Oscar waved his arms, though Luca figured the action was unnecessary. They were the only spots of color in a sea of white.

The helicopter descended slowly, so slowly Luca began to fear the pilot wasn't going to be able to set the vehicle down. Apparently, whoever Oscar had spoken to on the phone this morning assured him landing in deep snow was possible. Luca prayed that was correct because he wasn't entirely sure he'd be able to make a return trip to the cabin, if not. His legs had gone completely numb.

As it got closer to the ground, the whirling blades kicked up the snow, producing white-out conditions. Luca closed his eyes and lowered his head against the freezing bits of ice pelting him all over.

Finally, after what felt like a year and a half, the helicopter landed, the blades slowing, then halting. The helicopter sank until the belly of the vehicle nearly touched the snow, particularly the underside of the nose.

As the snow began to settle, Luca looked up and saw the pilot open the side door, gesture for them to approach, then jump back into his seat.

Somehow, Luca managed to make it the last twenty-five meters to the vehicle. Oscar helped Selene and then him inside, before climbing in himself and closing the door. The second they were sealed up in the helicopter, Luca felt the hot blast of air coming from a heater at the front of the vehicle. He'd never been so grateful for warmth.

There was a bench seat with room for three. Selene had claimed the spot directly behind the pilot, Luca the center, and Oscar, the place on Luca's right.

The pilot gestured to the headphones tucked into the back of the cockpit seats, then to his own headset.

They put them on as the pilot worked his magic and the blades began to rotate once more, kicking up a mist of snow all around them.

Once they all had the headphones on, the pilot twisted around to look at them once more, pointing to bags on the floor at their feet.

"Dry clothes," the pilot said. "And blankets. We aren't cocked, so change now." The pilot seemed to realize they were freezing and confused. "We have time. While the rotor speeds up. Change."

After issuing his command, the pilot turned back to the control panel, pressing a series of buttons before picking up the handset of a radio. "Pickup confirmation. Skids in sky, approximately four minutes."

Selene reached down for the bag at her feet, but her hands were trembling so badly, she was struggling to grasp the strap. "I've never been this cold in my life."

Luca pulled off his wet gloves, bending over to grab her bag. He placed it on her lap as she smiled gratefully. Then he got his own.

Oscar was already pulling off his shoes and socks,

unfastening his jeans. Luca watched as the other man lifted his ass and fought to peel the wet, frozen denim down.

Oscar caught him watching. He started to say something, then his gaze drifted to the pilot. With the headsets on, everyone in the helicopter could hear what everyone else said. Instead, he shut his mouth and winked.

Luca chuckled, the sound catching Selene's attention. She watched Oscar strip, then blew a kiss before fighting her way out of the thick coveralls.

With much wiggling, struggling, and, of course, cursing on Oscar's part, the three of them managed to replace their wet clothing with the sweatpants, soft long-sleeved Henleys, and thick socks in each bag.

"Seat belts." The pilot's hands were moving over the levers and buttons.

Selene unfurled a blanket—there was one at the bottom of each bag—and tucked it over her waist after she buckled her seat belt. Oscar and Luca followed suit.

The pilot turned then. "Ready?"

Oscar gave him the thumbs-up and Luca took a deep breath as the sound of the rotor shifted. The world outside went white.

"What's going on?" Oscar demanded.

"Recirculating snow for a tower takeoff. Gotta take it slow. Snow takeoffs are tricky."

"Not comforting," Selene muttered.

The pilot barked out a laugh before focusing all his concentration on getting them off the ground.

The helicopter began rising from the Earth at a snail's pace.

Luca reached over and grasped Selene's hand. She

smiled and squeezed it, letting him know she appreciated the support.

Luca was surprised when Oscar took his other hand. The three of them sat quietly, Selene with her eyes pressed closed tightly for the first few minutes, as the pilot expertly maneuvered the chopper off the snow.

And then, they were flying.

"We should be in Boston in about two hours," the pilot said after a few minutes. "So just sit back and relax. We'll be back on the ground before you know it. By the way," he said, turning to look at them, "there's no snow in Boston, but with the wind chill today, you're going to be disembarking in negative temperatures."

Luca sighed. "In Dante's Inferno, hell burns with cold, not fire."

Selene looked at him. "Are you saying being trapped with us was like being in hell?"

Oscar unsubtly pinched him.

"Ouch. No. Of course not," Luca stammered.

"Danger," the pilot said.

They all froze. "What danger?" Oscar demanded.

"The guy with the accent is going to choke on his own foot if he shoves it any farther into his mouth."

"Fuck, dude. Do *not* say danger unless there's something wrong with the fucking helicopter," Oscar snarled.

"Oh, the helicopter is fine."

After that demonstration that anything they said would be heard by the pilot—who also apparently had no reservations about joining in—there were no further conversation attempts during the trip.

Instead, Luca sat replaying the past several days in his

mind. If he wasn't in such a sexual haze, he might have used the time preparing himself for what was to come.

But he couldn't do it. He'd spent too many years of his life worrying about the future. He realized now that was probably because there was nothing in his past worth remembering.

He startled slightly when, after nearly two hours of silence, the pilot said, "We're ten minutes out if you want to start gathering your stuff. There will be a car waiting at the landing pad for you."

Selene and Oscar exchanged a look and he could read the concern on their faces. Then Oscar placed his hand on Luca's knee and gave it a comforting squeeze.

"We got this," Oscar said, unconcerned if the pilot heard them or not.

Twenty minutes later, they were on the ground, safe and sound. Peering out the window on Oscar's side, Luca saw that there was indeed a car waiting only fifteen meters away.

"I'm not putting my shoes back on," Selene said. They were speaking normally now—sans headphones, though the rotor hadn't completely stopped yet and was humming above them.

"I say we make a run for it in our socks," Oscar clearly agreed. Their shoes weren't only damp, but still sopping wet and freezing cold. Luca nodded. Though they'd been ensconced in the warmth of the helicopter for over two hours, he hadn't completely shaken off the cold that had gone bone-deep.

And when Oscar opened the helicopter and their heat was whisked away by air so cold it took Luca's breath away, he suspected it might be years before he ever shook off the frigidness of winter in northeast America. For the first time since he'd left on this venture to find his tablet and the plans to the bomb, he found himself actually missing Italy and its mild winters.

They each grabbed the bags containing their wet clothing and shoes and sprinted toward the waiting vehicle.

The driver opened the back door of the town car for them and they slipped inside.

Once the driver was back behind the wheel, Oscar leaned forward. "Where are you taking us? Hotel? Because we need to get cleaned up. Need clothes and shoes."

Luca knew that was wishful thinking on Oscar's part. He was certain they would be given no reprieve for such comforts.

The driver shook his head. "I'm not at liberty to reveal that." He twisted from the front seat then and held out what appeared to be a black pillowcase. "I need you to place that on Mr. Campisi's head."

"You've got to be kidding," Selene said hotly, just beating Oscar, who had opened his mouth to issue a complaint as well.

"It's okay, Selene," Luca said, taking the bag from the man's hands. He saw a brief moment of surprise on the driver's face. "I expected this."

Luca pulled the bag over his head on his own, not wanting either of his lovers to feel guilt over the simple task.

"Stupid fuckers," Oscar muttered as the car engine turned over and they started to move. "Did the same goddamn thing to me."

Luca didn't know what to make of that, but now that they were on their way to meet the Masters' Admiralty, the assurances he'd given Oscar and Selene about his having made peace with what he'd done, what he'd become, faded away. He did what they'd wanted in order to protect his sister, and it hadn't mattered to him because he'd had no future, either in this life, or in the fiery afterlife he had stopped believing in long ago.

That had been true a few days ago. He'd been determined to do whatever it took to keep Joli safe, and to someday, hopefully rescue her from the Bellator Dei. There had been plenty of days he'd considered ending his own life—it would be easy to make it look like an accident, a bomb defusing gone wrong—but he couldn't protect his sister from beyond the grave.

Still, he knew the price for his crimes would be death. And death at the hands of their enemy, the Masters' Admiralty, would make him a martyr among them, which, he was sure, would insulate her from any repercussions if, after he was gone, they managed to discover he hadn't been as devout as he'd pretended.

His life had no future—a white blankness to pair with his black past.

But now...

Now, as stupid as it was, he wanted a future. Not one in which he lived lies in order to protect Joli. Not one in which he did horrible things for other people.

He wanted a future.

A real one.

Because now he had something worth living for.

CHAPTER TWELVE

The room, a cave perhaps—he was fairly sure they were underground—was dramatically lit. The edges were shrouded in darkness, while a cone of light illuminated a huge medallion embedded in the stone floor. It bore a Celtic triangle symbol.

Luca hadn't bothered to try to track where he'd been taken, or how he'd gotten where he now was. There hadn't been a need to because Selene and Oscar had been by his side. As long as they were with him, he was safe.

But ten minutes ago, he'd been separated from them. He'd been brought into what he was fairly sure was an elevator, a man's hand on his shoulder guiding him since he still had the hood on.

He was sitting in the centermost of three chairs that abutted one half of the medallion. His guide had, after removing the hood, faded into the darkness.

If they killed him here, now, would Selene and Oscar grieve for him? The idea that there would be someone left behind to mourn him was actually comforting. The Bellator

Dei would celebrate his death if he died at the hands of the Masters' Admiralty because it would be a sign that he'd paid the ultimate price for the cause. They wouldn't let Joli show any sadness.

Footsteps clicked on the stone, and then a robed, hooded figure appeared from the darkness.

When the person spoke, he was surprised to realize it was a woman, though he shouldn't have been. He thought he'd heard Oscar and Selene referring to the person they called the Grand Masters as her/she.

"Luca Campisi," she said. "We've been looking for you."

He remained silent. There was, after all, nothing he could say that would change what was about to happen.

"You build bombs. You design bombs so horrific that the idea of them keeps me awake at night."

"The bomb does not work," he said softly.

"Yes. But that wasn't by design, was it? Not the same way the flaw that allows it to be disarmed was."

Luca nodded, just to show he was listening.

"When we looked at the bomb plans, we realized the person who designed it wanted it easily disarmed. We concluded it was designed under duress." She took a half step, the hem of the long black robe brushing the edge of the medallion. "Mr. Hayden and Dr. Tanaka tell me that we were right. You hold no loyalty to the Bellator Dei, only to your sister."

Luca didn't respond immediately, touched by Oscar and Selene's defense of him. Oscar had offered reassurances in the helicopter. "We got this," he'd said. It was the word *we* that Luca still couldn't quite wrap his head around.

"I have done terrible things to protect Joli. I do not deny that, or that I deserve to die for my crimes."

Emotion choked him. He knew he was facing the end of his life, but his final thoughts weren't worry for his sister. Instead, he felt regret. Regret that he had shared only a few days with Oscar and Selene.

"Do you prefer death to facing what you've done?"

That snapped his head up. "You're calling me a coward."

"There's a phrase—suicide by cop. Is that what you were doing? Running all over the eastern seaboard, attacking my people in hopes that we would end your life for you?"

"No, of course not. All I wanted was my tablet back. I needed the bomb plans. It needed to be *my* bomb that they tried to build."

He'd revealed more than he should have.

"Your bomb…" The hooded Grand Master was silent for a moment. "Because your bomb could be disarmed."

Luca leaned forward, too weary to sit up, so he propped his elbows on his knees. "I was not the only child they trained to make explosives."

"How many others?"

He'd told Selene and Oscar about these things, but telling them to this woman in the hood, to a person who was, according to everything he'd grown up being taught, his enemy, was so much harder.

"Three or four when I was there." Thinking about the others caused his chest to tighten because he knew them well—had spent countless hours in classes and in the laboratory with them. He knew their hearts, knew they were truly committed to the Bellator Dei's cause. Unlike him, they were determined to see their bomb designs succeed. The bigger the death toll, the better. "But there are many more. The technical institute is still operational, still recruiting, training. They have to be stopped."

"The more you say, the more it seems that you're our ally rather than our enemy."

"I am no one's ally."

"You say that, but do you believe it? You would not consider yourself Selene and Oscar's ally?"

A horrible thought occurred to him. "Please! Please do not punish them for…"

To his surprise, she laughed. "For sleeping with you?"

Luca froze.

"I know the signs. Their vehement defense was not purely intellectual."

"I did not turn them against the Masters' Admiralty," Luca said quickly. His heart was slamming against his ribs. "I…I coerced them and—"

"You didn't. The Hayden brothers cannot be coerced, only bribed or outmaneuvered." The Grand Master walked to the center of the medallion. "There is something you do not know, which I feel it is time you learn."

Luca tensed, waiting for a blow.

"We—Selene, Oscar, Langston, Mina Edwards—are not members of the Masters' Admiralty."

"What?" Luca's hands curled into fists, and he began to look around the room, pissed off at himself for failing to take in his surroundings. If they weren't the Masters' Admiralty…

His stomach clenched as he considered too many unsavory options. Then he thought of Oscar and Selene. Had they intentionally lied to him? Before he had time to consider the possibility of their betrayal, the woman spoke again.

"You didn't really think the Americans would submit to being members of a society based in Europe, did you?"

Luca blinked, then cursed. "There are two societies?"

She gestured at the cave. "Welcome to the headquarters of the Trinity Masters. America's oldest and most powerful secret society."

The Trinity Masters. He'd simply assumed, when he saw Langston with a man and a woman, and associating with known Masters' Admiralty member Milo Moretti, that they were part of the same society.

It also meant that Selene and Oscar truly *had* lied to him. He'd told them all his deepest secrets, and they'd let him continue to assume they were members of the Masters' Admiralty, not correcting him when he said so.

Their betrayal cut deep. He'd given them his trust, his truth, while all along they'd lied to him, deceived him.

Distracted by his heartbreak, Luca didn't look up until the Grand Master repeated her next words.

"Mr. Campisi, I have a proposition for you."

He took a moment to gather himself. To think. "You want me to return to the Bellator Dei as your spy."

"No, though I won't say that isn't something either I or the leader of the Masters' Admiralty might ask of you."

"What is your proposition?" Luca asked warily.

"In exchange for your loyalty to our members and laws, in exchange for your obedience to my orders and your acceptance of an arranged marriage…I offer you membership to the Trinity Masters."

. . .

OSCAR WAS on his fourteenth trek across the floor of the stone "conference room," which could have doubled as a dungeon, when Selene cracked.

"Sit down, Oscar."

He glanced up, then walked over to a chair, sinking down heavily. The scowl on his face had grown darker with each passing minute. It had been nearly two hours since Sebastian had led Luca away from them, and the Grand Master—in full robe regalia—had quickly questioned them before leaving them alone with a terse, "You will remain here."

"We should have stayed with him," Oscar barked.

"We weren't given that option. It's going to be okay." Selene wasn't sure she truly believed those words or if she was merely saying them to comfort herself.

"What the fuck could be taking them so long?"

Selene shrugged. "I suspect the Grand Master had a great many questions to ask him about the bomb. Though I assume she wouldn't have a technical discussion without me there."

"What if the Masters' Admiralty is here?" Oscar asked.

The same concern had crossed Selene's mind as well. While she felt relatively sure no harm would come to Luca at the hands of the Trinity Masters, she wasn't familiar with the Masters' Admiralty or the way they operated. The fact that Luca was a member of the Bellator Dei, a very real enemy of the other society, could outweigh the fact that he didn't believe in their "cause" and was being forced to work for them.

"Luca is of more use alive than dead, Oscar. To both societies. You know that."

He nodded, then he said what Selene suspected had

been bothering him the most. "We should have told him. About the Trinity Masters. I didn't like lying to him."

"We were under direct orders from the Grand Master." And while that was true, their deception wasn't sitting well with her, either. Just because she didn't like an order didn't make it optional.

"Fuck that!" Oscar said hotly. "We should have told him."

Selene sighed, but before she could reply, the door to the conference room opened. Both she and Oscar sprang to their feet, and Selene found herself able to take the first real deep breath since Franco left them here as Luca walked in, followed by Sebastian and Franco.

"We'll give the three of you a few minutes to talk, then we'll be back to continue, Luca," Sebastian said.

"Continue what?" Oscar asked.

Sebastian didn't respond. Instead, he turned around and left the room. Franco merely gave them all a big smile, then slipped out as well, closing the door behind him.

"Are you okay?" Selene asked, walking over to Luca, placing her hand on his forearm.

Luca pulled away from her, offering only a brief nod.

Selene shared a glance with Oscar, whose guilt was practically oozing out of him.

"You know?" Selene asked. "That we are not..." She hesitated to say it, in case he didn't know.

Again, Luca nodded.

"We're sorry, man," Oscar started.

Selene rested her hand on the back of one of the chairs to stop herself from reaching for him again. She wanted to touch him, hug him. She hated the distance she suddenly felt between them. "The Grand Master ordered us to…to…"

"To lie to me."

Selene didn't bother to nod. Regardless of what they were asked to do, things between them had advanced well beyond the point where obeying those orders rubbed against the grain.

However, if there'd been another longstanding member in the room, someone who had heard the horror stories, they would have known that obeying the Grand Master's orders didn't have caveats and footnotes that allowed disobedience because you disagreed with the orders. Oscar was too new, and too stubborn.

And Luca…well, he'd grown up in an organization even more rigid than the Trinity Masters, and he'd rebelled.

"If we could have told you…" she said softly.

Luca didn't reply, didn't offer forgiveness. He pulled out a chair, moving to sit down, but the glint of something caught her eye, drawing her attention to the ring on his finger. The ring he hadn't been wearing before.

"What is that?" she asked even though she knew. She recognized the triquetra, the symbol of the Trinity Masters. She tried to reconcile what that ring represented with reality. "Luca," she whispered.

"What?" Oscar asked. He clearly hadn't seen what she had, but the shock in her expression, in her tone, had him on full alert. "What the fuck is it?"

Luca lifted his hand. "I joined the Trinity Masters."

Selene blinked. "You did *what?*"

Oscar's eyes widened. "Holy fuck."

Luca sank down in the chair. "I was shocked when your Grand Master offered the invitation."

Oscar pointed to Luca's hand. "You're wearing the ring, dude. She's your Grand Master now too."

"Why?" Selene asked quietly.

"Why would they want someone like me to join?" Luca asked, the hurt in his eyes unmistakable.

Selene responded quickly, hating that his thoughts had gone that direction. "No, why would you say yes? Did she not give you a choice?"

"The choice was mine. Unlike the Bellator Dei, there were no threats."

Oscar slammed his hand down on the table. "Just spit it out. Tell us what happened and then you can be pissed at us."

"I'm not angry."

"Clearly, you are," Oscar countered.

"I'm hurt," Luca said quietly. "I understand that you were ordered to not tell me the truth, but I told you...I shared everything. Every truth I had to tell. And I know that I've told countless lies, done truly horrible things, and that I don't have a right to feel..." His words fell away.

The silence that followed was painful. Damn it, Luca deserved, for once, to not hurt. Not be in pain.

"Power," Luca said after a moment. "I joined because I've spent my life being, feeling, powerless. If I am a member, I am no longer powerless."

Selene nodded. "And you're not alone. You have every other member."

"You traded a shitty cult for a less shitty cult," Oscar said.

"You think I'm a fool," Luca said softly.

"No. I think you're incredible."

Selene shot Oscar a look. He rolled his shoulders as if uncomfortable.

"Perhaps I can make up for some of the evil things I have done. Perhaps…I can…" He paused for a moment. "I would very much like to make a positive difference in the world, like that trinity you told me about in the cabin. The ones working together to save the environment."

Oscar grinned. "I get that."

"And perhaps I can rescue others from the Bellator Dei."

"Like your sister." This time, Selene didn't stop herself. She placed her hand on top of Luca's, and he didn't pull away. Instead, he turned his hand over and grasped hers, held it.

Luca nodded. "For the first time in my life, I will not be powerless."

"You were never powerless," Selene said softly.

"I was. And I was a fool to think that…" Luca glanced first at her, then Oscar.

Selene squeezed his hand. "Everything that happened in that cabin was real. We weren't lying about the things that mattered."

"As I said, I am not angry with you. I understand that lies are necessary to protect secrets." Luca was quiet for a moment. "But I won't lie to you now. I've done enough of that to last a lifetime."

"Then get pissed at us. You have every right to," Oscar declared.

"I told you I am not angry—"

"—just hurt." Oscar rose and grabbed a chair and thrust it at Luca. "Here, smash it against the wall."

Luca blinked. "Why?"

"It will make you feel better. It's therapy."

"Therapy is something people go to years of school in order to learn to do," Selene said in exasperation. "You can't just tell people to do property damage and call it therapy."

"My family are great believers in smashing shit." Oscar thrust the chair at him. "Break it."

Luca's air of resignation and hurt faded a little as he stood and took the chair, but then carefully set it down. "I know you might not believe me, but I'm a pacifist. I don't believe violence solves anything."

Oscar clearly didn't agree, but he didn't say anything more.

"If you're a member," Selene said softly, "then you need to really understand that you cannot disobey an order from the Grand Master. Even if your heart wants to."

Luca looked at her, his posture straightening. "Your heart."

"Yeah, yeah, we fucked until we all caught feelings because this is the shit that happens when you join a cult." Oscar sat in the chair. "I still think you should smash something."

Selene resisted the urge to smack Oscar upside the head. Actually... "You could spank Oscar," Selene suggested. "I'll watch."

"Are we...uh. Can we still have sex?" Luca asked, the last of his bad feelings fading away.

Selene smiled. "Yes, and now that you're a member, it's practically your moral obligation to practice ménages for when you get married."

"Married." Luca dropped into a chair. "I hadn't...I mean. Wait, do people have children together?"

Oscar snorted. "When a man and a woman and a man love each other very much—"

"Maybe just slap him around a little," Selene suggested.

The door opened. "I'll help if we're talking about smacking around one of the Haydens," Sebastian said as he entered, Franco behind him. "You two go wait in the changing rooms or in the great hall. We have to finish onboarding the Italian."

"Wait, before they go, I had an idea." Franco dug in his pocket, then walked over to Luca. "Congrats!" He threw a handful of confetti into the air. It rained down on Luca.

"Jesus Christ," Sebastian muttered.

Franco took another handful of confetti and threw it on Oscar. "Here's some belated confetti for you too."

The look of her guys, the stupefied expressions on their faces with confetti in their hair and dusting their shoulders, was one Selene would treasure for a long time.

CHAPTER THIRTEEN

A massive round wooden table had been set up in the grand entrance hallway of the underground headquarters. There were eight chairs, seven of which were occupied by members of the Trinity Masters, including their newest member. Besides Luca, there was, of course, the Grand Master, her face hidden beneath the deep hood of her dark gray knitted shawl, as well as her advisors, Franco and Sebastian, Oscar and herself.

The seventh person was Owen Fraser, whom Selene recognized from one of the all-society galas, though it had been years since that particular event.

She glanced at Owen, who returned her smile before quickly shifting his attention back to Luca.

She and Oscar had taken seats on either side of Luca, who was quiet, though she wasn't sure if it was from shock at his new status or prudence. She had to suppress the urge to reach over and pluck an errant bit of confetti from the back of his hair.

The last, unknown attendee was a rather stoic man,

sitting ramrod straight. He had thick curls that just brushed his collar. His hair and his sharp, penetrating eyes were almost the exact same shades of medium brown with flashes of gold. He was broad and stocky, in a muscular way, not a fat way. He'd been introduced as Percival Knight, and he was the Masters' Admiralty's representative.

"Mr. Knight," the Grand Master said. "You speak for the Masters' Admiralty at this…gathering?"

"War council," Sebastian said quietly.

That statement echoed slightly against the arched ceiling above, grand columns, and stone floor.

"I do, within limits." Percival looked around. "I may need to be above ground to contact my fleet admiral if there are matters I cannot make statements on without confirming with her."

"That can be arranged," Sebastian said. "Do you each know why you're here?"

"Yes," Selene said.

"Of course," Owen murmured.

Luca and Percival nodded.

"No. Can I leave?" Oscar grumped.

"Pinch him," Selene whispered to Luca. "He's being a dick."

"Ouch, fuck," Oscar yelped. "Also, I heard that." He sat forward slightly to glare at her.

"You are here, Mr. Hayden—"

"Apparently as comic relief," Sebastian muttered.

"—because you were instrumental in the first part of this investigation." The Grand Master had raised her voice slightly. "Also, you are standing in as a proxy for your brother Langston, whom I believe we will need to call on sooner rather than later."

"Still on his honeymoon," Oscar said shortly. However, his nod told her he would accept the need for his presence if it meant his brother could remain with his new spouses a few days longer. He settled back in his chair, arms crossed.

Sebastian sat forward, forearms on the table. "If we're being frank, the other reason you're here," he looked first at Oscar, then at her, "is because Mr. Campisi is comfortable with you."

Selene resisted the urge to sputter. "I'm a theoretical atomic physicist. You're saying my expertise is secondary to a discussion about a nuclear bomb?"

"A bomb that doesn't work," Sebastian pointed out.

"Pardon?" Percival, who already had excellent posture, went even stiffer. "It doesn't work?"

"We told you about the engineered flaw." The Grand Master gestured to Luca. "Mr. Campisi has confirmed that it was intentional, and that he designed the bomb under duress."

Percival frowned. "Be that as it may, we believe it is in the best interest of both organizations for Mr. Campisi to return to Europe with me—"

"Not possible," the Grand Master interrupted. "Luca Campisi is a member of the Trinity Masters."

Percival looked like he might shatter, he was so tense and stiff. "Pardon? That's not possible. Since when—"

"About an hour ago," Franco said cheerfully.

Owen winced, but then his expression smoothed out. "It'll be fine, Percy. The task force means that whatever information I have, you have."

Percival didn't seem appeased. "I very much doubt that you will be given all the information."

"And your admiral tells you everything?" Owen asked mildly.

"Luca is ours," Sebastian said briefly. "He's intelligent, resourceful, and cunning. All traits we look for in our members. The Grand Master identified his potential and offered him membership. It has nothing to do with the Masters' Admiralty."

"What a load of shite," Percy muttered loud enough that everyone in the room heard him.

"Imagine what he'll be able to do when he's not all alone," Oscar said quietly. "When he's got us at his back."

Everyone looked at him. Beside her, Luca had gone perfectly still. Selene reached for his hand under the table and squeezed it. Oscar's words had caused a little lump in her throat, so she could only imagine what Luca himself was feeling.

While Selene had been the one to suggest they continue "practicing ménages," there was no denying she had feelings for Luca and Oscar. Walking away from them at the end of this nightmare was going to be...difficult.

No. Not difficult.

Impossible, her mind whispered.

"Watch your tone in the presence of the Grand Master." Sebastian was staring down Percival.

"Grand Master, if I may?" Owen leaned forward, as if he could physically intercept the tension crisscrossing the table.

She nodded to Owen.

"And may I talk freely about the MPF?"

"Yes."

Owen looked at Percival, then to her, Luca, and Oscar. "For the first time in our histories, the Trinity Masters and

Masters' Admiralty have a formal mutual aid agreement and a way to take action against any threat to both societies."

"The Bellator Dei doesn't know about the Trinity Masters," Luca said softly.

"Something we didn't realize until they brought you in," Owen acknowledged. "However, the Bellator Dei and their associates have made moves on U.S. soil, so they are now a threat to all of us."

Percival had composed himself. He cleared his throat and Owen motioned for him to take over. "Mr. Fraser and I are the joint heads of this combined task force. The Masters Protection Force."

"MPF," Selene said.

Percival nodded. "This is the first time we've been called on to act, and our original mission was to apprehend Mr. Campisi."

"Well, you did a shit job of that," Oscar said, sounding weirdly cheerful. "A computer nerd and an academic did that for you."

"Not helping," Selene hissed at him.

Owen's lips twitched. "Now that we know that Mr. Campisi—can I call you Luca?"

Luca nodded.

"Thanks," Owen continued. "That Luca isn't really a member of the Bellator Dei, our focus has shifted."

"There are two main issues," Sebastian said. "One that matters more to the Masters' Admiralty, and one that's more pressing for us."

"We need to dismantle the Bellator Dei," Percival said, making it clear which was their priority.

Beside her, Luca stiffened.

"There are innocent people in that cult," Selene said hotly.

"They beat children, murder people," Oscar added with a snarl. "We need to get those fuckers, but rescue the kids."

"We are not proposing slaughter," Percival said. "But the Bellator Dei has grown many heads since we disposed of the man who was manipulating them."

"What?" Luca demanded. "Who was it? How did you—"

"Go back and read the earlier books," Franco said.

"Dismantling the Bellator Dei, and helping people who were brainwashed or coerced by them, is what the Masters' Admiralty is focused on. We have a smaller but connected issue. Who were the mercenaries who attacked you in Pennsylvania?" Sebastian asked.

"At first, our assumption was the Bellator Dei hired them to find Luca," Owen said.

Luca nodded. "They think I am loyal to them and the cause. I may not be a full numerary, living on the compound, but my profession is one they chose, and I tithe fifty percent of my salary, as is expected of everyone in our congregation. There should be no reason for them to suspect me. They shouldn't even know I've left Italy, as I told them I had to go no-contact for several weeks."

"Someone clearly knows," Percival pointed out.

"The Serbians," Oscar added.

Luca whispered what sounded like a prayer, or maybe a curse, in Italian.

"We had to turn over the people we captured to the authorities, but before we did, we discovered several things that concern us. First, all but two of them were American." Owen raised his finger.

"Boss and Henchman Two," Selene said. "Those were my pet names for them."

"You gave them...pet names?" Percival looked alarmed, probably for her mental health.

Owen ignored them both. "Second, they had Serbian passports but have no ties that link back to Bellator Dei. They do have some very distant ties to Serbian dissident groups. But the connections are tenuous. One of them is the neighbor of a man whose brother-in-law's cousin is a paramilitary rebel in the ultranationalist Serbian Action Organization, who are believed to be neo-fascist and neo-Nazis. They have the resources of a small government and have used bombs."

"Did you design bombs for them?" Percival asked.

"No." Luca shook his head. Then paused. "Not that I... I don't make car bombs or suicide vests, if those were what was used."

"If they have the resources of a government, I'm thinking they have access to components." Owen raised both eyebrows.

Luca sat back, blinking behind his glasses. "I was never told where the Bellator Dei got the bomb-making materials. I had some in the lab I used for my job, but that is a known facility, and everything I brought in was regulated," Luca said. "But I overheard a few things that made me suspect weapons and bomb supplies were purchased from a Serbian or Ukrainian source."

"A paramilitary organization would be a good source for those kinds of things," Owen said.

"You never interacted with them directly?" Percival asked.

Luca shook his head.

Percival leaned forward slightly. "But they might have figured it out. If I was selling bomb supplies to someone, I might get curious as to who was designing and building the bombs for them."

Luca rubbed his jaw wearily. "But I am not the only one they trained to do it. I focused on experimental bombs. There are others who build package explosives, car bombs—"

"They're still rebuilding the villa that particular device destroyed." Percival sounded stiff once more. "And of course, the families of those who died are still grieving."

The table went silent, and while her heart hurt for what those people must have suffered, Selene's thoughts were focused on putting together pieces of what she knew, and what Owen and Percival had said.

"The neptunium." Her voice broke the silence.

"Fuck." Oscar sat up straight. "Of course."

Luca looked back and forth between them, realization stamping his features. "If they supplied it…"

"Much better to have that for themselves," Selene said.

"Exactly," Oscar echoed.

"Would you like to share with the rest of the class?" Owen asked mildly.

Selene turned away from her lovers to look at the rest of the people around the table. All of whom, with the exception of the Grand Master, were leaning forward with either frowns of concentration or confusion on their faces.

"Let's say I'm the leader of a military rebel group—"

"Aka, a supervillain," Oscar said.

"—and I'm selling guns and explosives to a funky little religious cult. That's fine. They're terrorists, I'm a terrorist, it works out for both of us."

Luca didn't flinch when she called the Bellator Dei terrorists, and she was glad she hadn't hurt him, even if she was, unfortunately, correctly labeling both him and his sister.

"Then one day, they ask for something different. Neptunium. You get it for them, but then you start to wonder why they need it."

"Ahhh, yes. Shit." Owen sat back. "Nice one, Selene."

She nodded, but kept going in case the others hadn't figured out where she was headed. "So I do some research, realize it could be used in a nuclear device. Suddenly the little cult I've been supplying has something I don't—the ability to make a nuclear bomb, using an element that isn't as heavily regulated as uranium and plutonium.

"I want that bomb. But how to get it?" Selene continued. "I could go to the cult and offer to buy a bomb or two. Or...I figure out who's playing the role of Oppenheimer and kidnap him. If I have the bomb maker, I have as many bombs as I want. I don't have to pay for them, and the threat from those bombs isn't diluted by another terrorist organization having the same thing I do."

Owen tapped his fingers on the table. "Luca, do you have neptunium?"

"Yes. I didn't make the bomb, but I could. I had everything I needed."

"How did you actually get ahold of the neptunium?" Owen asked.

"It was delivered in person. The courier never spoke. I cannot confirm he was Serbian."

Owen clearly believed they now had a lead they could work with as he continued with one follow-up question after another. "But it would be a logical assumption…if the Bellator Dei gave the address of your lab to the Serbians so they could deliver it—I assume special handling is needed?"

"Yes. In addition to being radioactive, it's pyrophoric, which means it's capable of spontaneously catching fire at room temperature."

Owen closed his hand, lightly hitting the table with the side of his fist. "It's possible, even probable, that they know who you are, and given that your actual job is bomb analysis and forensic disposal, they could assume you were also, secretly, the man who created bombs for the Bellator Dei."

"The Serbians may have tracked you to the U.S.," Percival said. "The risk of kidnapping you in Italy may have been too great."

"But if they have ties to an organization we've labeled terrorists, then their known members can't enter the U.S.," Owen pointed out.

"So they find someone who isn't on our watch lists," Sebastian said. "Send them over."

Owen nodded slowly. "The Americans in the group are part of the Serbian gangs of Chicago."

"So the two who come over recruit some Americans with ties or sympathies to act as muscle," Sebastian added.

"That would explain why they were so fucking dumb," Oscar added.

"This changes things." Owen looked at Percival, who nodded.

"How?" the Grand Master asked softly, less as if she

needed an answer and more as if she were prompting him to explain.

"Now we have three issues. The Bellator Dei, the Serbians, and the bomb plans themselves."

"It doesn't work," Luca reminded them. "My calculations were wrong."

"But no one knows that besides us," Sebastian pointed out. "And frankly, Luca, even if you told your people that it didn't work, they might not believe you. And the Serbians will probably assume it *does* work, even if they're told it doesn't."

"Because they want it to work. And even if they kidnapped Luca, and he told them it didn't, they would assume he was lying to stop them from having a nuclear bomb."

"Exactly."

"We release the plans," Oscar said. "Put them up on the dark web."

Sebastian nodded. "Alert the intelligence community first to be prepared to track the sale and movement of neptunium."

"Find the bad guys when they go shopping," Oscar added.

The Grand Master stood, and they all turned their attention to her. "Owen, you coordinate with Percival to address the issues of the Bellator Dei and the Serbians."

"Yes, Grand Master."

Beside Selene, Luca stiffened. "My sister is innocent. She doesn't know what they really are."

"Our goal is no loss of life," Percival said, not unkindly. "We would like your assistance in listing their members and describing their compound."

"If you save them," Luca said quietly. "The ones you can. My sister, the people who never had a chance to learn anything else. The children."

"With your assistance, that is a likely outcome," Percival said.

Selene noticed neither he nor Owen promised that Joli would be okay.

"Oscar, Luca, and Selene. It's clear the three of you function well as a tri—together."

For a heart-stopping moment, Selene thought the Grand Master was going to say "trinity." The overwhelming sense of disappointment that washed through her when she didn't told Selene exactly how bad this was going to hurt when they all parted and returned to their homes and jobs.

"You will work with our primary CIA contact to orchestrate the release of the plans." While the hood hid her face, it was clear the Grand Master was pleased. The hood turned as she looked at each of them. "Well done."

With that, the Grand Master turned and walked away, Sebastian and Franco at her back.

CHAPTER FOURTEEN

O scar gave Selene a casual one-armed shrug when they found themselves back in the same hotel they'd left...fuck...was it really just five days ago? It felt like they'd lived a lifetime since.

After Luca's hours-long meeting with the leaders of the MPF, Sebastian had ordered them to return to the Boston Park Plaza. They'd been set up in the penthouse suite his brother Langston had shared with Mina and Rich a couple weeks earlier. Apparently, this suite was reserved for the Trinity Masters year-round.

Franco said it was typically used by newly formed trinities, part of their get-to-know-you month right after the initial binding ceremony.

In their case, Oscar, Selene, and Luca were here because it was a three-bedroom suite, and the Trinity Masters knew how to protect it. There was currently one of their Warrior Scholar dudes, Andre, standing sentry in the hall.

Sebastian had pointed out they'd probably only use one

of the bedrooms. Luckily, the Grand Master hadn't been there when he'd said that because Oscar wasn't sure how Juliette felt about him and Selene hooking up, let alone how she felt about them adding Luca.

Of course, Oscar had been taking his cues on Trinity Masters stuff from Selene, and she just laughed at Sebastian's joke, so it was probably cool.

"This is a very beautiful room," Luca said, taking in the kitchenette, the mini baby grand, the bar. Given what he'd told them about his upbringing, it was safe to say there'd been precious few luxuries in Luca's life. Not that Oscar was accustomed to this kind of high living, either.

"Oh!" Selene cried out. Oscar followed her line of vision and understood her sudden happiness. Their luggage had been retrieved from the safe house and was sitting at the end of the hallway, waiting for them, along with…

"My laptop. Fuck yeah." He rushed over and picked up his battered laptop case. "Come to daddy, baby. I've missed you, girl."

Selene rolled her eyes at him, but he didn't give a shit. The past few days were the longest he'd ever gone without touching a computer, and he had been about five minutes away from some serious DTs.

Luca's eyes widened when he realized his suitcase was amongst theirs.

Selene recognized his surprise. "The security team who captured the Serbians must have gone through your rental car and recovered your belongings as well."

"I suspect they searched it all first, but I don't care. I'm grateful to have clean clothing. And dry shoes."

They'd been forced to put their cold, damp shoes back on when they'd arrived at the library. The first thing Oscar had done when they'd walked into the suite was kick his shoes off by the door. Glancing down, he realized Selene and Luca had done the same.

Selene reached for the handle, intent on dragging her suitcase down the hallway, and Oscar started to follow suit. They both stopped when Luca sank down on the couch, his elbows on his knees, his head in his hands.

"You okay?" Oscar asked, walking back to the other man.

Luca started to nod, then released a shaky breath and shook his head. "No. I'm still struggling...trying to make sense of..."

Though Luca seemed incapable of gathering his thoughts, of forming a complete sentence, Oscar understood immediately.

How many months had Luca spent finding a way to accept that he could be killed for his actions? Oscar tried to put himself in Luca's shoes. While death was inevitable, he was still young and, because of that, he assumed he had decades left before he had to worry about dying. He wasn't sure he would have been able to come to grips with the idea of living on borrowed time, sacrificing his life before he'd even gotten close to hitting forty. As far as he was concerned, he still had a shit-ton of stuff to do and too much life to live.

Oscar sat next to him on the couch and gripped his shoulder tightly, trying to comfort Luca. "I get it, man. You weren't expecting this. Don't take this the wrong way, but you've been running with the wrong crowd. It's skewed your perception of people. Not everyone in the world is a psychopath, seeking to cleanse those they deem evil through explosives."

Luca laughed, and Oscar could hear how rusty the sound was. Luca hadn't had a lot of stuff to laugh about in his life. "That's good information to have," Luca joked.

Selene claimed the other side of Luca. "You're one of us now, Luca. The Trinity Masters will protect you, help you."

"I still don't understand why your Grand Master invited me. It seems…strange to me."

Selene smiled. "You're brilliant. The Trinity Masters seek out the best and the brightest. You definitely qualify."

"But my bomb design didn't work."

Selene waved that argument away. "Yet. The concept is solid. What doesn't work is our current technology. You were wrong about the speed an atom could obtain with that particle accelerator, based on current particle accelerators, even modified ones. You're like John Michell, predicting the existence of black holes long before we had the technology to see them."

Luca's face hardened. "Even if the technology existed, I will never try to make that bomb work."

She grasped his hand and squeezed it. "I know that. But that doesn't mean you can't design something amazing that could change the world in a positive way. I think that's why the Grand Master invited you to join. You can help me try to make a fusion energy generator."

"Isn't that the thing you said could blow a crater in the Earth?" Oscar asked in alarm. "How about no?"

"I hope you are correct, Selene," Luca said softly. "I was wondering if it was *Tieni i tuoi amici vicino…ed i tuoi nemici… ancora più vicino.* Keep your friends close, but your enemies closer."

Selene shook her head. "No. Our society doesn't work that way."

"I figured she was just nabbing Luca before the Masters' Admiralty could," Oscar added. "Like you said, our dude here is brilliant, and the Grand Master is still pretty tweaked at Eric, the fleet admiral, for stealing Sylvia away."

"Tweaked?" Luca asked, unfamiliar with the expression.

"Pissed off. Mad. Annoyed," Oscar clarified.

"That's *also* not how the Trinity Masters works," Selene said though Oscar could tell she was less confident his argument was wrong.

"You saw how that Percival guy reacted when the Grand Master told him she'd recruited Luca to the Trinity Masters."

Luca shook his head. "I don't believe the Masters' Admiralty would ever want me. I am their enemy. It is different here. The Trinity Masters don't have the same violent history with the Bellator Dei."

Selene tilted her head. "I think you're wrong, but it's a moot point. You're ours now."

For a split second, Oscar grinned, his fucked-up head and heart mistaking the meaning of those words. Selene meant Luca belonged to the Trinity Masters, while Oscar wanted Luca—and Selene—to belong to him.

Apparently their pep talk worked, as Luca's expression cleared. "It will take me some time to become accustomed to that, to truly believe it, but…" He broke into the biggest, brightest smile Oscar had ever seen. "I am certainly going to try."

Jesus, Luca was seriously hot…and Oscar couldn't

believe he'd actually thought the man somewhat nondescript the first time they'd met.

Selene rose, tugging Luca up as well. "Let's go find the biggest bedroom."

It occurred to Oscar he wasn't the only one struggling with the hourglass on this relationship. The sand was flowing and there was no stopping it, no avoiding what would happen once they released the plans on the dark web and the Grand Master told them they were free to return home.

He didn't want to leave Selene and Luca. It was as simple and as difficult as that.

Oscar had spent half his life with his head stuck up his ass, thinking—convinced—that Faith was the only woman for him.

He'd lived with that broken heart for two years. And now, in just a few short days, Luca and Selene had not only mended his heart, they'd almost completely erased the memories—and the pain—of his first love as well.

Talk about conflicted. He was a man with a new lease on life…and there was a guillotine blade poised right over his neck.

The three of them grabbed their bags, placing them in the master bedroom. The bed was fucking huge, which made sense considering this suite belonged to the Trinity Masters.

Oscar pushed away the realization that this was where his brother, Langston, had celebrated his honeymoon. This was no honeymoon, but he sure as fuck wished it was.

"So…" Selene said, sitting on the edge of the bed, running her hand over the duvet suggestively. "Where are we on our list?"

Luca glanced over at Oscar, who grinned. A smart man —a man who'd spent years wallowing in the pain of a broken fucking heart—would put some distance between himself and his next shattered heart.

Oscar wasn't that fucking smart. "I'm not sure we fully explored all the aspects of bondage. Why don't I tie you both down?"

"I agree. We should explore further. However, I would like…" Luca's gaze traveled to Selene, who rolled her eyes, not in anger but amusement.

"Of course," she said. "You want your turn to play lord and master."

"If you are not comfortable—" Luca began.

Selene's soft laugh stopped him. "Sweet Luca. I love submitting as much as I love giving orders. Get undressed."

"That doesn't sound like submission to me," Oscar said, even as he pulled his shirt over his head. "Luca, get in my duffel. I have a belt in there. We'll use that to tie her up."

"Or you could spank me with it," Selene offered helpfully.

"No topping from the bottom, Tanaka. We're running the show here. Get onboard or we'll have to gag you," Oscar murmured.

The threat did little to tame their sexy scientist, who simply gave him a superior look that made Oscar think the gag was probably her goal all along. The woman's kinks were off the charts and hot as fuck.

Luca's eyes went dark with desire, and he moved to open Oscar's bag, rummaging around until he found the belt.

Oscar looked at Luca, recalling how much he enjoyed

role play. "Are we playing this straight, or do you want to set a scene for us?"

Luca glanced at where Selene sat on the bed. "Capture. Claiming," he whispered.

"Fuck, yeah," Oscar groaned. "We'll need a safe word."

"Fermi," Selene suggested.

Luca smiled. "A man born in Italy, but who became an American."

"I know one of you wants me to ask who Fermi is so you can geek out, but I'm not going to." Oscar folded his arms. "Say that, and it will make us stop. Otherwise…"

Luca studied Selene's face closely, and Oscar was continually moved by the man's constant concern for their safety, their happiness.

Oscar walked over to Selene and cupped her cheek affectionately. "Give our boy the affirmative one more time, Selene. He won't truly let go until he knows you're okay with all of it."

Selene rose slowly. "Don't hold back, Luca. I know what a safe word is for, and I won't hesitate to use it if I need to. This is one of my fantasies as well. I expect you—both of you—to make it good for me."

Luca stepped closer to Selene, his voice dropping. "We followed you home from the store. You're beautiful and you caught our eye. You didn't see us walking behind you, lurking behind the shrubbery, finding out where you lived. You didn't realize we were waiting outside for night to fall, for our chance to break in. You've just turned the lights out, and you're getting ready for bed."

Jesus. Luca's deep, quiet voice, the way he created the scene, developed the story, had Oscar's dick rock-hard.

"We're going to go out to the living room for a couple

of minutes while you remain in here. You hear a noise. You realize you're in danger. You know you have to hide."

Selene's mouth was open slightly and Oscar wasn't sure she was breathing. Her nipples were tight beneath her T-shirt, betraying how much Luca's role play turned her on. "I'm going to fight you," she whispered. "Hard."

Luca gave her a slight grin, though Oscar wasn't sure if it was meant to be comforting or...sinister. Either way, it fucking worked. He'd never really tried role play before these two—Faith's sexual appetites were far more vanilla—but damn if he didn't love it. "We wouldn't have it any other way."

Oscar was suddenly grateful he was still in the sweatpants the helicopter pilot had provided. If he'd been wearing jeans, he would have been in serious pain.

Luca turned and left the room. Oscar stood still for a moment, then shook his head in amazement. "We created a monster."

Selene laughed softly. "Or maybe *we* are the monsters."

"Who gives a fuck? The sex is amazing."

Oscar went out to the living room where Luca was standing at the front door, talking to Andre.

Luca closed the door, throwing the chain and the dead bolt before looking at him. Oscar noticed his face was slightly flushed. Was Luca blushing?

"I, uh, told him if he heard anything questionable in here, it was okay."

Oscar chuckled. "What did he say?"

Luca grinned. "He told me to have a good time and use lube."

Oscar was still shirtless, so Luca pulled his T-shirt off as well. Luca wasn't well-defined by any stretch of the imagination, but he was trim, with a smooth, bare chest, and Oscar, who hadn't thought he could get any more aroused, was proven wrong as his dick twitched.

They looked like twins in their matching gray sweatpants. That might have been funny if Oscar had any air in his lungs to laugh. As it was, he was too excited, too worked up, too fucking ready for this.

"Guess we should give her time to hide. So you wanna work up a game plan, or are we just winging it?" Oscar asked.

"I think we should follow our impulses. Do…what feels right. What feels good. Oscar…" Luca hesitated, and Oscar saw the wealth of emotions written in his expressions. He recognized them for what they were because he'd been feeling the same way.

Oscar reached out and gripped Luca's shoulder, squeezing it. "I know, man. This is…"

"Perfect," Luca finished. "The three of us…we're…"

Oscar sighed and nodded. "Perfect."

"I just gave your Grand Master the right to marry me to anyone she chooses."

Oscar grimaced. "Yeah. I'm still trying to get that part of the membership requirements to sink in too."

"You really are new to the society?"

Oscar sighed. "I know we lied about being part of the Masters' Admiralty. I fucking hated that, by the way. But nothing else has been a lie. I've been a member of the Trinity Masters almost a whole week."

Luca's eyes widened.

"We'll talk more later. Right now," Oscar glanced over his shoulder, "we have a woman to ravish."

Luca chuckled, then stepped around Oscar, stealthily sneaking toward the bedroom.

Oscar was hot on his heels, not wanting to miss a second of this action. He figured he could anticipate what most women would do in this situation.

But Selene Tanaka was not most women. She was in a league all to herself, and he was—no, he *had* fallen head over ass for her.

Luca hadn't made it one step inside the bedroom before Selene was there, launching herself at him in an all-out tackle.

Luca hadn't expected the attack, so he fell back into him. The three of them teetered for just a moment, but Selene had come at them with enough force, and there was no defying gravity. They wound up in a heap on the floor, and because he'd been at Luca's back, Oscar had caught the brunt of it, hitting the floor hard while cushioning the other two.

"Fuck!" He'd landed mostly on his ass, and it hurt like a son of a bitch. Before he had time to reorient himself, Selene was up and racing toward the hotel door. Luca had obviously fared better because he was only two steps behind her, catching her before she could reach the doorknob. Not that she could have escaped anyway. Luca had wisely thrown the chain and the dead bolt.

Oscar rose slowly, gingerly, then followed, his eyes glued to his lovers the entire time.

Luca had Selene pressed firmly against the door, his chest hard against her back.

"Fight all you want. You're still ours," Luca murmured in a menacing tone that was completely at odds with the man Oscar had come to know over the past few days.

Oscar stepped beside them, reaching out to grab a handful of Selene's silky hair. He pulled it roughly, forcing her to look at him.

Her eyes were glazed with desire, the arousal in the room so thick, a knife couldn't pierce it.

"Carry her to the bedroom," Oscar said harshly. "We'll take her there."

"No!" Selene cried, struggling against Luca's hold. She almost broke free, but Oscar grabbed her hands as he twisted her, gripping them firmly behind her back.

Selene bent forward quickly, freeing her hands for just a second while nearly headbutting Luca in the process. Fortunately, he'd managed to dodge it, or he'd have ended up with a broken nose. It had definitely been a close call though.

Oscar regained his grip on her wrists with one of his hands, the other wrapping around her shoulders so that he could pull her against his chest. "This one's a wildcat," he said to Luca.

Selene was still fighting them roughly, kicking out and catching the side of Luca's thigh. Damn. She hadn't joked around about fighting back.

The next time she tried to kick, Luca caught her ankle, and if Oscar hadn't been holding her, she would have taken a backwards tumble. Once Luca had a secure grip on one leg, it was easier for him to grab the other.

Together, they carried a squirming Selene to the bedroom. Throughout it all, she called them a steady stream of nasty names, promising to cut off valuable parts of their bodies once she got free. The only thing she didn't say was her safe word.

They dumped her on the bed, both of them ready for her.

Selene didn't disappoint. The second her hands and feet were free, she sprang up. And met two immovable walls.

Oscar straddled her legs, holding them to the mattress to prevent her from kicking. Then he grabbed her wrists. "Grab the belt."

Selene's hair was a tangled mess, her face red from her exertions, her chest rising and falling rapidly from the fight.

She'd never looked more beautiful.

Luca returned with the belt, looping in around one wrist, then threading it through a slat on the headboard, and finally fastening her second hand.

With her arms secured above her head and Oscar trapping her legs to the bed, the fight slowly drained out of her.

"Good girl," Oscar said, running the back of his fingers along her cheek, provoking her to shudder, even though she narrowed her eyes at his words.

"Get your hands off me!" she yelled, turning her head away from his touch.

Oscar clenched his fist around a handful of her hair tightly. "You're ours."

She tried to shake her head, but he tightened his grip, refusing to allow it.

"Ours," he repeated. "Say it."

"Never," she spat out.

Oscar ignored her denial, reaching for the neck of her T-shirt. He ripped it in half, fighting hard not to laugh when he heard Luca's muttered "holy mother of God."

Even Selene struggled to remain in character, the edge of her lips tilting upwards.

The ragged ends of her shirt hung open at her sides,

revealing her lacy bra. Oscar roughly palmed both her breasts, squeezing them until Selene groaned, the sound a perfect blend of pain and desire.

Reaching into the cups of her bra, he pulled her breasts out and over the tight lace. Luca lost no time taking advantage of what Oscar had just uncovered.

Bending his head, Luca sucked one of her nipples into his mouth.

While Luca distracted her, Oscar slowly peeled her pants and panties down, moving with them, constantly alert in case she started kicking again.

She didn't. Obviously Selene had passed the fighting stage. Her eyes were closed and her hips gyrated in search of more.

Oscar pressed her knees apart, kneeling between. Leaning down, he ran his tongue along her wet slit as Selene hissed.

Through his peripheral vision, he saw Luca lift his head to see what he'd done, so he repeated the action.

Luca shifted so that he was lying on the bed next to Selene. "Make her come with your mouth."

Oscar wasn't used to Luca giving orders. Typically, that was Selene's department.

He looked up at both of his lovers, gave them a wink, then bent down to do exactly that.

Oscar pressed his tongue against her clit before sucking it into his mouth. For several minutes, he drove Selene's arousal higher, tormenting her with licks and bites and sucks before fucking her with his tongue.

A quick glance up proved Luca wasn't idle, either. He was kissing Selene like it was his last day on Earth, his fingers toying with her taut nipples.

Oscar could tell she was getting close, her breathing erratic, harsh.

"She's there," Oscar said, prompting Luca to break the kiss so that he could watch.

Oscar drove three fingers deep, the impact fast and hard and the catalyst she needed. Selene's back arched beautifully as she flew away on the wings of her orgasm. Oscar stroked her through it, drawing the climax out even longer.

"I need you," she said after a moment, her voice hoarse from her cries.

Oscar stood quickly, stripping off his sweatpants. Within seconds, he was deep inside her, fucking her with all the strength, all the desire, all the love in his body.

He didn't bother with finesse or stamina. He couldn't. He needed her, and so he took, driving in, pounding in, grabbing every ounce of pleasure he could steal. He came hard, bright flashes of white light blinding him beneath his closed eyes, and Selene was right there with him, her pussy clenching around his cock tightly.

Oscar fell to the side, aware that Luca had taken his place. It took several minutes for him to shake off the effects of his own climax before he could focus on his lovers. When he did, he knew Luca was there too.

He lifted himself up on his elbow and watched his lovers come.

Fuck him. There was nothing more incredible than the image of Luca and Selene in the throes of passion.

Every single thing in his life had driven him here, to this moment, to this bed, to their arms.

And they weren't his to keep.

CHAPTER FIFTEEN

"Remind me again why we're outnumbered, outmanned?" Ridley Phillios asked mildly as he checked his weapon and hummed a number from *Hamilton*.

"We can bring more people on," Owen replied, "but it would take time to get them all to Rome."

Jennika was using the side of the van, the sliding door pushed open as a seat. She was wearing a headset and had a computer perched on her lap. "I'm about to link us in with their comms, so get it out of your system now."

"Saddle up," Rhys Fletcher said.

"No." Jennika pointed at Rhys. "No stupid cowboy terms."

"Aww, darlin'—"

"I will delete you from all known digital databases. Good luck trying to convince the government you're alive again." Jennika didn't look up from the computer screen as she issued the threat.

As an NSA agent, she could carry through on that.

"As long as you don't mind a top spot on Homeland's watch list," Rhys countered.

"Now, now, let's all try and get along," Ridley said with a grin. He was laid-back and approachable—which seemed counterintuitive since he was 6'5" with a shaved head.

"Fine." Jennika pointed to her own headset. "Earpieces in."

"Fine by me," Rhys paused, then very deliberately added, "darlin'."

"Could you not?" Owen asked the Homeland Security agent.

Rhys shrugged and put his earpiece in.

"Besides." Ridley put in his own earpiece. "I could rendition both your butts to a CIA black site."

"Literally the opposite of helpful," Owen said.

Then there was no more banter because the comms went live.

Owen, along with Jennika, Rhys, and Ridley, stood by a white van with a cartoon plumber's logo on the side.

Two black vans, bearing logos for an Italian internet provider and a locksmith, respectively, were parked on the other side of the parking lot. Nine men and women stood outside or sat in the vans, and now that the comms were on, they could hear an occasional comment or quick conversation in a variety of languages.

Percival was standing at the open door to one van, talking to Sidika Arslan, a Turkish woman who worked for a private security company in Istanbul. She was running comms for the Masters' Admiralty team.

He shouldn't think of them as two separate teams, especially since the plan he and Percival had developed, with information from both satellite photos and a detailed interview with Luca, had them grouped into three entry teams, with a mix of Trinity Masters and Masters' Admiralty people on each.

"English, please," came Percival's clipped accent though the earpiece.

"Load up," Owen commanded.

"See you on the flip side." Ridley held out a fist, and Owen bumped it with his own.

Rhys touched two fingers to the brim of an imaginary hat. Jennika made a disgusted noise, but she smiled slightly.

Rhys and Ridley walked away from their van, each man heading for one of the two black vans. The Trinity Masters portion of the MPF was only five people, and one of those was Franco, the Grand Master's advisor. Since the man had no combat experience, and was still recovering from a nearly fatal gunshot wound, Franco hadn't come to Italy with the rest of them. With Jennika on the comms with Sidika, that left just himself, Rhys, and Ridley to join the strike teams.

Jennika hopped into the van, taking a seat at the small desk bolted to the side wall.

Rodrigo Santiago and Vadisk Kushnir came over to join Owen. Rodrigo looked like he'd walked out of a Spanish perfume ad—hair that was long on top, an "anchor" mustache and beard, and a long, lean body.

From what Owen had pieced together about him, Rodrigo was a "security officer"—which seemed to be a formal title in the Masters' Admiralty—for the territory of Castile. On paper, he worked for a small and highly sought-after security company based in Madrid.

Vadisk was also a security officer, but from the territory of Hungary, which had to encompass the Ukraine, because

Vadisk had full sleeves of uniquely Ukrainian tattoos—linear geometric patterns that almost looked like embroidery or quilting in black and red, with the Ukrainian coat of arms front and center on his right forearm.

"Vadisk, Rodrigo." Owen shook each man's hand. "This is Jennika."

Jennika turned around and waved.

In his earpiece, Owen could hear Rhys and Ridley introducing themselves. The white-van team—Team P, for plumbers—was a three-man unit. They would be going over a wall on the east side of the compound, where some tree cover would hide their approach.

Team L—for locksmith, since they were riding in the van with that logo—were going to enter through the front. Rhys was in that van, which was being driven by Kristin Riddari from Kalmar. Claudette Chevalier from France was riding shotgun, and the hope was that seeing two women would keep the gate attendant from sounding the alarm. The fourth member of that team was Konrad Rycerz.

Claudette, Kristin, and Konrad's last names all translated to "knight" in their territory's primary language.

Sarah Ritter—another knight—Milo Moretti, Percival, and Ridley were in the Team I van, which would approach from the back, where the walled compound had an unmanned gate beside the area where they kept the dumpsters.

"Confirm that your teams are ready," Percival said.

"Confirmed," Owen said.

"Confirmed," echoed Kristin.

"Move out."

It was a twenty-minute drive to the headquarters of the Bellator Dei. They had a walled compound several hours outside Rome. The compound had, in a previous life, been a large farm. The main house had been turned into offices, a grain barn into a church, and the outbuildings and stables into classrooms and dormitories for the members who lived full-time on the compound.

The low walls around the estate had been topped with metal fencing and barbed wire, turning what would have been a beautiful old-world estate into an ugly, industrial place completely worthy of being called a compound.

Owen turned off onto a side road just as the compound came into sight. Five minutes later, he was parked behind a bush, and Rodrigo and Vadisk hopped out.

"I'm not picking up any kind of signal I can grab," Jennika said.

"Possibly it's the range," Sidika said through the comms.

"We're moving toward the wall," Owen announced.

"We'll move when you're in position," Percival responded.

Vadisk went first, as planned. He held a beanbag rifle in both hands, the butt near his shoulder, so in a moment's notice he could snap it up. Less lethal weapons were one of the concessions they'd made to the fact that there were a lot of innocent people on the compound, including children. As an FBI agent, Owen had no desire to be responsible for an Italian Waco situation.

Within ten minutes they had reached the wall. The stone fence had toppled in places, probably thanks to the roots of the massive oaks that pushed up from the ground.

Rodrigo took the lead, dropping to a knee and pulling out a few stones, widening an existing gap, and then snapping through the bottom of the chain-link fence until there was a gap wide enough for them to slide through, even with their bulky bulletproof vests and gear belts on.

"Ready to breech," Owen whispered, trusting the comms to pick it up.

"We're pulling up to the front gate," Kristin said.

"Ready at the back," Percival added.

Owen waited, breathing steadily to keep himself calm and alert. Adrenaline was a wonderful thing, but it could be distracting.

The minutes ticked past, and he reached a Zen-like state of waiting.

"No guard." Kristin's voice was tight with tension.

"What?" Owen snapped into the moment, alarm bells going off in his head.

"No guard at the front gate."

"Sidika, can you get into their security system?"

"There's nothing. It must be analog."

"All teams, go," Owen ordered. "Extreme caution."

Rodrigo slid through the gap in the wall, Vadisk's gun raised to fire through the chain link if anyone approached.

Owen did the same as Vadisk slid through the opening, then finally Owen went through.

They'd chosen this spot because it was hidden, thanks to both trees and a large shed just inside the wall.

Owen took point as they walked quickly along the back wall of the shed. He checked around the corner with a mirror, but there was no one in sight.

All the comms had gone quiet as the teams used hand signs to communicate, though there were occasional sounds —a heavy "snap" that was probably bolt cutters opening a lock, the squeak of a car gate being opened.

His team reached the front corner of the shed, where

they were still partially protected but could see the center of the compound. The rear entrance was at their four o'clock, the main entrance at nine. The position of the buildings matched what they knew from satellite and Luca's description.

There was a large flagstone-paved area that acted as a sort of central courtyard. The flagstones themselves looked oddly clean. The rest of the ground was dry, sunbaked dirt with an occasional patch of grass or weeds.

And there was not a soul anywhere.

"Do we have visuals on any targets?" Owen asked.

"Negative."

"Negative."

Fuck the fucking fucker. This was bad.

"The basement," Percival said. "He said that was where they'd retreat."

He, meaning Luca.

The locksmith van approached from the direction of the front gate, appearing from around the corner of a barn that had blocked their view. The sliding doors on both sides were open and the van was driving slowly enough that the people inside could jump out to take action.

Owen's attention went back to the flagstones.

"The church," Claudette said. "They might be in prayer."

"The I team will take the church," Percival said. "Team L, you're support."

"Understood," Kristin said. The locksmith van picked up speed.

Owen stared hard at the flagstones. "Stop."

The van jerked to a stop, the front wheels a foot away from the edge of the flagstones.

"Team L, back up. Team I, stay where you are." Owen turned to Vadisk. "Can you get on the roof?" Owen pointed to the shed.

Rodrigo raised an eyebrow, but when Vadisk nodded, he made a stirrup with his hands and boosted the Hungarian security officer up.

"I want you to shoot the stone courtyard. Three in from midpoint, the darker gray one. It's raised slightly."

"No," Percival countered. "A shot will warn them."

"It's too late for that," Owen said. "Either we're too late or…"

Vadisk shouldered the beanbag gun, sighted, and fired. The "pop" of the gun was audible for only a second before an explosion rocked the night.

"Fuck!" someone shouted.

"Booby-trapped," Owen snarled. "The fucking place is booby-trapped with land mines."

"Retreat," Percival snapped. "Retrace your exact steps."

Owen didn't take a deep breath until he was back in the van with a grim-looking Jennika.

"They knew we were coming," she said.

Owen nodded and reached for his phone. He needed to call the Grand Master.

Someone had told the Bellator Dei they were coming. It hadn't been him or anyone in Trinity Masters. Unless…No.

The Grand Master trusted him. Petro, the now dead Mastermind probably had people within the Masters' Admiralty still devoted to his cause. They could have warned the Bellator Dei about the upcoming raid.

He'd get with Percy—could he trust Percy?—and talk about the possibility of there being a traitor within the MPF ranks on the Masters' Admiralty side. But he already knew what Percy would say. The same thing that had first occurred to Owen.

A traitor within the Masters' Admiralty was possible, but it wasn't the most probable. The obvious suspect, the person with known loyalty to the Bellator Dei and knowledge of their operation, was Luca.

Luca Campisi had warned the Bellator Dei they were coming. They'd abandoned the headquarters and rigged the place with land mines and probably a few other nasty surprises.

The Trinity Masters' newest member was a traitor.

CHAPTER SIXTEEN

Selene stood by the window, dry-erase marker in hand, laughing at the list she'd compiled on the hotel window. Oscar and Luca were sprawled out on the couch, shirtless, barefoot, both wearing the sweatpants provided by the helicopter pilot, rather than bothering with real clothing.

The three of them had been sequestered in the hotel suite for three days, living on room service, wine, and sex—not necessarily in that order.

None of them had expected to be in Boston for so long, but the Grand Master wanted her counselor, Devon, present, along with Norah Douglas, a Trinity Masters' member and brilliant hacker and dark web specialist, when they released the bomb designs.

There was some groundwork to lay prior to releasing the plans to make sure there were eyes and ears on all the stores of neptunium so they could follow the trail and discover any lunatic assholes who thought building a city-killer bomb would be a good idea.

It was taking time to get everything in place, but Selene wasn't complaining. She was having the best time of her life and she wasn't anxious for the real world to intrude on that.

"Not happening." She drew a line through a couple Kama Sutra positions that involved her being upside down and supporting herself with her hands. The sex was too good, so there was a good chance she'd lose focus and crash to the floor if they tried those. Besides, she preferred kinky.

Oscar growled in disapproval, but didn't argue.

Selene tapped one finger against her lips. "So what should we attempt next?" she asked. "Fem Dom or some new role play?"

They'd begun an actual list of sexual positions and fantasies they all wanted to try when it became apparent they were going to be together for the foreseeable future. They'd taken "practicing ménages" to the next level.

Oscar chuckled and shook his head. He'd made fun of the list ever since Selene found the dry-erase marker and started writing things down on the hotel window. Mercifully they were on a top floor, so no one on the street far below could read what she was writing.

Of course, she noticed Oscar's teasing didn't stop him from adding his own suggestions. Hell, half the things on the list were his, including the just-nixed Kama Sutra positions. He'd added those after watching her do yoga yesterday morning and realizing she could hold herself in a handstand for an extended period of time. He'd immediately fired up his laptop and started researching positions for that particular talent.

Luca stood up under the pretense of studying the items still remaining. Not that she was fooled when he slipped his hands under her T-shirt so that he could cup her breasts.

Luca was definitely a tit man, while Oscar seemed to enjoy both packages equally, dividing his time between slapping asses—hers and Luca's—pinching her nipples, or cupping Luca's balls.

"I think we should—" Luca mused.

Before he could express his opinion, there was a knock at the door.

"People here to see you," Andre called through the door. "Y'all decent?"

Selene laughed. Andre and another Warrior Scholar, Tate, had been guarding their door in shifts over the course of the past two days. Which meant they'd gotten more than an earful of some of their activities.

Oscar rose and peered out the peephole. "There's a generic-looking white dude and a Latinx woman with Andre."

"Our dark web experts are here." Selene looked longingly at the list. Still, working with a CIA agent and a hacker to release flawed nuclear bomb plans was its own kind of exciting.

Oscar bent down to pick up the shirt he'd shed just before their last round of sex and tugged it over his head. Luca followed suit.

"I'm going to go put on some pants," Selene said, heading for the bedroom. "And a bra," she added begrudgingly. She hadn't worn a bra in three days and it had been glorious.

Yeah. Reality sucked.

She quickly dressed and listened as Oscar opened the door. When she returned to the living room, she was introduced to Norah. She had socialized with Devon Asher—of the New York Ashers—at past Trinity Masters events as both of them were legacies. Devon worked for the CIA, so Selene assumed it had been his job to coordinate monitoring of worldwide supplies of neptunium.

Devon was an attractive, rather imposing man with brown hair, cut in a stylish if boring side-part fashion, appropriate for a banker or lawyer. He also had shrewd steely-gray eyes that seemed to take in everything at once. Selene suspected there wasn't much the man didn't notice.

She flushed when she saw his gaze shift toward the list on the window. Dammit. Apparently he didn't miss anything.

"Keeping ourselves busy, I see," Devon deadpanned.

Luca tried to step between the window and Devon's line of vision in a feeble attempt to stop him from reading the entire list, while Oscar just crossed his arms and looked pissed off. Except there was a slight smile on his face, the barest curl to his lips that anyone who didn't know him as well as she did wouldn't have noticed.

Norah glanced toward the window, and Selene could tell by her raised eyebrows and the way her gaze slipped back to Selene, she was impressed.

Sebastian had called a couple days earlier to give them a status report. According to Sebastian, Norah was a dark web expert and had previously been a "hacktivist," but now freelanced for the FBI cybercrimes division.

"Let's do this, bitches." Norah had arrived with a sleek, expensive leather laptop case, which she set on the dining room table before taking a seat. She also had a bright red backpack with the cactus, eagle, and snake of the Mexican flag printed on it. The dichotomy was…weirdly compelling.

She pulled out a completely matte black laptop with no

logo on the lid. Oscar made a weird noise and rushed over to her side, examining the computer.

"Can I help you?" Norah asked in a "who the fuck are you?" voice.

"Is this custom?" Oscar demanded.

"Of course it is. Also, who the hell are you? Wait, I forgot, I don't care." She turned to her computer and began to tap on the keyboard rapidly.

Devon had followed her to the table. He put a hand on Oscar's shoulder and eased him back. He was standing directly behind Norah, who glanced over her shoulder and frowned.

"I can't stand it when people stand behind me. Sit down, dude." With her left foot, she pushed out the chair next to hers.

Devon hesitated for a moment, clearly unaccustomed to being ordered around. Then he sat.

Norah glanced at Oscar. "You're the data-mining expert?"

"Yes," Oscar all but snarled.

"And you've never seen a custom laptop?"

"I've never seen that casing." He pointed at her laptop, which, now that he mentioned it, had weirdly angular sides, almost as if it had been designed to look like an objet d'art.

"Yeah, okay, I hear you. I have friends at Falcon. They made it for me. I pretend it's just a gaming laptop if people get weird. What do you have?"

Oscar crossed his arms. "Two desktops I built, and my original custom Origin. I travel with a Maingear."

They stared at one another and seemed to reach some sort of computer nerd understanding.

Norah tilted her head toward the chair on her right, which Oscar claimed, his eyes glued to her screen.

Oscar had mentioned more than a few times that he'd heard of Norah, assuming she was who he thought she was. He'd explained that she was a pure hacker. She went after information that was purposefully hard to access. While Oscar did some of that, he focused on creating digital tools that could access and analyze data, both public and private, in order to answer questions, find patterns, and "mine" all available data for information.

Norah, he'd explained, was the kind of person who could dox misogynistic, racist, and homophobic assholes.

With Norah well-flanked, Selene and Luca exchanged a glance, then took the remaining two seats across the table. They couldn't see the computer screen, but Selene didn't mind. She sort of preferred to study the other faces at the table.

She had been unaware of her knee bouncing nervously underneath the table until Luca reached down and placed his hand on it, stilling the motion. She gave him a quick, apologetic smile. Her sudden case of the nerves wasn't based on what Norah, Devon, and Oscar were doing, but rather the end result of what loading those designs to the dark web meant.

Her time with Luca and Oscar was about to end. She was mere hours away from…a broken heart. A shattered heart.

Luca gave her leg a squeeze and murmured "it's fine," in a low voice meant just for her. While neither Norah nor Devon appeared to hear, Oscar's gaze shifted to the two of them, his brows furrowed with concern.

She gave him a quick wink, hoping to set his mind at

ease. It worked. Oscar's lips tipped up in what Luca had dubbed a grumpy smile. Only Oscar could pull off such a look, and just the sight of it sent a sharp, piercing pain through her heart.

Selene had been playing fast and loose ever since arriving in Boston, acting on her immediate attraction to Oscar, then Luca, inviting the latter to their bed. She'd assumed she could keep her physical desires for both men tucked safely in a box where emotions didn't come into play, simply because she'd always been able to do so with other lovers in the past.

She'd been a fool.

"Okay, I scrambled all the public networks around us, and the hotel Wi-Fi is down for everyone but us." Norah looked up. "We're cleared to talk."

Devon cleared his throat. "For the sake of clarity, and also to remind all of us of the gravity of this situation, I'll restate the purpose of this meeting." He looked at each of them in turn. "We are here to discuss the possibility of releasing a set of flawed, but still dangerous schematics for a backpack-sized nuclear bomb."

Devon let that statement hang for a moment before continuing. "Agencies around the world are already monitoring known supplies of neptunium, which is the heavy element used in this design; however, if we release the plans, there are no guarantees that someone won't attempt to create this weapon, and in the process, create something horrific."

"Nothing can happen until my sister is safe," Luca said. "I was promised—"

Devon held up a hand. "We are just discussing our options."

"But you already have people watching neptunium," Oscar countered. "Seems to me your mind is made up."

"The fact that Mr. Campisi used neptunium in his design is evidence enough that we should have been monitoring it already."

Norah looked up from the computer. "So what's your deal, dude with the sexy accent? You evil or what?"

Selene narrowed her eyes. *Hands off, bitch.*

"I am well aware that I am not a good man," Luca said slowly. "I am…"

"He grew up in a cult. They tortured him for being bi, forced him to learn how to make bombs, and are essentially holding his sister captive to keep him in line." Oscar didn't look away from the screen as he spoke. "How do you have access to all these sites on the dark web?" He pointed at her screen.

Luca made a choking sound, and Selene squeezed his hand.

"Damn, dude. I'm sorry." Norah shook her head. "That sucks. We got him out?" Norah looked at Devon.

"Yes, Luca is our newest member, and a task force has been sent to raid the headquarters of the cult. They will rescue his sister."

"Any word?" Selene asked, knowing that was what Luca had been waiting for.

"We'll let you know," Devon said.

Luca released a long, slow breath. Selene knew he wouldn't rest easy until Joli was no longer on the Bellator Dei compound.

"Back to this…" Oscar tapped his fingers on the table beside Norah's laptop. "How do you have this kind of access?"

"I used to be a merchant on Silk Road. And I'm a moderator on a lot of these sites."

Selene blinked. "Isn't Silk Road like eBay for drugs?"

"Yup."

"You…sold drugs on the dark web?"

"You got it," Norah said cheerfully. "But just the good stuff. High-quality weed, and prescription drugs that Big Pharma uses to extort people. Epi pens. Antibiotics. Nothing addictive." Norah glared at them. "None of you are dumb enough to think weed is addictive, are you?"

Selene shook her head. Luca just looked confused. Devon seemed slightly pained.

"You still operating?" Oscar asked with interest.

"Why? People who couldn't get insurance and needed me now can. Universal healthcare, baby. It's not perfect, but it's better. And pot is legal."

"Not in South Carolina," Oscar grumped.

"I'll hook you up, friend."

Norah and Oscar bumped fists.

"Did he just buy drugs?" Luca asked. "Can I… Can I try some drugs?"

"I'll put it on the list," Selene joked.

"It was one of those no-drug cults?" Norah shook her head. "That makes it all so much worse. At the very least, it could have been one of those new age shroom cults."

"Ah, no. No drugs. No alcohol. But we already tried that," Luca said, pointing to Oscar and Selene. "I liked the gin. And the bourbon."

Norah's attention had shifted to the list on the window. She smiled. "Get it, boy. Get it. I have a couple of suggestions if you're looking to expand your horiz—"

"Bomb. Dark web," Devon interjected.

"Right." Norah dragged her attention back to her computer. "Okay, so what are the bomb plans? I mean, are we talking about an image? Do we want to encrypt it?"

"I had it encrypted," Luca said.

"How hard was it to break?" Norah asked.

Oscar shrugged. "It took me a minute."

"Okay, so that works." Norah looked around. "One more time, the bomb doesn't work, right?"

"No, but it took a DARPA supercomputer to run the numbers and figure that out," Selene said. "The flaw is only evident in the math, and the calculations aren't part of the schematic."

"My question to you, Norah, is where within the dark web would it be released?" Devon asked.

"Depends on who you want to find it. And who do you want to have posted it? Dark web people are paranoid. They're not just going to think some asshole posted this out of the kindness of his or her heart."

Devon's phone rang. He glanced at it and frowned. "Excuse me." He rose from the table and walked over toward the door.

Norah looked back at the list on the window. "Okay, if you want to stay natural, I'm suggesting you try some MJ in a vape, then an edible, then maybe peyote."

"How the fuck is an edible the stepping stone to peyote?" Oscar demanded.

"You a peyote expert?" Norah asked. "Because I'm not, but I could be. I have a fucking spiritual connection to it. It's from the earth. It's natural."

"If he starts tripping balls and has flashbacks—"

Oscar's rant was interrupted by the sound of Devon

opening the door. He said something they couldn't hear to Andre, and then swung the door wide.

Owen Fraser walked in with a dark-haired, uber-handsome man who looked like he'd stepped off the pages of *GQ* and an equally dark-haired, medium-complexion woman with dramatic eyebrows and full lips that Selene would have needed filler to get. She was gorgeous even with her hair scraped back in a low bun and wearing a simple black shirt and jeans.

For a moment, Selene was struck by the arrival of the three gorgeous people.

Then she registered their expressions. Particularly Owen's.

Anger. Cold, hard anger.

And they were looking at Luca.

"Luca Campisi, stand up." Owen's voice was cold.

"What's going on?" Oscar was the first out of his chair, and he glanced from Owen to Devon, who stood off to the side, expression grim.

Then Oscar backed up, around the table to their side, and put himself squarely between everyone else and Luca.

Norah closed her laptop and scampered out of the way.

"Oscar, step aside," Devon said softly

"Fuck that."

"Luca Campisi," Owen began, "you are under arrest."

"What?" Selene jumped out of her chair and joined Oscar, another barrier between Luca and whatever was happening.

"Where's my sister?" Luca pushed between her and Oscar. She expected him to be confused or scared—she was both—but Luca was pissed. "Where is Joli?"

Oscar grabbed Luca, holding him back.

"You have the right to remain silent," Owen went on. "You have the right to—"

"What charges?" Selene asked. "Why are you arresting him, and what happened to the Bellator Dei?"

"I think the fucking Trinity Masters lied to him," Oscar said. "Tricked him."

Selene went cold. "No, they wouldn't."

"We did not," Devon said. "Oscar, Selene, I know you may have developed a relationship with this individual, but I need you to step away from him."

Luca jerked from Oscar's hold. "What did you do to them? They were innocent! Most of them, my sister—" His words tumbled to a stop, and Selene could feel the grief and anger pouring off of him.

The dark-haired man said something in Italian. Luca responded in the same language. Within thirty seconds, it turned into a loud argument, which she didn't need a translator to understand.

"Milo, English, please," Owen said.

"He continues to pretend he doesn't know."

"Pretend he doesn't know what?" Oscar demanded.

Devon stepped up, a calm, cool presence amid the anger and accusations. "There was no one at the Bellator Dei compound. We need to assess the possibility that perhaps Luca warned them we were coming."

"What?" Selene demanded.

"No, he didn't, you dumb fucks," Oscar countered.

"My sister wasn't there?" Luca staggered as if he was going to collapse. Oscar yanked him back, held him up. "Where? Where is she? Is she still alive?"

The dark-haired woman's eyebrows rose. She looked at Owen, whose expression had gone blank.

"The compound was abandoned," Milo said through gritted teeth. "It was rigged with explosives. The whole thing was a trap to kill as many of us as possible."

"Booby-trapped?" Selene asked in shock. She shook her head. She may not have known Luca for long, but no part of her doubted his honesty. "No. Just no."

"Land mines," the woman said in a lovely accent. "If Owen hadn't spotted the disturbed stones, we would have driven over one."

"I didn't," Luca said softly. "I didn't tell them, but if they knew…do they know I betrayed them?" Luca began to curse quietly in Italian. Selene put her hand on his arm. He was shaking.

Milo took a half step forward, his attention on Luca.

"What's he saying?" Owen asked.

"He's scared his sister is being…tortured. Because they know what he's done."

Oscar turned Luca around, hugging him and letting Luca bury his face against his shoulder.

"I'm going to use small words, you stupid fucks," Oscar snarled. "He didn't contact them. I've been with him the whole time. Yes, even at night. We fucked like rabbits and ate room service. He didn't contact them, which means something *you* did spooked them. And maybe got his sister…"

Luca shuddered.

Killed.

The unspoken word hovered in the air. Owen and Devon were looking at each other. Milo appeared uncertain, and the woman who'd come in with Owen and Milo walked over to Oscar's computer, which was on the coffee table.

"I'll verify that he hasn't communicated with anyone."

"Touch my computer, I'll deck you," Oscar said.

The woman held out one finger, then very deliberately poked the black laptop.

"Hold him." Oscar thrust Luca at Selene.

"Sidika, don't provoke him," Milo said softly.

"You okay?" Selene asked Luca.

"How long have they had her?" Luca's eyes were wild. "How long has my sister been tortured while I was here…"

Oscar yanked his computer away from Sidika and hauled it over to the table. He thrust it at Norah. "Here, I'll let *you* touch it, but not *her*."

Norah shrugged, took Oscar's laptop, and sat down. Sidika pulled up a chair beside her.

Thirty minutes later, Norah and Sidika both confirmed that Oscar's laptop, Selene's laptop, and their phones hadn't been used to write any emails—in draft form, by SMS or internet-based messaging system, by any PHP or other code-writing program—which might have allowed Luca to leave a text message hidden within the code of a website or program—or several other things Selene didn't understand, which was rare for her.

Luca had sat still as a stone throughout their search at the dining room table, his elbows on his knees, his head in his hands. Selene had never seen a person so wracked with guilt and despair. All her attempts to comfort him were met with silence.

"Satisfied?" Oscar demanded.

"And they never left the suite?" Devon turned to Andre.

"No, sir."

"No calls from the hotel landline?"

"We monitor those. Any calls and we would have known right away," Devon said.

"I didn't contact them. I..." Luca's bowed head rose, and anger made his features sharp, more angular somehow. "I joined you...I trusted you to keep her safe. And now she's, she's..."

MILO SNARLED SOMETHING. Owen yanked his phone from his pocket, and Devon surveyed the room.

"If you didn't contact them..." Owen's thumbs were flying over the screen. "Then we need to know who did. It might mean there's a traitor in the Masters' Admiralty side of the MPF."

"And," Selene said, "we need to know where they went."

"New plan," Owen said. "This is no longer a raid. It's a rescue mission." He looked up. "Everyone have their passports?"

"Why?" Oscar demanded.

"We're going back to Italy. All of us."

CHAPTER SEVENTEEN

Luca didn't pray—they'd beaten any belief in a higher power out of him long ago—but on the seemingly endless trip from Boston to Rome, he hoped that his sister wasn't in too much pain.

The compound had been abandoned and booby-trapped. Somehow, they had discovered his betrayal, which meant Joli was no longer safe. The Bellator Dei wouldn't hesitate to punish his sister for his crimes. He'd learned that lesson the hard way when his love affair with Roberto had been revealed. Signore and Signora Campisi had been quick to threaten Joli's future in order to force his obedience and compliance. God only knew what they'd do to her now.

Selene and Oscar had both tried to assure him she was probably fine, but their words had felt hollow, offering no reassurance or comfort. Eventually, they fell silent and left him to his thoughts.

They landed at a small airport outside of Rome. Luca practically flew down the steps from the large private jet. A man and a woman, both wearing polo shirts with an emblem he recognized—that of *Cohortes Praetorianae*—were waiting near two black SUVs.

Milo, who had been Luca's point of contact when he'd worked for *Cohortes Praetorianae* for years, walked over to them.

Luca wasn't aware that he'd stopped dead until Oscar bumped into him from behind.

"Luca?" Selene was at his side, and she laid a hand on his arm.

He stared at Milo. Could it be that simple?

"What did you just figure out?" Selene was peering at his face.

"I…" Luca squashed the hope blossoming inside him. Hope was dangerous. "I need Owen."

"Owen," Oscar called out.

The FBI agent turned around, examined their little tableau, and walked over, his steps quick. "What's going on?"

"Who…who helped you enter the compound? Them?" Luca jerked his chin toward Milo and the two other *Cohortes Praetorianae* staff.

Owen shook his head. "No. The MPF, but *Cohortes Praetorianae* staff assisted with logistics—airport pickups, physical recon to ensure that our planned approaches matched what we could see with satellite surveillance."

Luca exhaled and relief made him weak. He leaned back against Oscar, who stiffened to help support his body weight. "I know how they knew. And it wasn't me." Luca briefly closed his eyes.

"How?" Owen snapped. "Wait. Milo, come here."

Something in Owen's tone made Milo whip around and then jog, not walk, toward them. "What's wrong with him?"

Milo asked.

Luca stood up so he wasn't leaning against Oscar. "I think I know how they were alerted."

Milo shifted his body weight ever so slightly, but in that micromovement, it was clear he was ready to fight if needed.

"The Bellator Dei know that *Cohortes Praetorianae* is a part of the Masters' Admiralty."

Milo bristled. "What do you mean?"

"The benefactor told them, the leaders. It was why I was allowed to move off the compound and get a job—so that I could find a way to make you my client." Luca gestured at Milo. "They monitor your company." He didn't admit that the "they" in that sentence was actually his sister. "If they learned you were suspicious of them, sending people to do surveillance…"

"Fucking Petro told them about us," Milo snarled. "Why didn't you tell us this before? Why didn't you tell us everything they knew about us?"

Luca heard the unspoken accusation that went along with the two voiced questions. *What else are you hiding?*

"You didn't ask," Luca said simply. "I answered all your questions in Boston, but it wasn't until now, until I saw *them*," he gestured to the people by the vehicles, "that I remembered."

"The devil is always in the details," Owen breathed. "Okay. Clearly you need to do a debrief with Milo since you two have a history. That's on me and Percival, we should have looped Milo in since we did talk about you having contact with him."

Such a simple thing, and if Luca hadn't been so

emotionally distraught back in Boston, he might have thought to mention it.

"What changes?" Owen asked, then answered his own question. "Nothing. We still go in as planned. If they're still monitoring *Cohortes Praetorianae*—"

"How?" Milo demanded, this time in Italian. "They have a spy?"

"How could they have a spy?" Luca countered. "You're all members."

"Actually, that's not accurate. A few of us…people who have certain security positions within the Masters' Admiralty, are, but most of the people, and all of the support staff, don't know about the society."

"Oh." It was humbling every time he realized exactly how much he didn't know about the Masters' Admiralty. "Apps," he told Milo. "Game apps, with built-in spyware. Enough targeted ads, and they can get almost anyone to download an app, even if it's just to try it once." Joli had told him that.

Milo blasphemed—creatively—and turned away, his own phone in his hand.

"English, please," Selene said.

"I'll tell you in the car," Luca assured his lover.

His lover.

Luca still struggled to believe the past week had been real. The days and nights spent in Oscar's and Selene's arms felt like a dream.

One he was about to wake up from. They weren't his, and once all of this was over—if he survived—the Grand Master would place him in a trinity with strangers. Strangers he feared he could never love. He'd already given his heart away to these two incredible people standing next to him.

"Everybody in the car. I'll let the rest of the MPF team know en route." Owen's attention shifted to Oscar. "We have some backup coming too. He had to catch a commercial flight from Texas, but he's only a couple hours behind us. It gives us time to stop by your lab, Luca. I assume you'll need equipment to help dismantle the explosives. We'll wait to breach until we have the last member of the team."

"Who?" Luca asked.

"Texas?" Selene said at the same time.

Oscar sighed. "Fuck. They're talking about my brother. Langston's coming to help defuse some bombs."

Luca froze. "Is he coming…alone?"

Owen nodded. "Yes. His spouses wanted to come, but there was no reason for them to make the trip."

Luca breathed a small sigh of relief. That meant he didn't have to face Mina Edwards yet. The woman he'd forced to wear a bomb. A bomb that he would never have detonated.

But even if he told her that, did it excuse what he'd done?

No.

He'd emotionally tortured her, and the memory of the fear in her eyes that day had haunted him ever since.

Being with Oscar and Selene these last few days, he'd managed to push away the things that hurt him to remember. Now, faced with seeing Langston, the past was catching up to him. And the reality was, he'd done evil things.

For good reasons, but still, truly evil things.

Suddenly he was glad for the reminder, the reality check. Because when this was over, once his sister was safe, he would walk away from Oscar and Selene, knowing it was the right thing to do. They deserved better than to be tainted by his presence.

"Load up," Owen said again. "It's time to go."

Luca went first, and instead of sliding into one of the rear seats, he took the front passenger seat. That way Selene and Oscar couldn't sit next to him.

It was time for him to start distancing himself from his lovers.

LUCA STOOD at the front gate, flanked by Owen and Rodrigo, the controls for one of his robots in hand. He also had at his disposal the rest of the things he had grabbed from his lab, including some smaller blast walls, a bomb suit —which he hadn't bothered with, and a small bomb box that had fit in the back of one of the SUVs.

He was the bomb expert with the front gate team. The rest of the MPF people were stationed around the edges of the compound as combination lookouts and guards, posing as a road crew and diverting traffic, or in one of the vans working the communications system, or watching a live satellite feed of the area. The fact that someone in the MPF had enough pull to re-task a satellite was both alarming and impressive. And strangely...it instilled in Luca a small sense of pride.

After all, he was now a member of the same society as the satellite re-tasker. Within the Bellator Dei, he'd been treated as a subordinate, a pawn to be used, someone without a voice, without a choice, in his actions.

Today, however, while in the company of some of the most brilliant minds he had ever met, he'd been treated as an equal, and even deferred to as they made decisions regarding this mission.

It had given him emotional whiplash from first being the main suspect to then being a part of the discussion about who the potential traitor within the Masters' Admiralty side of the MPF might be. Background checks had already been run, so unfortunately there was no clear suspect, but he'd carefully looked at the dossiers Owen and Devon had given him, looking for anything that might indicate a Bellator Dei connection.

There hadn't been anything, but those hours of working with them had made him really feel like a member of the Trinity Masters. He was here because he wanted to be, because it was the right thing to do. The Bellator Dei needed to be stopped.

There was a second bomb disposal team at the back gate. Langston was with them, but Luca had yet to see the other man. Oscar also hadn't seen his brother. He and Selene were in a van with Sidika, the woman who'd come to Boston with Owen and Milo, and they were helping watch the various camera feeds that had been set up to monitor the areas around the compound for any incoming problems via satellite images.

"We're ready." The speaker was Jennika Davis, an American NSA agent—and a very likely candidate for the person who had enough power to re-task a satellite.

She motioned him over to a second van that was pulled up near the gate. Luca hopped inside and put on the headset when she passed it to him.

"This is the live satellite feed." She pointed to one of several monitors. "It's cropped so you're only seeing the compound. Here, here, and here are the feeds from our snipers."

Three people—Sarah, Vadisk, and Claudette—had managed to make it onto the roofs of buildings closest to the wall, Vadisk by retracing his exact steps from the first raid, and Sarah and Claudette by jumping from the tops of the chain-link fences onto the roofs. He'd watched their jumps via video feed from their body cams, and it had been both impressive and horrifying.

"Hit this button to talk to them." Jennika pointed at a small panel with a dozen identical silver switches. A piece of tape was stuck to one of them. "Flip it down to come back on the main comms line." She pointed at his headset.

Luca nodded, then scooted his small stool back and unfolded a printed image of the compound on his lap. He'd drawn over the top of it, outlining the main building in thick black lines. Owen had helped him number them, then taken a picture of his map and sent it to everyone. They would use his map to guide the whole operation. It seemed insane that they were putting their faith in him, considering Owen had tried to arrest him for lying to a federal officer twelve hours earlier.

Luca looked at the image then closed his eyes, thinking back to what he'd been taught about land mines. Undoubtedly the curriculum had been changed and updated since his time in "school."

But what hadn't changed was the layout of the buildings, or the way they thought. Bombs were blunt instruments, land mines especially so.

He opened his eyes and looked at the map, studying the location of the first land mine, which they'd found only because Owen had noticed the recent disturbance of the flagstone.

Luca flipped the switch so he could speak to the three people on the rooftops. He took a breath and started giving directions.

"At the steps of building two, is there a cross?"

After a second there came a reply. "No." The voice was female, with a Nordic accent.

There had been a cross there. If they moved it, it was because they didn't want to risk it being damaged.

"There," Luca told them.

"I have it," a second female voice said with a French accent. "The base of the steps." A second later, there was the cracking sound of a rifle being fired.

Followed shortly by the loud boom of a land mine detonating.

On the satellite feed, a puff of dirt appeared, the delay only a matter of seconds.

Owen leaned in. "Nice one, Luca."

Luca nodded, looked down at the map, and gave the next direction.

It took over an hour and forty beanbag rounds to explode nine land mines. With each one that went off, the mood of those around him grew a bit grimmer. Nine land mines.

There would be more. Other traps, other ways the Bellator Dei leadership would try to keep the cult's secrets.

Jennika tapped her own headset then pointed to the switch. Luca flipped it, tuning into the comm link that everyone else was on.

"Woohoo! That last one was a good one," Oscar said enthusiastically.

Luca blinked. That was Oscar's voice, but it didn't *sound* like Oscar.

"It's not a fucking fireworks show," Oscar grumped.

Wait, *that* was Oscar, which meant the first voice had been Langston.

Luca's stomach knotted, but he didn't have long to dwell on his guilt over what he'd done to Langston, Mina, and Rich.

"Clear the channel," Owen commanded.

"Aye, aye, Mr. FBI," Langston said.

"We have clear pathways," Owen continued. "But there are no guarantees. Breaching is a risk, clearing the buildings is a risk. There's no shame in backing out."

Through the open door of the van, Luca saw Owen looking around at the handful of people who had started to gear up—strapping on vests, checking tool belts, and putting on helmets. None of them looked up or acknowledged what Owen had said.

"This is your chance to take a step back, and there is no shame or cowardice in it," Percival added.

"Out teams?" Owen asked.

"Ready."

"Ready."

"Last call."

Luca could see Owen putting on his vest while his voice came over the comm link.

"We're all going in, boss."

"Let's find these people, rescue the ones we can."

Luca didn't know who any of the voices belonged to. They were strangers to him, but they were willing to risk their lives to go in and search for any information they could find about the Bellator Dei. They had just spent an hour listening to land mines being detonated, and they were still willing to go in. The cynical part of him said it was because they wanted to put an end to the Bellator Dei. They were, after all, enemies of the Masters' Admiralty, and, by extension, the Trinity Masters.

But part of him, perhaps the part of him that had taken a leap of faith and joined the Trinity Masters, believed that the members here today wanted not just to stop the Bellator Dei, but to save those people, like his sister, like his younger self, who were trapped. Victims. Even if they didn't realize it.

Luca passed Jennika his headset and stepped out of the van. Oscar and Selene were waiting for him. Neither one of them had on protective gear, and Oscar looked pissed, especially when Owen passed Luca a helmet and vest.

"They won't let us go in with you," Selene said quietly.

"Good. I don't want to risk you." He looked at them. "Either of you."

"Be safe." Oscar's voice was gruff as he helped fasten the Velcro of the vest.

"Is your robot ready?" Selene asked.

Luca picked up the remote he had put down in order to guide the land mine clearing effort. He clicked a button and then used the joystick to guide the robot forward, toward the open front gate.

Selene put his helmet on, and once more he could hear chatter on the comms. "We'll be here. Come back to us." Selene blinked, as if she'd surprised herself. Oscar was frowning at her, but it was a frown of concern.

Luca allowed himself one moment—one brief, quick, beautiful moment—to pretend he *was* coming back to them. Then he shut those feelings down hard. He needed to concentrate on the job at hand, do what needed to be done in that compound to save innocent lives.

And when it was over…all of this was over. He wouldn't be coming back to them. He couldn't.

"We're taking building two," Owen said. "We're going on a separate channel, and if needed, Jennika can patch us through to the other team. As you suggested, Luca, they're taking building four, the, uh, school facility."

Luca was going to the main building that housed not only the dormitory, but the Prelate and clergy offices as well. He was hoping there would be records there, something that would give them a clue where they'd gone.

Where his sister was.

Those buildings were also the most likely to be rigged with some kind of explosive.

Owen looked at Luca. "Ready?"

He nodded, the helmet heavy on his head, and guided the robot forward. He walked behind it, fifteen feet of space between him and the small machine. Once they were through the doors, Luca could see the back gate, at the far side of the compound. Though the view was somewhat obscured by a few buildings, he could see the open rear gates and a team of people following their own robot, which looked considerably nicer than Luca's.

For a moment, the man walking behind the other robot paused, staring across the courtyard at Luca. His face was in shadow, hidden beneath the helmet, but the breadth of his shoulders, his height, was achingly familiar. Even with the distance between them, Luca could feel Langston's animosity.

All the more reason he needed to distance himself from Selene and Oscar. He didn't want Oscar put in the middle.

While Oscar understood and accepted the reasons for Luca's actions, the same wasn't true for Langston. Nor should it be. Luca had deeply hurt someone Langston loved. Luca would want to commit murder if anyone ever hurt Selene or Joli in such a way. There was a reckoning coming for Luca and Langston, and he didn't want Oscar forced to watch or take sides.

It took a painstaking forty minutes to get to the building, mostly due to the slow speed of the robot. Having the robot go first meant that it would trigger any remaining land mines, but for safety, he also chose a path that went over the craters *left* by the land mines, which slowed them even further.

They reached the steps of the dormitories. He looked up at it, shocked that it was just…just a building. Somehow knowing that it was empty, that the Bellator Dei leadership, the men who had controlled his life and shaped him into something he had never wanted to be, weren't there, took away the power of this place. He no longer feared it. Now it was just a building.

A potentially dangerous building.

Luca navigated the robot up the steps, but now that they were so close, the painfully slow pace was aggravating. He hurried forward, ignoring Owen's shout, and lifted the robot up the steps. As he set it down, he glanced at the doors and froze.

There was a red wire peeking out from above the stone lintel around the door.

He'd known there was going to be something, but seeing it, being so close to a bomb built by someone he knew, someone who had been trained by the same people who'd trained *him*, was jarring.

"Opening the door will trigger a bomb," Luca said very carefully. He eased back and gently nudged the joystick to send the robot forward.

Behind him, Owen was talking, his voice buzzing in Luca's ear as he asked to be patched in to the other team to let them know that the door here was rigged. Luca was focused on what was in front of him. There was a small screen on the control, which gave him a grainy feed from the camera on the robot.

Defusing bombs wasn't what he'd been taught here. It was a skill he'd had to learn on his own—with the Bellator Dei's support—in order to get his job with *Cohortes Praetorianae*. A job he'd walked away from in a desperate attempt to retrieve his tablet, something he had yet to think about or really deal with. He was out of work, homeless, and facing certain heartbreak.

Luca shook his head as if he could physically drive the dark feelings out.

Too many thoughts ran through the back of his mind as he methodically worked the robot. He found where the red wire disappeared though a small hole beside the doorway that they must have drilled just for that purpose.

Learning to defuse the bombs, even if it had been done to serve the Bellator Dei's needs, had been a small rebellion.

He shifted the robot and got a better look. It wasn't just wire. It was thicker than he'd first thought. Detonating cord? But why would they have that around the door? Det cord was used as a transmission medium in commercial explosions—construction. But it was also an explosive in its own right.

Deep down, he'd clung to the hope that maybe he'd be able to secretly disarm the bombs made by the Bellator Dei.

Between that and the flaws he always built into his own bombs, he'd been trying to minimize the damage he'd done.

To change what he was.

There was nothing else he could do from out here. Time to open the door.

He held his breath, ignoring the chatter of people talking though the comms as he slowly opened the door with the robot arm. It was unlocked. Given the blasting cord, the unlocked door was by design.

And suddenly, Luca knew what was waiting for them.

Even as he piloted the robot forward, he backed up, walking blindly as he kept his eyes on the screen.

Hands grabbed him, guiding him back, and then there were people around him…protecting him.

"There's going to be a fire bomb inside," Luca murmured. He didn't realize he was speaking in Italian until he heard someone repeating what he'd said in English. Since there was someone to translate, he didn't bother wasting the brain power and kept speaking in Italian.

"You see it?" Owen asked.

"No, but I know…it's something they taught us." He divorced himself emotionally from what he was saying. The world had narrowed, focused to just him and the small, blurry screen. He found the pressure plate, hidden under the corner of an industrial-style rug, a mat put down to keep the floors from becoming wet or muddy when it rained.

It took him several tense minutes, but he carefully disconnected the det cord from the pressure plate.

"You step on the pressure plate and the det cord

explodes. The door collapses. You're trapped inside. Then…"

He flipped the rug aside and followed four thinner ignition wires. It took some maneuvering before he found where they went up the walls, where they were connected to long black boxes mounted where wall met ceiling. They looked like they could have been some odd heating or cooling element, the wires added to an older building, *on* the walls rather than in them.

"Then the fire bombs ignite. They're filled with gas that drops even as it ignites. You're trapped inside a burning building."

Luca pulled the robot back and, one by one, cut the wires.

"It wasn't enough for you to die. They wanted you to burn." Luca looked up, blinking to focus his eyes. Around him, people were looking back with expressions ranging from grim to horrified. "To suffer as you died. To burn in hell for your sins."

CHAPTER EIGHTEEN

Oscar sat on the floor of the van, his feet on the ground outside the open door. Jennika, the woman from NSA, had outfitted both him and Selene with earpieces so that they could hear what was happening on the compound after Oscar had apparently hit the limit on times he could ask her "what the fuck is going on now?"

After that, he'd begun pacing outside the van, listening with his heart in his throat as Luca and Langston drove their robots through the compound to the buildings. He'd spent every single second holding his breath, waiting for an explosion, fearing one misstep that might steal his brother or his lover from him forever.

He'd never liked Langston's chosen career path, though he'd never said as much to his brother. He, Langston, and Walt were all too much alike, marching to the beat of their own drums. So Oscar understood that, like it or not, he had no choice but to accept that Langston was going to spend his life working with bombs. Reckless fucker.

And because fate was a heartless bitch, she decided to have even more fun at Oscar's expense, ensuring he fell in love with a man who did the exact same goddamn thing.

Oscar's legs had finally given out when he heard Luca describe how the Bellator Dei had intended to kill them all with fire.

He'd sunk down in the open door of the van, sitting with his elbows on his knees, staring at the ground.

Selene had been silent and intent throughout the entire operation, standing as he paced, and now sitting next to him. Though she hadn't said a word, he felt bolstered by her presence, drawing strength from her closeness.

He wasn't sure how she knew he didn't want to talk. Their time together had been ridiculously short, yet he felt like this amazing woman knew him better than people he'd known his entire life. She definitely understood him better than Faith.

Faith.

Up until a month ago, he couldn't think of her name without a piercing pain stabbing at his heart. Now…now it was as if the blinders had been lifted and he was suddenly seeing things he'd never noticed before.

Faith couldn't stand the times when he went quiet as he dealt with anxiety or stress. He wasn't the type of guy who talked out his emotions. Talking about shit like that just made him more anxious and pissed him off. He'd always preferred to deal with the bad stuff on his own, in his own head, working through it until it went away.

Faith never got that, always accusing him of shutting her out, of being a moody bastard, emotionally distant. He could never make her understand that his feelings had nothing to do with her—or with them as a couple—and that he just needed some time and space to work it out.

Somehow, Selene got that. She could see that he was barely holding his shit together. Rather than push him to talk about it, she was simply remaining close. Letting him know she was here if he needed her. Otherwise, she was letting him deal with it in his own way.

The minutes crept by slowly as Oscar listened to Luca and Langston and their teams make their way through the buildings. He could tell from the frustrated tones no one was finding anything of use.

Finally, a decade and a half later, Oscar heard Owen tell Luca and Langston to lead them out, the bots going first, even though they'd retrace their steps.

Oscar didn't move, didn't even bother to breathe. He wasn't going to feel easy again until both Langston and Luca were off that fucking compound and in his line of sight. They were in the van at the front gate, so they saw Luca first, though Oscar heard Langston's voice through the comm, reporting his team was heading for the back rear entrance. The plan, based on the chatter, was for everyone to reconvene at the front where he and Selene were.

Oscar saw the robot, and then Luca. Rather than lead the party out, Luca stood off to the side, robot controller in hand as he watched the rest of his team steadily walk out. Only when the last person—Owen—had cleared the gate did Luca himself actually leave the compound.

When he took off his helmet, he looked completely wiped out, despondent. In addition to facing down death for the past hour, they were still no closer to finding his sister.

Owen placed a hand on Luca's shoulder, halting him

just outside the gate. Oscar couldn't hear what the man was saying, but he could read body language well enough to know Owen was offering reassurance.

Luca nodded, but the heaviness in his face didn't lift. Oscar suspected Luca wasn't going to find peace until he had his sister back.

Considering the unbearable stress he'd suffered this past hour, Oscar could relate.

Owen walked on, while Luca put the robot controller and helmet down so that he could pull off his heavy vest.

Selene found her sea legs first, rushing over to Luca, pulling him to her in a shaky embrace that proved Oscar hadn't been the only person terrified out of their wits at the van. He'd been so wrapped up in his own fears, he'd failed to see how scared Selene had been too.

Oscar rose and followed, taking a moment to hug Luca as well. After a few moments of silent reassurance, Oscar pulled back a bit to look at Luca. "Did you find anything?"

"Files, papers." Luca sighed. "They're going to look through it, but everything important was gone." He looked up. "There was a box of old laptops. Would you…"

"Of course. Whatever you need," Oscar assured him.

"We'll find her," Selene assured him.

Caught up in the moment, Oscar ignored the sound of a vehicle pulling up and stopping somewhere behind him. He needed to touch them again, so he wrapped Selene and Luca up in a bear hug, gripping them tightly.

They returned the embrace, the three of them locked together. If Oscar could freeze time right here, he would. They were all together, safe, alive.

"What. The. Fuck?"

And just like that, fate stepped in to kick Oscar in the teeth.

He released Luca and Selene, turning so that they were both tucked safely behind him.

God only knew what Langston was going to do. Of the three of them, Langston was the most cheerful and easygoing, but the flip side of that coin was his fucking explosive temper. And right now, Langston was pissed. Whatever his brother was about to do, Oscar didn't question for a moment it would involve violence. His brother was gunning for Luca, but he wouldn't hesitate to take Oscar down as well if he stood in the way.

"Langston," Oscar said, holding his hands up in front of himself. The position was one where he could either hold Langston back or return a punch if his brother wasn't in the mood to talk first.

They were evenly matched when it came to fighting, which meant, while there wouldn't be a winner, they'd both be bloody and beat to hell at the end.

Langston was a smart guy, observant, so it didn't take him more than three beats to put one plus one plus one together and come up with the right answer.

"Are you fucking kidding me?!" Langston yelled, his attention focused solely on Oscar.

He was glad. As long as his brother was looking at him, tossing his anger in his direction, Luca was safe.

"I just need a minute to explain."

Langston shook his head. "Not gonna be anything you can say that'll explain this."

Oscar hoped that wasn't true, but when Langston was this pissed off, his ability to listen and reason vanished completely.

"Goddammit, Langston. Calm the fuck down and let me—"

That was all Oscar managed to say before Luca threw a monkey wrench in the works, stepping to the side and around Oscar, putting himself directly in the line of fire.

Langston and Oscar moved at the exact same time.

Oscar shoved Luca out of the way and met his brother in the middle. Langston had been mid-swing, but he didn't bother to pull back when his original target was no longer there.

Oscar was ready.

He reared backwards, Langston's fist glancing off his jaw. If it had connected, he probably would have broken Oscar's nose.

Though he'd managed to avoid most of the force, his ears were ringing from the hard blow. Oscar pulled his arm back, looking for revenge, when strong arms circled him from behind.

Oscar fought against the restraining grip, but Luca wasn't letting go.

Owen had appeared from somewhere and now had Langston in a similar grip.

"What the fuck is going on?" Owen yelled, struggling to maintain his hold as Langston fought like the devil to get back to...fuck...Oscar didn't know who Langston was gunning for at the moment. Didn't look like he cared who he got to first, either. His brother was out for blood.

"Let. Go," Langston said through gritted teeth when it became obvious he wasn't going to be able to break free of Owen's grip. Oscar had stopped fighting, but Luca still held him tightly, apparently not trusting his sudden stillness.

"No," Owen said.

"This doesn't have anything to do with you," Langston said. "This is between me, my brother, and that fucking psychopath."

"He's not a psychopath," Selene said. Oscar growled when she put herself between him and Langston.

He was going to have a little word with his lovers once all this was over, make sure they understood they never stepped between the Hayden men when tempers were high.

"Get behind me, Selene," Oscar said darkly.

She glanced at him over her shoulder and—fuck—rolled her eyes. Then she turned her attention back to Langston. "Your brother asked for a minute to explain."

"And I told him—" Langston started, his voice raised.

Selene cut him off with a wave of her hand. "Langston. Stop now. You don't have the whole story."

Langston stopped trying to break free of Owen's grip, his breathing heavy from his exertions. His face was flushed and his eyes still flashed murder, but at least he didn't resemble a runaway train barreling toward the station anymore.

Owen slowly released him, though Oscar knew the man was on the offensive, ready to reclaim his hold if Langston made even the slightest move.

"Somebody going to explain what's going on to me?" Owen asked.

"It's a family matter," Selene said simply.

Owen nodded slowly, his gaze traveling from Langston to Luca. "I'm guessing this is the first time you two have seen each other since Boston."

Owen Fraser was thorough. While he hadn't been involved in the operation to save Mina, who'd been kidnapped by Luca, it was clear he knew the story, knew what Luca had done to Langston's wife.

"If you know about Boston," Langston said, "then you understand why I'm angry."

Owen didn't respond. Instead, he turned his attention to Selene. "You got this, Dr. Tanaka?"

Selene nodded. "I do."

"Then I'll leave you to it. But just in case," Owen pointed at Langston, Luca, and Oscar in turn, "I'm reloading the beanbag rifles and I won't hesitate to shoot." With that, the FBI man turned and walked away from them.

Langston took a step toward Luca, but Selene and Oscar moved together, placing themselves in front of him.

Langston shook his head, his anger giving away to something worse. He looked genuinely hurt by what he viewed as their betrayal. "You too, Selene? You were both there…you know what he did to her."

Once again, Luca tried to step around them. Oscar stopped him, but he knew Luca wasn't the type of man who could hide behind another, let someone else fight his battles. Oscar stepped to the side so that Luca could stand between him and Selene.

"Langston—" Luca began, his face etched with guilt.

"She still has nightmares," Langston said. "Wakes up in a cold sweat in the dead of night, trembling. You strapped a *bomb* to her."

Luca nodded miserably. "I never would have detonated the bomb. I swear to you, I—"

"Fuck that!" Langston yelled. "And fuck you!"

The last he hadn't directed just at Luca. Langston's gaze

traveled to Oscar as well. "Mina's family now, Oscar. I don't...I can't..."

Oscar couldn't stand to see his brother's pain. Or Luca's. "He did it for his sister," he blurted out.

"What?" Langston asked, confused.

Oscar continued. "The Bellator Dei has his sister. They'll hurt her if he doesn't deliver the plans for that bomb. He had to get the tablet back. He had no choice."

Luca took a step closer to Langston, and Oscar got the sense he was inviting Langston to throw another punch. Not that it would be a true fight. Luca would never hit back. He would stand and take the beating, thinking it was his due. "That still doesn't excuse what I—" Luca started, but he stopped talking when Selene placed her hand on his arm and drew him back.

"Luca," she said softly. "Don't."

"His...sister?" Langston shook his head, though Oscar wasn't sure if it was because he didn't believe them or because he was struggling to maintain his anger. There was nothing—absolutely *nothing*—he, Langston, and Walt wouldn't do for their sister, Sylvia.

"Her name is Joli," Selene said. "And she's in danger. Luca did what he did to save her."

Langston ran a frustrated hand through his hair, cursing steadily under his breath. "Goddamn, motherfucking, son of a bitch." Finally, he looked back at Oscar. "I gotta hit something."

"I see you and your brother share the," Selene air-quoted her next words, "smash-stuff gene."

Langston studied her face for a moment, then finally, the tension broke and his brother grinned...or maybe grimaced. Either way, he didn't appear as angry as he'd been a few minutes earlier.

Luca, however, couldn't let it go. "You should hit *me*. I…want you to hit me. I deserve it."

Langston appeared to consider the invitation, his fists clenching by his side.

Oscar shook his head. "No. If you've gotta throw a punch, I volunteer as tribute."

Langston snorted and said, "Jesus," at the same time Luca asked, "Tribute?"

Selene smiled, amused by his literary allusion, and shook her head. "*Hunger Games*? Seriously?"

"We lost a bet to our sister, Sylvia, a couple summers ago. She made us watch all four of those damn movies with her. An all-day marathon," Langston explained, and the memory of spending the day with Sylvia, devouring platter after platter of what their sister referred to as "fun food" like wings, cheesy tater tots, pepperoni rolls—wiped away the last of his brother's anger.

"I hope I get to meet your sister one day," Selene said. "She sounds very cool."

"You put a fail-safe in your own bomb," Langston said, looking at Luca. Now that he was calm, he was starting to recall that he'd been the one to figure out Luca's Galen Erso move.

"I did. Not that it matters. The math was wrong. The bomb won't work."

Langston's eyes widened as that fact sunk in. Then he smiled in relief. "Rich and Mina are going to be damn happy to hear that."

Luca sighed sadly. "I would like to…if you think…I

would like to tell Mina how sorry I am for what I put her through."

Langston considered his request, then shrugged. "Might need to let a little more time pass. I'm not sure she's ready, and Rich wouldn't fight fair like me. He's from Texas. Shoot first, ask questions later."

Luca nodded. "Okay." He bent down to pick up his robot as Selene grabbed his helmet. The two of them walked back to the van, but Oscar held back with Langston. The two of them still had things to say to each other.

"I figured out you and Selene were hooking up before I left, but where does Luca Campisi fit in that?" Langston asked.

Oscar stroked his jaw, drawing his brother's attention to where he'd punched him.

Langston grinned. "Not gonna apologize for that. You had it coming."

Oscar narrowed his eyes but decided to let it go. He'd get revenge one of these days. He was a fan of the "when you least expect it" model. He was going to reorganize everything in Langston's lab and then switch the language of his computers' OSs to Mandarin.

Langston narrowed his eyes suspiciously when Oscar merely gave him a menacing smile.

"It's a long story, bro, that started right after you left for Texas with Rich and Mina. Selene and I kind of stumbled into some shit that meant spending time in a safe house. Luca showed up looking for you. Then there were these mercenaries, a blizzard, butt stuff—I'm a fan, by the way— and this impromptu trip to Italy to defuse a bunch of bombs set by a cult full of psychopathic religious nutjobs.

Oh, and Luca and I are now members of the Trinity Masters."

Langston stared at him, speechless for nearly a full minute. Oscar got the sense his brother was waiting for him to say "gotcha!"

When he didn't, Langston shook his head. "Dude. It's only been two weeks."

Oscar laughed and placed his hand on his brother's shoulder, the two of them walking back toward the van. "I'll fill you in on all the details at the hotel."

CHAPTER NINETEEN

O scar took a swig of wine. He would have preferred beer, but when in Rome—or when several hours outside of Rome. "And then the next thing we know, we're all on a plane headed for Rome, ten minutes after Owen tried to arrest Luca. It's been a crazy month, and it started with you getting called to the altar."

Langston was leaning back against the headboard of the bed in his hotel room, three pillows behind him, as Oscar sat in the desk chair, his socked feet—he'd kicked off his shoes earlier—propped up on the bottom of the mattress, crossed at the ankle.

Oscar had left Selene and Luca in the suite next door an hour ago, both of them lying down in the bedroom, looking like a couple of zombies. It had been a long, emotional, stressful-as-fuck day, and he suspected they were both sound asleep by now.

Oscar couldn't shut his brain down, so there was no point in trying to sleep. There was too much rambling around in his head. Besides, Langston hadn't been willing to give him a bye on filling in the blanks, and he'd been grateful for the distraction from all the shit stressing him out.

So he'd covered his lovers with a blanket, given them both a kiss, then ventured over to Langston's room to split a bottle they'd ordered from room service and tell his brother about everything he'd missed after taking off on his honeymoon.

"Told you you'd join," Langston said smugly, once Oscar had finished his story.

He hated when his brother was right. Oscar had spent the past few months swearing off the Trinity Masters, calling them a cult and claiming the society wasn't for him. "I was coerced," he grumbled.

Langston rolled his eyes. "No, you weren't. You're a stubborn bastard, and you never do anything you don't want to. You can protest until the cows come home, but you and I both knew you were always going to join. If anyone is a loose cannon, it's Walt. Who the fuck knows what he'll do? Or where he is."

Oscar chuckled. He and Langston both lived on their family's land, behind the house they'd grown up in, and before the Masters' Admiralty and Trinity Masters had crashed into their lives, the two of them had frequently hung out at one of their places each evening, chatting over a few beers and a frozen pepperoni pizza or three. Walt also had a home there, but he was never in it.

"I've missed this. Hanging out with you. Shooting the shit," Langston said, his thoughts clearly mirroring Oscar's. Not that he was surprised. Mama claimed he and his two brothers shared a hive mind.

"Me too."

"So you've basically caught me up on all the stupid boring stuff."

Langston's perspective on life was pretty skewed if he found mercenaries and blizzards boring.

"Let's get real here. What's the deal with you, Dr. Tanaka, and, uh, Luca?" Langston asked.

Oscar took a long sip. He'd been expecting this question, and he was actually glad to have Langston here in Rome to bounce some of his concerns off. He and his brothers didn't have secrets between them.

"I fucked up," Oscar admitted.

Langston frowned and sat up straighter. "What do you mean? I thought the three of you looked pretty happy, considering everything that's going on."

"I'm in love with them, bro."

Langston's eyes widened. "Oh shit. Nice!"

"That's not a good thing, Langston. For God's sake, I just joined the Trinity Masters. I don't get to fall in love and pick who I marry. I literally just agreed to that, then went and fell in love."

"Maybe the Grand Master will put you with them."

"I doubt Juliette's going to do that, and I'm pretty sure she's not a fan of mine after I kept a copy of the bomb design and triggered that webcam."

"Pro tip, call her the Grand Master, not Juliette."

"I've been careful around Selene and Luca."

"You haven't seen her in scary mode yet, but trust me, she can be." Langston made a face.

"She strong-armed me into joining a cult. I've seen the scary mode."

"Mmm hmm." Langston shrugged. "Anyway, she

recruited you *after* that. And if not Selene and Luca, she definitely won't put you with people you're incompatible with. Sort of defeats the whole purpose of the secret society."

"I know, but…I can't see myself with anyone but them."

Langston climbed off his bed and reached for his laptop case.

"What are you doing?" Oscar asked. Here he was baring his soul to his brother, and the asshole was what? Checking email?

"This is too good to keep to myself. We're Zooming Walt and Sylvia."

Oscar snorted. "Jesus Christ. Do we have to get the whole family involved?"

"If I thought Mama and Papa could figure out how to get into Zoom, I'd link them in, but I don't want to waste an hour talking them through it."

The computer started to ring.

"Walt's busy with work. He probably won't—"

"Well, this is a surprise."

Before Oscar could finish his thought, he heard Walt's voice through the speakers. Langston had climbed back on the bed, so Oscar moved his chair to his side of the mattress so he could see the screen too.

"Hey, you're together," Walt said, when Oscar entered the screen. "Thought you were in Texas, Langston."

Sylvia's face popped onto the screen in another window, and she squealed with delight when she saw all three of them. "Oh my God. You're all here! Did I forget my birthday or something?"

Prior to this month, it hadn't been uncommon for

Oscar to Zoom with his siblings a couple times a week, usually one at a time. It was rare for all four of them to manage to get online at the same time.

"Wait," Sylvia said. "Where are you and Langston? I thought you were still in Boston, Oscar."

"We're in Italy. Outside Rome."

Sylvia blew out a loud, disgusted breath. "Seriously? Why the hell wouldn't you tell me you were crossing the pond? Do you know how close you are to me?"

"I'm in North Africa, Sylvie," Walt pointed out. "You haven't come to see me once."

Sylvia rolled her eyes. "The last time I visited you when you were in Haiti, you had me proofreading grant reports and unpacking boxes of weird medical supplies. No, thanks. Rome, however, would be a lovely trip."

Oscar and his siblings hadn't lived in the same house in many, many years, and they'd grown accustomed to Walt, who'd spent most of those years in other countries, and his virtual visits. But with Sylvia living in England now, and Langston moving to Texas with Rich and Mina, Oscar would be the last Hayden at home, and suddenly, he was homesick for his siblings.

"Okay, simmer down," Langston said. "This isn't exactly a social call. I have news."

Oscar crossed his arms. "Fuck you."

"Given Oscar's response, I'm going to go out on a limb and guess it's actually *his* news," Walt mused. "Wait. Is this about Faith? Did the two of you get back together again?"

Oscar hesitated to respond, hung up on Walt's tone. His brother didn't sound upset, exactly. Rather, his question was posed with almost no inflection at all, completely wooden.

"Faith?" Sylvia's face seemed frozen in a polite smile.

Oscar wasn't totally surprised by Walt and Sylvia's assumption. After all, he and Faith had been somewhat notorious for their breakup/makeup routine, and while they'd been split up a couple years now, this actually wouldn't break the record for their longest time on the outs.

"Nope," Langston said gleefully. "I think our Faith years are finally behind us for good."

"For good?" Sylvia asked almost hopefully.

Oscar studied the screen and witnessed the outright relief on both Walt's and Sylvia's faces. What the fuck was that about? "I thought y'all liked Faith." His siblings had never said anything negative about his ex that he could recall, never alluded to the fact they didn't care for her.

Walt didn't reply to Oscar. Instead, he focused on Langston. "Be very sure, bro. We start trash-talking her and he goes back, we'll all be in the doghouse."

Langston's smile never faded. "He's not going back. He's in love with someone else. Two someones."

"What? Who?" Sylvia asked.

At the same time, Oscar grumbled, "Doghouse? One of you fuckers better tell me what you're talking about."

"No one liked Faith," Langston explained almost gleefully.

What? "What?!"

Walt shrugged. "She wasn't good for you, Oscar. None of us thought so, but you never wanted to hear that. After the first breakup, we all did the usual you're-better-off-without-her pep talks, listing all her faults, of which there were many. Two weeks later, you were back with her and pissed as fuck at us for talking bad about her. You didn't speak to me or Langston for nearly two months. After that, we learned it was better to just keep our mouths shut."

Oscar frowned. "I don't remember that at all."

Sylvia laughed. "I do. Y'all had just graduated from high school and, Oscar, you read both of them the riot act for being assholes about your girlfriend. You even told Faith what they said, which just got her to dig her claws in deeper. Suddenly, you were doing family holidays and crap like that with *her* family, not ours. So after that, the rest of us sort of made a pact to never talk bad about Faith until we were sure—really sure—you weren't going back with her."

"But you *wanted* to say bad things about her?" Oscar asked.

Langston sighed. "Dude. She kept your dick tied up in knots for years. She was selfish."

"Had to be the center of attention," Sylvia added.

"Insecure, and every time you did something awesome, she made it about how she was worried she wasn't good enough for you so that you'd stop talking about your awesome thing," Walt provided.

"Vain," Langston said.

Oscar raised his hands to cut them off when it became clear they could keep the list rolling for a while. "You're right," he said. "She was kind of a bitch."

"I object to the use of bitch as a derogatory term," Sylvia declared.

Oscar ignored her with the ease of practice.

"She was…Faith was all that and more." Admitting it felt like a catharsis. Freedom. "God. I was a fucking idiot."

There was nothing fake about Sylvia's smile now. "Wow. Breakthrough."

"So, who do we have to thank for this miraculous change of heart?" Walt asked.

"Dr. Selene Tanaka," Langston said cheerfully before his tone darkened a bit. "And the guy who strapped a bomb to my wife."

"The guy who set off all those trash can smoke bombs in Boston?" Walt asked, alarmed.

"Wait, what?" Sylvia demanded.

Oscar narrowed his eyes. "Thought you understood why," he muttered to Langston.

Langston shrugged. "I do. I get it, and in his place, I would have done the same. To protect you, or Walt, or Sylvie." Langston took a breath. "But…but Mina has nightmares. And I'm not sure how Rich will handle this."

Mercifully, Sylvia moved them away from the stickiness of that topic. "You're in love? With both of them? Wait. Did you join the Trinity Masters?"

Oscar nodded.

"Congratulations," Walt said. "Figured it was just a matter of time."

"Everybody thought I was going to join?" Oscar asked.

All three of his siblings nodded.

"Yep," Langston said. "Knew it would happen once you managed to pull your head out of your ass over Faith."

"And now you're in love," Sylvia said with a happy sigh. She was a poet with the heart of a true romantic. "But…" Her expression changed, and he felt the weight of his sister's eyes on him even through the computer screen. "Oh. Oh my."

Oscar stroked his beard, grateful it was hiding the tender bruise his brother's punch had left behind. Otherwise, he and Langston would have been subjected to one of their kid sister's speeches on why violence never solved anything. "Yeah. They aren't my trinity. They're not mine."

No one spoke for a moment as those words sank in. Sylvia had fallen in love with Hugo and Lancelot before she even knew the Masters' Admiralty existed. But she'd gotten lucky. The fleet admiral, Eric, had seen the budding romance between the three of them, and he'd used it to lure Sylvia away from joining the Trinity Masters. Oscar had been there to witness the posturing between the leaders of the two secret societies, and he and his brothers had also been offered membership to the Masters' Admiralty.

"What are you going to do?" Walt asked.

Oscar shook his head. "What *can* I do? I knew the price I would pay when I joined. I just…didn't…"

"Expect to find them," Sylvia said, the compassion in her voice reflective of someone who'd been there. "Maybe you could ask Juliette to place you in a trinity with Selene and…I'm sorry…I don't know the bomber's name."

Langston and Walt chuckled as Oscar reluctantly grinned. Leave it to Sylvia to find a way to make him smile.

"Luca," he said. "His name is Luca Campisi."

"Is he a member?" Walt asked.

"He is," Oscar said.

"So I'll ask again," Walt said. "What are you going to do?"

"Tell them I love them. And then, somehow, someway, find the strength to walk away from them when all of this is over."

"When it's over?" Leave it to Walt to tackle the tough stuff.

"Walt—" Oscar started.

"Bro," Langston interrupted. "I've seen you with them. You're in too deep."

"What are you saying?" Oscar asked even though he knew the answer.

Sylvia, never one to shy away from emotions, gave him a sweet, sad smile and said the words he needed to hear, even as they broke his heart. "Love isn't absolutes of black and white. It's a gradient. The more time you spend with them, the deeper the love will root."

Oscar swallowed. "You're saying I need to…"

Sylvia didn't bother to hide her tears as she said, "Don't wait until your time in Rome is over. End the romantic relationship now. Tonight."

OSCAR QUIETLY LET himself back into the hotel suite. Neither Selene nor Luca was in the sitting area, so he figured they must still be asleep. He crossed to the bedroom and peered through the open doorway.

Selene was on her side, her arm wrapped around Luca's bare waist, sound asleep. Luca was on his back, and until he spotted Oscar, he'd been staring at the ceiling, a million miles away.

He gave Oscar a small smile.

"You okay?" Oscar whispered.

Luca nodded, but Oscar knew the response was a lie, Luca's attempt at setting Oscar's mind at ease.

"We'll find her," Oscar said softly.

Selene shifted and blinked her eyes a few times. Late afternoon was giving way to evening, and the room was only dimly lit by the slightest bit of remaining daylight.

"How long was I asleep?" she asked.

"Couple of hours, maybe a little longer," Oscar replied.

"Was coming in to see if y'all wanted to order dinner from room service?"

"That sounds good." Selene slowly pushed herself up. She'd stripped down to her bra and panties for her nap, her gorgeous breasts drawing his attention. Oscar figured he could look at Selene for years and still never get enough.

"Is Langston eating with us?" Luca asked.

Oscar shook his head. "No. Said he was wiped out. Got the red-eye to Rome, forced to fly coach since he bought the ticket last minute." Oscar gestured at his build. "I'm afraid these bodies need more legroom than the few measly inches of space they give you on commercial flights, so he couldn't get comfortable and didn't catch a wink of sleep. Poor guy's dog-tired, too beat to eat."

Luca smiled. "You have an interesting accent. I very much like listening to your expressions."

Selene laughed. "Our Oscar is what we Americans call a redneck."

"Damn Yank," Oscar threw back at her with a grin. "Come on. Throw some clothes on and we can call down an order. I'd...I need to talk to y'all."

Selene paused in the middle of pulling a sweater over her head. "Everything okay?"

Oscar pasted on what he hoped was a reassuring grin. "Yeah. It's fine. Just find it hard to concentrate with the two of you half-naked and looking sexy as hell in that bed."

Luca chuckled, throwing on his jeans. He didn't bother with a shirt, and instead wiggled his eyebrows suggestively as he walked by Oscar into the sitting room.

"Tease," Oscar said, slapping Luca's ass as he passed.

Selene decided to add her own fuel to the fire, not bothering to put on pants. Her teasing earned her a quick, hard kiss as penance before he let her pass by.

Once they were all seated, Oscar took a deep breath and said the words he'd only ever said to one other person —the wrong person, according to his siblings. "So here's the thing. I, uh…I've fallen in love with both of you. I didn't mean to, but—"

"Oh God," Selene said, cutting him off. "I was so afraid it was just me. I've been lying to myself, trying to pretend…" Her voice cracked as she looked at Luca and then Oscar. "I love you too. So very much."

She and Oscar shared a sad smile. "We called it practice, but it's all too real. We fucked up, Tanaka." Oscar swallowed hard, trying to dislodge the lump in his throat, trying to beat back his sadness with a lame attempt at humor.

Luca, who'd been grinning as they professed their love, suddenly sobered up. "Perhaps the Grand Master will place the two of you in a trinity together."

Selene reached over, grasping Luca's hand. "Luca, we don't get to choose our partners. The Grand Master forms the trinities, and while compatibility comes into play, love isn't the predominant deciding factor and members don't get to ask."

"Wait. What? Just the two of us?" Oscar asked. "What about you?"

Luca sighed. "I am not worthy of your love."

Selene, who was next to Luca on the couch, turned to face him fully. "Don't say that. Don't even think that. Of *course* you're worthy. You deserve so much love."

Luca shook his head. "No. I've done terrible things. You

heard Langston. Mina has nightmares. When she closes her eyes, it's me there, terrorizing her in her sleep."

Oscar scowled. "Dammit, Luca. We'll visit Mina, explain it to her. You can say you're sorry and we'll all move on. It'll be okay."

"I hope that is true, but…"

"It *is* true. Now," Oscar said, rising from his chair and perching on the edge of the coffee table in front of Luca. "Say it back to us."

Oscar watched as Luca tried and failed in his attempt not to smile.

"When I was young, I believed I was in love with Roberto. And maybe I was, but what I felt for him was lukewarm compared to this. I will never regret what we've shared. You saved me in ways I can never explain. And even if our destinies take us on different paths, I promise you now…I will love you both until the day I die."

Selene tried to discreetly wipe away a tear, and Oscar had to turn his head away. He couldn't see her cry without adding a few of his own tears to the mix.

"We can't…" Selene's voice broke, but neither he nor Luca needed to hear more.

Oscar nodded slowly. They couldn't keep going on this way. The pain of losing them was already more than he could face. To continue…

Fuck. This couldn't be completely over. Not after today. Oscar had spent too many hours, holding his breath, terrified. He needed…more. Selfish or not.

"We all knew going in this couldn't be forever. I knew when I met you," Oscar said, looking at Selene. "You were a member and I wasn't. I knew someday you'd belong to someone, someones, else. But now…"

"But now our hearts are involved." Luca's voice was soft.

"Which means we have to stop. Cold turkey." Even saying that made Oscar feel ill.

"Stop loving one another?" Luca shook his head. "No."

"Stop sleeping together," Selene said. "We start there. We have to put some emotional distance between us."

"We're still going to be together," Oscar said slowly. "Until we find Joli. Until the Bellator Dei are stopped."

"But the day will come when we have to walk away from one another." Selene's voice was watery. "And that will be much easier if we stop sleeping together now."

"Can we have…tonight?" Luca asked softly.

"One more night. I can't let this be over without… fuck…" Oscar ran his hand over his head.

Luca reached over and grabbed it with his free hand, Selene still clinging to the other. "One more night," he agreed.

Selene merely nodded. Speech seemed to be beyond her right now.

The three of them stood together and walked to the bedroom. To hell with dinner.

Unlike their previous sexual endeavors, this time they weren't playing roles, trying new positions, "practicing" ménages.

They were simply Oscar, Selene, and Luca.

And they were in love.

The masks were off and none of them held back as they took their time, kissing, touching, undressing.

Night had fallen, the room bathed in moonlight.

Once they were naked, Oscar pulled back the duvet, the three of them climbing beneath the sheets. Luca reached for Selene, pulling her under him. Oscar stroked Luca's back and ass as he made love to their woman, the two of them rocking together, fighting off their climaxes, neither wanting it to end.

When it did, Oscar was certain he'd never seen anything more beautiful than the pleasure, the utter bliss on their faces.

Luca fell to the side, clearing the path for Oscar. Selene twisted at the last minute, flipping onto her hands and knees, giving him a sexy smile over her shoulder. She'd remembered him claiming that doggie style was his all-time favorite position.

He pushed in hard and fast, both of them gasping. While Luca preferred sweeter, slower lovemaking, Oscar needed a rougher touch, and Selene matched him in those desires.

She arched her back, thrusting back to meet his forward motion, the action driving him deeper inside her.

Luca sat up to watch, tracing his finger over the tattoos on Oscar's arms, his back. Oscar could feel him tracing the letters of his Faith tattoo. Luca had found a way to make him feel better about the damn ink a few nights earlier, proclaiming the word—the noun—was one he felt described Oscar perfectly. Luca saw him as courageous, confident...faithful. And by stroking that tattoo now, it was as if Luca was telling him to have faith, to believe.

Oscar turned his head and kissed Luca even as he continued to move inside Selene. She watched them over her shoulder, her eyes dark with desire...and love.

When they broke apart, Luca reached beneath her, playing with her breasts before his fingers drifted lower, to her clit. Selene jerked at the first touch of Luca's fingers there, and her pussy clenched tighter around Oscar's dick.

"God. Yes," Oscar hissed. "Fuck, Selene. Love you. Love you both."

Luca began alternating between stroking Selene's clit and cupping Oscar's balls, ensuring both of them were completely out of their minds when their orgasms struck.

Selene collapsed facedown on the bed, giving them an exhausted grin when they reached out at the same time to caress her perfect ass.

They lay in the darkness, whispering secrets and sweet nothings, refusing to give in to sleep.

After an hour or so, Oscar got up to rummage through his luggage. He found the tube of lubrication he'd packed. Selene helped him work it into Luca's ass, each of them pressing a finger inside him as he panted and begged for more.

Then Selene slipped beneath him so that Luca could take her once more as Oscar knelt behind him. Placing one hand on Luca's hip, he guided his cock to his lover's ass and they all moved together, their bodies completely connected, the perfect union.

When they came, it was powerful, moving. Bittersweet.

One last night.

And now it was over.

CHAPTER TWENTY

"**D**oes anyone need more tea?" Percival picked up a white teapot and turned to survey the room.

Everyone shook their heads, so he poured more into his own cup, then took a seat at the head of the long conference table. The hotel was a modern style, large enough to accommodate all of them, with several meeting rooms. Late last night, Owen had called to tell them that they'd be having a "war council" in the morning in the largest of the conference rooms.

They'd arrived half an hour ago to find what looked less like a war council and more like a casual breakfast meeting. There was even a buffet set up off to the side. Luca had taken a seat, ignoring the food. When Oscar put a plate in front of him, Luca objected—fear for his sister had tied him in knots—but when Oscar shoved a piece of fruit into his mouth, Luca chewed it, then realized he was starving.

Now most of the empty plates had been pushed to the side or toward the center of the conference table. Owen sat at one end of the table, Percival at the other. The three American representatives in MPF were seated near Owen. Four of the eight MPF officers from the Masters' Admiralty were seated near Percival, the other four lounging against the walls or, in Claudette's case, sitting on the countertop where the coffee and tea was set up.

That left four spaces in the middle of the table, two on each side, for himself, Selene, Oscar and Langston. Oscar had opted to sit next to his brother, and listening to the two of them bickering had been the meal-time entertainment, at least until Percival called the meeting to order.

"Thank you all for joining us this morning," the Englishman said. "Given that each person here has unique expertise and perspective, rather than myself and Owen making decisions and identifying assignments, we'd like to solicit input from each of you."

There was a beat of silence, then Owen said, "Suggestions for next steps?"

Luca reached for Selene's hand under the table. She tangled her fingers with his and squeezed.

"Continue reviewing security camera footage of the roads," Milo said. "There's not much near the compound, but if we expand the net, put more people on it, we might be able to find likely vehicles."

The Bellator Dei had several cars used by the numer-aries who lived on the compound. They were communal vehicles, which had all still been on site. Everyone on the compound had left, and they'd taken everything from computers to some of the most important religious iconography. Because of that, they had to have used either larger vehicles or a dozen smaller ones.

"My parents' house?" Luca asked. Prior to yesterday's

mission, he'd given his parents' address to Owen and Percival and they'd sent a team to check on not only the house he'd grown up in, but the homes of other supernumeraries—married couples or individuals who didn't live at the compound. All had been abandoned and stripped of computers.

"We have a forensic team coming in to do sweeps. We'll start with your parents' home," Milo explained. He was lounging against the wall, looking elegant and brooding and a lot like the imaginary men Luca had conjured during his guilt-filled fantasies as a teen.

"Thank you." Luca nodded in Milo's direction, and the Italian answered with a smile.

Selene leaned toward him. "I'd be cool with one more night if you still want that gang bang. I vote we get Milo and maybe Rodrigo to join us."

Luca tried to turn a startled laugh into a cough.

Oscar glared at them from across the table. "Hold it together, you two."

Luca's brain was tossing up detailed images of Oscar and Milo together, and it was destroying his focus.

Oscar made an aggravated noise. "Really, Luca? Time and place, dude." But he was smiling.

Luca had felt crushed by sadness and fear this morning, worrying about Joli and devastated by the knowledge his time with Selene and Oscar was over. Leave it to his amazing lovers to find a way to break through all those bad feelings and make him smile.

Everyone let their byplay go, though a few smiled at either him or Oscar. Luca studiously avoided looking at either Milo or Rodrigo.

The meeting progressed with various people providing

updates or making suggestions. The updates made Luca realize that some of these people had been up half the night trying to figure out where his sister was.

It was still difficult for him to truly believe there were people this genuinely good in the world. In his experience, no one did anything without expecting something in return.

"I'm going to work on the laptops," Oscar said.

"They're old models, and if they had anything useful on them, they would probably have taken them," Percival warned.

"Still worth a try."

"I'd like to help him." Luca looked back and forth between Percival and Owen. He wasn't really sure which of the men he should be asking.

"There's a smaller meeting room down at the end of the hall." Owen pointed. "Ridley, can you bring them the box of computers?"

The big American saluted as he pushed up from his seat. The discussion continued as various possibilities for tracking the Bellator Dei down were debated. It was both fascinating and horrifying how many options there were and how little privacy people really had. The Bellator Dei's paranoia and distrust, taught to them by their benefactor, whom Luca had heard referred to as Petro by several people, made them a little harder to track, but by no means impossible.

For those at the table, it wasn't a question of "if" they would find them, but "when."

Ridley returned, holding the plastic storage tub full of old laptops. They were uniform and basic black, and Luca thought they might be the "school" laptops that he and the others at the technical academy had used as part of their instruction.

Oscar rose, and Luca followed suit. Selene squeezed his hand as he stood up. He smiled back at her, then followed the other two men out of the meeting room.

Ridley led them to the far end of the generic hotel hallway, then used a keycard to unlock the door. "I stopped by the desk and got these after I grabbed the box out of storage."

This room had only a small rectangular table with six chairs around it. Ridley set the box down on the table. "What else do you need?"

Luca had expected Oscar to open it immediately, but instead, he bent and peered at the laptops through the clear side of the storage bin. "Respirators, gloves, face shields, maybe some plastic to cover the table."

"Damn, son, that's paranoia. I like it. You thinking Anthrax?" Ridley asked.

"Better safe then fucking dead." Oscar straightened.

"Milo's people are paranoid too, so the vans were outfitted with damn near everything. I'll go check. If I find a hazmat suit…?"

"Nah, but if they have Tyvek coveralls, I wouldn't say no."

When Ridley left, Luca went to stand by Oscar. "You think this is a trap?" he asked.

Oscar slung an arm around his shoulder. "You tell me? In addition to bomb and programming school, did they have a poison school?"

"Not that I know of, but it's possible. Almost anything is."

"Hey." Oscar squeezed him. "We'll find her."

Luca hadn't realized he was letting the worry he felt come through his words. He'd tried to put it aside, to separate his fear so he could focus. Or maybe Oscar just knew him that well.

It had barely been a week, but for Luca, it felt as if he'd known Oscar and Selene his entire life. He'd held nothing back from them and since he'd joined the Trinity Masters, they'd done the same. This was a relationship unlike anything he'd ever imagined. Perfect. Pure.

Ridley returned with an armful of stuff, dropping it on the far end of the table, away from the box. "If you need anything else, call us." He pointed at the phone mounted by the door, near the emergency exit diagram. "You have a cell phone too, right?"

"Yeah." Oscar was sorting through the supplies. "This is perfect, thanks, man."

"No problem." Ridley smiled. "Hope you find something useful."

When the door closed behind him, Oscar ripped open one of the clear plastic packages and shook out a set of white coveralls. "Suit up."

Ten minutes later, they were covered head to toe in white Tyvek suits, gloves, goggles, and respirators. They'd draped the table in plastic and even taped up the HVAC return so if they did unleash something, it wouldn't spread to the rest of the hotel.

"We don't have a way to test for any poison," Luca pointed out as they stood shoulder to shoulder, looking at the box.

"Technically we do. If we fucking die, there was poison." Oscar sounded uncharacteristically cheerful. "Ready?"

Luca nodded.

Oscar flipped the latches that secured the lid of the storage box and yanked the top off and—nothing happened. Of course it didn't. Even if the box was full of poison, they wouldn't see it.

Oscar took out the first laptop, turned it over in his hands, and then set it to the side. After the third computer, Luca was too antsy to just watch, so he grabbed the fourth one. All in all, there were six computers in the box. As he walked around the table to set the last one down on the plastic, Luca frowned. He turned the computer over to confirm what his sense of touch had told him. This computer was missing the plastic panel that covered the battery compartment. Newer computers didn't have battery compartments, but these did.

Oscar must have seen him looking at the back. "Yeah. These have replaceable batteries. Well, technically all laptops do, but these are old enough that it was back before the industry perfected laptop batteries so they wouldn't wear out fast. It's also why they're so heavy."

Luca touched the patchwork of black electrician's tape that covered the battery compartment. "I did this."

Oscar sighed. "Luca, none of this is your—"

"This." Luca pointed at the tape. "I taped this up, for Joli. This is her old computer. The one she used for school."

Oscar cursed, but it was a happy *fuck*. "You sure?"

Luca's own excitement was building, though he didn't know why. Maybe it was just that this represented some tenuous connection with his sister.

He put the computer down and opened it. There, right where he remembered, was a sticker of a cartoon cat stuck to the casing just to the side of the trackpad.

"Yes, I'm sure."

Oscar hurried around to him, carrying one of the charging cords that had been in the box. It took the computer several minutes to boot up, during which Oscar drummed his fingers on the table in impatient irritation.

"How old was she?" Oscar asked once the screen lit up. "When she had this computer?"

"Fourteen, fifteen, maybe. Normally they didn't educate girls past twelve, but because she was so good, and they saw that, an exception was made. She came to school at the compound, but lived with our parents since there were no dormitories for girls. She even took advanced classes online."

"If we had my laptop from that age, we'd see some shit like crappy attempts at programs, saved bits of code..." Oscar's fingers slid over the trackpad, his voice slightly muffled by the mask.

"And this might help?" Luca was far from computer illiterate, but he was having trouble figuring out why Oscar was excited, an emotion that had transferred to him.

Oscar didn't take his eyes off the screen as he spoke. "When my sister first started sketching and writing poetry, she had this one pen she loved. It was just a normal pen, but it had this pattern on it, and she glued a flower to the top. Even when she started drawing more seriously, when we knew that she was really fucking good, and that the handwritten first drafts of her poems were important and needed to be saved, instead of using nice pens or artist pencils, half the time she still used this old-ass ballpoint pen. Langston would take it apart to put refills in it even though it was supposed to be disposable."

Luca put his hand on Oscar's shoulder, touched by the

personal story his lover was sharing. "And you think that there may be something on here, perhaps a programming signature, that you can use to find her?"

"Exactly…but I think we might have something even better than a signature I'd have to go and find." Oscar had half a dozen windows open, but he pulled one to the front. "See this? It's a private FTP site—and according to the log, it was last accessed two days ago."

"She's still using it," Luca breathed. "Can you tell where she was?"

"No. Not without the risk of crashing it since it's custom. If she created this, and has been using it since she was young, I might destroy it if I mess around too much." Oscar turned to him. "But we can leave her a message."

"What?" Luca's breath caught. "How?"

"A text file. We write a brief text file and upload it. It will get through since this computer is a terminal for the site. It can't be a picture or a video. That would be too big." Oscar shifted his chair, turning to look at Luca. "If you had twenty words. A sentence or two, to talk to your sister, what would you say?"

"Um, should we clear this with the MPF first? Call Owen?"

Oscar rolled his eyes. "And if they say no?"

Luca frowned. "I would still send it. I need to contact her. I need to know…"

"This falls under the category of it's easier to apologize after than ask permission before. So what are we sending?"

Luca sat back. It would have to be something that only she would understand. He had so many things he needed to explain to her—mainly that he had stopped believing a long time ago, but had stayed in the hopes he could protect her. That he'd learned so much about the world, the real world, and knew far more than the Bellator Dei would have ever let her learn.

"I...I don't know..."

"I know this is hard, but there has to be something just the two of you know, or would say?"

Luca thought for a few minutes, then he sat up straighter. "Egle, the Queen of the Serpents."

"What?" Oscar asked.

"It was a story I used to tell Joli when she was little, whenever she was scared. My mom used to tell it to me before she died. Joli was a baby and didn't have any memory of our real parents. I started telling her the story when we were at the orphanage and continued after we were adopted and moved to Italy. Signore and Signora Campisi...they weren't overly affectionate people."

Oscar leaned over and kissed Luca on his forehead, the impromptu, sweet gesture catching him off guard.

Luca smiled.

"Your childhood fucking sucked, man. I wish...I wish I could erase all that bullshit from your memory."

Luca nodded, too touched to reply.

"So what's the story? What should we say?" Oscar asked after a moment.

Luca considered the old folk tale. Since they didn't know who or if anyone was watching Joli's computer, he wanted to be careful not to say anything that might put her in more danger.

Oscar passed him the computer.

Luca stared at the keyboard but didn't type yet, considering his words carefully. "My dearest Egle. If you're alive, may the sea foam milk. If you're dead, may the sea foam blood."

"Jesus Christ, dude. That's from the story you told your sister when she was scared? What the fuck does that even mean?"

"If she's safe, she'll say milk. If she's in danger, she'll say blood."

"Ooookay. But is there something you can add to figure out where she is? Where the Bellator Dei is?"

"Oh. Of course." Luca considered the story once more. "Where are your serpents?"

Oscar gave him a funny look until Luca explained that the serpents were Egle's family. "She'll understand," Luca reassured him. He turned to the computer and typed out the message, then passed it back to Oscar.

Oscar saved the file, then glanced over at him. "Here goes."

Oscar dragged the file to the FTP upload. They watched in silence as the progress bar crept toward completion.

The computer dinged and it was done.

Oscar sat back. "Now we wait and see if anything pops up."

"A reply file?" Luca asked.

"Possibly that or some other kind of message. She'll have more options on her end than we do on ours."

There was a brisk knock at the door, and then a man's voice announcing he was with the hotel.

Oscar and Luca looked at each other, then around the room, which looked like it had been prepped to dismember a body.

"Fuck," Oscar breathed. "We can't let them in here."

"Just a moment, please," Luca called out in Italian.

"We have your lunch service," the polite voice called out.

Oscar glanced at his phone and realized they'd missed a text from Owen, telling them that lunch would be delivered to the room for them.

"We, uh, will be ready in a moment."

Oscar was throwing laptops back into the box. Luca started to strip off his protective gear.

"I'll just grab it from them," Luca told Oscar. "So we don't have to hide everything."

Oscar paused and glanced around. "Maybe if I just get rid of the plastic drop cloth…"

Luca stepped out of the coveralls, then opened the door just wide enough for him to see the man on the other side. Wearing a hotel uniform, he was pushing a large catering cart covered by a white tablecloth. There were three platters covered by silver dish domes on it.

"I'll take those." Luca held out a hand.

"I need to set them up." The man had an Eastern European accent and the politely distant look of an experienced hospitality worker. Immigrants from Eastern Europe worked in many of the hotels and service industries in central and western Europe.

"We're in the middle of something," Luca said apologetically.

Behind the waiter, a member of the housekeeping staff appeared, slowly pushing a massive laundry cart down the hall. Another witness to their rather illegal-looking activities firmed Luca's resolve. He reached for one of the plates. "I'll take that and—"

The man grabbed his arm and yanked.

Luca's head cracked against the doorframe and pain blinded him. He was vaguely aware of stumbling back and falling to the ground as something hot and sticky flowed over his lips.

"What the fuck?" Oscar snarled.

Luca looked up in time to see the waiter and housekeeper rushing into the room. Oscar fought, but they pinned him against the wall in seconds. Then a syringe appeared from one man's pocket and plunged down into Oscar's arm.

"Get the other one," the waiter murmured in Serbian.

Luca's head was ringing, his nose—probably the source of the blood coating his lips—was throbbing, but he forced himself to his feet even as Oscar sank to the floor, his eyes closed. He lunged for the phone on the wall, only to be knocked to the side. He'd seen the blow coming enough that he'd been able to turn, minimizing the impact so instead of knocking him out, it merely threw him off-balance. He used that, stumbling toward the table and Oscar's cell phone. His fingers closed over it. A roomful of dangerous people were just down the hall. All he had to do was call them.

There was a sharp pinch at the top of his shoulder. In his peripheral vision, he saw a thumb depress a plunger. The drugs burned his trapezius muscle, and though he was still conscious, he collapsed, landing hard on his knees, then falling to the side.

He watched with ever-fading awareness as the waiter and housekeeper calmly wheeled their carts into the room. Then Luca's eyes closed, and by the time they stuffed him into the catering cart, he was unconscious.

CHAPTER TWENTY-ONE

Selene knocked on the door to Langston's room. With each passing minute, she was becoming more and more worried about Luca and Oscar. No one had seen them since they'd left the "war council" room this morning, and the room they were supposed to be in was empty, as was their hotel room. Now, it was nearly dinnertime and she couldn't shake the feeling that something bad had happened.

"Hey, Selene. What's shaking?" Langston asked as he opened the door. Even though she knew it was Langston, not Oscar, she felt a split second of relief when she saw his face. It was truly uncanny how much the Hayden brothers looked alike.

She glanced over his shoulder hopefully, sorry to see Langston was alone. "Have you seen Oscar?"

Langston shook his head. "Not since he and Luca went to work on the laptops. They're probably still there. Once Oscar gets started on a project like that, he's like a dog with a bone."

She shook her head. "No. I went to check on them an hour or so ago and the room's been cleaned up, everything gone."

Langston shrugged. "Does Luca know where he went?"

"I can't find Luca, either."

Langston frowned. "Did you try his cell?"

She nodded. "No answer." To any of the seventy-two times she'd called.

"Weird. Come in and we'll call Owen."

Selene nodded, grateful for the invitation. She'd done so much pacing in her room the past hour, she was going to wear a hole in the carpet. "Thanks."

Langston stepped back so she could walk in, then closed the door. She sat down on the desk chair, while Langston perched on the end of the bed.

"I can't shake this feeling that something is wrong," she said.

"Did you call down to the front desk? Maybe…" Langston paused, then gave her a sad smile. "I know Oscar was going to break things off last night. Maybe he and Luca decided to get their own rooms."

She shook her head. "Their luggage is still in our suite." She didn't bother to add that she didn't believe they would switch rooms, no matter what they'd decided last night. At least, she hoped they wouldn't. While the wisest course was pulling back, Selene wasn't sure she was going to be able to follow through with that agreement.

Langston studied her face. "You doing okay with…everything?"

She sighed sadly. "I'm in love with your brother. And Luca."

Langston's wide smile filled his face. "I think that's awesome."

"Even though we're barreling straight toward certain heartbreak?"

"Yeah. I know it's not ideal, but…well…I want to thank you."

"For what?" Selene asked.

"The past few years have been pretty rough on Oscar. Faith kind of made drop-kicking his heart a habit. And when she broke things off just before he proposed, it changed him."

"Changed him how?" she asked.

"He was angry all the time, bitter."

"Faith hurt him badly. I think he just needed time to—"

"No," Langston interjected. "Time wasn't going to heal him. But you…and Luca…you brought my brother back. Even with all the shit going on right now, he's happier than I've ever seen him. And more at ease. I mean, that guy's a powder keg on a good day, but I don't see any of that white-hot rage anymore. You're good for him."

"He's a good man," Selene said. "And very easy to love. They both are."

Langston's grin faded. "I just wish that the three of you…"

Selene nodded, perfectly aware of what Langston was wishing for. "So do I."

They sat in silence for a few moments as Selene considered Langston's words and the subtle changes she had seen in Oscar since the day she'd met him at Trinity Masters headquarters. He'd been led into the conference room with a bag over his head because he hadn't been a member at the time, and he wasn't allowed to see where headquarters was located. Langston pulled the bag off, Selene took one look in his eyes, and felt as if her heart recognized him.

She stood up and walked to the window, glancing down at the street below. "Something is wrong," she said. "I can feel it."

Langston rose and stepped next to her. "Let's make that call to Owen. Maybe Oscar and Luca found something and they went to tell the MPF."

She'd grown so accustomed to the three of them being on their own the past week that she hadn't even considered Luca and Oscar would go to Owen first if they'd found something. "I bet that's it. Please call."

Langston grabbed his cell from the nightstand and found Owen's number. He put it on speakerphone.

"Fraser," Owen answered.

"Hey, Owen. It's Langston. I've got Dr. Tanaka here with me. We're worried about Oscar and Luca."

"Why?" Owen asked.

"I can't find them," Selene answered. "The conference room they were using has been cleared out and they never came back to the suite. Have you talked to them?"

"Not since our meeting this morning. How long has it been since you've seen them?"

"Since they left to work on the laptops this morning."

"Damn. We had some internal conflict going on about the possibility of a traitor in our midst and it pulled my attention away from the case. I meant to check on them earlier." Owen sounded alarmed. "I'll call you back momentarily."

Owen disconnected the call. Selene was grateful he was willing to help because she'd already decided that if he'd brushed off her concerns, she was going to start walking the damn streets to look for them on her own.

Langston scanned the street below, and she could see he was worried as well. "Not like Oscar not to answer his phone."

Ten minutes later, Owen called back. "No one's seen them since this morning. Jennika is checking with hotel security. We've been monitoring all hotel entrances and exits since we got here last night. There are surveillance cameras in the hallway with the meeting rooms. Ridley confirmed they not only went to the smaller meeting room, but were planning to work there. He also brought them protective gear. In the meantime, Vadisk and Claudette are going to take the vans and start canvassing the surrounding area. Your boyfriends picked a bad time to go MIA without checking in with someone."

"You don't think the Bellator Dei got to them, do you?" Selene asked, finally voicing the fear that had taken root when she'd discovered the conference room they'd been using empty.

"Unlikely. As I said, we're monitoring the hotel security system. If they stayed in the hotel, they're safe."

"And if they didn't?" Langston asked.

"If the Bellator Dei was waiting for one of us to walk out of the hotel, we have bigger issues."

"Bigger issues than them missing?"

"Yes. Because if the Bellator Dei are outside, it means they know who we are, where we are, and had the capacity to kidnap two fully grown men from a public street without raising any kind of alarm or creating a disturbance we would have heard about."

They ended the call, and Langston looked at Selene.

"That actually makes me feel better. The Bellator Dei aren't direct-confrontation people. That's why they like bombs."

Selene nodded, trying to feel the same, but the knot in her stomach tightened with each moment that passed.

Half an hour later, Selene's nerves were shot, and the normally smiling Langston looked grim when there was a knock on the door. Langston leapt across the room and yanked it open.

A grave-looking Owen, with Jennika at his side, was standing in the hallway.

Selene's legs trembled as she sank onto the edge of the bed.

Owen and Jennika walked in, the latter walking to the dresser and setting a computer on top. She opened the lid.

"Everything we have on video confirmed what we already knew." Owen nodded to Jennika.

Selene and Langston crowded around the computer. The low-resolution video showed Ridley, Oscar, and Luca walking down the hall. Jennika fast-forwarded to show Ridley leaving and then coming back with an armful of stuff, then leaving again.

"You two might want to sit down," Jennika said gently.

"No," Langston snarled, sounding so much like Oscar. "Just show me what happened to my brother."

Selene put her hand on his shoulder, both as a sign of support and to restrain him.

Jennika looked at Owen, then fast-forwarded again before hitting play.

They watched as a room service waiter knocked on the door. The angle of the security camera meant that they couldn't see who opened the door, especially since it wasn't opened all the way. There was a flash of a pale hand—

Luca's—reaching toward the food on the catering cart, but the waiter grabbed his arm.

A second later, the waiter shoved the door open and walked into the room, leaving the cart in the hall. A member of the housekeeping staff, who'd been pushing a laundry cart, followed him in.

Two minutes of nothing, only eerie silence as they watched the video. Then, the staff members appeared again and calmly pushed their carts into the room. Several minutes later, they wheeled both carts out of the room and closed the door behind them.

"Oscar, Luca…they were in those carts, weren't they?" Selene asked woodenly.

"Dead?" Langston's question was flat.

Jennika closed the laptop and glanced at Owen.

"No." Owen was calm and composed. "We lose sight of them briefly, but then we have video of a linen company truck pulling up at the service entrance of the hotel. Two carts are rolled into the back, the staff jump in the back with the carts, and the truck drives off. We've confirmed that today is not the regular pickup day for the hotel linens, and that the men on the videos aren't hotel staff."

"Not dead?" Selene asked, needing to hear it again.

"We don't believe so. This reads like a kidnapping."

"Kidnapped. The fucking Bellator Dei kidnapped them. Do you know where they are? Where they went?" Langston demanded.

Selene backed up until she was sitting on the end of the bed, mind racing. They—she, Luca and Oscar—been so consumed with the Bellator Dei, they hadn't thought about or discussed what had happened in Pennsylvania.

"We can't assume it was Bellator Dei," she said.

Langston frowned. "What do you mean?"

"Less than a week ago, someone tried to kidnap Luca," she replied. "Shouldn't we assume that another kidnapping attempt might be from the same people? The Serbians?"

"The Bellator Dei have good reason to want to kidnap him too," Jennika pointed out. "He's one of them. And if they infiltrated *Cohortes Praetorianae*..."

"But if they know he's here, with us, they know he's not loyal," Langston pointed out.

"No, they may think they rescued him," Owen said slowly. "And they might have taken Oscar as either a hostage or out of necessity."

"If they don't need Oscar..." Langston sank onto the bed.

"But the Bellator Dei don't kidnap people. They use bombs. You just said so yourself, Langston." Selene jumped to her feet and started to pace. She didn't know why she was so sure this wasn't the Bellator Dei.

Owen considered that briefly. "The professionalism of this operation indicates that it wasn't Bellator Dei members themselves who did it. If they're responsible, they hired someone."

"Maybe they hired the Serbian mercenaries to kidnap him back," Selene said. "Or it's just the Serbians attempting to get Luca again, this time closer to home."

Owen nodded. He didn't seem surprised, which indicated he'd probably already thought of that. "I've already called the Grand Master. Boston is sending over everything they have on the people who attacked you in Pennsylvania."

"So, we're going to Serbia?" Langston demanded. "Or do we think they have them here in Italy? A search party?"

Owen walked over and put one hand on Selene's shoulder, stilling her pacing. With the other, he reached out and grabbed Langston's shoulder in turn. "We *will* find them, but we have to take action, not just react."

"Meaning?" Selene demanded.

"Meaning that for the next twenty minutes, I want you two to take showers, change into something comfortable—because this might be a long night—and then meet the team in the conference room." Owen released them and followed Jennika, who headed for the door. "We'll find them," Owen assured them.

When the door closed behind him, Selene and Langston looked at each other, but neither spoke.

Their fears were too big for words.

LUCA ROLLED OVER, vomited, and then gagged. His head was clearer than it had been, enough that he knew it wasn't the first time he'd been sick, a fact made painfully clear, considering there was nothing left in his stomach for him to throw up. This was, however, the first time he'd been aware enough to then sit up and look around his surroundings.

The walls were dusty, uniformly gray concrete, with heavy plastic sheeting where there should have been doors. It was dusk, and the only light filtered in through plastic that covered what he assumed would be a window. He was in a construction site of some kind, though there were no useful tool boxes lying around he might use to free his hands from the cuffs. The cuffs were looped around some roughed-in plumbing sunk into the concrete. He wasn't going anywhere.

He had a vague memory of men checking on him, and

at some point, someone had thrown water on him, probably to wash away the vomit, because his hair was wet.

The last thing he could recall at the hotel was the man attacking Oscar, plunging the needle into him. He was gripped by terror as the image of Oscar falling flashed through his mind.

Where was Oscar? Was he okay?

His lovers had shared their fears with him last night, Selene and Oscar talking about the panic and unbearable fear they'd felt when he was on the compound, defusing the bombs, both of them far too aware that he could be killed at any moment.

Last night, he'd been touched by how much they cared for him, and the realization that there was someone in the world, besides just his sister, who would grieve for him.

But now that he found himself in the same position, uncertain if Oscar was alive or…no.

No.

Luca pushed that thought from his mind, unable to consider something so truly horrifying.

The sound of voices pulled him from his dark thoughts. A second later, light flashed over plastic. Then two men, speaking Serbian, pushed through a plastic-draped doorway. They had guns slung across their backs, and one of them held a flashlight. They held the plastic aside, and two more men came in—carrying Oscar.

Luca's heart stopped.

Where Luca had on only handcuffs, Oscar was trussed up in what looked to be layers of silver duct tape. They dumped him on the ground beside Luca, and Oscar grunted, his eyes bright with rage.

There was tape wrapped completely around his face

and head, covering his mouth. His wrists were crossed at the small of his back, bound with more tape and a pair of handcuffs. His legs were bound at the ankles and knees.

One of the men took a fresh pair of cuffs and crouched, locking it around the same looped pipe that Luca's hands were bound to. He reached for Oscar, who head-butted him. The man's nose broke with an audible pop, and Oscar's eyes crinkled in a smile, until the man sucker-punched him in the stomach.

Oscar bent, sucking in air through his nose and groaning. The man with the broken nose and blood on his face locked the free end of the cuffs to the chain between the pair Oscar was already wearing.

Luca realized the wave of happiness washing through him was foolish. They were in very grave danger and it was obvious Oscar was hurt. But he was alive. Simply seeing him here, watching the brave, crazy man fight back against unbeatable odds made Luca feel better.

They were both still alive. And they were together.

He wanted to talk to Oscar, to tell him he loved him, but there were four enemies in the room, and Luca knew that silence was always safest. He met and held Oscar's gaze. Then turned away.

The men were standing near the light from the window, the flashlight now dark. One was looking at his phone. They made no attempt to keep their voices down, so they must not have been near enough to another building for that to be of consequence, but they did seem to be worried about any light being noticed.

They were speaking openly in Serbian, which indicated they had no idea he understood the language.

"I still think we shoot him in the head and bury the body."

"Don't be stupid. A missing man is…" The speaker shrugged. "But a body?"

"Then we kill him and dissolve him in acid. No body. We only want the little Italian man."

"We have to wait." The one with the phone looked up. "The lawyer our American family hired for my sister's husband's cousin is going to call back with information. The black man matches the description they gave of the bodyguard for the other interested party."

Luca blinked. Oh.

Selene and Oscar's insane bluff back in the farmhouse no longer seemed so insane. They thought Selene was someone to be feared.

And that was keeping Oscar alive.

"Do we know who she was?" another of them asked.

The one with the phone shook his head. "American accent, but Asian."

"Chinese," one of the men spat. "They can't have our bombs."

"No, but we don't want a fight with any of the Triad, especially not 14K."

The men nodded in agreement, several of them looking over at Oscar.

The phone pinged, and the man holding it grunted. "Andrej says the lawyer is speaking with my sister's cousin-by-marriage now. We will have more information soon."

The four men walked out, their conversation turning to what kind of wine they were planning to drink while they waited, a ridiculously mundane discussion, considering they were just deciding whether or not to murder someone.

When they were out of earshot, Luca looked at Oscar.

"Mercenaries," he whispered. "Serbian mercenaries. This time it's the real ones, not their stupid relations."

Oscar closed his eyes and nodded, the expression saying clearly this was what he'd expected.

"They don't know who you are and are trying to figure it out. That, and who Selene is."

Oscar's eyes popped open and then he winced.

"I'll do what I can to keep us both alive and buy time," Luca said softly. "Oscar, I am so sorry."

Oscar shook his head, then winked. He might be down, but Oscar was far from out.

CHAPTER TWENTY-TWO

Selene wanted to do something—walking the streets with flyers, reviewing satellite imagery, maybe beating information out of someone. Unfortunately, flyers wouldn't help since they'd been kidnapped in a van, people more experienced than her had already reviewed all satellite footage, and there was no one she could beat up.

Selene listened as the men and women around her talked about plans and strategies. There was urgency in their voices, and she knew they were working hard, but it wasn't enough. She wanted to scream at all of them.

Langston was seated beside her. They were now comrades in battle, tied together by the same paralyzing worry. However, unlike her, Langston didn't look like he necessarily needed a reason to beat someone up. His fist was clenched tight and he was pounding it lightly on his thigh. He studied every single person at the table, and she could almost imagine him sizing them up, debating who would put up the best fight. The Hayden boys had an unnatural love of smashing things.

"I have preliminary IDs on the kidnappers." Sidika's voice broke through the chatter. The flat-screen TV on the wall clicked on and two mugshots appeared, side by side, their names written below their faces.

Miroslav Zoran and Vlado Milica.

Selene studied the pictures. "Who are they?"

Owen answered her question. "Miroslav and Vlado are high-ranking members in a paramilitary organization called Serbian Action. We're dealing with the same group who already attempted to take Luca once. With one critical difference."

"What?"

"The men you were dealing with in Pennsylvania were low-level members of the American Serbian mob out of Chicago, and individuals with loose affiliations to this main group. People with clean enough records they made it through U.S. immigration."

They already knew that, but Selene bit her tongue to keep herself from snapping at him to hurry up and get on with it. There were people around the table who didn't know this, and she wanted every single person here to have all the information needed for them to bring Luca and Oscar home safely.

"What we're dealing with now is the main group. These are dangerous individuals—neo-fascist, neo-Nazis. They're very good at hate and violence, and they're well-equipped, experienced fighters."

"What's their poison?" Rhys asked in his cowboy drawl.

Several people frowned in confusion, but Percival understood and responded, "Guns, drugs, and they're mercenaries for hire. They're all military trained, and the organization espouses ideals of a free Serbia."

"And they sell bomb-making supplies," Selene said. "That's how they know about Luca. The Bellator Dei buys bomb stuff from them."

Owen took over from there, going over what the Trinity Masters had discovered about the paramilitary rebels, both from questioning the men before handing them over to the authorities, and in the ensuing investigation afterward.

"How did they know he was here?" Konrad asked when Owen was done.

"That's the question we need to answer. If we find out how they're tracking Luca, we trace it back to where they are now."

"We are sure Luca and Oscar aren't working with them?" Vadisk asked.

Langston snarled and launched himself across the table at the Hungarian man.

Selene accidentally on-purpose got in the way as Kristin, seated on her other side, tried to grab Langston. Rodrigo managed to nab him and haul him back across the table. Vadisk didn't move, didn't even uncross his arms, which was both impressive and alarming.

"We are sure," Owen said, a hint of anger in his voice. That he too was pissed made Selene feel better.

Percival cleared his throat. "Every member of the organization is on a watch list—Interpol, Serbian BIA. As Owen pointed out, none of these men were part of the kidnapping attempt in America. They wouldn't have made it through customs."

"So if they're being watched, where are they?" Langston demanded.

"They are on watch lists, not under constant surveillance," Percival said primly.

On the long wall of the conference room, under the TV, was a bank of cabinets. The top of them served as the food service area, while inside were supplies for both catering and business meetings.

From inside the cabinet came the sound of the printer turning on.

Milo, who was closest, turned and opened the cabinet, pulling out the sheet of paper, while the rest of them continued to discuss the latest intel they had on the Serbian Action group.

"Who printed this?" Milo's sudden sharp question cut through the chatter. Everyone looked to the people who had laptops open in front of them—Jennika, Sidika, Ridley, and Sarah.

They all shook their heads.

"*Merde.*" Milo turned the paper around. A single question in large black typeface was printed on the paper

"I don't read Italian, what does it say?" Selene demanded.

"Can you save my brother?" Milo translated.

"Shit!" Jennika's finger tapped against the trackpad of the computer. "The printer is on the hotel's guest Wi-Fi, not the secure network I set up for us."

"Luca's sister? But how?" Selene asked.

"Do we have any idea what Oscar and Luca did before they were kidnapped?" Sidika demanded.

"They had the old computers from the Bellator Dei compound." Langston sounded hopeful, and that got her hopes up in turn. "Oscar can do a lot of damage with a computer."

"Can we send a message back to whoever sent this?" Owen demanded.

"I'm going to the hotel office." Sidika closed her laptop and raced for the door. "I'll try to trace it back."

Percival nodded at Konrad, who rose and followed her.

"Maybe, maybe…" Jennika's fingers were flying over the keyboard. "If we can, what should it say?"

Everyone looked at her. Selene blinked, her brain briefly and terrifyingly blank.

"Yes," Langston said. "Just say yes, and ask if she knows where they are."

"Wait." Selene closed her eyes, mind whirling as she went over everything Luca had said about his sister. "Say… say…" She took a breath. "'Yes, but not if it means risking you.' He wouldn't want that."

Milo leaned over and typed out the message in Italian.

"How are you getting it to her?" Langston asked.

"I'm putting the document in the print queue and pausing it." Jennika looked up. "The printer equivalent of writing a draft email in an account both parties have access to."

"Did it work?" Selene demanded.

"I don't know yet." Jennika tapped and then a mirror image of her screen appeared on the TV. The window showing the printer queue was up, a single untitled document listed as "paused."

Selene had a sudden vivid flashback to all the times she'd had to call university technical support because she was having trouble printing. That life seemed so far away.

A second document appeared, and a moment later, the printer started up. Milo ripped the paper out of the tray as a black wall of code appeared on the other half of Jennika's screen.

"'He has strayed from God's path. I cannot save him,

but know it would be His'—Capital H—'work for you to do so.'" Milo looked up.

"The sister is a card-carrying believer," Langston said grimly.

"But she loves her brother," Claudette said softly.

"Ask her where he is," Selene demanded.

"And how she knows," Percival said.

"No." Selene looked around, ready to fight anyone who dared suggest they do anything that put Oscar and Luca's lives at risk. "How doesn't matter. If she knows, *that's* all that matters. We get them back safely and deal with the rest of it later."

"Agreed," Owen said. "Our priority is their safety. I know we have outstanding questions as to how our adversaries are obtaining their information, but we deal with that after we get Oscar and Luca back."

Milo glanced at Percival, then Owen. When Jennika slid the laptop toward him, he typed up a simple message.

"What did you say?" Langston asked.

"'Where is he? I will save him.'"

They watched as Jennika dropped it into the print queue, a digital drop spot. The reply came faster this time, the printer whirring to life.

Again, Milo grabbed the paper. "It's an address." He passed the paper to Jennika, who pulled up the location on a map.

"That's an hour away from here," Milo said.

"Is this a current image?" Claudette asked. "It looks like a construction site."

"Yes, from a few days ago," Jennika said.

The image resolution wasn't great, but it was enough to

see a gray building surrounded by dirt with yellow heavy equipment parked around it.

"Let's go." Langston stood.

"We need a plan." Rodrigo hadn't shifted from his position, lounging sexily against the wall. Selene recalled she and Luca joking just this morning about adding Rodrigo to their gang bang wish list. Her heart lurched and she forced herself to take deep, slow breaths because there was no way she was going to fall apart. Her men needed her. And she needed them.

"This is a trained military force. We need a plan. Milo, does *Cohortes Praetorianae* have a military strike team?"

"We do, but they're on a job. I have contacts with *Arma dei Carabinieri.*"

"We need to go in *now*," Langston countered. "They might be..." His voice trailed off and he swallowed.

Oscar and Luca might be subjected to torture. Or they might already be dead.

The need to act made Selene tremble.

"A firefight is the last thing we want," Rhys drawled.

"Then we create a distraction and send in an extraction team," Kristin said. "I've done distractions before."

"Langston, you could build us a bomb?" Owen asked.

"Always, just point me toward a kitchen."

"It's still high risk," Rodrigo countered. "They'd be trained for that. They're not amateurs. A distraction and they'll close ranks, making it harder to get to our people."

"I can distract them," Kristin said again, with an arched brow and slight smile.

Rodrigo blinked. "I'm sure you can."

Kristin was one of those stop-men-in-their-tracks beauties.

"I'll redirect a sewer line and flood the building," she finished.

Rhys choked on a laugh. "That is not where I saw that going."

Selene tuned them all out for a moment. She had an idea, a messy, uneven prism of a thing that wasn't pretty or elegant. But it might work. It might mean they could walk in and see what shape her boys were in before either shit flowed or bullets flew.

"What do these guys know about what happened in Pennsylvania?" Selene asked.

Everyone looked at her.

"Why do you ask?" Owen was studying her.

"I have an idea."

Selene took a breath and started talking.

CHAPTER TWENTY-THREE

"Someone's coming," Luca whispered to him. Oscar didn't say anything in reply, mostly because he couldn't thanks to the half a roll of duct tape wrapped around his fucking head.

"Not more of the crew. Someone new. They sound worried. They're using some slang I don't know and—"

Luca stopped talking abruptly, and a second later, the sound of footsteps heralded the arrival of their kidnappers. The group had swelled from four to six people, and one of the two newcomers was clearly the boss. He couldn't understand what anyone was saying, but he heard the boss called Andrej.

Andrej dropped his cigarette and stepped on it. The fact that the dude was smoking while wearing a tracksuit with a gun tucked in the back, and was basically a walking, talking Eastern European stereotype, was seriously pissing Oscar off.

Being pissed was a lot easier than being scared.

Though Andrej looked less intimidating than the others,

who were in what looked like all-black military fatigues, it was obvious he was the leader. And right now, he was barking orders.

With the bad guys in the room, Luca couldn't translate for him, so Oscar had to try to read everyone's body language. Whatever was about to happen was bad. Really, really bad, based on the way Luca had stiffened. Oscar grunted—the only noise he could make—to remind Luca that he had to act like he couldn't understand when they spoke Serbian.

Luca turned his head, his eyes wide.

What the fuck was that expression supposed to mean? Dammit. Oscar had no fucking idea.

Andrej continued giving orders, and two of the five men ran out, one returning rather quickly with a chair, setting it down. Andrej took a seat and crossed his legs, ankle on knee. Then he seemed to change his mind and sat up straight, taking a fresh cigarette from his pocket and sticking it in his mouth. The other men arranged themselves, one just behind Andrej's chair, the others near the windows.

Andrej adjusted his position again. What the actual fuck was going on?

The sound of footsteps grew louder, and Oscar frowned. At least one of the people coming in was wearing high heels.

One of the two guards who'd left entered again, holding aside the plastic.

A mountain of a man stepped through—6'5" with a shaved head, medium-tone skin, and wearing a belt with a gun and knife, one on each hip.

Oscar froze because he knew the man. It was Ridley.

One of the MPF. Was one of the task force members a traitor? Working with these guys, the Bellator Dei, or both?

That would explain how the mercenaries had found them.

Ridley moved to the side and a woman stepped through.

Dark hair fell in a perfect curtain around her lovely face. She wore a blood-red dress, a white fur stole, and black fuck-me heels.

Selene.

Jesus. Fucking. Christ.

More men came in behind her—Owen, Vadisk, Rodrigo. They arranged themselves around the room, each one armed to the teeth.

Another Serbian man brought up the rear, and Vadisk bared his teeth at the man as he skirted around from behind them to join his compatriots.

"Am I hallucinating?" Luca breathed.

Oscar made a noise and shook his head.

"Any idea what she's doing?" Luca asked again, his lips barely moving, though no one was looking at them.

Selene surveyed the room, chin held high.

It was a really good supervillain look.

Oscar swallowed the hysterical urge to start laughing and was now glad for the presence of the duct tape.

"Do you speak English?" Selene demanded.

"Yes." Andrej lit his cigarette. "Do you speak Serbian?"

"There is literally no reason I would bother to do that."

Andrej bared his teeth. "I'd watch your mouth, pretty lady."

Selene made a face like she'd just watched a dog eat its own poop. "First of all, secondhand smoke kills. Put it out."

Andrej took a deep breath and blew it at her.

Selene tapped Owen on the shoulder. "Shoot him."

Owen hesitated for half a second before raising his gun, and Oscar saw his gaze slide toward her, knew the moment Owen realized this plan was probably insane because Selene was the best kind of nuts.

The Serbians all whipped out guns, pointing them at Selene.

In turn, Vadisk, Rodrigo, and Ridley pulled *their* guns.

The tune to *The Good, the Bad, and the Ugly* started playing in Oscar's head.

Selene rolled her eyes, walked over to Andrej, and ripped the cigarette from his mouth. He surged to his feet with a snarl and everyone raced forward, but before anyone could reach her, Selene put the cigarette out on the hand Andrej had reaching for her throat.

Andrej stumbled back, spitting a word at her.

"Bitch," Luca translated.

Oscar looked at him and blinked slowly to indicate that he'd gotten that.

Andrej drew his own gun and raised it, pointing it at Selene's face. "I'll keep you alive and—"

Selene sighed and dropped the cigarette. "Yes, yes, threats of violence and rape."

Was the woman on drugs? What on God's green Earth was she thinking? The man had a gun pointed at her fucking head. If he had to watch the woman he loved get shot, he was going to...well, he didn't know what the fuck he'd do, but it would be something.

"Moving on." Selene pushed his gun down. "Do you need me to tell you that I have this entire building surrounded, or have you figured it out on your own?"

Andrej looked at the man standing by the window. He shifted the plastic to look out then jerked back. He looked at Andrej and nodded slowly.

Andrej sucked in air through his nostrils. "That won't do you any good if you're dead."

"If your solution to everything is to kill someone, it's no wonder you're not a major player. Killing lacks imagination."

If they survived this, Oscar was going to put Selene in therapy. Anti-supervillain therapy. Was that a thing? Maybe Walt could do some shock therapy or something.

"I am—"

"No one." Selene's voice cracked. "You stumbled upon something valuable, and you treat it like that?" She gestured to Luca.

Oscar blanked his expression when everyone glanced their way.

"And look at what you did to *him*." Selene's eyes met Oscar's for the first time, and he knew he was the only one who could see the desperate fear she was hiding. "He's my favorite. If you kill him, I won't have a matched set anymore."

"What?" Andrej demanded.

"There is a man who looks just like him outside," the man by the window muttered.

Andrej put his gun away, which indicated he was smarter than he looked. "Who are you?"

"You can call me Selene Gallio."

Oscar leaned his head back against the wall and just barely refrained from banging it repeatedly.

Selene Gallio made sense as an alias. It was her real first name after all. But it was also the name of the oldest-known mutant in the Marvel Universe. Selene, the comic book character, was, of course, a villain.

Oscar opened one eye. Selene was looking at him and smiling. He closed his eye.

This was either going to work, or they were all fucking dead.

"Selene is a beautiful name. You are…American?"

"Yes."

"And you're with a triad."

Selene stopped, frowning. "Excuse me? You mean the Chinese gang?"

Andrej nodded like he was so smart for figuring that out.

"First of all," Selene declared, "that's racist. I'm clearly Japanese." She pointed to her features.

"Asian people look alike." Andrej shrugged.

Selene sucked in an outraged breath. Die. They were all going to die because, shockingly, the Serbian mercenary was racist.

Oscar slid the heels of his shoes across the floor, making just enough noise to draw her attention. Selene pressed her tongue to her lip and held up a hand.

"You are not worth teaching. You, third favorite. Go get my favorite." Selene tapped Rodrigo on the arm.

"I think that makes me second favorite," Luca whispered. "Because we were going to invite Rodrigo to the gang bang."

Oscar looked at him. Fucking *what?* Was he the only one who wasn't completely unhinged in this relationship?

"I fail to understand why you think you have the power here," Andrej said coldly. "You have men outside? Fine. What is to stop me from taking you hostage?"

"Do the thing with the dots," Selene said, waving one finger in the air.

Owen pulled a phone from his pocket just as Rodrigo dropped to a knee beside Oscar. He took a knife from his pocket and started cutting through duct tape.

A red sniper dot appeared on Andrej's shirt. Then half a dozen more dots appeared on the floor around him.

Everyone froze.

Rodrigo took a set of cuff keys from his pocket and undid first Oscar's cuffs, then Luca's. Oscar started working on the tape around his mouth.

"You are smart," Selene said softly. "You saw what the cute Italian man could do. Saw his potential." She stepped closer to him and the dots slid away from her, one hovering on the side of his head, but none touching her. "If you could dream of greater things, we could be...allies."

Oscar ripped off the last of the tape, taking the top layer of skin off his lips and half the hair out of his beard as he did so. He dragged in a deep breath through his mouth.

Andrej sighed and his body language shifted. The man was smart enough to know when he'd been out maneuvered. "I've never heard your name."

"Exactly. If I were you, I'd start making sure no one knows yours." Selene stepped back. "I'm sorry to take your prize, but I want him."

Rodrigo hauled Luca to his feet and started dragging him across the room. Oscar got up more slowly. His legs were slightly numb.

Luca started babbling in Italian and pulling against Rodrigo.

"He doesn't want to go with you," Andrej said mildly.

Good job, Luca, play along.

"I'm sure he doesn't, but I didn't ask. Did I?" Selene smirked.

"You're going to steal from me and leave me nothing? We had a deal."

"I would, but I've been told that's no way to make friends." Selene snapped her fingers and held out her hand. Ridley handed her a small tablet. "The plans for his bomb, as promised. We located them. I, of course, kept a copy, but I have no interest in using it in this part of the world."

She passed Andrej the tablet. He tapped it against his palm. "What if we share him?"

"I don't share," Selene declared. "Just be glad I'm not asking for a gift. I like the look of that one." She pointed at the man behind Andrej's shoulder.

The man's eyes widened in a mix of alarm and...interest?

For fuck's sake, Selene.

Andrej was looking at the tablet screen, his fingers flicking over it.

Oscar made it over to his group, and without any sense of shame stood directly behind Ridley, who was big enough to be a human shield in case things went south. He couldn't believe they'd made it this fucking far.

"You can have him if we share the Italian." Andrej tucked the tablet into his pocket.

"I still don't share. It was a problem when I was in school, I'll admit." Selene cocked her head, examining the man in question, then shook it. "No, I have a similar-looking one back home. I'll be leaving now."

Andrej smiled, his disposition as sunny as a fucking military anarchist could manage, now that he had the bomb design. Oscar was grateful the bomb wouldn't work because God only knew how much damage these assholes could do with a true city killer. "It was a pleasure doing business with you, Selene."

"And with you." She offered the scary mercenary who now possessed a nuclear bomb a saucy wink.

Then Selene turned and calmly walked them all right out of the building and into two waiting vehicles.

Oscar plopped down in a middle bench seat. Luca sat beside him. Selene had claimed the front passenger seat with Rodrigo, and Owen sat in the back. The others, including people who'd been outside, piled into the second car.

Oscar and Luca looked at one another, then at Selene, who was twisted in her seat to check on them.

"What. The. actual. Fuck. Was that!?" Oscar demanded, all his feelings bubbling up inside at once.

"That was not the plan we went over." Owen sounded hoarse. Probably from repressing the need to shout at someone. Selene, undoubtedly.

"I improvised," she said primly.

"I nearly shat my pants," Rodrigo said from the driver's seat.

Luca started to laugh. It had a hysterical edge.

Selene wiggled her eyebrows. "I am such a good supervillain."

Oscar leaned back, put his hands over his face, and started to laugh too.

CHAPTER TWENTY-FOUR

Luca sat between Oscar and Selene in the same conference room far beneath the Boston Public Library where he'd been onboarded as a member of the Trinity Masters. The three of them could have walked onto the set of any zombie movie as extras right now without needing a bit of makeup.

It had been twelve hours since Selene—with the help of the MPF—had bluffed her way into a meeting with some seriously dangerous men and managed to rescue him and Oscar.

As they drove away, Owen and Selene had quickly filled Luca in about how Joli had helped them find him and Oscar. Though he still had a million questions, Selene grasped his hand and assured him that Joli was okay.

They hadn't even returned to the hotel afterwards. Instead, Rodrigo, who'd been driving the SUV, had dropped the three of them and Owen off at a small landing strip, where they'd boarded a private plane back to Boston. Luca dragged his feet, insisting on remaining in Rome until they found Joli, but Owen had shaken his head, promising that his sister was fine where she was.

Langston had remained with Rodrigo, who would take him to Fiumicino Airport to catch a commercial flight back to Houston. Langston had only been brought in to help defuse the bombs. His part in all of this was clearly finished. He and Oscar had said a quick goodbye before they'd boarded, hugging and promising they'd find time to visit each other again soon, when things weren't so crazy.

Upon landing in Boston and arriving at headquarters, he, Oscar, and Selene had been ushered into this room and instructed to wait. He didn't have a clue where Owen had gone.

Luca tried to brush some dirt off his shirt, but all he did was spread the stain around and make it larger. He was on day two—he thought it was day two, though it felt like twenty years—in this outfit, which was wrinkled and, well, he was pretty sure he stunk. He'd gotten sick numerous times from the knockout drugs the mercenaries had used on him. He'd been sitting in his own filth so long, he wasn't even sure if he smelled. Oscar and Selene had claimed the seats on either side of him, which gave him hope he was wrong. Of course, it also gave him even greater hope that they loved him enough not to care about how badly he needed a shower right now.

Their luggage had been retrieved from the hotel and delivered to the airport, but someone had stowed it beneath in the cargo hold, so they hadn't had the opportunity to change. Not that any of them had been thinking about that when they'd boarded the plane.

Oscar looked even rougher than Luca felt. Selene had found a washcloth on the plane that brought them back to the U.S. and cleaned up the gummy residue on his face. His beard looked patchy from where the duct tape had pulled out large chunks of his facial hair. Like Luca, his clothing had seen better days, stained and filthy.

Selene, however, took the prize. She looked like a night-club singer—the kind who got the job because she slept with the mob boss—the morning after a long set. She'd slipped off her white stole and hung it on the back of her chair when they'd entered the room, refusing to give it up upon landing because she needed the extra layer. The Boston air was teeth-chattering frigid, a rude awakening after the mild temperatures in Rome. Her mascara had smudged, leaving her with raccoon eyes, her hair was pressed flat against her head on one side from where she'd fallen asleep on Oscar's shoulder, and her bright red dress looked completely out of place in this conference room.

The second they'd boarded the private plane and the door was closed behind them, Oscar had reached for both of them, pulling them tightly into his embrace, kissing Selene's forehead, then Luca's, over and over, as he swore he was never letting either of them out of his sight again. Owen had excused himself to talk to the pilot, though Luca suspected the man had merely wanted to give the three of them some privacy for a few minutes.

They'd remained there, locked together, kissing, touching, hugging, until Owen returned and said it was time to take their seats for takeoff. Oscar and Selene sat next to each other, while Luca claimed one of the seats facing them. Owen opted for a spot near the back of the plane, a row all to himself, and two seconds after they'd reached their cruising altitude, he'd opened up his laptop and didn't look up again.

After the initial flurry of relief and kisses, the three of them fell silent. They were headed back to Boston. And from there, Oscar and Selene would return home.

The heaviness of having to part so soon wiped away their relief, their joy at being together again, safe and sound.

A flight attendant had delivered hot tea and offered him and Oscar painkillers. Luca had accepted, suffering a skull-splitting headache, an aftereffect of the drugs, he assumed. He'd closed his eyes to let the drugs work and the next thing he knew they were being instructed to fasten their seat belts for landing.

He, Oscar, and Selene didn't speak as they waited in the conference room. In fact, they hadn't said more than fifty words since takeoff, the weight of what the next few hours would bring crushing them into silence.

"Whatever happens," Oscar started, speaking quietly, as if he suspected the walls had ears. "I don't regret a second of it. I never will."

Luca reached over and grasped Oscar's hand. "Neither will I."

Selene tipped her chin up. "I swear to God, if you two make me cry…"

Luca clasped hands with her as well, sharing a sad grin with Oscar when she refused to look at either of them. He understood Selene well enough to know she prided herself on her strength, her confidence, her steadiness in stressful situations. The idea that she could walk into a room and face down half a dozen men with guns pointing in her direction and never once lose her composure, but she couldn't look at them right now without falling apart

completely, moved him deeply. He'd never felt such powerful, abiding love.

They fell silent once more, and Luca stared at the bare
stone wall across the room from where they were sitting, his
mind whirling a million miles a minute.

What was he supposed to do now? He was homeless,
jobless, and...family-less. He jerked in his seat as his brain
engaged.

"Joli. I need to know what you know about my sister,
Selene," Luca started. He'd let them reassure him on the plane.
If it had only been Owen's word, he would have fought harder
to remain in Rome, but Selene had promised she was okay too.

"She's fine," Selene said, but before she could say more,
the door opened. The Grand Master, her face hidden once
more by the hood on her large shawl, entered first, followed
by Sebastian, Devon, and Franco. Owen was the last to
walk in and he shut the door behind him.

"Joli," Luca said before the others had properly settled
in their seats. "I need to go back to Rome. My sister is
still—"

Owen held up his hand. "Your sister is not in any
immediate danger."

"So you keep saying, but how do you know that?" Luca
asked.

Owen sighed. "She contacted us. It was your sister who
told us how to find you."

"She did?" Luca asked, though his lack of surprise was
obviously noticed by Owen.

Owen narrowed his eyes. "She contacted us at the
hotel...through the printer."

Devon's eyebrows rose. "Perhaps we should start at the

beginning, unpack what happened in Rome for us. What you found at the compound."

Luca described the way the Bellator Dei had booby-trapped the compound and what he and Langston had to do to defuse the different bombs set there. Owen went into detail about what they'd found—precious little—and then Oscar explained how they'd found Joli's old school laptop and used it to contact her.

"Where are those laptops now?" Sebastian asked.

Oscar and Luca looked at each other and shrugged. "They weren't still in the room we were using?"

Owen shook his head. "No. I think we can assume the men who captured you took everything with them. The room was cleaned out by the time we discovered you missing."

"Apart from the ability to contact Joli, I'm not sure we would have found anything on the machines. The Bellator Dei wouldn't have left anything behind that might lead to them," Luca said.

Selene explained how she'd become concerned when Luca and Oscar didn't return to their hotel suite.

"How did the Serbians find Luca?" the Grand Master asked.

"Informant in the hotel. She had a set of photos, including Luca's, and had instructions to call it in if anyone on the list showed up," Owen replied. "We believe they— Serbian Action—have people in every hotel within a wide radius of the Bellator Dei compound."

"They've been watching the Bellator Dei for a while." Devon tapped his fingers together. "Did we get a copy of that list?"

"Yes," Owen replied.

"The informant was a Serbian National?" Sebastian asked.

"She was. There's at least one Serbian or Ukrainian employee at every hotel we checked with." Owen shook his head. "That's hardly unusual. Interpol is looking into it. It's possible Serbian Action is blackmailing or threatening people into working for them."

"No hotels in Europe, for any of our members," the Grand Master declared.

"Yes, Grand Master," Owen replied.

Luca cleared his throat. "When you discovered we were missing...Joli contacted you?"

Owen nodded, opening a file folder and pulling out several sheets of paper. He handed them over to Luca, who read them, so grateful to be holding proof that Joli was still alive, still safe. If she had access to her computer, the Bellator Dei obviously hadn't realized her loyalties were divided because she loved her brother.

"Those were sent to us, to the very room where we were holding our meeting, through a hotel printer. I was hoping perhaps you could provide us some information about your sister's particular skill set when it comes to either her own programs or access to tracking programs, databases, and information security."

"I don't know everything she can do. I know the names of some of the apps they made."

Everyone had already gone through and deleted most of their game apps, though the Bellator Dei apps weren't available in English language markets...yet.

"It is not only her. There are others in the organization with dangerous skills." Luca looked at Oscar. "They have a protocol, a program they made for me and others who have outside jobs. The program works on less-secure information sources. I was able to activate it on a computer here in the library to access Boston traffic cameras." Luca pointed at the ceiling. "That is how I followed Oscar, when I thought he was Langston. If she helped you," Luca said, leaning forward, "then why didn't you save her too? Why did we leave Rome without her?"

Owen rubbed his jaw. "She is still committed to the Bellator Dei cause, Luca. She seems to think you've lost your way."

Luca nodded. He knew that, knew that he would have to work very hard to convince Joli to betray the Campisis and the Bellator Dei. They'd fulfilled her desperate desire for a family, and they'd recognized and supported her academic pursuits even though it went against the "traditional" marriage model they espoused. While he'd seen their evil deeds up close, Joli had been sheltered from the bad stuff.

"We can't rescue a woman who isn't in danger, Luca," Devon said. "Who doesn't want to be rescued. To do so is kidnapping."

Luca wanted to argue that point, but he wasn't sure how.

"I'll find a way to contact her, Luca," Oscar said, reaching over to place a comforting hand on his shoulder. "I'll hack into whatever I have to. I'll make sure the two of you have a safe way to communicate."

Luca nodded slowly, grateful for Oscar's help. His lover knew how much his sister meant to him, how much he longed to see her removed from the grips of the Bellator Dei. "Thank you," he said softly.

The Grand Master turned her attention to Selene. "I

understand you were quite convincing in your role as a... what did you call it, Owen?"

"Supervillain," Franco replied before Owen could respond. "Totally fits. Selene Gallio. Did you know she was active in the Hyborian Age?"

"Which age?" Luca asked, more than a little confused.

"He's talking about a comic book; please ignore him," Sebastian said with a sigh.

Selene smiled. "I sincerely hope that was my swan song. My parents insist I was named after the Lunar deity, so I'll probably try to put away my supervillain powers. I've intimidated my last mercenary."

Franco was visibly disappointed. "With great power—"

"If you quote Spider-Man one more time—" Sebastian snapped.

Devon leaned forward, ignoring the byplay. "Norah released the bomb design on the dark web the moment we received word Oscar and Luca were safe."

"What about Luca?" Oscar asked. "Do the Bellator Dei know he's turned? Sorry about the phrasing."

Luca shrugged.

"Did they try to contact you before they abandoned their main facility?" Devon asked.

"I don't know."

"That means one of three things. First, they know you are now a member of the Trinity Masters and therefore lost to them. I doubt this is the case, since even if your sister is somehow tracking you—and we have to assume that's why she knew where you were—knowing your location would not be enough for them to uncover our secrets."

"We swept him for implants," Sebastian said.

"I thought about that, how she found me, us..." Luca

said. "I think…I think perhaps she was watching the mercenaries. The leadership always knew they were dangerous, and she may have been tracking them, even if she wasn't asked to. Oscar and I sent her a message from the hotel. Then the mercenaries went to the same location."

"She grabbed the location of the hotel from my FTP upload information?" Oscar asked.

"Jennika believes so, though there's no way to know for sure."

"If she knew they and I were in the same location, she could have assumed I was in danger."

"The hotel had cameras. It's possible she found footage of you arriving with us, so she knew you had allies in the hotel." Owen nodded as if he were putting things together as he spoke. "We can look into the possibility that Joli was tracking the Serbians. That might allow us to try a digital trace for her."

Devon nodded, then added, "The second option is they tried to contact you before they ran, but couldn't get ahold of you. They think you're dead or at least missing."

"But—"

"If that were the case—"

Devon raised his hand to stop the protests. "I agree. Unlikely, unless we take into consideration the third possibility."

"Which is?" Luca asked softly.

"Your sister is covering for you."

Luca closed his eyes. "I think…she shouldn't risk herself."

"I think we need to assume Joli knows more than she should, and she's not telling the Bellator Dei everything she *does* know."

"Could your sister access passport records?" Owen asked. "Know you've flown back and forth to the U.S. a couple times?"

"I don't know...I don't think so. The things she can access are smaller."

"She's deeply indoctrinated," Owen reminded everyone.

"But she loves her brother," Selene said.

"What do we do next, to find the Bellator Dei? Joli?" Luca asked.

"You?" Owen shook his head. "You do nothing. We've debriefed you, and if you think of other things we, the MPF, need to know, you call me. But you've done your part. Let us take it from here."

"But—"

"Trust," the Grand Master said. "It's time for you to trust us."

Luca nodded. The Trinity Masters had stood by him, believed in him, had his back, defended him. The trust she requested was easily granted. "Yes, Grand Master."

"And with that, I believe your part in this mystery is concluded," the Grand Master said, looking at Oscar and Selene. "You're free to return to your homes, to your lives. And, Luca, we will help set you up here in the States."

The Grand Master stood, so everyone else at the table did as well. Sebastian opened the door as Selene, Oscar, and Luca gathered their things and left. "Your luggage as well as a car are waiting for you outside. It will drive you wherever you wish to go."

Franco appeared next to Sebastian. "The suite at Boston Park Plaza is available if you need a day or two to..."

Luca forced a smile, then followed Selene and Oscar to the waiting car.

"Hotel?" Oscar asked.

"Hotel," Selene agreed.

Luca nodded, not sure how he felt about walking away from the hunt for the Bellator Dei. But then Oscar put his arm around Luca's shoulder, Selene took his hand, and Luca thought that maybe, just maybe, it would be okay for him to find some happiness for himself.

For however long it lasted.

AS THEY TOOK the elevator up to the penthouse, Oscar felt like he was coming out of his skin. The silence that had lingered between him, Luca, and Selene had gone on for too long. He'd fucked up in Rome, telling them they needed to walk away.

He'd been wrong to tell them this needed to end. If he left right now, returned to Charleston without them, or without a plan to see them, it would feel like he was ripping off his own arm. He couldn't do it.

Once they'd entered the room, he shut the door with more force than he'd intended. Luca and Selene both looked his way, Luca confused, Selene concerned.

"Oscar——" she started.

"No." He raised his hand to cut her off. "Just hear me out. Forget everything I said in Rome."

"Everything?" Luca asked, and Oscar shook his head, aware, that as always, he was letting his temper, his anxiety, keep him from saying shit right.

"Not everything," Oscar said, trying to calm down.

"Jesus. I still love you, okay? That's solid, that's not changing or going away. It's all the other bullshit I said."

Selene sank down on one of the chairs in the living room. "It wasn't bullshit, Oscar. You were right to suggest we protect ourselves, our hearts."

"Fuck that. I'm already in too deep. Shit, I don't think I can fall much deeper in love with you."

Luca smiled at Selene. "I believe we are in love with a very romantic man."

Oscar rolled his eyes, but Luca's joke helped break the tension that had been building up inside him. Oscar's shoulders relaxed slightly. "Smart-ass. Come here."

Luca chuckled as he moved closer to Oscar. They kissed deeply, passionately. And when they parted, Selene was there, kissing Oscar, then Luca.

"Maybe we could just run away. Do you think the Trinity Masters could trace us to Bora Bora?" she asked.

Oscar knew it was ridiculous to feel this happy considering everything was still so fucking wrong. There were a shit-ton of really bad people with the designs to a nuclear bomb—and while it didn't work, that didn't mean there wasn't some soulless asshole who wouldn't try to find a way. The Bellator Dei was still MIA—with Luca's sister. While Luca was putting on a good face, Oscar knew he wouldn't rest easy until she was away from the cult completely.

And…while they were here now, together, Oscar knew the day would come when one of them would be called to the altar, and after that…

Jesus. He couldn't even begin to think about that.

"I say we fucking lean into it," he announced.

Luca gave him a curious glance. "I do not understand 'lean into it' in this context."

Selene reached out and cupped Luca's face, kissing him softly. "He means we're going to stay together until we can't anymore."

Luca grinned. "I like this idea. Because the truth is… I'm homeless."

"Come live with me," Oscar said quickly. "In Charleston. Langston's place is next door and he's got a whole bomb-building lab set up there. I bet he wouldn't mind if you worked on your experiments there."

"That sounds ideal," Selene said softly.

Oscar looked at her and realized that, while moving Luca in would be easy, Selene had her work, a life she loved, in upstate New York. "Selene—" he started.

"You know," she said, cutting him off. "I have a standing offer from SECNAV for grant funding to review the nuclear protocol manuals and emergency plans for the submarines. Perhaps now would be a good time to request a sabbatical from Cornell. I could read and rewrite nuclear manuals from anywhere. Even…Charleston."

Oscar picked her up and spun her around. "Are you serious? Are you sure?"

Selene laughed as she struggled to get down. Oscar wasn't letting her go until she promised she was going to ask for that sabbatical.

"I'm serious. Now let me down, you lunatic, and get in the bedroom. I might have lied about hanging up my supervillain hat. Selene Gallio has plans for you two."

Luca's eyes widened. "Fem Dom?"

She tapped her fingers together and gave them a wicked smile. "Take off your clothes. Now."

EPILOGUE

Walt stretched his arms overhead, working the muscles in his shoulders. He'd been reviewing slides of bloodwork, something most doctors didn't do again after college biology, or maybe a virology class in med school.

In his type of medicine, he often had to do it all. Normally, there'd be some shiny new doctors around to help—working in an understaffed clinic was a great way to get tons of experience—but he was between rotations right now.

The Zoom call with his siblings the other day had made him slightly homesick. Langston was in love and married. Oscar was in love—which was great because this time it wasn't with Faith, but not great because he was in love with two people he couldn't marry, since he had joined the Trinity Masters.

Walt would join too—the Trinity Masters or Masters' Admiralty, he didn't actually care which—at some point. But it wouldn't be any time soon. Right now, he had to chart and then do a bit of cleanup before locking down the clinic for the night and falling facedown on his bed in a room on the other end of the long rectangular building.

He stripped off his **PPE** and washed before grabbing his computer and taking it out onto the concrete patio. The patio area served as a waiting room, a triage center if things were really bad, and his living room, since every bit of space in the clinic besides his bedroom was devoted to medical care.

He sat back in one of the woven chairs and popped open his computer. He'd only been working for half an hour when he heard footsteps approach.

He repressed an exhausted sigh and stood, turning back to the building, where various doors led out onto the large patio. Instead of his "lab" room, he headed for one of the exam rooms, leaving the door open behind him.

This was another reason he sometimes sat outside at night. There were people who wouldn't come to him during the day. Oftentimes women with more personal concerns, but sometimes the occasional man who was experiencing everything from embarrassing ED, to injuries they'd ignored, so that by the time they came to him, it was a salvage situation.

"Come on in," Walt called out in English, then again more hesitantly in French and Spanish, just in case. One of the nurses at the clinic was local and acted as a translator. She'd taught him a few helpful phrases, but not enough. He'd call her to come in if needed.

He listened to the sound of footsteps on concrete as he put on a fresh mask and gloves. Whoever was coming was a large person, most likely male, and wearing shoes.

It was surprising how much information something so simple as a footstep could reveal.

"Hey, Doc."

Walt frowned in surprise and turned. A massive figure stood in the shadows just outside the door, where the overhang of the roof kept the bright light of the moon and stars from reaching.

The voice had a distinct Scandinavian accent. Danish, maybe. And it was familiar.

It took him several seconds to place it. "Oh, uh, Eric?"

Eric was the leader of the Masters' Admiralty. According to Langston, he was seriously terrifying when angry. Walt had only met the man once, and he'd found him to be irreverent, though clearly commanding.

"Yep."

"What are you doing in Libya?"

"That's a long story. But not why I'm here."

"Sylvie?" Walt's heart stopped.

"Your sister's fine, but I need your help."

"What's wrong?"

In response, Eric stepped through the open door and into the electric light of the exam room.

At well over six feet and heavily muscled, his nickname of "the Viking" fit him.

Especially now.

Because Eric was covered head to toe in blood.

ARE you looking forward to Walt's story? You can preorder Wrath's Storm now.

. . .

SEE WHERE IT ALL BEGAN! Be sure to read the entire Trinity Masters series.

Elemental Pleasure

Primal Passion

Scorching Desire

Forbidden Legacy

Hidden Devotion

Elegant Seduction

Secret Scandal

Delicate Ties

Beloved Sacrifice

Masterful Truth

Fiery Surrender

Necessary Pursuit

AND IF YOU'RE interested in reading more about Erik, Sophia, and Milo, be sure to check out the Masters' Admiralty series as well.

Treachery's Devotion

Loyalty's Betrayal

Pleasure's Fury

Honor's Revenge

Bravery's Sin

JOIN THE SOCIETY! Hey fans of Facebook! Did you know there's a Trinity Masters/Masters' Admiralty fan group? Come join the fun—behind the scenes news, exclusive sneak peeks, cover reveals and (gasp) too many screenshots of texts between Mari and Lila.

DEAR READER

We hope you enjoyed reading this book as much as we enjoyed writing it. It's lighter than the rest of the series—verging on comedy—because in the middle of a pandemic that is the book we thought you wanted to read and we wanted to write. We will return to our regularly scheduled mystery and mayhem with Wrath's Storm.

And don't be alarmed! Oscar, Selene, and Luca will get their happily ever after! We just aren't quite finished tormenting those Hayden triplets yet.

Mari and Lila

ABOUT THE AUTHORS

Virginia native Mari Carr is a *New York Times* and *USA TODAY* bestseller of contemporary sexy romance novels. With over one million copies of her books sold, Mari was the winner of the Romance Writers of America's Passionate Plume for her novella, *Erotic Research*.

Join her newsletter so you don't miss new releases and for exclusive subscriber-only content. Find Mari on the web on Facebook | Twitter | BookBub | Email: mari@mari-carr.com.

Lila Dubois is a top selling author of contemporary erotic romance. Having spent extensive time in France, Egypt, Turkey, England and Ireland Lila speaks five languages, none of them (including English) fluently. She now lives in Los Angeles with a cute Irishman.

You can visit Lila's website at www.liladubois.net. She loves to hear from fans! Send an email to author@liladubois.net or join her newsletter.

f

Made in the USA
Middletown, DE
23 March 2022

63058082R00210